REAPERS

Reapers

Lorne McDougall

2014

Reapers

ISBN: 978-0-9947366-0-4

First Printing: 2014

Lorne McDougall
317 Dundas St. West
Belleville, ON, K8P1A9

Ordering Information:

Special discounts are available on quantity purchases by corporations, associations, educators, and others. For details, contact the publisher at the above listed address.

Trade bookstores or wholesalers: Please contact Lorne McDougall at mcd.lorne@gmail.com for inquiries.

Dedication

To Caitlin Cook and Marilyn McDougall. Thank you. You are my inspiration, my demo audience and my very first editors. Without you, this would have never happened.

Contents

Acknowledgements

I would like to thank my editor, Ann Louise Bailey, as well as my teachers, family and friends without whose help this book would never have been completed.

Thank you for your patience, guidance, and putting up with me talking about my book incessantly.

Chapter 1

Rain. It tumbled through the night sky, falling in great torrential sheets, and burying the expansive city beneath its cold weight. The rainclouds, pregnant with water, hovered forebodingly in the sky. They blocked the moon and the stars, leaving the city centre illuminated with the artificial halos of streetlights and passing cars. The deluge flooded its dark alleys, its storm grates and its crevices, drowning where light would never reach.

Regardless of the poor weather, and the fact that it was almost midnight, the city still bustled with life. Pedestrians navigated the soaking sidewalks, holding their umbrellas close to their bodies, as if the canvas could protect them from the cold as well as the rain. Cars sped through the streets with water cascading around them as they motored through the ever-deepening puddles. This level of activity, during such forbidding conditions, proved the city never slept.

The buildings in the downtown core towered over the citizens like massive concrete trees. Some of them were well lit, either from the glow of the city or independent lighting, but this only accented the sinister shadows that gathered at their corners and windowsills as they endured the assault of the rain

One imposing brownstone building stood out in this forest of skyscrapers. Its wide walls loomed over a crowded intersection, where the two busiest streets met. The incandescence from the traffic bathed its bricks in a golden aura, in stark contrast to its dark and secretive windows.

The upper half of the landmark was mostly hidden in shadows, but four enormous gargoyles were barely visible, perched on the edge of the otherwise barren rooftop. These fearsome guardians watched over the city in silence. Battered by the rain, water poured from their extruding beaks, claws and wings, a sight that would be beautiful if it weren't so dark and threatening. They were carved in marble, and stood rigidly defiant against the downpour, utterly still.

And yet, if one looked closely enough, one might see a slight movement, a distortion on top of the largest, gryphon-like, statue. It resembled an outline, almost as if the rain were colliding with some invisible... *something*.

On the physical plane of existence, there was nothing there; how-ever, an examination of the spiritual plane revealed something far more interesting.

Our world is composed of two distinct realms: the physical and the spiritual. The physical plane is where humans live, it is where we build our homes, where we raise our children, and where rain falls and sun shines. The spiritual plane is the realm of, well, spirits. Souls, ghosts, angels, even Paradise itself, exist on the spiritual plane. Those same spirits can interact with one another, much like humans do in the physical realm. They can touch, hear and see each other. They can think, and most, can feel.

This spiritual plane exists in harmony with the physical plane, yet is separate. Think of it as a hidden layer, which is superimposed onto the physical plane. In the spiritual world, all of the characteristics of the physical world exist. The mountains we see and climb in the phys-ical plane still exist in the spiritual plane, as do our rivers, buildings and even the people we see. If you were to exist on the spiritual plane, the world would seem exactly the same to you, except you would be invisible to those on the physical plane.

Despite this linked existence, the rules that govern the spiritual plane are very different from the rules for the normal world. The spir-itual realm is dominated by pure energy. The laws of physics do not apply; anything can occur if a being has enough energy to do it.

The *something* that rested on top of the gargoyle clearly had an impressive amount of energy. Somehow, the rain was hitting it, even though it's form did not occupy any space in the physical plane. The outline caused by the rain suddenly shifted, changed shape. Whatever it was had adjusted its... his... position.

For it was a man who occupied the space; gazing into the spiritu-al realm made that clear as day. He was crouched on top of the gargoyle, wrapped in a dark hooded robe. His frame was slender but tall, and the set of the shoulders dispelled any notion that he could be female. The energy he was employing was prodigious.

Forcing any object to occupy both the physical and the spiritual planes at the same time requires a remarkable degree of power and control. Navigating the threshold between realms is tricky, even for the all-powerful angels.

But the man did not seem to notice the strain, as he effortlessly lifted his face towards the sky, allowing the enchanted rain to caress his face. His hood slid off, revealing further features.

The man, although this term is applied loosely for he appeared to be no older than eighteen, was handsome, with shoulder-length silver hair. When it was dry, it fell like curtains on either side of his face; but now it was slicked back, weighed down by the rain. Despite the dark night, the pale fairness of his skin was evident.

Lance, for that was the boy's name, closed his grey eyes and embraced the cool feeling of the rain showering his face. He revelled in its cleansing touch, a luxury he chose to allow, even though it was technically against the rules.

It was forbidden for mortals to see him; he was to remain on the spiritual plane at all times. Unfortunately, human sightings of spirits were becoming an increasingly greater problem, as they developed more advanced ways of taking photos and spreading news. Lance sighed and turned his attention from the soothing rain back down to the busy intersection below. He had a job to do.

As always, there was a steady stream of people flowing through the intersection. Lance watched carefully, but his quarry was not to be found. Each pedestrian existed only on the physical plane; they were humans, not ghosts. He could not detect the spirit he was seeking.

Lance scowled and surveyed the cityscape. This metropolis, constructed completely of iron and stone, was a perfect hiding place for spirits on the run. They could use the immense buildings and cold metal to protect themselves from the vigilant eyes of spiritual enforcement—from spirits like Lance.

Annoyed, Lance abandoned his crouching position and jumped down onto the rooftop. Being a reaper was a difficult task, and one which few spirits embraced. The rain continued to fall onto Lance, and his mind slowed to match its rhythm. The water always affected him this way, with its calming and nostalgic patterns. It made him reflective, recalling memories of a distant past. It made him think back to how it all began, to the start of his journey... as a reaper.

Chapter 2

He grew up just like any normal kid. He had parents and a younger brother who loved him, although little Jeffrey would never admit it. He had a house, a sizable one, in the neat and tidy suburbs. It was the perfect location for Miles; all his neighbours had kids his age, friends he would grow up with.

That was his name back then. Miles, not Lance. He attended Jackson Secondary School, just a ten minute walk from his home. At Jackson he was a good student, a procrastinator to be sure, but an intelligent boy.

Not a remarkable athlete, he still tried out for and made the school's football and basketball teams, largely because his father and friends wanted him to. At the age of seventeen, Miles was enjoying a truly good life. It really was a shame, that it would abruptly come to an end.

It all started on a rainy Tuesday afternoon in September, the day Miles was destined to become Lance. It was a day he thought was going quite well. He had just received word from his football coach that he would be a starting wide-receiver. The team was stacked, and a promising season lay ahead. He had also discovered that his lab partner for the rest of the semester was his long-time crush, a certain Jessica Roberts.

School was over and Miles was sitting on the front steps leading to Jackson High's driveway. The rain was falling fairly heavily, and Miles was drenched, along with his backpack which he had slung down beside him. Miles didn't seem to care, as evidenced by the slight grin on his mostly acne-free face. The rain felt good on his skin, and soaked into his dark brown hair.

He had forgotten his Ipod and cellphone at home that day, so he ran no risk of damaging any electrical gadgets. He simply waited, gazing serenely into space.

If someone had asked him what he was doing, Miles would have said:

"I'm reflecting on how the day has unfolded and how my senior year is shaping up to be the best of my entire life."

But this would only be half the truth; Miles *was* looking forward to a great year. But as he sat there and the rain poured down, all he could think about was Jessica. Miles was so relaxed and distracted that he forgot to be angry when his parents arrived, late, to pick him up.

Finally, his Dad drove up in their red minivan and stopped directly in front of him. Miles opened the side door and jumped in. The first thing he noticed was his brother, Jeffrey, sitting in the seat beside him. Miles grinned, perplexed.

"Shouldn't little Jeffey be out running in a race?" he enquired, not addressing anyone in particular. Jeffrey gave his brother the evil eye; he hated it when Miles teased him and called him *Jeffey*. Their father turned around from the driver's seat to address his eldest son, whom he closely resembled. They had the same basic features and eyes, though his own face was more weathered.

"Jeffrey actually just finished 3rd in the district! We were delayed because of the awards ceremony! And more good news: we've decided to take the family out for a celebratory dinner."

At this point, Miles' mom turned from the front passenger seat, flipping hair that was identical in straightness and sheen to his.

"We heard from Coach Callaghan about the starting position. Congratulations, dear!"

"Thanks, mom" Miles replied, smiling, as his Dad put the van in gear and headed through the outskirts towards the city centre.

Sure he was soaked, but dinner sounded really good. He stared out the window, contently watching at the houses flew by. The sound of the rain grew almost deafening, and soon Miles could barely see the sidewalk, let alone the homes, through the relentless downpour.

His mother grew slightly agitated in the front seat because of the poor visibility.

"Slow down John!" she ordered, anxiously. "The bridge is narrow!"

Miles realized they must be approaching the downtown; they just needed to go over the river that twisted through the middle of the city. He looked out the front windshield expectantly, but only saw the misty gray fog of rain and a pair of intense yellow headlights in the opposite lane. Miles focused on the headlights.

As the car moved forward, he noticed that peculiarly, their position didn't seem to change. Instead, they simply grew rapidly in size as his family's van drove closer and closer. Suddenly worried, Miles yelled out.

"Those headlights aren't moving!"

At that moment, an ominous shape erupted from the fog, no more than a couple of meters from the van. A huge tractor-trailer, hauling a giant chrome fuel tank, had jackknifed at the very top of the bridge, blocking both lanes. Its driver was trapped in the front seat, unable to warn the oncoming traffic of the silent danger.

Miles' heart froze as he realized there was no time to stop. His mother screamed, his brother closed his eyes, and his father jerked the wheel to the side in a desperate attempt to avoid a head-on collision.

The noises of screeching rubber and bending steel filled the air as the van jerked into a ninety-degree turn without a chance to slow, and promptly flipped on the wet pavement. It rolled over and over, violently throwing its occupants around within the confines of their thankfully fastened seatbelts. The windows shattered and glass cascaded around them as they were pummeled, screaming for their lives. The van finally slammed against the side of the truck, coming to rest upside down.

Everything went eerily silent, save for the sound of the harsh, merciless rain and the rumble of distant thunder. Inside the car, Miles slowly regained consciousness.

The first thing he noticed was searing pain, spiking through his right leg and shoulder. Miles opened his eyes and swallowed, convincing himself not to look down at his injuries; if he did, he feared his resolve would fail.

He was suspended upside down in his seat, his seatbelt having kept him securely in place. With his hair hanging around his face and his arms suspended limply, Miles attempted to find the release.

From the front of the vehicle, Miles heard a loud thump and a guttural groan. He looked up to see his father, now freed from his harness, slowly crawling around inside the overturned vehicle. His dad turned to Miles; his face badly cut from the shards of glass.

"Miles? Miles! Are you ok, son?" Miles nodded as he found the release to his own and pressed it. His body fell to the ground and immediately the pain increased exponentially. Despite his best efforts, Miles let out a scream of agony.

"Miles!" cried his father, who moved forward in a bid to reach him.

"I'm fine dad," Miles responded weakly, having recovered from the initial shock of impact. "You... your face..." His father turned to look at Jeffrey, who was still suspended in his seat.

"It's nothing. Check on Jeffrey. Let me know..." his voice trailed off as he refused to acknowledge the possibility of losing his son. He turned his attention over to his wife, and immediately jolted towards her. "Your mother is breathing! She's still alive! I'm going to get her out of here."

Miles obeyed his dad's orders and turned to Jeffrey, who wasn't moving. Miles stared at the face of his brother, so similar to his own, wearing a countenance of total peace. The face, uncut from the glass all around, seemed so calm to Miles. And he dreaded what that calmness meant.

Then Miles saw it, an almost imperceptible movement that meant so much. Jeffrey's chest had moved, drawing air in to breathe. Miles could barely believe it; his entire family had survived.

The pain he was feeling melted away. He completely forgot about his injuries as he surged forward to help his brother. Moving faster than he ever had before, Miles quickly undid his brother's seatbelt and pushed him towards the van's side window, which was now a convenient escape route. Glass littered the van floor, cutting Jeffrey as Miles forced him along.

In a second, his dad reached into the car, grabbed Jeffrey and pulled him out towards the side of the bridge. Miles' resolve hardened; now it was his turn.

Miles pushed along the ground, feeling the small bits of glass cut into his belly, ripping at his abdominals. As he emerged halfway from the vehicle, his father dragged him away from the wreck and towards the side railing of the bridge, where his brother and mother already lay.

"They're both in rough shape," he said bluntly. "I can't tell what's wrong either." The worried father turned his gaze towards the remnants of his crushed metal vehicle, which was still being gently sprinkled by the rain. "We need to get out of here; that was a full tank of gas. We need to move, now!"

Miles nodded, but felt immobilized. The jolt of adrenaline that had given him the strength to escape from the van was wearing off, and his pain was returning in terrible waves. Miles had the courage to do what was necessary, in spite of his condition.

"Dad, just take care of mom and Jeffery. I can manage."

His father stared at his son for a quick second, before nodding his head. Then, despite his own wounds, Miles' father grabbed his wife and son and slung them over his shoulders.

It was surreal, superhuman, but he was motivated by a dual desire to save not only the woman he loved, but his whole family as well. He limped slowly towards the end of the bridge.

Miles closed his eyes for a second, gathered his strength, and in pure agony, pulled himself up onto his left leg, quickly realizing that his other was unable to bear weight. Ignoring his pain, Miles slowly moved forward, clutching the rail and hopping his way down the bridge.

It would have made an amazing tale. The kind of story that makes the news, spreads through the churches and goes viral on popular websites. An entire family surviving a horrific crash. The heroism of the father—the bravery of the eldest son. Certainly inspiring stuff. Unfortunately, it was not to be.

As Miles drew closer to his father, a small spark burst from the damaged electrical equipment inside the twisted metal of the wrecked van. This spark fell into a pool of gasoline, which had seeped from the van's ruptured fuel tank, and ignited.

The explosion, though horrifying already, was drastically magnified by the truck, which carried a full load of explosive petroleum. A brilliant crimson fireball bloomed up into the sky, accompanied by a sonic boom rippling through the immediate area. The deadly blast threw Miles to the ground and with a brutal impact, ripped the bridge in half.

The remains of the bridge trembled and shook in limbo as the concrete and metal that held it together began to crumble. Miles was trapped. The blast had robbed his legs of any remaining strength, he believed they were both broken, and he had lost sight of his family. He desperately looked around for an escape.

With a dreadful sinking feeling penetrating his stomach, Miles realized there was none.

He did not cry, did not scream or wail. He simply looked up to the stormy sky, felt an incredible sadness engulf him... and closed his eyes. He felt the mist of rain on his face. Its gentle kiss was the last thing he would ever feel.

With a violent groan of tortured steel, the bridge collapsed. It's entire frame was torn asunder as it, along with Miles, plunged into the awaiting abyss. As he hit the water, Miles was nothing more than a body, being carried deeper and deeper into the depths of the river, entombed in debris. He had left his happy life as a teenager, forever. Miles had passed away.

Chapter 3

The blaring honk of a car horn underneath him brought Lance out of his reverie. The stormy night sky still surrounded him, but with his mind focused elsewhere, the magic he had worked faded. The rain no longer existed in both planes, and instead fell through Lance, leaving him alone on his watch. The faint outline of the reaper had disappeared; he was completely invisible to the material world.

Lance shook his head, trying to snap out of his reflective mood. He looked down, causing his black hood to once again fall over his face, obscuring his features in deep, mysterious shadows.

He cursed inwardly, not knowing if he had missed his prey during his jaunt down memory lane. He had a job to do, a spirit to track, and he was allowing useless memories to not only keep him from fulfilling his task, but also place him in danger. There were malevolent things out there, prowling in the dark.

Lance stared down into the city streets, almost desperately, scanning for his target. There was nothing to indicate that he had missed his charge, or that the spirit known as "Cody Tremors" was in the immediate area. If Cody had passed, Lance would have seen his residue down below, on the spiritual plane.

Residue is a substance that does not exist on the physical plane but would closely resemble a scent. If scents were visible, that is. It is the remnants of spiritual power—the energy source that allows all spirits to manipulate and control the spiritual plane.

This residue, best described as a kind of light dust, shimmers in the air on the spiritual plane and floats around long after the source of its power has dissipated. The stronger the force, the greater the residue and the easier it is to track. Residue is also unique to each individual energy source, meaning it is a very useful tool for a reaper, if he is hunting for a spirit.

Tracking is the biggest part of the job for the reapers, who are constantly searching for rogue or wandering spirits. Cody was a spirit of the latter variety, a poor soul who was so attached to his life on earth that he remained there when he died. He was trapped in the spir-

itual plane, unable to traverse into the second realm of existence—
Paradise.

Lance had seen it many times before. Some spirits had suffered a
violent death, and the drive for vengeance, or the pure terror of the
unknown, trapped them in the mortal world. Others were madly in
love and could not bear to leave behind those they cared about. And
others still were just silly or stubborn enough to fight the gentle tug of
Paradise, a force applied to all spirits, which lightly pulls them to the
other side. It was rare for a human to possess the spiritual strength to
resist this pull, but it did occasionally happen.

Lance didn't care about Cory's story. To him, he was just another
target, just more prey for him to catch, just another way to fulfil the
pledge he had made a year ago, after dying in the rain.

He shook his head again, trying to focus. If he continued to be
distracted, he would definitely miss Cody and waste the important
lead he had just recently secured. Luck had been on his side recently,
and he knew that luck always favoured the alert and prepared.

The big break for Lance in his pursuit of Cody had been the arrival of a portion of Cody's residue in Paradise. Some of his spiritual
power had become detached, which showed Lance exactly what he
was looking for.

Think of a soul resisting the pull of Paradise like sugar being
dropped into water. Typically, the pull dissolves the soul, bringing all
of it away from earth. For weak or willing spirits, this process happens in seconds, but for others, it can take a lifetime, or even eternity.
Despite his ability to resist, Cody lacked the strength to continue
holding his spirit together, and it was quickly dissolving. The particles
of his power that did reach Paradise coalesced and formed residue,
which was collected. Then, a sample had been given to Lance to examine.

This residue was the key to bringing Lance's week-long search
for Cody to its climax. Tracking it, like a dog would follow a scent,
Lance was able to use his keen spiritual power to seek out and find its
point of highest concentration.

That had led him to his perch on the head of the gargoyle, poised
above the bustling city centre. The flooded intersection down below

was absolutely teaming with a wide variety of spiritual residues. Obviously, this was a very popular hang-out spot for spirits.

Lance ignored the others, focusing on Cody's own personal dust. It had been everywhere in the intersection, fanning out in all directions, following streets and entering alleys and shops.

Some trails were smaller, fainter, and harder for Lance to detect, while others were vibrant and thick, indicating less time had passed since the residue was deposited. If Lance hadn't been alerted, the track could have dissipated over time, and the search for Cody would have been much more challenging.

By studying the residue, Lance had identified a pattern. Cody was wandering around the city, always returning to this specific intersection, making long, winding and circular rotations.

Instead of wasting his time trying to follow the most recent trail—about ten hours old at this point—Lance had decided to wait it out, on top of the gargoyle.

He again cast his eyes around the intersection, looking for any fresh signs of residue. Even if he didn't see the spirit itself, Cody's dissolving power would leave a thick trail which Lance could follow easily when fresh, like a trail of slime left by a snail inching along the ground.

However, he saw nothing. Just the mundane passage of people and cars. His temper began to flare as Lance realized just how much time this could take. The difference in intensity between the two most recent trails indicated that they were made close to a day apart. He could be in for a frustratingly tedious wait.

A jarring scream from nearby rang out below, a desperate pitch, breaking through the soft sound of rain tickling pavement and brick. Lance leapt to his feet, quickly turning towards the noise, finally breaking away from the view that he and his gargoyle mount had shared for most of the evening.

The scream was shrill, definitely female. Lance, with his senses heightened far beyond that of any human, was able to quickly locate its source.

She was in a poorly-lit alleyway located between a grimy concrete building and his own brownstone perch, just off the intersection.

The darkness would be a problem for a normal human, but the absence of light no longer affected Lance's vision.

The woman was being attacked by two menacing figures, who clearly intended to rob her, or worse. Lance moved from his position on the gargoyle to the side of the building nearest the alleyway, to secure a better vantage point. He wanted to see how this would play out.

The woman, a young girl whose features were obscured, was struggling valiantly against the attackers. They were covered in black clothing to ensure that no one would be able to identify them, in either video camera footage or a police line.

They assailed her viciously, intent on preventing a second scream. Lance watched it all with detachment, almost as though he were viewing a movie, or some play that was clearly make-believe. He hadn't felt emotion for the plight of humans since after the bridge had collapsed, and certainly wasn't about to start now.

The excitement below elicited no anger, no fear, not even empathy. Just impartial, cold, curiosity. What would happen next?

The muggers, restraining the girl with brute strength, focused on grabbing the large and luxurious purse that she gripped fiercely. One man pinned her struggling body against the wall of the brownstone, while the other covered her mouth with one hand, reaching for her purse with the other.

Sensing a small window of opportunity, the victim bit down on the man's hand, making him howl with pain, withdrawing it instantly.

Unmuffled, she screamed once again, her panicked cry filling the night air, before the man abruptly clamped his hand back over her mouth, rectifying his mistake.

Lance shifted his attention towards the main intersection. He noticed that several onlookers had stopped their progress and were peering down the alleyway, unable to deduce exactly what was going on.

Not one of them moved. Not one of them took action to assist another human, who despite any confusion was clearly in danger. Lance frowned and looked back to the scene unfolding directly beneath him.

Humans, he thought. *Pathetic.*

The entire human race was degenerating, losing all sense of morals, respect and dignity. Today's self-absorbed generation had an unearned sense of entitlement, and ultimately, the planet and civilization were paying the price.

Lance could see this clearly, as a dispassionate bystander. Humans were no longer stewards of the planet. They had no compassion, they had no faith, and they no longer rushed to the aid of a screaming woman in a dark alley.

Down below, the men were able to wrestle the struggling girl's purse out of her grasp and were searching the pockets of her torn coat. The rain continued to fall as hard as ever, mercilessly soaking the desperate scene. The sound of a car horn disrupted their pillage, and they decided, in unison, that it was time to run.

They took off, sprinting down the alley, away from the intersection, with the expensive purse and a few electronics in tow. Lance did not move; he simply watched them flee, impassively, for a few short seconds. He then turned back to the victim, who had collapsed in a puddle in the alley. She was shaking and crying, now that the adrenaline rush of the attack had subsided, as she waited for the help which the car horn had signaled.

Lance knew better. The driver was simply honking at another vehicle in the intersection, and now that the screaming had subsided, the other people in the intersection had lost interest and returned to their lives.

Disgusted, he turned away from the ledge of the brownstone, heading back to his old seat on top of the gargoyle, which maintained its quiet vigil over the city centre. He didn't even bother to walk as he brooded. Instead, he used his powers to float towards his perch. Taking his place, he turned once again to inspect the intersection, and immediately snapped to full awareness.

Excitement flooded his veins as he noticed a thick trail of residue leading from a side alleyway, going through the intersection, and heading down a main street. The trail could not be more than a minute or two old. Lance smiled, revelling in his empowering discovery. The waiting was over.

Now he could really hunt.

Abandoning his levitation, Lance ran to the edge of the building closest to the street where the trail had become visible. Lance peered down the avenue, which was busy with pedestrians and traffic.

There was no spirit in sight, only more residue. The trail followed the street for a few blocks then abruptly turned to the left, heading into an alleyway between two stores. Lance gathered his strength, and then leapt from his station, his black, silken robes billowing in the air.

His leap was surreal, superhuman. Lance sailed through the forbidding sky, a shadow in the night, before landing on the other side of the street. It resembled the leap of a superhero, revealing the kind of impossible power that humans believe only exists in fantasy.

Racing now, and taking long powerful strides, Lance blistered over the roofs of the few remaining skyscrapers and found himself overlooking the alleyway where the trail ended. It seemed identical to the one where the earlier attack had taken place.

Another filthy, narrow concrete path with the same claustrophobic sense of neglect that filled all the dark places within these man-made jungle. Down the middle of the alley, Lance spied his target: the soul of Cody Tremors.

He looked like a human in his mid-thirties, slightly chubby with curly brown hair. Except that he wasn't a human at all. He didn't exist on the physical plane. Cody was surrounded by a narrow but bright outline, composed of the same residue which Lance had been given. Lance paused, silently spying on Cody, who continued to slowly trundle through the alley.

The shuffling stopped briefly and Cody, who had been staring at his feet, straightened up and moved his head around to briefly observe his surroundings. Lance did not bother retreating to the centre of the building to hide; if his prey could spot him, so be it.

Lance could now see Cody's face, which was strained and upset. His eyes were bloodshot. He had been crying, which was still possible, though pointless, on the spiritual plane. He yelled out in anguish.

"Cindy!" His voiced was high pitched, full of sorrow and desperation.

Now Lance knew exactly why Cody Tremors' passage to Paradise had been interrupted. He was searching and upset, the typical signs of someone who has been trapped on earth due to a bond of love.

Cody's feelings for this *Cindy*, whoever she was—wife, child, secretary, who knew—had kept him on earth. Now, more than anything, he wanted to be close to her. Cody would search for her for years before his soul dissolved, if he didn't get caught by a reaper first. Or something worse.

Cody hopelessly cast his eyes around once more and began to sob.

Lance shook his head. The pathetic spirit hadn't even noticed him observing from the skyscraper above. Not what he would call dangerous game. It was time to end this chase and put Cody exactly where he belonged. Lance reached into himself, closing his eyes and feeling his power. He prepared to bring havoc and instill fear.

Fear is the greatest weapon in the hunting reaper's arsenal and a necessary element in every attack. It instantly saps the spiritual power of others, making them feel heavier, more sluggish and easier to trap. It can paralyze, and lead to poor decision making. Most importantly, it keeps everyone afraid.

When a human spirit, like Cody, is frightened, it affects all the humans near him—they subconsciously absorb the fear of remaining on earth, and thus fewer spirits resist the pull of Paradise. This also produces a side-effect: humanity's universal fear of death.

Gathering all of his power, Lance expanded it rapidly, into a turbulent black wave. It threw the alley into utter darkness, snuffing out all light until any details disappeared from sight.

Cody instantly stopped moving and spun around, his eyes wide like a panicked animal.

"H-Hello?" he stammered weakly, slowly backpedalling.

Lance opened his eyes, which were no longer gray. They had turned bright red, hiding pupils, iris and any manner of colour distortion to form two malevolent orbs.

Abandoning his running-jumping method of movement, he rose from the skyscraper and flew towards Cody, with his sinister cloak billowing behind. This time Cody saw him—an unearthly figure diving towards him with his wing-like arms spread wide and his face warped into a feral snarl.

The terrified soul screamed loudly and turned, sprinting as fast as he could towards the other end of the alley. Lance cursed. Why did they always insist on running? He opened his mouth and emitted a tremendous roar, layered with darkness and violent undertones.

"Cody Tremors! Your end has come!"

"Nooooo!" wailed Cody, his voice trembling as he ran. Lance continued his chase down the alley, which seemed to last forever.

Cody suddenly made a wild turn to the left, into another connecting sidestreet. Lance flew upward, over the building that made the corner and then back down into the chase.

Wooden scaffolding provided a latticework roof to this area, stretching over it at odd angles everywhere. Lance simply flew through it; the scaffolding only existed in the physical plane, after all.

He noticed that Cody was moving rapidly, at a rate a normal human, or even a regular spirit, wouldn't be able to achieve. Apparently, he had a natural affinity to use his spiritual power to enhance his speed. Lucky for him. But Lance was in no mood to race.

He willed some of his power forward, and it shot ahead in a dark red coil of energy towards Cody. Lance disliked using spiritual attacks like this against weak spirits, it was beneath him. But he had tired of his pursuit.

The coil bolted forward, far faster than any spirit could move, and wrapped itself around his victim's leg. Cody lurched and immediately fell forward, tripped by the wrapped tendril that began to pull him ruthlessly towards Lance, who had alighted on the floor of the alleyway and was standing erect, arms crossed forebodingly before his chest. Lance breathed out one word, enhanced with power.

"COME."

Cody sobbed and clawed at the ground with his hands, a feat that accomplished nothing since he was a weak spirit and therefore unlikely to affect the physical realm. Lance's victory was inevitable.

He was eventually dragged to Lance's feet, where the tendril tightened, keeping him tethered to the reaper. Cody tried weakly to break free, but couldn't. His fear and Lance's supernatural control had combined to rob him of his last vestiges of spiritual power.

Lance looked down at the spirit and prepared for the final step to move Cody to the afterlife. He once again reached into his reserves of power, and this time concentrated on his hands. His mind focused, he channeled his energy, manipulating and forming it. Slowly, the red energy began to take shape.

It was the outline of a scythe, with a shaft of close to six feet in length and a blade a third as wide. The red glow slowly dulled, as the outline became darker, finally assuming the appearance of a real scythe. Its shaft was comprised of dark wood, knotted and lined with age. In two lines along the shaft were a series of dark red runes, in a language foreign to all who perceived it. Its blade was made of steel, which managed to glisten menacingly, even in the heightened darkness.

The blade hung silently in the air, while the shaft stood at an angle across Lance's body. The weapon was called a *manta*, and it was an impressive manifestation of power.

This manta was given to Lance when he assumed his duties as a reaper. Mantas are forged by angels, the guardians and peacekeepers of the spiritual world, and when the scythe was given to Lance, it was sealed inside his very spirit, allowing him to call upon it by exerting his spiritual strength.

The weapon was an ingenious creation, because it existed on the spiritual plane, giving its owner the ability to damage other spirits without exerting their own spiritual power.

This advantage is invaluable for battles between powerful spirits, where energy management is critical. Mantas also possess the ability to return the fragments of spirits they destroy to Paradise, making it the weapon of choice for reapers, and essential for when a reaper strikes the death blow.

Cody did not know any of this, but due to human lore and the very intimidating situation he was in, he still understood that the scythe signaled his end. In anguish he tried to move, tried to open his mouth to shout or scream or beg, but simply couldn't.

He was finished, his outline beginning to blur as steady streams of spiritual power leaked from his body. Cody's essence was gently being peeled away from him by the pull of Paradise.

Lance stared down at his prey and couldn't help but feel a certain level of satisfaction. He had always liked to win, and once again he was successful. Cody had proven to be resourceful, but he could not outrun the master hunter. Lance smiled, savouring the sweet feeling of triumph.

He raised the scythe above his head, poised to strike and send the spirit to Paradise. He looked directly into Cody's eyes, which were the only parts of the spirit that were still active. They trembled with dread, and seemed to be imploring the reaper, in all his darkness and power, to take pity.

But Lance felt no pity towards the spirit, the once-mortal soul who no longer belonged. He glared intensely at him, and spoke the customary words.

"Your time has come!"

And with that phrase, Lance prepared to swing his manta into the spirit, but was interrupted by a startling noise that came from directly behind him.

It was a voice. Rough, like sandpaper, but not particularly low pitched. It was exactly the kind of wheezy and irritating voice that would annoy anyone within earshot.

"That's my dinner, reaper."

Lance whirled around to face this new threat, with the twisted fabric of his black shroud flapping and writhing.

He knew he need not tend to Cody immediately; the spirit had no energy to fight, let alone flee. However, this interruption was an instant threat to the success of his mission and had to be dealt with.

As Lance faced the source of the voice, and recognized the spirit from which it came, his alarm immediately morphed to annoyance.

Facing Lance was a spirit that looked like a mix between a lizard and a man. It possessed the bodily dimensions and humanoid shape of a very short person, but also had thick green scaly skin, and spines which traveled from the base of its skull down its body and along a limber tail which sprouted from its lower back.

The head itself was the most disturbing part of the spirit; it resembled the visage of a spiny lizard, but with clearly visible and sharp teeth.

Despite its rather fearsome appearance, Lance was not at all worried about the threat this spirit posed to him. He knew its kind immediately—it was called a revenant.

Revenants are spirits, formed whenever evil emotions or acts occur near a source of intense spiritual power, like a holy site or a powerful spirit. The strength of a revenant varies. Typically, its strength follows the power that was the catalyst to its formation, just several times weaker.

Revenants do not pose a threat to strong and experienced spirits like Lance, however they can be dangerous to wandering souls who are not used to the spiritual plane.

If allowed to, Lance knew this revenant would eat Cody, after all it had called the human spirit *dinner*. That's one of the two ways revenants grow. They can absorb spiritual energy by consuming other spirits, effectively adding some of that spirit's strength to their own. Alternatively, revenants can merge with others of their own kind, though this process typically involves the presence of a new source of power.

This makes revenants the equivalent of the insects of the spiritual world. Since they grow near power, they are drawn to it just as bugs are to light. Lance figured the revenant facing him must have tracked Cody's essence just like he had, hoping to find a meal. He stared at the creature, bemused, wondering what it would do.

The revenant, clearly confused by Lance's lack of movement, fidgeted slightly and tried to talk to Lance, once again employing the aggravating voice.

"If you don't move, spirit, I'll chow down on you too! Pretty boy!" Lance couldn't help himself; he opened up his mouth and snickered, baring startlingly white teeth.

This revenant had no idea what it was talking about. That was the problem with mentally weak spirits; their lack of intelligence made them easily disposed of, and that same stupidity also led them to greatly overestimate their own strength. Lance could tell by the creature's size that the revenant lacked the power to defeat him.

Most spirits who do not receive formal training are unable to control the surge of their power, and therefore inhabit a form on the spiritual plane that is in direct proportion to their strength. This particular revenant was actually much larger than the typical ones that Lance had encountered. Most were about the size of an average dog. Lance figured that explained how the revenant had been able to sneak up on him. It must have been employing its enhanced power to hide itself from Lance's spiritual senses.

The revenant roared, angered by Lance's dismissive mannerisms. The creature was probably used to terrorizing pathetic human spirits and had never been challenged. In a blur of speed, it charged toward Lance, who ditched his grin immediately and gripped his manta with strong, steady hands.

Even though the revenant was no match for Lance, as long as it was anywhere near Cody, it posed a threat to his mission and had to be dealt with. The revenant rapidly advanced on Lance, raising its front arms, revealing hands with long and sharp claws, intent on mauling him. It never got a chance.

Lance watched the revenant with the steady eye of an expert, employing a level of discipline the revenant would never appreciate. As soon as the he was within striking distance of the creature, Lance spun and sidestepped its brutal charge.

In one fluid motion, using the momentum of his spin, he slashed his manta through the air, in an attempt to impale the revenant in the back. But his efforts were disrupted by a sudden shaking, as the spiritual plane shuddered jarringly. The commotion was enough to spoil his attack, as his scythe missed by a fraction of an inch.

Lance continued his spin and came to a rest uneasily, facing the monster. Realizing the charge had failed, the revenant completely ignored Lance, and leapt for Cody, who lay completely exposed, immobilized by Lance's binds.

Flustered, Lance hesitated. He couldn't believe he had missed, he had never seen the spiritual plane act like this before. It reverberated, like it was some taught string that had just been struck.

But there was no time to think; the spiritual plane was presently unpredictable and Lance needed to complete the hunt. He tried to focus by ignoring the shaking, which was getting progressively worse, and channelled his power to move Cody to safety. He yanked at the tendril that was still wrapped around Cody and whipped the helpless spirit to a protected position directly behind him.

Though Cody had flown right past the revenant, the shaking plane disrupted its movements, and it tumbled to the ground empty-handed.

Lance, perturbed, took his eyes off the creature to assess the immediate surroundings. He was confused; the spiritual plane had never acted like this before, and he could barely believe what his senses were telling him. Power was running rampant through the area!

It flowed everywhere, filling Lance's reserves with an unprecedented boost of strength. He tried to use some of his power to stabilize his surroundings but couldn't; the shaking shredded it easily. He couldn't help but sense that someone, some*thing*, was coming. Something really powerful, exponentially stronger than he was.

Lance felt an urgency to finish this scuffle with the revenant now, reap Cody, and move to safety before the situation deteriorated. With each second, the shaking intensified, magnifying the difficulty of every task. He needed to move, now!

Facing the revenant, Lance knew he needed only one blow to destroy the struggling creature. The shaking was quickly matching the intensity of an earthquake, and though Lance was unsteady, he was more than strong enough to do battle.

He raised his scythe above his head and swiftly charged towards his defenceless foe. Lance grimaced as he brought his scythe down through its prone body. This was not how he was meant to fight, how reapers were meant to fight. This revenant could not defend itself, overwhelmed as it was by the pandemonium in the spiritual plane. There was no challenge, no hunt.

Nevertheless, Lance continued his strike. He had no choice. This time, his aim was true, his blade cleanly cleaving his foe in half.

The creature spasmed for a few seconds, as the fatal wound took its toll. It began to glow slightly, and its features became less and less distinct. Its body slowly evolved into a bright shape in the basic form of the revenant, just as if a child had been given an outline and simply coloured everything in with a gold crayon.

The glow did not last long, for the body was quickly shaken apart, and thousands of particles of spiritual power, still glowing luminously, were scattered into the night sky.

Lance did not stop to appreciate the artistic nature of the revenant's demise, as he was distracted by the increasingly violent movement of the spiritual plane. He had still not finished his task. He turned around to check on Cody. The spirit was no longer there.

Looking down, Lance noticed that the tendril of power, which had tethered Cody to him during his battle with the revenant, had been severed by the fluxing spiritual plane.

He hadn't paid too much attention to Cody, and failed to realize that the random bursts of power that had restored his reserves, could have done the same to his target. Fresh with energy, Cody would be able to escape. How could he have been so careless?

Now it would be nearly impossible for him to track Cody; there was too much power overloading the area. It would be like trying to hear running water in the midst of a hurricane.

Lance looked around the alleyway, which had been freed from his artificial darkness, trying to find something, anything, to help. He immediately became aware that the sky was steadily becoming lighter, as if the sun where rising, but it was still the middle of the night. Lance had no idea what was going on, but he had to find Cody.

He charged forward, no longer able to channel the power to fly, simply sprinting through the passageways. He scanned the other alleys, desperately hoping to see the glow of Cody's spirit, or maybe a clue as to his whereabouts. There! A flash of colour down one corridor was all Lance needed to engage.

The reaper barreled down the alley, losing sight of his charge behind a façade of decaying buildings. Lance rounded the corner and finally spied his prey in an area that was like an open terrace, littered with boxes. Cody was actually moving backwards toward Lance, not knowing the reaper was directly behind him. Lance ran up to him, raising his scythe and preparing to repeat his line.

"Your time has c-, come on!" he yelled, as he now saw precisely why Cody had been backpedalling.

A large group of revenants, each about the size of the one he had defeated earlier, was slowly advancing on Cody like a pack of wolves. Each had a distinctly different appearance.

One was a lizardman, just like the first. A second resembled a huge dog, but had massive goat horns sprouting from its head. Beside it, one appeared to be made completely of fire and another was a green skeleton.

All of them were crawling, barely capable of moving due to the vibration of the spiritual realm, but hungry for Cody's power. Lance realized that the event was actually destroying not only their spiritual power, but his own as well. Though his superior energy was more resistant to the pressures of the spiritual plane, he felt his essence being torn apart as the apocalyptic shaking continued.

The terrace was now being engulfed in bright light. It seemed like it was the middle of a sunny day on the spiritual plane. Lance could feel intense heat, and the pressure of the power that was being released into the area weighed him down, as though gravity had suddenly been introduced to the spiritual dimension and multiplied by four.

Lance bared his teeth and struggled to move his scythe. He had to transfer Cody before the spirit was destroyed. He had to deal that death blow. But he could barely move, as the pressure and shaking intensified.

He was reminded of the bridge, where the concrete and steel shook and trembled beneath him. But this wasn't the bridge; this was an entire plane of existence. The light in the plane became painfully fluorescent, as if the sun had landed on the spiritual plane.

Suddenly Lance connected the dots—the brightness, the heat, the vibration, the power—and finally, he looked up. There, in the sky, was a great ball of energy.

It was massive, wreathed in flame, blazing just like the sun. It was hurtling directly towards him. It was too close.

Lance barely had to time to think, let alone react, before the mass reached him. The light got brighter and brighter and the pressure got stronger and stronger, until Lance reached his breaking point.

Then blackness. Total blackness.

Chapter 4

What is death? Is it the end of the journey? The final stop, on the great road of life? Or is it just the beginning, the launch point, the departure into a universe beyond comprehension?

Humans may never know exactly what happens when their hearts beat for the last time, when their physical lives truly end. Science tells them that there is nothing after death; once the electricity in their brains recede it's like turning off a light switch; their sense of themselves, their humanity, simply ceases to be.

Many believe that death is the single most grim force on the planet; an unescapable reality. But some believe in other scenarios, alternate realities where a part of the human soul survives, carries on through to a new world, and proves stronger than death itself.

Spirits, however, know precisely what happens after that last breath. Most of them, the ones who were once human at least, have experienced it firsthand.

The others have watched it, witnessed the process when the soul departs from the body. Humanity's obsession with science and facts and what they can see and touch, has led them to forget about the divine, to forsake the supernatural. But the spirits know.

Miles didn't know. When Miles slowly plunged into that frigid water on that rainy day in September, he was armed only with a teenager's knowledge of death, and only a vague notion about what might happen. Miles truly believed it was the end, and just prayed that he would get to see the people he loved, and wanted to love, at least one more time. Alas, it was not to be.

As the bridge crumbled around him, his weak frame was crushed, his body obliterated mercilessly. Thankfully, he died before he felt any pain. His nerves severed, ending his journey long before his broken body slowly sank to the bottom of the river, which splashed as fragments of the collapsed bridge pierced its icy depths.

For humans, rest is the only state of being that resembles death, which for a time appears to be a deep, dreamless sleep. A sleep from which the physical body never awakens. And so Miles drifted away as his body and mind died, slipping into a dark, everlasting, void. Miles did not see a tunnel of light, nor angels, nor trumpets nor heaven. He saw nothing—nothing at all.

Miles awoke to the soothing sound of water. He was perfectly at peace, with the feeling you get when you wake up, knowing you have plenty of time to sleep in, and it's a glorious Saturday. There was nothing occupying his blissfully clear mind. No stress, and no worry. It was wonderful.

He opened his eyes and noticed calm grey skies above. He watched contently as the wind blew lightly, pushing away the swirling clouds and beginning to expose small beams of sunlight. Everything was changing.

However, in an instant that peaceful feeling was shattered as memories of the accident came flooding back. He immediately sat up as a wave of terror washed over him.

He cast his eyes to his left and saw the city. Before it was the calm, flowing river, no longer the frothing monster from before. He looked straight ahead and observed the ruins of the bridge.

The two main supports, on either side of the river, were still standing. They were warped, but remained upright, testaments to the violent collapse of the main bridge itself. It left an odd-looking gap above the river, where the pavement used to be, before the explosion and the agony of the accident. Miles started. His pain, where did it go? He felt fine.

Back at the bridge's disjointed sides, Miles could see flashing lights. Emergency vehicles had arrived to assess the damage and assist anyone they could. People were running around agitatedly at both ends, but Miles was too far away to make out their features.

Despite the activity, Miles heard only the gentle lap of the river. As he finished turning his head, he looked to his right to see... the river again.

That didn't make sense. The river again? He doubled checked. Left, river before the main city. Right, river before the suburbs. Ahead, more river. Where was he?

In his confusion, Miles looked down at his body, which was totally intact, bearing no signs of his violent demise. He was even clothed, wearing the same jeans and t-shirt that he had been sporting that day at school.

But, more importantly, he solved his positional conundrum. He was sitting on *top* of the river. Suddenly the water, which had felt as solid as a rock just seconds before, gave way, and Miles fell in with a splash.

The water was ice cold. Miles flailed, trying to stay afloat. He thrashed his arms and kicked fiercely, fighting to keep his head above the wash so he could breathe. As he fought, his mind raced. *What happened*? Miles had thought... no, had been sure, that he had died. The bridge collapsed around him; there was no way anyone could survive that... right? And yet here he was, swimming in the river.

If he had survived, then so had his parents! And his brother! For the first time since he had awakened, Miles smiled and felt somewhat hopeful. The shocking chill of the water faded away as he pictured his family in his mind. He had to get to them, reach them somehow. In his excitement, he forgot that he had been standing *on* the water.

Miles began to swim, propelling himself towards the bridge, and help. His family was probably there right now, being treated by the response team. He buried his head in the water, straining to gain those extra inches, fighting the current, in his haste to get to shore.

When he raised his head, he noticed that the bridge appeared to be no closer. *The current must be strong*, Miles decided. He would take a different route, trying to reach the shore to his right, and then walk to the bridge. He should get out of the water quickly, he reasoned, or he would end up with hypothermia.

Curiously, Miles then realized that the water was no longer cold. But as he thought about it, the temperature began to drop, almost as though some invisible hand were turning the thermostat down lower and lower. The intense cold bit into him, and he shivered violently.

Panicking, Miles knew he had to reach the riverbank before weakness set it. Adrenaline fueled him as again he surged forward with all of his might.

He pushed through the water, certain that he was gaining against the current. He was beginning to feel tired, but surprisingly, his muscles didn't ache at all.

After a while, Miles looked up once again, and noticed to his dismay that he was no closer to the shore. Confused, he stopped swimming. What was happening?

Then, Miles heard a chuckle. The laugh seemed modified. It sounded artificial, as if someone were speaking into an auto-tuned microphone with the settings all set to "spooky".

"You aren't moving, you know."

The voice came from directly behind Miles, who spun around in the water and beheld a horrifying image of a hooded man. Miles instantly lost all of his strength, all of his willpower, and all of his remaining hope. Standing there, on top of the water, was a sight that all humans dreaded.

Robed in black, the figure was much taller and slightly wider than the average human. His flowing robes were held in place by a frayed rope belt, from which dangled a series of eerie skulls. They were affixed by smaller ropes that were threaded through gaping holes cut into through their sizable craniums. Miles gulped: the skulls were clearly human.

The robes covered the man's arms up to the wrists, where pale, veined hands were visible, with long, dirty fingernails. The right hand of the figure clasped the rough shaft of a massive scythe. He held it upside-down, like one would hold a walking stick, with the curved top of the blade laying on the water. A mysterious hood was pulled up over the man's head but only cast his face into partial shadow, making his features largely visible.

The face was that of a mature man, about the age of fifty, with bushy white eyebrows and a massive white beard. His skin bore many scars, memories of past battles which stretched across his cheeks, giving him a rugged appearance.

But to any observer, the feature that would stand out the most was his eyes. They had no pupils, and no irises, instead shining a single shade of clear blue. They were the same colour as the middle of the ocean, where all you can see is a solid wall of blue for miles and miles. Even more peculiarly, these eyes emitted light; they glowed softly from beneath the shadow of the hood.

Miles knew immediately who the figure was. He protested, his voice weak and broken.

"But... I'm not dead." The man grinned with the corner of his mouth, still not showing any teeth.

"If you aren't dead, how do you see me?" Miles shuddered. The implications chilled him more than the water ever could.

"I don't... I don't know who you are." Miles winced as soon as he said it; he did not sound convincing. The presence of the reaper stifled him; it pressed down upon him and stole the energy from his body, like a wet blanket smothering a flame.

"You know *exactly* who I am, child," the reaper stated. His voice echoed with the ghostly vocal effect. "Do not insult me with lies. I have been watching you for some time now, Miles. I have come for you."

At this point the reaper paused, and suddenly abandoned the modified voice, revealing instead one that sounded old, but also rich, deep and powerful. "But not in the way you think," he added.

With that statement, the unsettling glow of his eyes grew dull, then faded away. Miles felt the oppressive fear and darkness that the reaper brought with him suddenly uplifting, as though a weight was taken off his shoulders.

He could see the eyes of the reaper now, normal, blue, human eyes. They looked impossibly old. The eyes offset the face, which seemed positively juvenile in comparison. Within them, Miles perceived a glimmer of kindness. He knew that the reaper was not going to harm him.

"Now, get up so we can talk." Miles vainly tried to stand, having forgotten that he was treading water. He plunged deeper into the river, which in his distraction, he did not notice was now warm. Fighting back to the top, he glared indignantly at the reaper.

"You did that on purpose! How am I supposed to get up on water? And I don't take commands from strangers." The reaper looked down at Miles and grinned, displaying teeth that were surprisingly white and straight.

"You've changed your tune rather quickly, Miles. Be careful. Just because someone's eyes aren't glowing is no reason to underestimate them. But I suppose I do owe you an introduction. My name is Enigma, and I, as you have already so cleverly determined, am a reaper."

Miles frowned. *Enigma? What kind of name is that?* Deciding to ask, Miles spoke up, interrupting Enigma, who was clearly preparing to answer his earlier question about standing up.

"Is that your real name?" Enigma's grin turned into a frown, and Miles felt the ominous pressure and fear return.

"That is my only name, boy. Did no one teach you it is rude to interrupt your elders? I need not tell you anything. You are entitled to nothing. Consider what I am doing a kindness. Do not take it for granted. Now do you want your other question answered or not?"

With each of his emphatic points, Enigma seemed to increase the pressure on Miles. Despite his apparent kindness, the reaper was powerful and still wielded a horrible scythe. Miles looked up at the towering figure and managed to stammer, "Y-yes. I... I am sorry."

As soon as he had apologized, the pressure was gone.

"Good," replied Enigma, who stopped scowling and resumed a more neutral expression. "Now, the simple way of explaining how to stand in water is to understand that as a spirit, you exist on the spiritual plane, not the physical one. Water does not exist in the spiritual plane."

He paused here to observe Miles and started speaking again when it appeared the teen was attempting to talk. "Yes," continued Enigma, foreseeing Miles' question. "You are a spirit. This means that you are dead."

The statement disturbed Miles more than any other event since he had been thrown into the water after the explosion.

Dead.

The finality of it was suffocating. There was no doubting it, no arguing it. Even more than the appearance of the reaper, that last sentence truly convinced Miles that his life was over.

Despair, grief and anger all descended on him, threating to overwhelm his thoughts. He had to distract himself for a while, to compartmentalize, so Miles simply asked Enigma to continue.

"What do you mean water doesn't exist? It's everywhere! I'm swimming in it. I'm moving it," to prove his point, Miles splashed water at Enigma, and noticed with shock as the water went right through the reaper.

"This is often the case with new spirits," responded Enigma, ignoring the bewildered look on Miles' face. "You need to understand two things. The first is that although the spiritual and physical planes are separate, and they do not interact with each other, they are also symbiotic, and are aligned within one another. Everything you see here—the water, the city, the banks of the rivers—they look the same as always. Correct?"

Miles nodded, not totally understanding what the reaper meant.

"That is because they *are* the same. The spiritual plane has no natural features; it simply coincides with the features of the physical plane," responded Enigma. "The viewing only works one way. The spiritual plane lies on top of, and can view, the physical plane, but the physical plane has no way of observing the spiritual plane. That is why almost no one sees ghosts."

Miles thought about it for a moment, slightly baffled. That was a lot of information for a human to process. A second plane of existence. With ghosts, no less! It seemed so bizarre, and yet almost made sense.

"So... this water, it's on the physical plane," said Miles, talking as he thought, "and I'm on the spiritual plane? But then how do I move it?" Enigma smiled, and Miles realized this reaper took some joy in teaching.

"It's quite surprising that you can. It also brings me to my second point. The rules of the physical plane no longer apply here. There is no gravity, there are no solid objects. The only force that matters in the spiritual plane is spiritual power, an energy which every spirit, from the tiniest animal ghost to the most powerful angel, possesses."

Enigma looked at Miles before continuing, "You fell into the water because your mind insists on replicating obsolete physical rules within the spiritual realm. The only reason you fell is because you thought you should. The only reason the water is cold, is because you think that is as it should be."

As Miles heard this, he thought about the water, which suddenly became extremely cold. The reaper's explanation was compelling, and at this point, Miles was prepared to believe anything.

"But you still haven't said how I moved it. How can I affect the physical plane at all?" Enigma nodded in agreement.

"It's complicated. It is possible to manipulate the physical plane while in the spiritual plane by using vast amounts of spiritual power—levels of power which very few spirits possess. You seem to do this subconsciously, with ease even, which is very interesting." Enigma brought his hand up to his chin thoughtfully.

"What does that mean?" asked Miles.

"Very simply, it means that you are powerful, and moreover, useful. But I will not continue explaining until you are no longer swimming like some kind of otter. Come on up here."

Miles looked at Enigma, dumbfounded. "You told me why I don't have to swim, not how I accomplish it. I can't just *unlearn* gravity."

"But that is precisely what you must do. Close your eyes, disregard your senses, and believe that you are standing on a platform," instructed Enigma.

Miles diligently closed his eyes, trying to ignore the sound of the water all around him. He forced his mind to envision a concrete block underneath him. He then let himself drift down, and to his surprise, he felt his feet hit something solid.

"Excellent," said Enigma. "Now raise the platform up."

Miles did as he was instructed, and felt nothing. He kept his eyes closed, mentally raising the concrete block. Suddenly, incredible fatigue wracked Miles' body, as if he were trying to lift a weight that was far too heavy. Panic gripped him, and he opened his eyes, trying to get his bearings.

For a second, Miles realized that he was floating above the water, now at eye-level with the reaper, who had to be at least seven feet tall. That second lasted briefly, as with a cry, Miles' concentration broke fell back into the river with a splash.

As he plunged into the water, Miles felt a force pushing him back up. The force solidified into an invisible barrier on which to stand. As it rose, Miles turned around to face Enigma, whose eyes were softly glowing with the blue light.

"It was a good start, but I am impatient, Miles," explained Enigma. "There will be plenty of time to instruct you later. Now I need to explain exactly why I have come. Miles, you may have moved on from the physical world, but your death need not be in vain. There is a service here that you can render to us, to your family and loved ones."

At the mention of his family, Miles stiffened and stared at Enigma with renewed intensity.

"My family? What do you know? What happened to them, Enigma?" The reaper's expression softened, and there was genuine regret in his voice when he responded.

"I am sorry Miles, but I haven't the faintest idea about what has occurred to your family. You were the human we had interest in, so as soon as I felt your power, I came."

Upon hearing this, Miles suspiciously narrowed his eyes.

"What do you mean, interest? Did you know about me before I died?" Enigma nodded.

"Yes, collectively the reapers knew all about you. We have been following your life for some time now." Miles frowned indignantly, temporarily forgetting what the reaper had said about his family.

"How? How did you know about me? What gave you the right to spy on me!?"

"You misunderstand," said Enigma, shaking his head, "We have not been watching you on a continuous basis. We have merely exposed ourselves to samples of your power so we would be aware of significant events that occurred, like your death."

Miles nodded, slightly relieved that supernatural forces hadn't been following him around his entire life. But he was still worried and intrigued by what the reaper had said regarding his parents. He had said there was a way to help them!

"Why were you exposed to my... power? I was human back then. I couldn't use power to do things like make people levitate the way you can," asked Miles. "And what about my family?"

"Just because you could not use power, does not mean you did not possess it. When you were a human, your spiritual power radiated all around you. It was quite a sight to behold.

"You see Miles, you are *unique*. There are precious few humans with your gift of spiritual power. You were noticed by another reaper who was on a mission a long time ago, and you were immediately identified as special. In fact, your raw power greatly exceeds mine," stated Enigma. "I have never seen such natural talent in a soul before."

"If I'm so strong, how come I can't walk on water like you do?" blurted out Miles, before Enigma could continue. Once he realized he had rudely interrupted him again, Miles prepared for more discipline.

It never came. Instead, Enigma remained aloof, completely absorbed in his thoughts. He looked at Miles, and said quietly, almost to himself,

"This one has quite a thirst for knowledge. Just as important as power."

Then, addressing Miles, "I can do things you cannot merely because I use my power more efficiently. Your power is immense, but greatly unfocused. If my power is expressed by one-thousand units, then yours would be at least ten-thousand. But for me, I would require just one of my thousand units to levitate, while you would need to use nearly all of your reserves. That is why you fell when you attempted to float. You simply ran out of strength. But I will change that, I will teach you to be efficient."

"Teach me? Why would-"

Enigma made a dismissive motion with his hand, interrupting Miles' query. "The best way of putting it, the reason why I will teach you, is that we need you. And by we, I mean everyone. Every soul, every angel, every human. There are thousands of us here on the spiritual plane Miles, and uncountable multitudes beyond. And we all need you to be a reaper. You have more than enough power, and I will train you in everything else."

Miles felt something, he was not sure what, running through his body as Enigma said these words. Was it... fear? Perhaps. Excitement? Of course. But, also, a more profound sense of annoyance mixed with hope. All this reaper did with his explanations was make things more complex and confusing. Could he really help his parents? His brother? Miles decided he would let the reaper explain himself.

"A reaper? But I'm a human, not a spirit."

"Yes," responded Enigma. "A reaper. And you *are* a spirit now, Miles. In fact, all reapers, from the Grim Reaper himself, were originally human. I suppose I should describe to you exactly what a reaper is, in order for you to understand more clearly." Miles nodded; he wanted to know more.

"The heart of the issue is souls," explained Enigma. "At the beginning, there were relatively few human souls. A manageable number. They were brought to Paradise, or as many of you humans call it, heaven, through a force known as the pull of Paradise. This pull is actually strong enough to lift most souls to Paradise, with the exception being spiritually strong beings such as yourself, as well as people experiencing a profound connection to earth.

"Back before the human population exploded, these types of souls were rare. Angels, the spirits designated to maintain the peace and order within the spiritual plane, were usually able to handle these few exceptions by themselves. But as the human population grew, angels were not numerous enough to manage the increased number of earth-locked souls."

At this point Enigma paused, observing Miles to see if he had understood, so far.

"You see, angels do not reproduce like humans. They are spawned only when a human being lives a life free of wrongdoing."

Enigma grinned, "and that's pretty rare. So, the number of angels being created was low, far too low to match the growth of humanity. The angels had to find a way to deal with these wayward souls, for the strong ones had the ability to haunt and even hurt those on the physical plane.

"In their quest for a solution, they eventually turned to humans themselves. The angels found a unique human soul, who was known as Grim, and formed an agreement where he would ferry the lost souls to Paradise on behalf of the angels. In return, Grim was taught how to control spiritual power.

"Grim was powerful, learned quickly, and carried out his job exceedingly well. As the number of human souls continued to multiply, the Grim Reaper, for that was what he called himself, developed his own techniques and even created spiritual tools to assist him in his work of harvesting souls. For a time, he was the pinnacle of spiritual power."

Enigma paused, his features sombre as he reflected on the Grim Reaper, before continuing.

"Eventually more reapers were needed to handle the exponential growth of humanity. All souls who exhibited a certain level of natural power were given the option of becoming a reaper. That brings us back to you. If you agree to become a reaper Miles, you will be a hero to humanity. You will become powerful, extraordinarily so. And you will have the ability to keep your loved ones safe from the clutches of harmful supernatural creatures. You will have the privilege to work alongside the angels themselves to resolve all issues of spiritual security."

Enigma activated his spiritual power, having completed his story, and the riveting blue glow returned to his eyes. Strands of cobalt blue energy filled the air near the two, writhing and roiling in a magnificent display. Speaking now in a thundering voice, Enigma asked Miles the question that would set his path for eternity.

"Miles, will you accept the challenge and the honour of becoming a reaper?"

Miles stared at Enigma, barely noticing the glorious lightshow that surrounded him. A million competing thoughts and emotions were running through his head.

It was unfair of the reaper, to ask this of him, right after he had experienced the trauma of death. He really ought to decline. The reaper had said something about heaven. Wouldn't heaven be a nice place to go?

But if he agreed, it sounded like he would still be able to interact with the physical world. It was almost like cheating death. And his family... they could still be alive, and even if they weren't, there were so many others he wished to protect. So many needed his help. Help that seemed to be his to give.

He looked at Enigma, who stood tall and expectant. Everything the reaper had said, all of the answers he had given him, had been leading up to this moment.

"I'll do it," decreed Miles, understanding his response would change the course of his destiny. As Enigma had said, his death would not be in vain.

"Excellent," replied Enigma, allowing a smile to flash across his face.

"But I have one question," said Miles, looking deeply into Enigma's scarred face and thinking of his sad expression when speaking of the history of his order. "Where is the Grim Reaper?"

Enigma's gaze shifted, and he looked off into the distance.

"The Grim Reaper," said Enigma, speaking very slowly, as if each word weighed a ton, "was destroyed by the angels long, long ago. He had been channelling spiritual power into his son and that son's family, giving them inordinately long lives.

"When the angels discovered this, they demanded that Grim take the family's souls to Paradise, where they belonged. The reaper resisted and was defeated by three angels, but not before striking one down."

Enigma sighed, "This brings me to the seal. All reapers must undergo it, as a precaution. It prevents them from yielding to temptation. The seal transforms your human soul into one of a reaper, from a soul of the physical plane to one of the spiritual plane."

He hesitated, briefly, then continued. "It... it also prevents you from feeling any emotions. Any feelings for human souls, or concerns about what occurs in the physical plane, will be cast from your mind. You will no longer feel love, anger, jealousy or any emotion at all. To protect your family, to serve mankind, you must sever your connection with it. That is the price of becoming a reaper. That is the price of becoming an immortal spirit."

Enigma gazed into Miles' eyes, which had become dull, unreadable to anyone. Miles felt weak. This was the catch, and it was a big one. In order to serve humanity, he had to give up everything that made him human. It was a horrible fate, something Enigma had clearly decided to leave until the end, after he had made his decision.

But there was no turning back now. Miles knew he had to take this chance, this opportunity. He would commit to this unthinkable sacrifice for humanity. His time on earth had been too short; seventeen years was not long enough to experience the corporeal level of existence. He would have more time now. He would be immortal. He would be a reaper.

Miles gathered his courage and boldly said, with all the conviction he could muster, "I accept. I will be a reaper!"

Enigma looked at Miles for a second before answering, "Very good. I shall now cast this seal on you, but to do so there is one crucial step left. The transition of the soul cannot be performed without a focal point—something for the soul to concentrate upon."

Enigma's smile broadened, "So you must choose a new name! Here we go!" As Enigma spoke, the glowing light from his eyes reached blinding intensity. The blue energy surrounded them, and intensified in speed. Additional power seemed to be flowing from Enigma's mid-section, and it enveloped Miles in its glow. "Yell out your new name when I say *now*, Miles!" bellowed Enigma, who was forced to shout over the buzzing electrical sound of the power cascading around them.

The reaper raised his scythe above his head. The eye sockets in the skulls on his belt shone with the same blue hue of his eyes. A ball of the energy began to collect at the tip of Enigma's scythe. It pulsed there for a second, and then the whirlwind of energy reached a climax. "NOW!" cried Enigma as he brought the scythe down, slashing it towards Miles' head.

Miles had no time to react, no time to think. He had been trying to come up with a name, something epic and interesting like *Enigma*. But it was hard. As the scythe flew at him, Miles simply said the first name that came to his mind.

"Lance!"

He pronounced the name just as the ball of energy from the tip of scythe contacted his body. Miles' soul was filled with power, and his mind faded to blackness. His time as a reaper had begun.

Lance. It was not particularly creative or unique. It held no real special meaning to Miles, it was almost like a second thought.

Lance. That name would be his forevermore, it would be his identity. It would be his companion, his strength.

Lance. He liked the name; it would suit him well.

Lance.

Chapter 5

It was daytime in the physical realm by the time Lance came to his senses. He was lying crumpled on the ground in the middle of the alleyway with his face positioned upwards, exposed before the bright blue sky. All around were the sounds of a bustling city. The noise of engines waiting for that red light to turn green, the dull hubbub of construction and millions of voices all too far away to make out clearly.

As he became more lucid and focused, Lance noticed a distinctive humming in the air. The spiritual plane was still vibrating. The anomaly, which had so nearly ended his second life as a reaper, was obviously still present. But it was muted now, diminished, as if someone had thrown a blanket over a loudspeaker mid-song.

Something was different. He felt... different. It was intangible, something he couldn't explain. But it was strangely... familiar. Lance was sure he had experienced this sensation before, and his inability to identify it frustrated him.

He reached up with his hands and rubbed his eyes, an endeavor that Enigma had repeatedly explained was pointless. But Lance didn't really care; he always did that when recovering. It was a long lost habit from his human days. One of the few things his master could never correct.

Enigma, that old reaper, had taught him well. Lance had blossomed under his tutelage. He had prepared Lance perfect for his duties as a reaper, his sacred job of ferrying souls. Wait. The job!

Lance sat up immediately, preparing to search for Cody again as the reality of his situation set in. How long had he been down? Could the spirit, the one he had followed so painstakingly, have escaped his clutches? The thought maddened Lance, but did not last. As soon as he took his eyes off the sky and observed his surroundings, any thought of the rogue soul was extinguished.

There, standing in the grimy alleyway, were three spirits. Three great spirits. Lance gulped, recognizing them instantly. They were the kind of spirits that everyone knew. They stood there watchfully, quietly observing Lance as he recovered.

Lance could barely believe it. Three of the most powerful beings in existence were standing there in the alley with him. And each one was staring at him. This definitely was not good.

The spirits stood shoulder to shoulder, with the one in the middle slightly ahead of his two peers. Their combined power, though formidable, did not hum like whatever was dormant in the plane. Rather it shone like a beacon, glimmering out of their bodies in mesmerizing auras of brilliant colour.

It was an impressive display; a level of control which took thousands of years of practice and refinement. The three shone like stars, their strength almost blinding to Lance's tired mind.

Two of the spirits were angels, the one in the middle and the one to Lance's left. The other was a reaper, one who Lance knew well. It was Abyss, the head of their order.

Abyss was female, and maintained a slender frame. She wore completely black robes devoid of accoutrement, except for a grizzly bone-chain necklace. Her hands were hidden within the sleeves of her robes, but Lance didn't need to see them to know that they were clenched angrily. He and Abyss had never really gotten along.

The most intriguing feature about Abyss was her face, which Lance had never seen. She kept her hood up at all times, and Lance even suspected that it was infused with power just to guarantee that her appearance was never exposed. There was also a constant cloud of choking black smoke that shielded the front of the hood, making it impossible for anyone, be it spirit, reaper or even angel, to distinguish her face.

The power required to maintain the smokescreen never appeared to bother Abyss, who had steadily built a reputation within the reapers by coordinating the group and dealing with some of the world's most notorious rogue souls.

Unfortunately, Abyss had always seen Lance as an arrogant and overconfident reaper—a liability. She constantly heckled him, assigning him to tedious and boring missions, like his current hunt for Cody. Lance never argued, merely taking pride in easily completing the menial jobs and slowly rising in the ranks of the reapers, despite her opposition. He knew that Abyss felt threatened by his strength. Lance had far more raw power than Abyss. Or any of the other reapers, for that matter.

Lance did not know the angels personally, not like he knew Abyss, but he certainly could recognize them, as well as any person could recognize a celebrity.

Both of the angels were wearing white garments, upon which were fastened suits of golden armour. White feathered wings sprouted from their backs, although currently they were curled neatly behind their bodies.

They each wore a cloth tabard, which slightly obscured their gleaming golden breastplates and girdles. The fabric tucked under their belts and dangled in front of their groins, coloured pure white. Emblazoned upon the centre of each was a balanced, golden, cross. Gazardiel and Michael truly did look the part of angels.

Human souls take their appearance in the spiritual realm from what is called *residual self-image,* that is, their soul is subconsciously shaped into the form that they preferred on the physical plane. As souls grow in expertise, they can modify this image slightly, but it still retains a close resemblance to their original self. Angels were never human, so they, and the other spirits who never existed on the physical plane, are able to sculpt their forms to preference.

And because of this, the angels' physiques were perfect. They were both tall, close to eight feet in height, though Lance knew beings of their power were typically much larger. The angel's required un-parallelled control to keep their forms so contained.

Gazardiel stood to Michael's right. Lance did not know exactly his title, but he knew that Gazardiel, Michael and Gabriel were the three angels who had fought the Grim Reaper. Therefore, he deduced that Gazardiel was very powerful.

The angel's face was broad but extremely handsome, with a large nose and thick eyebrows. His eyes were baby blue, and his shoulder-length golden hair curled about his face untidily. He had a fairly large, messy beard, which matched the colour of his hair, and his thick lips were set in a neutral expression, neither angry nor happy. He stared pensively at Lance, who quickly turned his gaze to Michael.

Michael. The Archangel himself. Lance had heard so much about this one spirit, who by all accounts was the largest single reason the world remained intact. Lance had never seen Michael before, and to him, it felt as if he were looking directly at a legend, someone cut from the tapestry of myth, so fantastic and powerful that a reasonable man could not comprehend his existence.

Michael's bodily attire, though it matched Gazardiel's exactly, seemed to be brighter and more elegant. Unlike Gazardiel, Michael's face was slim and beautiful. It was angled, with high cheek bones and thin lips and eyebrows, but perfectly in proportion. His hair was not golden yellow like Gazardiel's, but was instead platinum blonde, almost white. It was completely straight, and spilled over the band of gold encircling his forehead before falling down his back to his shoulder blades. His eyes were also a startling shade of blue, and they were staring directly back at Lance.

"Ah, so you have awakened then, Lance? We were beginning to wonder about the extent of your damages." Michael's voice was deep and rich, not at all the type of voice you would expect to come from such a delicate face. It echoed in the spiritual plane, reminding everyone present of the Archangel's power. Lance did not quite know how to react, but he knew Michael deserved the highest level of respect.

"Archangel Michael," stated Lance, bowing low. Then, remembering there were others present, he turned to acknowledge them. "Angel Gazardiel." Lance performed another bow, and then turned to Abyss, who appeared to be waiting impatiently. He jerked his body unceremoniously towards his master. "Abyss."

Gazardiel smiled, either not noticing or not caring about the venom between Lance and the lead reaper, and spoke. His voice was also deep, and possessed an inspiring level of confidence. If Michael's voice made one think of the church, Gazardiel's conjured images of a barracks, or a great castle. "Well, Michael, it seems Lance has recovered his senses. And he even remembered to address Abyss and me. That never happens in your presence!" His joke fell on deaf ears, as Michael was focused on Lance, and, to the best of Lance's knowledge, Abyss had no known sense of humour. Despite the status of the spirits near him, Lance could not help but be curious.

"If it is not too forward, may I ask to what do I owe the honour of your esteemed presences?" he queried. At this point Abyss spoke, her voice cold and shrill.

"Our presence is due to no honour, reaper." She spat the last word out like it was distasteful. "We have come because of your failure, and because of the irregularity that occurred last night. We found you here, unconscious and vulnerable. I wanted to force you up, but he," at this point she jerked her head towards Gazardiel, "wouldn't allow it."

"Waking a damaged spirit risks permanent harm. You know this," stated Michael. "Gazardiel was right to advise us to wait. Lance still has potential." Gazardiel nodded solemnly. Lance's mind reeled. Michael was talking about him as though he had not succeeded, as if he could *become* a good reaper, not because he *was* one.

"I don't understand," exclaimed Lance, "Is something wrong?"

Abyss scoffed and shook her head.

"Of course there is. Do you see Cody anywhere?" A pit formed in Lance's stomach. He had forgotten about Cody as soon as he saw the three visitors.

Damn. His job. He had failed at his job. But more than that, he felt terrible for Cody. Poor Cody, he had relied on him! He had let him down!

And Michael and Gazardiel and Abyss knew it.

"What happened to him, Lance? What happened to Cody?" The question caught Lance off guard. He hadn't been listening because his thoughts had strayed to the strangest of subjects. His family. *Where were they now*? He hadn't thought about them in years. But now, considering the plight of vulnerable Cody, thoughts of his family invaded his mind, overwhelmed his consciousness. How could he have gone so long without even considering them? Were they just as exposed as his former charge?

"What happened to Cody?" Repeated Abyss, becoming audibly frustrated.

"You don't know?" asked Lance confusedly, sounding surprised. It was definitely the wrong thing to say.

"Don't know? I was not aware the spirit was our responsibility, reaper," Abyss again spat out the word *reaper* in disgust. "I was under the impression that you were given the task to take him to Paradise. But it is clear you are so incompetent that you have botched even that simple charge, and decided as an alternative, to rest your pathetic mind and take an idiotic nap." Lance winced. Abyss was angry, even angrier than usual. He had to focus, to de-escalate the situation. But that was easier said than done. His mother, his dad, his brother. How had he not checked, not at least *inquired*? He yearned for insight, just one little bit, into their lives.

No, he couldn't think about this now. Michael himself was standing a few feet away. This was very serious. He thought back to last night. What had happened with Cody?

"Lance," probed Michael. "Tell us what happened."

"He could have run off after I was incapacitated," suggested Lance.

"No," countered Abyss "We checked the surrounding area, his residue ends here."

"Then...," Lance trailed off, this was going to look very bad. "There were revenants. I destroyed one earlier in the night, and as I chased Cody, we ran into another pack..."

"That is exactly what we theorized," said Abyss, sounding very smug. "At least you were truthful; we could see the trail left by the revenants and came to that logical conclusion."

"That is inexcusable, Lance," chastised Michael.

"Not to mention pathetic," continued Abyss. "A pack of revenants? Subdue a reaper? For all of his so-called 'potential', it appears Lance is barely a glorified soul." This comment enraged Lance, having insulted his pride to his very core. Defeated by a group of revenants? Him? That was a lie and he would not stand for it.

"That is not true!" He exclaimed vehemently. "I am shocked that you, for all of your logic, came to the conclusion that a reaper was defeated by a pack of revenants. The very concept is patently ridiculous. I was subdued, yes, but not by them. No, I was taken out by a sudden spike in power in the spiritual plane, a mass of concentrated power that nearly hit me! It was incredible, like nothing I have ever seen. Surely you can all feel the tremors in the spiritual plane, even now," he finished, staring at Abyss indignantly.

"*That* is why you are here, not because of the loss of a single soul. Angels would never be involved with this type of issue. Gazardiel, Michael, you are both here for something else. And you think I can help." As he finished, Lance looked at Gazardiel, who had allowed a ghost of a smile to drift across his face.

Abyss was furious. She walked menacingly towards Lance, rounding on him aggressively. "How dare you speak to your superiors like this, I will..." but before she could carry out her threat, Abyss found herself cut off by Gazardiel who asked intently.

"A mass of concentrated power? Is that what caused this?" But before Lance could respond, Michael raised his hand to halt the conversation.

"Lance, you are correct in at least one respect. We are indeed very concerned about what has occurred in the spiritual plane. But that does not change the fact that, until we can prove otherwise, you have failed in your charge without extenuating circumstances. And you will be punished accordingly."

Lance could barely believe it. "Extenuating circumstances?" He exclaimed incredulously. "Can't you feel what's going on around you?

"These tremors, though worrisome, certainly could not incapacitate you," decreed Michael, his face remaining neutral. Abyss nodded energetically

"Nothing but an excuse to hide your incompetence," she said angrily.

"But Michael," interjected Gazardiel, looking at Lance with concern. "Lance told us this power was of a much higher intensity than it is now. If that is true, then little fault can be found in Lance. Angels themselves could not withstand such a high degree of pressure, let alone a reaper."

Michael shook his head slowly. "But it is clear that the power was never so intense. This energy is constant, not variable. Therefore, it must be a natural runoff of power, most likely from an unidentified spirit. This minor pulsing would never be strong enough to deal the damage Lance claims, and we know it has never been stronger. Sadly, Lance was incapacitated by a direct spiritual attack, and the only aggressive spirit nearby would have been a revenant."

"What if this power *is* an attack?" offered Gazardiel. "An extremely powerful spiritual attack would deal damage to an area similar to what Lance has experienced. It would also explain the change in strength over time. All attacks burn out eventually. In fact, that also accounts for the mass of power Lance talked about, that resembles a blast of some sort."

"Except for two facts," explained Abyss, showing a great deal more respect to Gazardiel than she did to Lance. "Such an attack would surely have run out of energy now, or would be almost completely gone. We seem to have reached a stable level of emission, and have yet to observe it change in some time. No attack exhibits such behaviour. And," as she said this she motioned upwards with her head, "an attack that powerful would have been felt by us."

Lance frowned. Although it seemed they had forgotten about disciplining him for the time being, it was still very frustrating that they dismissed his account, something they had spent time waiting for, as simply lies.

"What if the power... was absorbed somehow? Into a human? Human bodies cocoon their souls and emit a stable pulse, maybe it found its way into a human..." Lance's voice trailed off, the idea sounded silly. Gazardiel stared at him thoughtfully, but Michael was quick to explain exactly why that could not be the case.

"No human could contain this amount of power, it would rip them apart. In addition, this power is *spiritual*," he emphasized spiritual, as if he felt that Lance could possibly misunderstand, "It wouldn't affect anything on the physical plane."

Now Lance was really upset. Just because he had made a suggestion was no reason to imply he knew nothing about how the spiritual and physical planes worked. As impressive as Michael was, Lance was getting frustrated by his complete dismissal of Lance's opinions.

"Well," snapped Lance, "If you are so sure it is a spirit, why haven't you gone to the centre of this power and found him? That shouldn't be hard."

Michael nodded, apparently not noticing Lance's tone. "Normally yes, but this power is acting uniquely. It is a decentralized cloud of essence. It hangs over the entire city, like a fog. It doesn't change position at all. The centre of the cloud is the centre of the city itself. Whatever spirit is here, it is doing a good job at keeping itself hidden."

With this statement he turned away from Lance and looked to Abyss. "We had hoped that you could shed some light on the situation. Apparently not. We need to move quickly Gazardiel, things will soon get out of hand. Abyss, I leave Lance's discipline to your discretion."

And with that, Michael turned his back to Lance and began to walk away. Lance was horrified. Allowing Abyss to do what she wanted to him was practically a death sentence! In desperation, he tried to stop Michael, to keep him from leaving him alone with Abyss.

"Out of hand?" he asked, trying to keep his worry about Abyss from spilling over into his voice. "What do you mean?"

"Revenants." Answered Michael dryly.

Gazardiel nodded solemnly, apparently deciding to elaborate.

"Yes, this power, whatever it is, is more than strong enough to spawn them. And this is a city of several million people. There is a lot of evil going around. A lot of opportunities for revenant formation. The area is being flooded by them."

Lance opened his eyes wide, now fully understanding the seriousness of the situation. Revenants were deadly to souls. Mindless, violent, and hungry. Some could even be strong enough to affect the physical plane. People could get hurt, spirits could be destroyed!

He thought about a generic human, blissfully unaware, being attacked by a revenant. It was so unfair and terrifying Lance could not even stomach the thought.

"Can they merge?" asked Lance, now very worried. Michael, who had been slowly walking away from the group this entire time, turned to look at Lance once again.

"Let's hope not." Michael activated his power. His eyes became a dazzlingly bright colour of white. In front of him shot a massive beam of light, almost as if some spaceship high above him had activated its tractor beam at that location. He stepped into the light, which Lance recognized as a conduit to Paradise, and disappeared.

Abyss, who along with Lance had been watching Michael, turned to Gazardiel. "After you."

Gazardiel shook his head. "I will remain here to observe the punishment you deliver to Lance. I am curious to see how it is customarily done." Lance suddenly felt a huge feeling of gratitude towards Gazardiel as he watched the angel refuse to leave. Gazardiel was protecting him; Abyss would dare not give out a ridiculous punishment in his presence. Lance looked at Gazardiel, who did not return the gaze, but instead stared calmly at Abyss, who had noticeably stiffened.

"Very well," said Abyss, her voice level dropping a couple of volume levels. She turned to face Lance, who reluctantly brought his eyes away from Gazardiel to meet her.

"Lance, you have failed in the most sacred objective of the reapers: To shepherd the souls which we are assigned to give passage. Your incompetence and recklessness have resulted in the destruction of a soul, and I no longer feel confident in your ability to perform as a reaper," she paused, acutely aware of the presence of Gazardiel.

"So I now strip you of your title as reaper and demote you to the level of apprentice. Hopefully, by working with a *real* reaper, you will learn your place. I believe Pajetic, a senior agent, requires a servant. I will leave you to his care. You will be contacted." And with that, Abyss turned, walked briskly towards the beam of light, and disappeared.

It was now just Lance and Gazardiel present in the alleyway, which had, surprisingly, remained devoid of humans during the entire discussion. Gazardiel, who had remained fairly still, walked up to Lance. When he got close, he grabbed the ex-reaper's hand.

"I will not always be able to do that for you, Lance." He spoke with kindness. Lance couldn't help but smile.

"I know, sir. Thank you." Gazardiel nodded.

"I can see your power, Lance, I know you were not defeated by simple revenants. But things are changing rapidly, and you will need to be able to take care of yourself. From what you know, and what you do not. Use your time with Pajetic to get stronger. You and I both know that Pajetic loses accomplices regularly in his line of work. Don't become just another. This is an opportunity for you. Take it."

Lance knew exactly what Gazardiel meant. Pajetic was in charge of hunting down the most dangerous spirits bound to earth. He routinely worked with angels and was known to regularly clash with them, Abyss, and anyone else who got in his way. Lance had been given the most perilous job within the reapers' organization, but the punishment would have been worse without Gazardial's presence. After all, Lance had always craved a challenge.

"I know Gazardiel. I will not fail."

"Good," responded the angel. "I believe what you have told us today, Lance. And despite his superficial misgivings, I think deep down Michael does too. We will look into what you have said. I don't think it is a spirit that is causing this... but I have been wrong before."

With this statement he placed a knowing hand on Lance's shoulder. "If you learn anything. Let me know." And with that, he turned and walked into the beam of light, which disappeared completely behind him.

The alleyway suddenly seemed very empty, as Lance was left alone with his thoughts. He was in a bad position, it was true. Pajetic liked no one, and yet cooperating with him was essential if Lance was to survive. But still, he felt somewhat relieved. Gazardiel would help him if he could, and that knowledge was comforting.

With the departure of the angels, Lance could not help but think of the weird sensations he was still experiencing. His concern about innocent people. His preoccupation with his family.

Could... Could they be... feelings? No, Lance shook his head. They couldn't be.

And yet, he couldn't stop thinking about his family, about his friends, even about his old crush, Jessica. Could the seal have been broken?

Lance did not know if this was good or bad, but he had to act. Something was not right, and if he really was experiencing emotions again, this little meeting he had with Abyss would seem like a friendly chit chat.

The sensation was like an itch, constantly begging to be scratched, and his mind was clouded with doubt and wonder. Could his family really still be here, somewhere in this city nearby? It couldn't be ignored, and in an instant, Lance decided to leave. He would go. Go and find his family.

Chapter 6

It was weird, feeling emotions again, Lance thought to himself as he channelled his power and took to the air. He felt his mind race with the implications as he flew, rising up over the alley and packed city.

There were no clouds lingering from the heavy rains of a night ago, and the sun hung naked in the sky, warming all the land it touched.

In contrast, the spiritual plane seemed to be under a curtain of fog, onset as it was by the unrelenting and oppressive humming. As a reaper who tracked and hunted spirits, Lance was used to chasing unfamiliar power. But this was different. It wasn't a solitary trail, it was a storm.

The overwhelming haze didn't bother Lance; he was too full of happiness, and joy, and the million other emotions he had been stripped of for so long. Becoming a reaper didn't take away your emotions, far from it, but it did blunt them.

Especially when it came to anything relating to the physical world – Lance barely registered the plight of humans, and certainly hadn't thought like them. But all that had changed, just in one flash of power.

It felt to Lance like he was awaking from a trance, some kind of dream where he was being controlled by an unfamiliar entity, an alien, a creature without reference for or care of what it meant to be human.

But Lance remembered now. He remembered how cool it was to fly. How amazing it was, for him to be what he had become. A reaper, a godlike being in the eyes of mortals, a warrior of great skill capable of doing things no human would consider possible. His friends would have been jealous.

His friends... How old would they be now? How would they have changed? Lance didn't know and right now didn't care. There was another set of humans that meant far more to him now. They wouldn't care if he was a god, or that he gave up his afterlife to protect the innocent. They wouldn't be afraid, or intimidated, or hurt. No, they would just care that he was with them once more.

Lance was going to see his family.

A boyish grin lit up his face as he flew in-between a few of the skyscrapers that stood tall, defying gravity, in the downtown. He weaved between them, looping through the concrete jungle where he had sat so silently just a night before. How that night's events had changed him.

He yelled out loud as he dove down towards the city streets, melting through the cars and people that saturated the area on the physical plane.

Once the novelty wore off, Lance flew high into the sky, thinking about how far he had come since his first day in the water. He could fly effortlessly, conjure weapons, substances and even perform magic! He grinned as he contemplated this last bit.

No matter how many times the reapers referred to it as *power*, he knew the beams and rays and coils of pure energy were the *magic* people described in so many books.

Stopping his ascent, Lance looked down onto the city below. The alleys and streets resembled a maze to Lance's enhanced vision. Though he was far above, he could still clearly discern individual people moving about their business.

It was funny, he concluded, how the city was constructed. Certain areas were angular and straight, the roads intersecting each other at neat ninety degree angles, with buildings that were all perfect squares. These areas had always been planned, thought Lance. They were mapped out at the beginning.

But the majority of the city was complicated, with a thousand shapes and twists. So typical of humans, Lance thought. Of *us*, he corrected himself. Adapters and changers, who embrace the chaos of mortal existence.

Lance flew eastwards, maintaining his current altitude and simply observed the city. He viewed different sections, like the financial sector; with its glass buildings and air of importance, and the university in the downtown; the centre of learning. Lance also noticed several spirits wandering around the city, apparently unaware of his flight through the sky.

Lance recognized their odd, beastly forms immediately: revenants. There were a lot more of them than Lance had realized. He must have flown over a hundred at least.

A few were solo, but many were roaming around in packs, terrorizing streets and hoping to find an unlucky wayward spirit. Some were massive; too large to have appeared naturally. Only a merger would be capable of letting them reach such a size.

Lance frowned, this was a very bad sign. Things really were escalating in the city. It was not safe for souls, nor humans. What would happen if the revenants became strong enough to influence things on the physical plane? He knew it was possible. Enigma had told him about it when he first taught him about revenants. Back when Lance was just his pupil.

"Revenants," Enigma had said, "Are curious beings of energy. They are examples of spiritual power in the environment coalescing to form a sentient creature."

"What?" inquired Lance, who wasn't really interested in the different types of spirits. He had always wanted to do more practice with his power, and less work on the theory.

"Pay attention," instructed Enigma, who continued undaunted. "You know that powerful spirits and spiritual objects radiate power, correct?"

"Yes," nodded Lance.

"Well, when this power is released, and special circumstances are met, revenants come into being. An example of spiritual power, with a will of its own."

"Like elementals?" asked Lance, now slightly interested.

"No," countered Enigma, "you didn't let me finish. Elementals are formed when a spirit consciously exerts spiritual power into an element or form of any type, like fire, and then gives it a core of power to operate as its own independent entity. The circumstances of elemental formation are far different from revenants, who are created subconsciously, by humans."

"Humans?" asked Lance, his attention now firmly on the subject at hand, "But they can't control their power."

"Indeed they can't, hence the term *subconsciously* Lance." Enigma laughed, "Whenever a human commits a strongly negative deed, an action that is morally wrong, like murder or torture, near a source of spiritual power, a revenant is formed."

"But what about intention? Murder is sometimes justified." Lance thought of the Grim Reaper, and his battle with the angels, as he spoke.

"Justified, perhaps, but revenants are still produced, even if the intentions are honourable. Even intensely negative thought can be enough to spawn their kind. Revenants are inherently evil, since the malevolent energy used to create them consumes their very being. They will always try to harm you." After saying this, Enigma stared stonily at Lance, who met his teachers gaze.

"But if there are more humans, that means more evil..."

"And more revenants," continued Enigma. "In fact, it has been suggested by some reapers that revenants are the spiritual plane's counterpart for humans, just like demons are the opposite of angels."

Lance continued to ask questions, and Enigma continued to answer them. Just as he always had.

Lance smiled from his altitude far above the city. He would always be grateful towards that particular reaper; Enigma had prepared him well for the massive changes between life and... well... death.

Lance considered this as he flew over the outskirts of the city, while the tall buildings of the downtown faded away. This new area was a compilation of oddly shaped structures, many of which were falling into disrepair. It was the place where the poor were kept. There were no revenants here, at least none that he could see.

Far to the east, Lance could just make out the industrial sector, where hundreds of smokestacks belched foul fumes into the air. He shook his head. Even with the return of his feelings for humanity, he could never understand why his race so eagerly destroyed their home.

He was glad he had not taken a wider route to the suburbs; it would have been depressing to fly through the smog hovering over that industrialized sector of the city. Years could pass, maybe even centuries, before life would ever be able to reclaim that area, even if all human activity disappeared overnight.

Lance turned his attention forward, reminding himself to be happy, and that he was on his way to see his family. He focused on the line of blue which had now appeared along the horizon in front of him. The river. Lance increased his speed, knowing his family, and his home, were close.

The line of blue stretched and grew until Lance was almost upon it and could make out its cold waters. Its great current frothed downstream, swollen from the rainfalls of last night. Up the river just a slight bit stood the familiar bridge, a monument to his death.

Or at least, a rebuilt bridge. It was no longer torn in two, but had instead been repaired, with more modern suspension and an emphasis on steel, as opposed to the original model which had made liberal use of concrete. This new bridge was sturdy, would have fared much better in the event of an explosion, but to Lance, this was just a case of "too little, too late". At least for him, anyway.

A part of Lance wanted to go to see the bridge, to examine it, to see if all traces of his death had been scraped away. Maybe there would be a memorial in his honour? But the other, more sentimental side rejected the idea.

There was something about visiting your own place of death that was just wrong. He didn't know what he would find there, but he knew he would probably get upset.

Would his parents still use this bridge? He knew the nearest alternate crossing was more than a fifteen minute drive out of their way, but he sort of hoped they put up with it anyway. He wondered if they respected his memory every time they drove into the city. Would they even still remember him?

He continued to fly, occupied with his recollections. He had so many questions. So many memories about his past life. What would they be like? He hadn't even begun to speculate about what had actually broken the reaper's seal. There was too much to process, too many implications from what just occurred the night before.

Lance struggled for a moment to solve this mystery of the strange mystical power, but quickly abandoned his pursuit as the image of his family, smiling and beckoning to him, once again commandeered his thoughts.

How would he react to them? In his mind's eye Lance could see himself entering the physical plane, and letting his family view and talk to him. He could explain everything to them. How he died, what his new role was, and how he came back to protect them. He would hug and kiss his father and mother, and even his annoying little brother.

Lance smiled at the thought of seeing Jeffrey again; his brother would now be the same age as his immortal self. The little kid would seem all grown up.

The sun had reached its peak in the sky, indicating mid-day, before Lance reached a familiar area in the suburbs. The neat and tidy houses, with the manicured lawns and pristine swimming pools, beckoned to him. This development was new when Lance had been born. The school he attended was just a few minutes' walk away. It was all as beautiful as he had remembered.

Lance dove down, bringing himself to an altitude only slightly higher than the squat subdivision houses. Vivid memories accompanied his descent, each house representing something different to him.

The one on the right, with the red shutters and brick walls; His friend Jake lived there, and they would meet in front of that house whenever Lance decided to walk to school. To the left; the dead end street where he and the other boys of the neighbourhood would play road hockey for hours, safe from the threat of oncoming cars. And there, just ahead, the house he knew by heart.

His house looked mostly the same as he remembered, with its white exterior and black roof. It had the same two-door garage, with its doors painted a glossy black, matching the front enterance to the house itself. However, there were also a number of small, disquieting changes.

The garden was different. His mother had always grown tulips and daisies, but now there were shrubs and roses. Lance had never really appreciated the flowers, except maybe as a quick way to grab a gift to impress some girl, but his mother had loved them. Lance remembered the hours she spent each day painstakingly maintaining it. There was also a birdbath in the front yard, which Lance definitely did not remember.

Lance landed at the foot of the driveway. At this point, after being distracted with the nostalgia of seeing his house for the first time in forever, he noticed the car in the driveway. He was shocked to see a black sports utility vehicle, not his family's van. Instantaneously, he realized that there was no way the van could still be there. It had been destroyed in the crash. The sight caused reality to set in.

In a way, coming back home like this had made Lance feel like things would be normal. Almost as though he could walk through the front door and find his family there waiting for him, ready to resume the life he had left long ago.

He had tricked himself into thinking that his return would make everything right, that this would fix it all, that he would no longer have to be a reaper and have to deal with spirits, or responsibility. He had just wanted to be a teenager again. To go back to enjoying the best days of his life.

But sight of the SUV brought an end to it all. Lance knew it could never be fixed, he could never go back. Their van was gone. His parents would have changed, his brother would never be the same. They would have moved on without him. They needed to, after all they had no choice. He had been left behind.

His earlier giddiness tempered, Lance pondered the situation for a moment. He couldn't do that to them, couldn't shatter the world they have lived in for so long. Revealing himself to his family would have massive consequences. And for what? To indulge in his own self-pity? No. He wouldn't do it. After all, everything he had done up to this point had been for them.

Lance gulped down a knot that was forming in his throat and nodded slowly. He wouldn't speak, he wouldn't show himself. He would remain in the shadows, as always the silent protector. But he could still watch. Because, no matter the path he took or the burdens he bore, Lance was at his heart just a boy. And he wanted to see his family.

He ran up the driveway and along the walkway to the front door. It was closed, but Lance, being on the spiritual plane, simply passed right through. As soon as he entered, a chill passed through his body. Something was not right.

The inside of his house was different, completely foreign from what he remembered. That fact was evident as soon as he stepped inside.

The walls, which had always been brown, were now covered in flowery wallpaper. To his left, the table for keys and wallets was gone, replaced by a huge brown armoire which reached up to the ceiling.

Gone too were the family pictures that had lined the wall beside the staircase to the second level. His family had one taken every three years, and each had a story behind it.

The keepsakes had been replaced by paintings, one of a bowl of fruit, another, a portrait of some elderly stranger. He noticed there was a new arched opening to his right, which led to the dining room. It had only been accessible through the kitchen before. The familiar wooden plank table, where he had enjoyed thousands of dinners, was gone, and in its place was a huge modern piece, pristine and polished.

Lance raced through the house, becoming more and more agitated. He had worried he had been left behind, but only in a metaphorical sense. It was beginning to look like that wasn't the only way.

He checked the different areas of the house and found more distressing changes. The kitchen, renovated. The living room, new tv and furniture. Even the room with the fireplace was transformed, with the rough white carpet gone in favour of a new hardwood floor. Now full-on sprinting, Lance headed to the staircase. He had to see his room. At least it would be the same.

As he whipped around the corner, he bolted straight through a person who had been walking down the steps. The person felt nothing, but Lance flinched and turned, hoping to get a glimpse of a family member.

But it was not to be. The woman walking down the stairs, holding a basket of laundry and humming softly, was a complete stranger. She was wearing a flowing pink dress and had curly white hair. Her face was lined with wrinkles, and her step was slow and laboured. The sight of her dashed any of Lance's remaining hopes.

They were gone, his family, his parents, his brother, all gone without a trace. And Lance knew that they had never wanted to leave the city.

His parents couldn't have done that to Jeffrey, whose entire social life had been in this area. They wouldn't force him to leave his friends. Hell, they wouldn't want to leave *their* friends, let alone Jeff's!

Their entire life had been situated here, his mom had loved this house, his dad had worked hard to pay off almost all of the mortgage. They had ties here, connections. Their past and their future was here. But they weren't.

A sliver of Lance knew what this meant, and vainly tried to get him to leave, but it was overborne by the rest of Lance who couldn't accept the truth.

Lance continued to ascend the stairs, praying his room would somehow, miraculously, be the same. Of course it wasn't. The bed, gone. His desk, gone. The posters of basketball players, even the mirror in which he had examined himself every morning, looking for some trace of facial hair and lamenting his acne, was gone.

In its place were shelves stocked with books, and a carved wooden desk, covered with papers and a computer monitor. His room had been converted into a home office.

It was the last straw for Lance, who felt tears running down his face, tears that he knew no one could see. His family never would have chosen to leave. That left only one option.

He had never known if his parents had survived the bridge collapse, only assumed that they had. His father had been ahead of him when the thing gave way. Lance had always figured that they had lived. Now, the thought seemed like wishful thinking. His grief was unbearable as he began to realize how futile his actions were. He had given up everything! His emotions, his power, even his afterlife for them! And for what? They weren't even here to be protected anymore.

Lance floated out of the house, and vowed never to return. It hurt him too much to see the changes, to see that his family was truly gone. And it was as if no one even remembered them. Instantly, Lance knew exactly where he would go.

He began to fly south, towards the place his parents and brother must be. Long ago, when his grandfather had died, his parents had purchased the area surrounding his grave, to reserve space for the entire family. To Lance, or rather, Miles, it seemed like a silly idea.

Death seems incredibly far away for a child, a whimsical concept, something in the distant future. But now Lance understood the wisdom of the purchase. Now he knew where to find his family.

The trip to the cemetery seemed to go by in the blink of an eye. Lance was completely focused on paying his respects to his family, on giving those he loved the proper send-off. He knew exactly where he was going. The gravesite was on the far west side of the graveyard, on a hill that stood apart from the remainder of the graves.

Lance's senses as a reaper were going haywire. Although he was long gone from the throbbing of the spiritual plane in the city centre, cemeteries always had a great deal of latent spiritual power about them. The dead remnants of a thousand souls.

As Lance moved through he could feel them, sense the sadness of the area, the profound feeling of loss. It engulfed him, and he felt fresh tears fall down his face.

But he pressed on, through the grief of this place and his own mind, seeing the outline of six graves that dotted the hill where his family would be buried. Six graves? That wasn't right. Lance had expected four. But as he reached the hill, he remembered that the first two graves were the resting places of his grandparents. They were part of the family too.

As Lance reached the tombstones, his blood ran cold. He stared at them for a moment, reading the inscription on each one. Loving father, caring mother, happy brother. Reading each one broke Lance a little, as he realized he would never get to see them again. Lance paused at the final grave, knowing what he was about to see but afraid to do so.

There, engraved on the stone, clear as day, were the simple words *"Here lies Miles Lechler, A treasure who had not enough time."* The sight of the assembled gravestones sent ripples of anguish through his body. That was not something anyone should see.

He could now understand the reasoning behind the seal of the reaper, the removal of emotions. No person should go looking for his family's grave. No soul should stare upon the marker of his own death, to be reminded that he was gone.

Truly, completely, inescapably... gone. During his flight, during his thoughts, Lance's mind had focused on if his family would remember him. Now he realized that with his family gone, no one did. He was a ghost, in every sense of the word. His entire family just a minor footnote in the sprawling book of humanity. There was no one left to care.

Lance shivered, feeling more alone now than he ever had before, and looked with disgust at the ground beneath his feet. His body was somewhere down there. The vessel that had harboured his mind, the site where he had lived his life, was entombed beneath the dirt. He was buried! Buried! Rotting! Dismay filled Lance as he realized that his tomb might very well be an empty one, his body could still be decomposing at the bottom of the river.

Lance couldn't take it anymore. He took one last, longing look at the graves.

"I... love you." He said, his voice catching in his grief. He meant it. He had always disliked saying it to his family, but there was never a doubt that he did. And now he could never say it again. He was gone. *They* were gone. *Everything was gone*!

His mind clouded by his pain, Lance leapt into the air, doing whatever he could to put distance between himself and this place of mourning.

The reaper ran and flew and cruised forward, running from his past, fleeing from his death. It felt to him like he was being chased, by his past life and his life as a reaper, both at the same time. They pressured him, like two famished beasts, one demanding that Lance languish in a broken past, the other, a pointless future.

But now, Lance merely wanted the present, to be free of the forces of his past and future expectations, to simply exist. Not as Lance, or Miles. Just as himself. It was a while before he stopped, and was surprised to see where he was.

It was his school, Jackson Secondary. He stood now at the steps, the steps where he had been waiting on that day so long ago. School had apparently just ended, as a tide of students streamed down, towards the mass of cars and yellow school buses that awaited to ferry them home.

The site acted as a kind of painkiller to Lance. Nostalgia dulled the heartache and confusion of realizing his family was gone, and the horror of seeing his own grave. He recognized many of the faces. One kid, with orange hair, walked briskly passed Lance, and then stopped, looking back to the front of the school, and yelled at a friend who was at the top of the steps,

"I'll be back for football." Lance nearly fell over. He knew that voice. It was Jake, his friend, his companion. Jake was still here, and although his hair was a bit longer and he no longer had braces, it was the same Jake he had always known. The relief of a familiar face washed over Lance and reduced his angst. Not everything had changed. Lance decided to walk up the steps, now really enjoying the all-too-familiar school. Unlike his home, the school was almost exactly the same.

The doors were the same, the library entrance was the same, even the office, which was to the right side of the main entrance, was the same. The display boards had different bulletins, but the glass cases were familiar to him.

The continuity was comforting for Lance; it was like Jackson Secondary had been frozen in time. He turned left from the main entrance, which led to a hallway lined with lockers on both sides, dotted with classroom doors. He walked for about thirty seconds and made another right, heading towards the place where his old locker used to be. As he walked down this new hallway, he saw a brunette girl standing with her back to him, fiddling with her lock.

Lance approached, curious. All the other students had left the school already. What was this girl still doing here? Suddenly, she finished working with the lock and turned around, walking briskly past Lance, but not before he got a clear view of her. It made his heart stop. *Jessica.* He even caught the scent of her perfume, the same kind she had been wearing in biology so long ago.

Her face was as beautiful as he had remembered, with deep green eyes and high cheekbones. Her hair was curly and a rich, dark, shade of brown, which tumbled gracefully to the middle of her back. Lance couldn't believe it.

She was still here. After all this time, she was still at school. He wondered if she would have remembered him at all, or if he would just be another faceless person in the periphery.

It didn't matter, Lance suddenly realized, as he stood in the now empty school hallway. It didn't matter what he was to her. She had meant something to *him*.

Just like his family.

Jessica wouldn't be remembered by the world. She would be forgotten when she was gone, just like him. And yet she had changed his life nevertheless. Lance felt his will begin to harden, and for the first time since reaching his house, felt hope.

His father and mother never cared about being *remembered*. They cared about *him*. They cared about making the lives of people full. They cared about leaving the world in a better place than they found it. That was how their legacy would be measured, not by monuments, or memorials or poetic inscriptions on tombstones.

And he had a chance. Lance had a chance to do what they did for him, to thousands, no, millions, of others. The proof was right here, at the school.

His work had kept Jessica safe, had protected these students and teachers. Lance's heart beat stronger, with reinvigorated purpose and intent. He had made a difference. He had become a reaper to protect his loved ones, but his actions had also protected others. He had kept the world safe, and as a consequence shielded people he had forgotten, or never even known.

His thoughts expanded to all of the humans living in the suburbs, the city, even those across the country and world. He had protected them all. He would protect them all. He would not let them down! His sacrifice had not been in vain.

Lance closed his eyes, feeling power flow through him once more. His new mission would start with whatever mysterious force had knocked him out and was spawning the revenants. He would solve this, redeem himself, and work to protect humanity. He would make a difference.

Opening his eyes, Lance channelled his red power into a place on the floor, where a white beam suddenly appeared, springing from the ground and up to the ceiling.

It was the same kind of pure white light that Michael had summoned to transport the senior spirits to Paradise. It was in fact, identical to what Michael had done, although admittedly only strong enough to move Lance himself.

He would go to Paradise and find out exactly what he and Pajetic were to do. He understood himself now, and knew why he had made that decision back on that dreary day. It was for people. For Jessica. He had the strength to prevent their lives from crashing down. And so he would work tirelessly until they were all safe. He drew in his breath, and then with a determined air, stepped into the portal to Paradise. For Jessica.

Chapter 7

Paradise. The mere promise of such a place has had a more profound impact on humanity than all of its heroes and all of its wars. To the hopeful, Paradise is the eternal joy to which all that live are entitled, a path that guides humans towards a good life, and a reward for ignoring the temptation of evil. To the cynic, it is nothing more than a partisan bribe.

Whatever its true character, Paradise is doubtlessly elusive. Humanity never sees it physically manifested; they merely trust that it is there. The light at the end of the tunnel of life itself.

The reapers do not know why Paradise exists, or how it came about. That is a closely guarded secret. But that does not mean that the reapers have never seen Paradise, far from it. They simply do not know its designs. Very little is known of its creator.

There have always been whispers, quiet murmurs in the crevices of the spiritual plane, of that being. The forerunner, the progenitor. God. Perhaps is it nothing, just a fanciful manifestation of the belief that some greater force is in play. But perhaps there really is something more. Certainly these notions have neither been dispelled nor confirmed by the angels, who divulge nothing on such a sensitive topic.

But as Lance arrived, he felt certain of the existence of such a force. As he gazed over its peaceful entrance he was momentarily taken aback, as always, by Paradise's overwhelming magnificence.

Describing Paradise is difficult, particularly because it has many forms. To each individual human soul, Paradise appears differently. For some, it is a beautiful city built of clouds, with the soft sounds of a muted choir gently caressing the background.

For an increasing number, it is experienced as a mirror of life—an ideal existence where the soul is exactly as he or she wishes. Successful, lucky, attractive, strong, whatever. Anything goes in Paradise.

And yet for others, a dwindling group, Paradise is a simple, but perfect, home. It is large, large enough to house multitudes of friends, with a garden and green grass all around. And as that soul approaches, preparing to face a peaceful eternity, their faces light up as they behold all of their loved ones already inside, happily awaiting their arrival home.

Lance had never had the chance to experience any of these scenarios in Paradise, after all he had never passed on. But he knew which one he would pick. But Paradise would have to wait for a different time. Lance couldn't rest just yet. He was desperately needed.

Every temporary visitor's first view of Paradise is the temple. It is constructed of immaculate white marble, perched on top of a jagged and steep mountain, with an imposing central tower at its very edge. The temple is open-roofed and surrounded by an ornate golden fence.

The fence had widely spaced bars, with more than enough space for a human to fit through, and is altogether powerless. No, it is the force field of power, nearly invisible amongst the white décor and yet godly in its strength, that makes this fence more effective than any wall ever built.

The only manner of bypassing this impenetrable barrier is through a golden gate, placed at the very front of the temple. Directly through the gate, there is a clear view of the tower, which Lance had never seen entered or exited.

This gate is where Lance arrived, just outside in a small stone circle on the edge of the mountain. This circle is where all spirits travelling to Paradise arrive, apart from the human souls, who are immediately escorted to their personal Paradise. Of course, such an infinite number of Paradises would cause issue with the coordination of angels, so the default temple is presented to all transitory residents.

The way to use your power to create the portal to Paradise, Lance recalled, was complicated. Enigma had taught it to him in what seemed to be eons ago. You needed to focus your mind on light, and project it using your power onto a spot in front of you. If done correctly, a gateway to Paradise would be opened.

At first, the process seems very simple, but it is quite difficult for human souls. For this light is not the physical light one sees when looking at the sun, or an illuminated light bulb, but instead the pure expression of good and love. Lance grinned, as he recalled how frustrated he had been by such a vague definition. How was he supposed to know what the *pure expression of good and love* was?

But Enigma had been patient, explaining to Lance that the easiest way to do this was to picture an angel. Angels were spiritual manifestations of this light, and therefore worked as an image to open a portal to Paradise. These portals were the only way to reach Paradise itself.

Lance had struggled with opening portals when he was first learning the technique, but now, travelling to Paradise was simple, though it did require substantial exertion of his power. Even with his great strength, Lance could barely manage a small gateway, one big enough for only himself. The fact that Michael could produce a portal large enough for an entire host of souls spoke volumes about his talents.

Nevertheless, here he stood, facing the gates of Paradise. And there before him, it's unshifting guardian. Lance was not surprised by his presence. Peter was always there, screening the arrivals.

The angel was standing to the right of the gate, on the outside of Paradise, wearing flowing white robes. His hands were clasped behind him, and the hood of his robe, encircled by a gold band, was drawn up, hiding his facial features. His chin, more pronounced than the rest of his face, was slightly free of the shadow and poked out defiantly. It was covered in a trimmed blonde beard. Matching long locks of golden hair cascaded out from either side. White and feathery wings sprouted from his back, but were folded up, giving Peter a more human appearance.

Lance always found it odd to see an angel not wearing armour, be it in Paradise or not. To him, the armour signaled readiness for battle. And the angels, just as much as reapers, perhaps even more so, should always be ready to intervene. After all, it was their duty. That was why they were in the city now, trying, and as far as Lance could see, failing, to reestablish control.

The sight of Peter, silently standing in the safety of Paradise, seemed very wrong to Lance. He seemed so detached. It was a reminder to him that angels, guardians of peace and justice, were remarkably unhuman. They were an incarnation of pure energy, spawned from lives free of sin, taking a form that was easy for human souls to understand. They acted with regal, harsh logic, and Lance couldn't help but wonder if they truly were the keepers of humanity, or were instead humanity's kings.

Lance walked towards Peter, who silently met his gaze. Lance wondered for a moment if he was in the right place. Typically reapers met at their own sanctuary, a place formed on the spiritual plane where they would be given assignments and instructions. But Pajetic worked almost exclusively in the field, so the chances of finding his partner there were slim. Abyss had only told him that "he would be contacted".

He had the option to remain in the city and wait for Pajetic to find him, but Lance refused to sit idle. He wasn't some pathetic servant, regardless of what Abyss said. He would take the initiative and find his new partner himself. Thus, Paradise.

Invigorated with his renewed confidence, Lance strode towards the gate, raising his hand at its sentinel in greeting. Peter also raised his, not so much in greeting, but to prevent Lance from passing through the entrance.

"Hold your position reaper," demanded Peter, whose voice sounded old, but not frail. It was a powerful voice, one that echoed like the rest of his kin. "What is your purpose here?" Lance was not upset with Peter's reaction; he knew this was the angel's duty. Although perhaps he could have posed the question in a slightly more polite manner.

"I have an assignment Peter. I'm to meet with another reaper, it's urgent."

The angel nodded. Apparently he had been made aware of this beforehand. "Very well, Lance. Gazardiel has also requested that you should speak to him upon your arrival." The angel then made a motion with his hand, and the gates methodically opened.

What? Why would Gazardiel want to talk to him? Lance had spoken with the angel just a few hours beforehand. Confused, Lance strode past Peter to enter the inner recesses of Paradise, silently considering what he had been told.

Perhaps Gazardiel had learned something about the disturbance, or wished to question Lance further. Maybe the angel had been watching him, and had seen Lance's journey to his old home. That would be an interesting conversation to say the least.

Regardless, Lance had little choice but to speak with him. Lance directed his path towards the tower at the edge of Paradise, directly his eyes to its simple stone top. That is where he guessed Gazardiel would be waiting. The great keep of the angels.

As Lance walked through the temple, he began to notice how barren it was. Usually there were many angels, wearing their sparkling armour with their wings unfurled and glorious, talking and moving throughout. But now the courtyard was completely empty.

They must all be on earth, Lance realized. Either helping humanity or slowly watching them destroy themselves. Lance once again thought of Peter, who stood patiently in front of the gates of Paradise. Could he not be more useful elsewhere?

As he approached the tower he wondered if it would appear disrespectful to just waltz up to the front door and knock. Though Enigma had told him it was the residence of the angels, he doubted that Michael or Gazardiel actually *lived* there.

Spirits didn't really need a residence. They don't need houses or beds or food or shelter. Spirits don't even sleep. If they expend a great deal of energy, they simply limit their use of spiritual power to allow their reserves to recuperate. It made no sense for the angels to live anywhere at all. Certainly some spirits congregated in specific areas, and they might even raise spiritual structures, but that was just to facilitate their coordination or protection.

Therefore Lance wondered what exactly was in the tower, for it to be called a residence, and figured that it probably guarded information. Perhaps a record of all the events in all the histories of the world? That seemed like an angelic sort of thing. Lance knew such a place would not receive a reaper banging on the door kindly. Then again, he had been invited.

Lance continued to walk towards the tower, which now loomed over him. The silence was intimidating. All he could hear was the steady sound of his footsteps. He had never quite understood why everyone walked in Paradise, nor why his footsteps actually made sound. He had merely observed that every other spirit walked in Paradise, so he never tried to float or fly. It was a weird sensation; he was used to moving quickly, with no audible consequence.

Surprisingly, the wooden door to the tower seemed unsubstantial. It was made of smooth weathered wood, and had black hinges affixing it to the stone. Lance noted with surprise there was no door handle on the outside.

Before he had time to knock, the door swung open, revealing a dimly lit corridor with two spirits standing together conspiratorially on the other side. Lance recognized them immediately, but was slightly shocked to see them conversing together.

It was Enigma, standing and listening intently to Gazardiel, who smiled as soon as he saw Lance.

"Ah, Lance, just the spirit I was hoping to see. I was just speaking to your master," with this statement he motioned towards Enigma, who turned to face Lance and inclined his head in recognition. "We were wondering what you were up to."

At this point, Gazardiel stopped, apparently thinking that it was Engima's turn to continue. Lance's teacher took his cue and began to speak, but not before Lance's heart was gripped with panic. What had they seen him do?

"We've been looking for you, Lance," Enigma said, his eyes fixed on his pupil. "We were beginning to think that you didn't want to be found. So I came here to ask Gazardiel for assistance. You have an assignment. Pajetic is getting impatient."

Lance nodded in relief, thankful they hadn't been able to find him. All that they wanted was an explanation about where he had been, his visit to his old life making him elusive while others searched for him. Instantly, he decided against revealing that his seal had been broken. If he told them, they might be forced to reapply it. And now that Lance had experienced his emotions, his real, human emotions, he was loathe to give them up.

"I decided to observe the city," he said in a strong, confident voice. "I hid myself there so I couldn't be found by revenants. There are an incredible number Enigma, more than I ever dreamed possible." Lance then looked at Gazardiel. "I noticed several large ones, and even more hunting in packs. They are definitely merging."

Gazardiel nodded solemnly. "I saw that myself. It's quickly becoming dangerous down there, which is why, I think, Enigma was worried."

Enigma looked somewhat annoyed for a moment, and Lance was forced to suppress a grin. He knew that his mentor genuinely liked him, but would never express it openly like Gazardiel just did. Without commenting, Enigma turned back to Lance.

"Worried, certainly," said the reaper amusedly. "If Lance were unable to handle a few lowly revenants just last night, you can imagine my concern with this new threat." Lance rolled his eyes, knowing that this was how his old master would respond to Gazardiel's openness. Despite Enigma's lack of intent, hearing his teacher speak that way was aggravating. Enigma, of all people, should know that a few revenants could not incapacitate him. After all, Enigma had trained him.

So Lance responded, with a bit of an edge, "You know that a common revenant couldn't have-" his retort was cut off mid-sentence.

"Stop." commanded Gazardiel. "We have gone over this already today. Lance, you will be glad to know that both Enigma and I," as he spoke he turned his gaze to Enigma briefly, "feel that it is highly unlikely you could be incapacitated by revenants. But until we have proof, our opinions are immaterial, Michael will not hear us. Now, I believe, time is of the essence."

Enigma nodded, "Yes. Pajetic is waiting for you back in the city. There is an unfinished job there which has become much more important due to the recent events. Pajetic will explain the details, but the summary is that you will be dispatching a demon."

Enigma paused here, evidently expecting Lance to balk at such a difficult task, but to his surprise, Lance remained unphased. The young spirit even nodded calmly, not at all afraid of the daunting task of fighting the most powerful genus of evil spirits. To Lance, after the events earlier in the day, the risk meant nothing. This was his mission after all. He transported himself to heaven to protect humanity, and if that meant fighting a real monster, so be it. Lance was strong.

"Very good, I'll leave immediately." He said boldly. "Gazardiel, is there any other reason you requested to see me?"

The Archangel nodded. "When I heard about your assignment, I wanted to make sure you understood what it entailed. Enigma informed me that you have never faced a foe of that level."

Lance shrugged. "I have never fought a demon, but I know all about them. I know that they are human souls who have remained on earth for too long. And I know that they are very powerful."

"Lance is not prepared for this," interjected Enigma suddenly. Lance was shocked to hear undisguised concern in the old reaper's voice. "He is talented, but not to the point where he can do battle with a demon. Only angels possess such strength."

Lance couldn't believe what he was hearing, and found fear creeping into him.

"Lance has no choice," stated Gazardiel bluntly.

"Couldn't I go?" offered Enigma. "Pajetic has assisted in demon hunts before. He is an exceptional fighter. The three of us would stand a chance…"

"I can't make that order Enigma," said Gazardiel simply. "Abyss has spoken for the reapers."

"Why don't you go then?" asked Enigma quietly.

Gazardiel shook his head sadly. "I wish I could. But I'm needed elsewhere in the city. We are stretched too far as it is. If we knew where the demon was we would fight it but the trail is too cold. That's why this task was given to the reapers in the first place."

"So the reapers are to die, and their corpses will guide you to your foe? Their orders aren't even to simply find the demon and relay the information to a more capable spirit. They've been told to engage!" Enigma sounded furious. "Do Pajetic and Lance mean so little?"

Gazardiel raised a hand, halting future arguments. "The task is set Enigma. Although the demon has taken on added importance with the current upheaval in the spiritual plane, it remains a tertiary concern. I am needed for other duties, are you. More debate on the issue is pointless, and Pajetic is waiting. But do not despair. I doubt they will even find the beast. And even if they do, I believe they will prevail. You have taught your pupil well. I believe in Lance."

"Very well," said Enigma resignedly. "Let us depart Lance. I will walk with you to the exit of Paradise." The learned reaper turned to face Gazardiel once more, not upset with the angel's lack of assistance, but still disappointed "Thank you for your help Gazardiel. It is most appreciated."

Gazardiel bowed his head regretfully towards Enigma. "If only things were different. I wish you and your pupil the best of luck."

With that, he turned and walked down the stone corridor deeper into the tower, slowly disappearing from their sight.

"Follow," ordered Enigma, heading towards the exit. Lance remained close to his former master, but did not initiate any conversation. They were halfway to the gate before Enigma spoke.

"How did this happen? Losing a soul like this is a terrible failure!" Lance had been expecting this reprimand, but still felt wounded.

"You know as well as I do that the revenant story is nonsense. Some massive spiritual force knocked me out, the same source that is shooting off enough errant power to spawn revenants everywhere."

"Excuses," stated Enigma flatly. "For all of your power and potential, you seem to fall back on excuses every time. The greatest spirits control events. Events do not control them. And now look where it's got you."

Lanced sighed. This accusation was so unfair. Enigma was not speaking angrily, but in a steady low tone. It reminded Lance of how his parents would sometimes treat him when he misbehaved. They would tell him, "We're not angry with you, we're just... disappointed."

"I won't let you down this time," Lance promised. As they passed through the gates, Peter did not even acknowledge them. Enigma turned to face Lance.

"I know you won't Lance. You are a great student, but this is different. A demon... a demon is deadly. You and Pajetic both are at risk."

"I'm not afraid." Stated Lance boldly.

"You never are." Chuckled Enigma. "I suppose this isn't all bad news. Michael is no murderer. He must believe that you and Pajetic are capable of handling a demon. You are strong Lance. Stronger than most give you credit. Perhaps stronger than even I think you are. I believe in you Lance, and Gazardiel does too. This may turn out to be a chance, a way for you to redeem yourself. Precious few reapers ever cross blades with a demon. Do not let it pass you by. Pajetic will be waiting for you on top of the brownstone structure in the city centre, the one with the gargoyles. Do you know the place?"

Lance nodded. It was the same building he had perched on while waiting for Cody, before everything had fallen apart.

"Good," continued Enigma. "Pajetic is just like you, a promising young reaper with considerable reserves of power. And," Enigma added, a ghost of a grin stretched across his face, "he can't get along with Abyss either. Good luck!" With this, a beam of light encircled the ancient reaper, and he departed from Paradise.

Lance looked at the space Enigma had occupied for a second and contemplated what his teacher had said. Redemption was to be his, certainly. But also glory. He would defeat this demon and work his way back into favour. It was time for him to show the spiritual world exactly how powerful he truly was. And with that thought, a beam of light sprang up from the ground, enveloping Lance and transporting him away from Paradise, leaving the empty temple, Gazardiel, and Peter, all far behind.

Chapter 8

When Lance stepped out of his portal to the mortal realm the afternoon had faded away and dusk was descending upon the city. The falling sun splattered the sky in glorious combinations of orange and gold and red, and it seemed like the roof of the world was on fire. The city still operated exactly as it had the night before, its denizens clearly unaware of the upheaval brewing on the spiritual plane.

Cars clogged the streets, their drivers heading home after a hard day of work. They rushed through Lance at regular intervals, but he paid them no heed. Instead, he looked up from the centre of the intersection in which he was standing, to observe an *extremely* familiar landmark.

His eyes were fixated on the massive brownstone building, looming over the downtown, where he had earlier stood sentinel. He scanned its gargoyles, straining to detect spiritual power. The constant reverberation of the plane itself made it difficult to sense even the slightest trace of spirits. It had only grown stronger since his trip to Paradise.

This was the place. He, fittingly, was told to meet Pajetic here. And yet Lance had assumed he would have been able to sense his ally, feel Pajetic's presence in some way. After all, Pajetic was young, like he was, and wouldn't be able to suppress or contain his power nearly as well as more senior spirits.

But Lance ignored his misgivings, they were beside the point. Lance was told to meet Pajetic, so all he could do was follow those directions. Slowly he rose into the air and flew to the top of the building. He alighted on the ledge of the roof, alongside a large stone gargoyle. He placed one hand on its great stone wing, spread as if ready for flight, and cast his eyes around expectantly. There was no life on the roof. It was barren, without any traces of spirit or residue.

Lance began to worry again, as he strained to detect something, anything, that would signify the presence of his partner.

There was nothing.

This was wrong. Pajetic was supposed to be waiting for him, but it seemed clear the reaper hadn't ever been on this roof. Lance turned away and looked down upon the street below, pondering his options. His mind was distracted as he noticed sinister shadows creeping along the road. Revenants.

They dotted the city like ants, scurrying around and hunting for spirits. Hunting for him. Lance frowned. There were too many of them, crawling the streets and infesting the city. If they ever joined forces... everyone would be in grave danger.

Lance realized their numbers could very well be too great already. The city might already be past its saturation point. Lance had no idea, since his knowledge of revenants and their differing power levels was rudimentary. They were dangerous, of that much he was certain. And it was not going to get better.

Seeing the revenants renewed Lance's sense of urgency. It wasn't just spirits in danger, but the humans he saw as well. They walked along the streets, blissfully ignorant of the monsters pacing beside them. They would not be safe for long.

Lance fidgeted uneasily. He had wasted enough time already, and he wanted to take action. What if Pajetic had been attacked? Waiting around here would achieve nothing if that was the case, it would only serve to expose Lance to the same risks that might have been the end of Pajetic.

If Lance were unable to find his partner, at least he could be productive. He could clean up some of the revenants, hunting silently and staying in constant motion. Lance gathered his power and prepared to leap off the building, when suddenly a pressure prevented him from taking to the air, and a voice directly behind him whispered,

"Leaving already?"

Lance flinched, recoiling from the foreign spiritual force. He let his own power flood through him, and his eyes blazed red as he sent a shockwave across the rooftop, repelling the pressure and allowing him to turn. Now free, he spun around to face the threat.

There, standing directly in front of him, was a tall, thin figure wearing long black robes. He was male, with distinctive oriental features surrounded by sleek straight black hair that fell down to his shoulders. The eyes burned with intensity, their acid green light dominating his face. Lance knew who this was, even before the figure spoke another word. Pajetic had been here, after all.

"What the hell was that about?" yelled Lance, furiously. He maintained his crimson energy and scowled at Pajetic. "Is that the way you were taught to greet your partners in... wherever you come from!?" Lance finished awkwardly, not exactly sure where he was going with that last remark.

Pajetic shrugged, allowing the glow from his eyes to fade just slightly. His now visible eyes gleamed with keen intelligence and a surprising amount of apathy. This nonchalant demeanour only served to enrage Lance even more.

"I was told you were some sort of great reaper, so I figured I would test you," said Pajetic, crossing his arms and leaning casually on a gargoyle. "It seems I was deceived."

Lance knew Pajetic was trying to get a rise out of him, but wasn't able to stop himself. His pride was hurt, and he was truly raging.

"Pardon me for not trying to track someone who was supposed to be my ally. I figured you would meet me on the top of the building, as *ordered*." Lance concluded his statement by placing emphasis on the last word.

Then, coming up with a clever rebuttal, albeit slightly late, he added derisively, "And I was only looking for powerful spirits, so it's not surprising I missed you."

The jab worked. Lance could see Pajetic's face adjust slightly, betraying his annoyance.

"I didn't know powerful spirits advertised their power for everyone to see." He retorted, his voice full of disdainful venom. "You must not have experience dealing with high level spirits, which isn't very surprising from the looks of you."

This conflict was not at all what Lance had anticipated. Pajetic and he were supposed to be a team, working together to protect the spiritual realm. And destroy a demon, no less! But he was far too engaged in the war of words between them to pay heed to some grander purpose. He would be damned if he let this relaxed punk get the better of him.

"Well, I'm certainly not in the company of a powerful spirit right now," Lance shot back, "because right now, all of your power is in plain view, and it certainly isn't impressive. No wonder you tried to hide."

Lance knew he had really struck a nerve with this one, as Pajetic stiffened. Lance felt his fury subside slightly: the score was settled and they had both been properly humiliated. However, his blind rage returned after Pajetic's next comment.

"I'm surprised my power hasn't knocked you out yet, since apparently a little buzzing in the spiritual plane is all it takes to put you out of commission, lackey." Pajetic smiled cruelly, adding further insult to his coupe-de-grace.

His remark infuriated Lance, who was caught in the double frustration of dealing with his own failure while being unfairly judged. There was pure, uncalled for malice in Pajetic's voice, and Lance reacted as one who has been insulted to his core.

"That's it!" roared Lance, his rage controlling his spiritual power as much as his mind, as evidenced by the red energy expanding and whipping around the terrace of the roof. "You take that back or I *will* strike you down."

Lance accompanied his cry with a pulse of scarlet energy to broadcast his strength to Pajetic. The smile immediately melted from Pajetic's face. His eyes radiated brilliant green energy, which wrapped itself defensively around him.

"Are you insane? You would attack a fellow reaper? Someone who is supposed to be your teammate? We are expected to work together!" he exclaimed incredulously.

"Work together?" answered Lance, "How? All you've done since I've arrived is insult me!"

"What am I expected to do? I'm supposed to fight a demon with a failure of a reaper!" protested Pajetic, angrily. "I could be destroyed! You are a liability!"

"I am no liability! Face me in combat and I'll prove that to you clear as day!" By this point Lance had thrown all caution to the wind. He was no longer a guardian of the spiritual realm, a servant to all humanity. He was a wounded animal.

He stared at Pajetic, who boldly returned his gaze. Their resolves met, acid green against fiery red. There was no middle ground between the two, and neither side budged. Lance's eyes were intense, filled with his rage. Pajetic's eyes were forceful, but somehow composed and calculating. The language of battle was being communicated between the two, as both reapers prepared for the other to instigate the fight.

"Very well," agreed Pajetic, in a calm but tense voice. "I will show you why you do not belong. You'll just get me killed anyway."

Lance willed his power to flow through him, feeling strength accumulate in his extremities. He was prepared to counter any move Pajetic made. Lance would retaliate swiftly and brutally. He assumed Pajetic would use his own spiritual power to attack; since he had not seen the reaper summon his manta.

Pajetic made a quick movement, darting forward to secure a better position. Lance wasted no time, bringing his defenses up in a wall around him. Suddenly, a violent impact smashed into his barrier, to the left of his field of vision. His shield held, but the shock of the impact knocked him down. As Lance fell onto his side, he looked over to where Pajetic had been standing. The impact had come from the opposite direction. Lance was shocked; he had never seen an attack like that before!

But Pajetic was no longer in view; instead, the place where he had been standing was engulfed in residual spiritual power from a second attack.

It wasn't Pajetic's.

The dots were beginning to connect in Lance's mind. He apprehensively looked around to where the force had come from.

There, standing on the lip of the building, staring directly at them, were five menacing revenants. They were much larger than men, each standing at least ten feet tall. Lance knew immediately these revenants were not the trash he could easily dispatch.

Their humanoid forms were muscular and smooth, not bizarre and malformed. They wore matching black pants, and were shirtless, revealing rippled tattooed chests designed to intimidate, though physical strength had no actual affect in the spiritual realm. Their heads were completely hidden in massive metal helmets, with only small dark slots for sight.

The headpieces were adorned with massive horns in a variety of styles. They curled from either side of the helmet like ram's horns, or sprouted from the front like those of a demon, or jutted out seemingly at random. The largest revenant, standing in the pack's centre, had a single protruding plate on the top of his helmet, resembling the dorsal fin of a shark. Their limbs were still faintly pulsing with the energy from their earlier strike.

Lance's quarrel with Pajetic was immediately forgotten in the face of this threat. These revenants were a different breed; Lance imagined they were the result of tens, maybe even hundreds of merged revenants. He and Pajetic were in real danger.

Studying his enemies, Lance was surprised to notice that the revenants had not yet moved in on their prey. Instead thry merely lingered on the rooftop's edge, silently observing the scene. It was like... they couldn't see. Lance realized that the revenants attacks had interacted with the latent power in the shaking spiritual plane to throw up a screen of spiritual debris. Lance or Pajetic were cloaked within it.

They are showing caution, Lance deduced. Instead of rushing in to see if they had eliminated their targets, they were maintaining their range advantage and waiting. More than anything, that was the fact that truly scared the reaper. The only revenants that had ever exhibited such a high level of intelligence were creatures of legend. And the smokescreen he and Pajetic were hiding behind would not shroud them forever. The debris was begging to fade.

Lance needed to escape, to run, of that there was no doubt. But Pajetic complicated things. Lance had to save his partner. Even though they had nearly come to blows, even though the useless spirit had been knocked out, Pajetic was still his responsibility and his only lead to the demon. Lance didn't even know the monster's name!

Knowing the field would allow sight of them in a second and expose them to another barrage, Lance decided to grab Pajetic and flee. Lance looked over to where the reaper lay.

As Lance turned to Pajetic, the remaining dust dissipated. To his surprise, Pajetic was not lying down, incapacitated, but was instead crouching in wait. He had also realized the dust was offering him protection, for as soon as he could be seen, he sprang into action.

Bands of green power crackled over his body as he shot towards the revenants, who immediately fired balls of concentrated spiritual power at him in response. Pajetic dove down into the building, sinking through the roof, causing the onslaught to barely miss.

Now with an ally, Lance was not about to run. It was time to fight. Following Pajetic's lead, Lance bellowed loudly and let his raw power completely engulf his form. With their attention diverted from Pajetic, three of the revenants threw their arms up and unleashed a combined surge towards him.

Lance didn't bother dodging it like Pajetic. Instead, he allowed the storm to hammer into him. In his power-infused state, Lance shrugged off the impact from the projectiles and sustained no damage.

He grinned wickedly, as the other two monsters charged towards him. Lance readied himself for close quarters combat. He hoped Pajetic was doing what he thought he was doing, since this ultra-powered state, taught to him by Enigma, wouldn't last for long.

The back three foes continued to fire, but Lance focused on the two rapidly advancing towards him. They were in a staggered formation. Big mistake. The first revenant arrived long before the second. Its hands had morphed into claws as it prepared to rip Lance apart. It lunged, with a speed too fast for any person to react. But Lance was not a person, and was faster still.

Lance stepped to the side, and brought his left arm up high above him. Then, channelling his power into his elbow, he brought it down, just as the revenant hurtled underneath. It connected with the charging spirit with an explosion, and Lance felt the creature's essence shatter beneath the force of his blow. A fatal move, he thought.

He reflected for a second too long, however, and found himself flat on the ground as the second revenant reached him. Sharp claws raked against Lance's spiritual armor, drastically weakening his protective field. The shield wouldn't survive another direct blow.

Lance grabbed the arms of the revenant, and the two wrestled together, each struggling to gain the upper hand. Lance's face was only inches away from the helmet of the revenant, which brought its head back to deliver a finishing headbutt to Lance.

But the second it brought it back, Lance unleashed a beam of red energy from his eyes, draining the last of his power from the protective cocoon surrounding his body, which faded completely. The formidable blast hit the revenant directly in the face and burned through its head. Its body dissolved in a shimmer of light, and Lance knew he had won.

Aware that he had not a moment to waste Lance was immediately back on his feet, preparing to dodge further projectiles. Except, none came. In fact, there was only one revenant still remaining.

The shark fin helmeted enemy stood with his back facing Lance, arms morphed into some kind of sword-fin weapons. The revenant panted heavily and was wounded in its side, its two companions nowhere to be seen. And there, facing the revenant, was Pajetic.

The green energy field that had surrounded his body at the start of the battle was concentrated around his hands, which shone with luminous green light. His eyes crackled with power, and Lance knew he could just sit back and watch. Pajetic needed no help.

The revenant made a desperate lunge with one fin, but Pajetic dodged and stepped past it easily, aiming a swipe of his arm at the back of its neck. The revenant blocked the blow with its other fin, but Pajetic, smirking, grasped the blade itself, trusting his energy to protect him from its razor edge.

He then whipped the revenant over his head, throwing the creature towards Lance, who watched unflinchingly in amusement. Pajetic then fired an intense beam of green light towards the airborne revenant, who became engulfed in green flames. The defeated combatant crashed to the ground, sliding just in front of Lance, who observed one spasm of the helmeted head before it was engulfed in green and disappeared for good.

With the threat eliminated, Lance let his guard down and dropped to one knee. The combat had taken a toll on him, and he was short of breath. The crimson hue of his eyes dimmed and eventually disappeared. Pajetic strode towards him, also letting the green in his eyes fade.

"I was expecting them to chase me," said Pajetic, looking at Lance with an inquisitive air.

Lance looked up to Pajetic and said bleakly, "Well I couldn't let you have all the fun." Pajetic laughed, a sound so unexpected that it made Lance laugh as well. But the moment of gaiety did not last long, as Pajetic observed Lance.

"Did this fight take a toll on you?" Lance thought he may have detected a whisper of concern in the reaper's voice.

"Yeah, I took a lot of shots when I decided to be your distraction."

"Any... damage?" asked Pajetic.

"No," responded Lance. "I shielded myself. It's a technique I'm quite good at. I've just expended a lot of energy, that's all." He paused for a second, then, deciding not to allow the conversation to fall into an awkward silence, added, "They were strong."

"Indeed," agreed Pajetic, "the strongest revenants I have ever encountered. They must have been the product of at least fifty mergers. The city is becoming more overrun by the minute." Pajetic diverted his look from Lance to gaze over the city, before adding,

"They even used strategy. One of them tried to flank me. It was impressive and uncharacteristic of them, sneaking up on us." Lance winced slightly, remembering the circumstances which brought on the revenant attack.

"We weren't exactly focused on the environment though," he said dryly. Pajetic narrowed his eyes and stared at Lance.

"Good point. Behaviour like that-"

"-is counterproductive," finished Lance. "I know."

Pajetic nodded his head. "We'll die if we act like that again." Lance agreed wholeheartedly. After the stress of combat against revenants, fighting a duel with another reaper, a teammate no less, seemed idiotic. He needed to keep his temper in check.

"Agreed," he stated, rising up off his knee and bringing himself back to Pajetic's eye level. "Where do we go from here?"

"We find the demon. And Lance, don't be a hero when we fight him. I don't want to have to save you again." Pajetic's remark surprised Lance, who had figured through the course of battle their differences had been resolved.

But Lance ignored it, remembering both the concern he had heard in Pajetic's voice and their decision to work together. Pajetic still didn't think he could rely on Lance, that much was clear. But Lance resolved to prove to him that he was worthy of being his partner.

"I won't Pajetic. What's that demon's name, anyway?"

"Prufias," answered Pajetic.

"Prufias," repeated Lance, engrossed in thought. Prufias, his new prey. He smacked his right hand, enclosed in a fight, into the palm of his left. "His reign ends tonight."

"Yes, Prufias is his name." confirmed Pajetic, before addressing Lance's showmanship. "But the result of his reign, that remains to be seen."

Chapter 9

The battle with the revenants was over, but the shattered fragments of their power remained, slowly floating above the rooftop. Pajetic and Lance balanced precariously on its very edge, as the sun slowly set in the distance. Recovering their strength during the momentary lull, their faces thrown into shadow, they contemplated the view. Just another two watchers in the row of gargoyles.

"What's he like?" asked Lance, in an attempt to break the silence.

"Prufias?" answered Pajetic, "I'm not really sure. He's a demon, so he's powerful. Seems to keep to himself, he hasn't done anything noteworthy to humans. That's why the angels themselves haven't bothered with him yet."

That was odd. The demons Lance had been told about were horrific creatures, who possessed an unquenchable thirst for human blood. The legends of monsters like Succorbenoth and Thammuz were subjects of fascination to reapers and retold time and time again. Those demons had destroyed countless lives, overthrowing kingdoms and even devouring angels when they roamed freely on earth. Why was Prufias different? What was his plan?

"If he isn't a threat, why are we being sent after him?" Lance once again gazed over the city, still gently vibrating from the energy of the spiritual plane. It seemed to him as though the plane was bending slightly, sagging under the stress of all the unusual activity.

"His last known location was here, in this city. The angels are afraid that he might see the upheaval as a chance to attack." Pajetic paused for a moment, looking across the cityscape restlessly. "After all, I think he has just been waiting."

"Then why us?" Lance asked again, although he felt as though he already knew the answer.

"Do you ever shut up?" barked Pajetic, annoyed. "The angels are busy Lance; they have no idea where Prufias is, and view him as a minor threat compared to the revenants infesting the city. There isn't an angel available to handle Prufias, so they delegated the job to the reapers. And we both know why Abyss picked us."

The grim tone of Pajetic's voice left no doubt in Lance's mind. Pajetic knew as well. Abyss wasn't assigning them to this mission because of her faith in *them*. She was sending them because she had faith in *Prufias*. Lance took a moment to prepare himself mentally for the hunt, then asked, in a resigned voice, "Where do we begin?"

Pajetic stepped forward, over the edge of the building and into the evening air. Lance followed, finding it funny that he had found it difficult to lift himself out water once, a lifetime ago.

"We're on our own. We have to find him without help."

"The angels didn't give us anything?" inquired Lance, somewhat surprised.

"They did. Like I said, their last trace of him was here. Several months ago."

"Months?" exclaimed Lance, now completely incredulous. "Seriously? There's no way we can track a spirit whose trail has been dead for months! Not even Michael has the expertise to..."

An exasperated look from Pajetic silenced Lance's rant. He finished with a weak mumble then closed his mouth, assuming that Pajetic had a plan.

"There are other ways to track a spirit you know, Lance," said Pajetic, almost comically. "And I know them all. Just stick with me. We will find Prufias, but first we need to get out of here."

With this Pajetic jerked his head back towards the centre of the roof, which still glittered with disseminating spiritual power. "More revenants will be attracted to all this activity. They are likely already on their way. It's time to go."

Looking at Lance, he saw that his fellow reaper was about to formulate yet another question. Pajetic silenced him with an impatient gesture. "Just trust me, I promise I will explain everything to you when we get there. This isn't complex Lance, you just need to follow orders."

With that, Pajetic flew off towards the east end of the city, weaving through the tall skyscrapers. Lance maintained his position, pondering the situation. For all of his arrogance, it was clear Pajetic was keen. They had a chance.

Lance then looked around exasperatedly, noticing that he had lost sight of his partner already. Swearing under his breath, he tore off in the direction Pajetic was headed. He caught up with him quickly, and the pair of them shot through the city.

As they traveled Lance was taken aback, not only by Pajetic's hectic speed, but also by his erratic route. They made curve after curve, swinging around buildings, diving into alleyways and performing many challenging manoeuvres. What was he running from? It was only when Pajetic abruptly changed direction and backtracked that Lance understood.

There, directly in Pajetic's original path, was a group of maybe twenty revenants. They prowled along the ground, their heads moving slowly, scanning the surroundings. They didn't seem to notice the reapers, hidden as they were by their position in the sky, but Lance knew that they would be seen before long. Lance doubled back with Pajetic and rejoined the frenetic pace with renewed gusto.

Pajetic's path was an effective way to avoid the revenants. He knew that if they flew above the city, in clear view, their chances of being attacked were much higher. Weaving through buildings was a far safer route, even if it was inefficient. And Lance was developing the suspicion that the revenants themselves weren't Pajetic's only motivation.

He couldn't shake the feeling that something wasn't right. Run of the mill revenants wouldn't be too challenging, but the ones they had faced earlier, it almost seemed like they were hunting for the reapers.

Especially the way they silently snuck up on them. It was as if the attack had a defined purpose; it was all very unsettling. It felt like something was chasing them, something sinister. And Pajetic was doing his best to keep whatever it was off their trail.

As the buildings whipped by, and Pajetic surged onward, Lance considered the possibilities. Was a spirit looking to take him out? Or Pajetic? Even worse, could Prufias be behind the attack? Did Prufias know they were coming for him? Lance didn't know, but he felt that their chances of fighting the demon successfully would be substantially reduced if that was the case.

Pajetic looked back and made eye contact with Lance. They were getting close. Close to... Where exactly? Lance had no idea, but Pajetic had a plan. Lance figured they would go to where Prufias had last been seen and try to pick up some kind of clue from there. Prufias could still be in the area after all. For all Lance knew, the spirit could be watching them right now.

The thought of a watching demon intimidated Lance, and he nervously looked around, half expecting to see a dark and sinister figure crouched on a windowsill. Of course, he saw nothing.

How would Pajetic track this demon once they arrived? Any trail would have long grown cold. Unless Pajetic had some kind of trick up his sleeve.

Lance noticed Pajetic was slowing their pace down a fair bit, as they exited the downtown core. He seemed to think that the revenant threat had passed. Lance considered his partner.

Lance had stereotyped Pajetic as a tracker reaper, someone who relied on their sensory abilities to find their targets. Pajetic could very well be a decent tracker, but his skills in combat and his claims of special ways to find spirits made Lance suspect Pajetic relied on something altogether more impressive.

Lance had heard that some spirits could focus their minds and cast their power out, spreading it very thinly across vast areas of the spiritual plane. They could sense any activity in that region, and pinpoint its location. Lance figured that Pajetic could very well be applying that approach. It was very advanced, and powerful, letting Pajetic essentially see the entire city at once. Perhaps his partner did know the location of Prufias, after all.

Pajetic suddenly jerked to a stop, hovering in mid-air. Lance came to a rest beside him. Night engulfed the city in colours of cool blue, the rays of the sun having disappeared behind the concrete jungle to their west. This part of the city seemed much more dangerous in the dark.

The neighbourhood they were in was run down, with sporadic, neglected houses with their exits boarded up and garbage piled high at the sides of the road. Several shops lined the street, advertising their names in bright neon signs. Most had barred windows to deter theft. A rough end of town, to be sure.

Lance did not like it. It was too grimy, too desolate. The cheesy luminescent signs that glowed in the dark seemed unearthly, unnatural.

It was towards one of the signs that Pajetic headed. A particularly bright one, with an illuminated female stick figure, who had several extra legs. The lights behind the legs flashed on and off, to give the character the illusion of dancing, which Lance thought was a very lackluster impersonation.

Several of the sign's bulbs were burnt out, resulting in one of the dancer's legs being missing entirely. Not the way Lance would try and attract business.

But nevertheless, Pajetic slowly floated towards the entrance of the establishment, where he stopped and waited for Lance.

"Bring your I.D.?" he asked, smirking slightly. "You are recent enough to remember those, right?"

"Yes," answered Lance peevishly. "What the hell was Prufias doing at a place like this?"

"Prufias?" asked Pajetic, confused.

"You know, the demon we are looking for? You tracked him here, didn't you?" questioned Lance, now beginning to think that his hypothesis about the objective of the expedition was flawed.

"Tracked him?" asked Pajetic. "No. How could I? You said it yourself, the trail's long gone. This is our best bet: The Guardian Society."

Lance stared at Pajetic, completely nonplussed. "Looks like a dance club to me."

Pajetic sighed and shook his head, "I'm glad to know at least one of us can state the obvious. Of course it's a dance club. The Guardian Society holds their meetings on the inside."

"I honestly do not know what a Guardian Society is Pajetic." interjected Lance calmly. "I know what a guardian is, and a society, but I've never heard of a Guardian Society."

"Urgh," bemoaned Pajetic. "Did Enigma teach you nothing?" Before Lance had the chance to reply with a well formulated account of all the extraordinary things Enigma *had* taught him, Pajetic continued.

"A Guardian Society is exactly what it sounds like. It's a group of Guardian Angels, Lance. Of course, the use of the word *angel* is a bit of a misnomer."

Lance's eyes widened. He had heard of Guardian Angels before. It made sense now. Guardian Angel was the term humans tended to use to describe deceased family members who were supposedly watching over them, as angels, to make sure their lives turned out ok. Although this actually does happen, in a manner of speaking, the reality is far less glamorous.

Often, benevolent spirits who managed to avoid the search of the reapers ended up trying to become "Guardian Angels" for their family members. They would follow them around, trying to impact their lives in a positive way. Unfortunately, human souls typically had little spiritual power, and even less training. The chances of them affecting the physical plane were slim to none.

"So they join together to pool power?" asked Lance, who was now wondering why Enigma had never explained this concept to him before.

"Exactly," answered Pajetic. "One or two alone probably wouldn't be able to influence the physical plane, but twenty or thirty combined can typically accomplish minor things."

Lance nodded in understanding. Minor things would probably mean slightly shifting objects or subtly influencing strength. Changes a human probably wouldn't notice. But when a bullet is streaking towards you, slight shifts can make all the difference.

"They come to such a backwater place because it is off the grid," explained Pajetic. "It doesn't see the same spiritual traffic as the city centre. Plus I think they find the idea of having a club in a seedy bar kind of cool." With this statement he shook his head in disgust. Clearly Pajetic was not the type to ever play pretend. "Shall we go?"

Lance shook his head emphatically. He appreciated Pajetic's enthusiasm, but the reaper seemed to have forgotten the purpose of their mission.

"As much as we might like to clean this place up, we've got to find the demon, Pajetic. We can report this location to the angels, or even return to take them all to Paradise once this is finished, but I just don't think we can justify chasing all these spirits down with so much at stake." Pajetic faced Lance, and tilted his head to the side.

"Report them? Chase them? Lance, we are here to *learn from them.* How else are we supposed to find this demon?" Lance grimaced, completely shocked at Pajetic's suggestion.

"Learn from them? Are you crazy, Pajetic? These are earthbound human spirits! They are not supposed to be here. We swore that we would take our charges to Paradise!"

"Yes," acknowledged Pajetic. "But none of these souls are my targets. Nor are they yours, unless you've failed to capture a spirit?" With this statement, Pajetic regarded Lance derisively. Lance rolled his eyes.

"I told you, what happened yesterday was out of my control. I've never lost a spirit before then." Lance sighed. He hated even saying those words.

Pajetic grinned slightly and nodded. "I know you're not *that* incompetent. Since we have no charges here, we have no direct responsibility to take them to Paradise. Besides, all they try to do is help their families, a righteous nut like yourself can appreciate that right? The intelligence they give is quite handy. They are everywhere, and constantly vigilant due to their fear of reapers and angels. They see everything."

"Pajetic!" scolded Lance, "Even with your twisted reasoning, you should feel this is wrong! How do you even know their information will be useful?"

"Oh, I know," replied Pajetic, smugly. Lance completely ignored the lack of explanation. He was on a roll.

"Even if, by some miracle, the information were useful, they would never share it with us! You said it yourself. Reapers are their enemy! They would be afraid of us!"

"They won't be afraid of me," stated Pajetic laconically.

"And past that, what if the angels found out?" continued Lance, not really hearing Pajetic's last comment. Then he did a double take after finally processing it. "Wait... what?"

"I said," repeated Pajetic, "they won't be afraid of me. I've used them before. That's how I know their intel is good. I've used it to capture many of my charges, taking days not weeks. Believe me, this is our best bet to find Prufias."

Lance closed his mouth, bewildered, as he realized Pajetic was determined to have his way. Had the reaper lost his mind? If the angels, or Abyss, or anyone else for that matter, found them here it would be the end of it *all*. Their main job as reapers was to remove spirits precisely like the ones they would find in this place. Even though they had no direct obligation to do so, Lance knew turning a blind eye would violated the spirit of every oath they had sworn.

But part of Lance wanted to go with Pajetic, and take advantage of this new method of tracking. What if this Guardian Society led them to Prufias? Surely it would be worth turning a blind eye for now, in order to deal with a much greater threat. The lesser of two evils and all that. Lance focused inwardly, his resolve strengthening, and prepared for what would come next.

"Lead the way."

Pajetic nodded, and evaporated through the club's closed door. Lance followed. They emerged into a dimly lit corridor. The muffled sounds of music thumped through the air, emanating from a second door, just a few steps ahead of them. Lance took a breath and stepped through.

The inside of the club was completely different from what Lance had expected. The level of extravagance on display surprised him, especially considering the surrounding neighbourhood. There were people, hundreds of them, all dancing in the centre of a cavernous room. The air in the physical realm was heavy with smoke and fake scents and loud music blared from enormous speakers which lined the rectangular room's walls.

A song was playing, some fast remix of a popular tune, and the bass boomed loudly, shaking the walls. Brightly coloured strobe lights flashed a multitude of colours in the space of a few seconds. Women in lingerie and high heels strode confidently throughout, carrying trays laden with drinks to several designated seating areas. A D.J. was perched on a raised platform with a table, a laptop, and earphones pressed up against his head. He was pandering to the crowd, telling them to dance. It all seemed tacky and over the top to Lance.

Pajetic marched forward, ignoring the activity around him. Lance tagged along, walking through the occasional guy sporting sunglasses indoors, and the odd girl wearing far too little. Lance turned as one particularly scantily clad server passed him, and figured he had just seen all there was to see of that young lady. The sight of the women reminded him of Jessica. No, not in that way. Sicko.

He briefly wondered what she was doing, after all he had seen her only so briefly when he had returned to his highschool. But as quickly as the thought came, it vanished. Pajetic had stopped, directly before a wall which stood out amongst all the details of the dance hall. The wall glistened with a bluish haze, one that was only visible on the spiritual plane, like it had been sealed in a block of light blue jello.

Pajetic shouted at Lance, raising his voice above the music, as neither of them had bothered to focus their hearing on just the spiritual plane. "It's in there!" he said, jerking his head towards the spiritually protected wall. Lance didn't properly hear him, but decided against yelling "WHAT?", because he didn't want to look like a moron. Instead, he just nodded absent-mindedly.

"When we get in there, you need to disguise yourself. You can't look like a reaper. Most of them don't know what I am." This time, Pajetic was right beside him, and Lance understood. He nodded again. "So no robes and no hoods! Street clothes!" And with that, Pajetic's appearance morphed. His robes rippled and disappeared. He was now wearing a white sweater with tattered blue jeans. He beckoned to Lance, then turned and passed through the gelatinous barrier. In a second he had disappeared.

Lance shrugged, and wasting no more time, morphed as well. His clothes shifted, melting into a white muscle shirt and black shorts, as well as a baseball cap turned backwards. His hair fell to the sides of his face, an untidy and tangled mess. His wardrobe change made him look, and even feel, younger. Lance grinned; it had been a while since he had dressed casual.

He stared up at the barrier, impressed that humans could create such a thing. He could sense nothing on the other side, not even Pajetic's presence. Interesting. It probably extended, like a cube, all around the restricted area. Not only did it keep other spirits from entering, but it served as a buffer, preventing trackers from detecting their power. It was pretty advanced stuff for human souls.

Lance shrugged and pressed forward, squishing through the barrier. It felt like walking through water, and Lance enjoyed the sensation.

He emerged in a plain, dimly-lit room that juxtaposed considerably with the one he had just been in, so full of energy and flashing lights. There were large crates stacked haphazardly against one wall and a steel exit door set in another. The vivid blue outline of the cube surrounded the entire space, and muted music from the dance hall could still be heard.

Lance's attention was quickly drawn to the surprisingly large group of spirits that occupied the room. They were everywhere, at least ten or maybe even twenty, all broken up into groups. They had obviously been in the midst of conversations, but that had stopped with the arrival of the newcommers.

They stared curiously at Lance and Pajetic, who had entered before Lance and now stood rigidly beside him. The spirits themselves were arrayed in a variety of costumes.

Some wore clothes that were clearly modern, there were a few hoodies, jeans and hats. A sports team jacket here, an exciting and stylish pair of glasses there. One spirit, who looked like he was about forty five in his residual self-image, wore an exceptionally nice suit. But the more interesting ones wore nothing familiar.

Instead, their attire was decades old. There were bell bottom jeans, a peace sign chain, and even one gentleman who appeared to be wearing britches, a doublet, and a frilly white collar. Lance had no idea how old that specific spirit was, but it seemed likely that he had been eluding capture for at least a few centuries.

The spirits did not move. They continued to silently observe both Lance and Pajetic, almost as if they were preparing for a standoff. Lance was about to break the silence, to ask Pajetic what the hell they were going to do, when a large soul detached himself from the crowd and walked towards them.

He was masculine and tall, with broad shoulders and a powerful build. His arms were muscular, and inscribed with several tattoos, mostly bands which looped around from the wrist. His black hair was oiled and slicked back, and he had a thin moustache above his lip.

His face was middle aged, with a furrowed brow and a five-o'clock shadow. He was wearing unremarkable clothes, just a simple t-shirt with plaid pants and a belt. Lance wasn't very good at such things, but he figured the guy vaguely looked Italian. As he walked towards them, he raised his hands to the other spirits.

"Don't worry guys," said the spirit, in a rough voice bearing an unmistakably Italian accent, which made Lance almost want to smile. "They're with me."

With that statement, the spirits lost interest and resumed their conversations, although several continued to steal suspicious glances at the new arrivals. Lance focused on the Italian spirit who, despite his earlier remarks, did not seem very happy to see them. He quickly closed the distance between them, moving with authority. That, combined with the deference of the other spirits, led Lance to assume he was the boss.

Pajetic nudged him and whispered, "That's Marco. He's the leader of the society." Lance nodded as Marco reached them. The soul stole a quick peek at Lance, then immediately asked Pajetic, in an agitated tone, "What are you doing here, man?"

Pajetic answered calmly. "We need some help, Marco. Something I think you can assist us with."

Marco shook his head, then surveyed the room to see who was watching. "I think you better leave, man, you're not welcome here." Pajetic shrugged.

"I don't really care. We need to talk."

Marco shook his head again. "I'm sorry, I can't help you, man."

Pajetic frowned and took a step towards Marco. Employing a menacing whisper, Pajetic snarled, "You see my friend I brought with me?"

Marco nodded apprehensively, obviously intimidated.

"He's just like me."

Marco regarded Lance nervously. Lance stared back, trying to look as threatening as possible. He wished he had made his corporeal frame a little less scrawny. Marco was twice his size.

Marco completed his study of Lance, while Pajetic continued. "You know what that means for you, if you don't help us?" Marco narrowed his eyes. Lance could tell he wasn't used to being bullied. Marco appeared to be working up the courage to say something, but he seemed to change his mind, and his face relaxed when he replied.

"Ok, I see your point man. He's..." at this point, he dropped his voice conspiratorially, "He's one too?" Pajetic and Lance nodded. Lance smiled evenly at Marco, which seemed to bother the man further.

Lance could hardly be surprised, human souls stood no chance against the trained and superior power of a reaper. They hunted souls like Marco; that's what they did. Marco had been on the run from reapers since he had first died, probably for years. And now two of them, two of his mortal enemies, were right there in his safe house, the place he had obviously worked very hard to build.

It was beyond dangerous for any human spirit to be this close to a force that could destroy him in a heartbeat. The rabbit would not enjoy having a wolf in its den either.

No wonder he had told Pajetic what he wanted to know, realized Lance. Marco couldn't say no. Once Pajetic had found the place, Marco was placed at the reaper's mercy. To him it was either listen to Pajetic, or see it all taken away.

"Ok," muttered Marco, in a subdued tone. The other spirits, who despite Marco's orders had been paying close attention to the newcomers, were starting to notice the defeated posture of their leader. They stared unashamedly, and whispered to one another frantically. Lance wondered what they were thinking.

Pajetic noticed the increased attention as well, and stiffened.

"We can't talk here Marco. It's not good for us, and it's not good for you. Can you clear them out?"

Marco shook his head. "No man. I've got a room we can go to, above this one."

"Is it secure?" asked Pajetic, sternly. Marco nodded. "Are you sure?" pressed Pajetic. Marco shrugged, "Man I worked as hard on it as this one. It should be secure! Now, can we go?" Realizing he had been too bossy, he added, "Please?"

Pajetic agreed. "Go ahead." He turned to Lance as Marco began to float up, towards the ceiling of the room. "Keep your thoughts to yourself. Don't say anything until I give the ok."

"Whatever," said Lance. He hadn't planned on saying anything in any case. Pajetic seemed to be in the position to do all the talking.

Pajetic turned and ascended right after Marco, with Lance just behind. He was unsure about what would happen next, and he hoped Pajetic knew what he was doing. They were on the hunt at last.

Chapter 10

Marco eventually reached the ceiling of the large room, and quickly stealing a look at the reapers following him, passed through, disappearing from sight. Pajetic vanished as well, not bothering to look back for Lance. Pajetic knew he would be close behind.

Lance rose upwards, but then hesitated. He turned and observed the remaining spirits in the room. They were all standing in groups, with faces uplifted. They were watching him. Lance felt slightly unnerved by all of the attention. Did each one of these spirits elude the capture of reapers? How was that possible? How could the angels and reapers miss so many?

Absorbed in thought, Lance passed through the roof of the room, and was astounded to discover yet another spiritual barrier, this one a darker shade of blue. It was suspended in mid-air, cleverly hidden within the ceiling.

Lance was impressed. He had never imagined human spirits would be capable of such advanced techniques. The teamwork required for such a feat was incredible. It sort of made sense in a way, that it would be humans who pooled their powers to reach a common goal. Humanity had always viewed the whole as greater than the sum of its parts.

The first thing Lance noticed when he emerged into the protected room was that Pajetic had resumed his typical robed form. His dark hood was back over his head, once again concealing his face in shadow. He was standing with his arms crossed, facing Marco. Lance couldn't see Pajetic's facial expression, but his fellow reaper's posture seemed rigid and annoyed.

Lance also reverted back into his reaper persona, and then stood shoulder-to-shoulder with his partner. Marco glared at the pair of unwelcome intruders, but Lance and Pajetic remained unflappable.

This room was even more desolate than the previous one, if such a thing were possible. It was simply four stark white walls with one door, to Lance's right. It didn't even look like this windowless box had a light. Lance assumed Marco used it as an escape for the occasional, relaxing moment of peace and quiet.

Although Marco certainly didn't look very relaxed right now. His face was strained and if he hadn't been a spirit, Lance would have sworn he was sweating.

Marco opened his mouth to speak, then closed it abruptly, as though debating the wisdom of saying anything. Pajetic frowned slightly, and decided to resume the conversation by steamrolling right over any proverbial "bush".

"Marco, you know why we're here, right?" Marco nodded his head slightly, with a tinge of disappointment on his face, as if Pajetic's statement had extinguished any hopes of a friendly conversation. Pajetic's question also appeared to shift his earlier indecision, because this time when he opened his mouth, words came out.

"I won't do it. Not again, man." He shook his head vigorously. "No!"

Pajetic sighed, as if he had expected this would happen. "What's the difference between now and last time, Marco? Some arbitrary ideal you've gotten into your head? It's a little late to think about principles."

Pajetic spoke derisively. Lance stole a quick glance at him, surprised at Marco's resistance. By the way Pajetic had talked about them, Lance practically expected the Guardian Angels to be his partner's cronies. Now it appeared the issue was much more complex.

Lance turned back to Marco, who was still facing them. Suddenly he was grateful for the protective covering of his hood. He wouldn't want Marco to see his puzzled face. He and Pajetic were supposed to be immovable and completely selfless partners, united in strength and purpose. Not two confused rivals who had just met and nearly come to blows a few short hours ago.

Marco shook his head again, murmuring to Pajetic. "It nearly killed me the last time I betrayed a fellow spirit to you. They are my kind! I'd rather die than give you any more information! I sent Julio to his doom; he did nothing wrong! I won't do it again!" Abruptly, Marco looked away sheepishly, realizing too late that he had, perhaps, gotten a little carried away. Lance couldn't help but feel a bit sorry for the poor guy, having to betray his friends.

During Marco's rant, Pajetic's frown deepened and his body went unnaturally still. His retort was spoken softly, but dripped with malice. "Do not forget who you are talking to, Marco," he threatened. "If I were in your position, I would *not* defy those who hold your fate in their hands. You talk about saving spirits? If you are of no use to us, why should we not just eliminate your entire society? You must know you remain here at my whim only, don't you?"

Marco's eyes dropped to the ground and he muttered something under his breath. "What was that, Marco?" Pajetic demanded, daring Marco to repeat it.

Lance had heard what Marco had said, every word. When it was clear that Marco wasn't going to respond, he foolishly did.

"He said we weren't strong enough to get all of them." Lance immediately regretted passing on Marco's comment. The entire tone of the meeting changed, from politically charged to murderous. Pajetic's hands balled into fists and his spiritual presence ballooned outward, applying pressure to the entire room. Marco would pay dearly for what he had just said.

"Not strong enough?" spat Pajetic, his wicked grin just visible from his shrouding hood. "Want an example of our strength, Marco?"

In the blink of an eye he was upon the helpless spirit, who scrambled as Pajetic's iron grip enclosed upon his neck. The reaper raised his choking hand until Marco was lifted up off the ground, legs trashing in midair. "I could rip you apart, piece by piece until there is nothing left but the echo of your screams." Pajetic seethed.

"Enough Pajetic." Commanded Lance. Pajetic dropped Marco to the floor before slowly turning to Lance, who tensed himself in preparation for his partner's rebuke. Pajetic had specifically ordered Lance not to act, after all.

But to his surprise, when he met Pajetic's gaze he saw not the blind rage he had expected, but the countenance of someone in total, calm, control. It had been an act.

"You're lucky, Marco. My friend still thinks you might be useful. If it wasn't for him, I'd have ended you right here in this room. Then who would be left to protect your wife?" Lance saw Marco tense suddenly, and realized that this jab hurt more than any attack Pajetic could make. Marco was protecting a wife. One who was still alive.

"The easiest proof of our power was your pathetic little barrier." Pajetic taunted. "What was that barrier supposed to do, Marco?"

Marco mumbled something incoherent, thoroughly intimidated. "Speak up!" commanded Pajetic, angrily.

"It-" Marco hesitated, then raised his gaze to meet Pajetic and continued in a discouraged tone. "It was supposed to stop all non-society spirits from entering." He let his eyes drop again, the very picture of defeat.

Lance was shocked. Evidently, those barricades he had passed were supposed to not only contain spiritual power, but also to prevent entities from entering. But it had taken him no effort at all to move through! His earlier, favourable impression of the society's handiwork evaporated. Perhaps humans weren't so clever after all.

Pajetic hadn't been exaggerating when he said the two of them could destroy the entire society. Having witnessed Pajetic's abilities, Lance knew his partner could obliterate this entire location in seconds, and probably would if Marco didn't talk.

This gross imbalance in power bothered Lance, who was starting to feel less like a private investigator, and more like the secret police. Against his better judgement, he decided to speak.

As much as he disagreed with what Marco and the other people were doing, Lance could understand why. The poor human before them looked terrified, exposed as he was to the two reapers, and Lance felt guilty that he had repeated the remark that had prompted Pajetic's brutality.

"Paradise got its name for a reason, Marco. It's a perfect place, moulded to each person's fantasy. Spirits sent there are not sad. Not by any means. In fact, the real tragedy is when spirits remain on earth, clinging to what is familiar, instead of embracing their happy eternity."

Lance tried to speak with some degree of sternness, since Pajetic and he needed information from Marco, but he also attempted to convey some warmth and offer hope. Actually, Lance endeavored to mimic Gazardiel's approach, blending kindness with authority. As an afterthought he added, "Think of it this way: you actually did your friend Julio a favour."

Marco stared at Lance, surprised with the reaper's remarks. His expression was no longer as antagonistic, but he remained defiant, stating emphatically,

"It doesn't matter how great you think it is, sir. Everyone deserves a choice." Lance shook his head slowly. This human wasn't getting it.

"No, not when your choice is damaging to others." At this point, Pajetic rejoined the conversation, apparently sick of either the polite tone or the philosophic content.

"The issue is irrelevant either way. We aren't looking for a spirit, Marco." Marco looked at Pajetic eagerly. Lance smiled inwardly; they had finally found a way in.

"You aren't?" inquired Marco.

"Nope," said Pajetic, shaking his head, "We are trying to find something that is as dangerous to you as it is to us. We are looking for a demon."

"Ohhhh," Marco groaned, his eyes widening in comprehension.

"Its name is Prufias, and it's been in this area for a while, Marco," continued Pajetic, assuming a business-like tone now that the wrangling and intimidation tactics had passed. "You've noticed the change in this city, right?"

Pajetic paused as Marco solemnly nodded. "You felt the shaking in the spiritual plane?" Marco again nodded, and satisfied that the spirit understood, Pajetic continued.

"Prufias may see this as an opportunity. The demon has been in hiding for the better part of the century, but my sources tell me he is here, in this city, at this exact moment. The angels are distracted dealing with the upheaval. Most reapers are too. If the demon decides to show himself now, in the middle of all this, innocent people and souls will be hurt. We are going to get to him before he has a chance to get to us, but our trail has gone cold. We need something to work on."

Pajetic ended his explanation. He stepped forward, away from Lance and towards Marco. Lance could hear the intensity in his voice as he asked, "Have you or anyone in your society seen a demon?"

At the conclusion of his questioning, Pajetic stared intently at Marco, who remained silent for an instant. Both he and Lance knew that if Marco had no information, they were facing an impasse. They had few other options. There was a sense of anticipation lingering in the air when Marco finally answered.

"Yes," answered Marco with conviction, "I can even do one better. I've talked to a demon. I don't know his name, it's never been revealed to me. But there can't be that many demons in the city, can there?"

While Pajetic shook his head, Lance felt exhilarated. They finally had their lead.

"I wouldn't expect him to reveal his name, and yes, demons are very rare. How do you know he was a demon?"

"He told me he was," responded Marco, "plus I've been around long enough to tell the difference. I've never seen an angel. But I've heard stories of them, that their strength fills the air with light, and that their voices echo inside a spirit's head. This demon was like that.

"Only instead of hope it seemed like the world went dark around him, and there was a pressure, like he was squeezing the life from me just by being near. He was monstrous. Big, with a lizard's face. And spikes, spikes everywhere."

Marco's face contorted in fear, but Lance grinned inwardly. Typical demon, all spikes and scares. Pajetic knew this too, and pressed on with his interrogation.

"How did the two of you meet?" he continued. Marco froze, and suddenly all the excitement in the room was snuffed out. On his face was the look of a haunted man.

"I'm sorry," he said, with such a desperate tone that Lance winced. Something foul was afoot. "It was Maria!" he pleaded desperately. Pajetic nudged Lance slightly, and Lance realized Marco was referring to his earthbound wife.

"She was going to die! Painfully! It was cancer. I didn't know what to do! So I asked around, and I found myself at this abandoned church... with... with *it*."

Lance knew where this was going, and felt his pity for Marco morph into disgust for this spirit who was in the midst of revealing a terrible secret. Pajetic glowered at Marco ominously.

"You made a deal with it, a deal with the demon! What is wrong with you, Marco?" Pajetic raised his finger and pointed at the spirit, who had knelt on the ground. "Do you have any idea what demons do?"

"I'm sorry," repeated Marco, avoiding their gaze. "It... he," stammered Marco, as if unable to stop his explanation. "He said he would save her, if I agreed to return the favour. I had to! I had no choice! She was going to die!"

"So he cured her," finished Pajetic, grimly.

"Yes!" said Marco, smiling. "She is healthy and stronger than ever! He said he blessed her! She is the happiest I've seen her in a lifetime."

"But what did *you* have to do in return?" interjected Lance, not caring about the utility of a demon's work in the physical world.

Marco shook his head slowly. "I had to, I had to," he repeated, almost as if he were trying to convince himself. "At first it was simple. I had to make barriers for him. Strong ones to contain power." Pajetic looked at Lance, knowingly.

"That's why we have no trace of him, Lance! He couldn't construct his own barriers because his power is so easy to sense. But creating a hideout by using human power, that would fly under the radar! That's how Prufias' whereabouts has been protected! Our last trace of him is most likely when he used his power on Maria!" Lance agreed. This was the break they needed.

Marco, distraught, paid no attention to the reapers, but continued to ramble, as if revealing his sins might somehow redeem him in their eyes. "Then, then he... he demanded! I said no, I wouldn't do it! But he said he'd kill her! And the entire society! I had no choice. He would have done it!"

He then looked up at Lance and yelled, "It's not my fault!" Lance had wanted to leave. They had the information they needed, so it was no longer important. But he couldn't help himself.

"What did the demon make you do?"

"Take them to him," responded Marco. "Spirits. I... I led them to him. And he took them!"

"You sacrificed souls to it!" exclaimed Pajetic, furiously. "Are you kidding me?" Lance couldn't believe what he was hearing. Marco was stewarding the souls of innocent people to a demon! Rage filled him.

"How hypocritical can you get?" he yelled, letting his anger take control. "Claiming that you wouldn't allow us to take spirits to Paradise because of your high moral standards, and then turning around and delivering them to a demon! Do you know what he would do to them!? Have you any idea how you've damned them?"

Marco dropped his head in shame. Lance almost rushed forward but Pajetic swiftly raised his hand to prevent his advance. "Do you know what happens to spirits taken by a demon, Marco?" asked Lance, infuriated. "Can you imagine the pain? He'll devour them, slowly. Their world will be one of torture and fire. They will *never reach Paradise.*"

Marco didn't respond, his eyes closed. He simply muttered, "I had to," over and over again, as if that mantra absolved him.

Lance turned to Pajetic, who seemed slightly more controlled. "We need to leave," he said to Pajetic, quietly. "If we don't, I'm going to kill him." Pajetic nodded.

"I agree, but before we do we need to know one more thing." He turned to Marco. "Where did you take them, where did you lead these souls?" Marco turned to face them once more, before stating quietly, "Mercy Chapel." He then sank to the floor, covering his face with his hands.

"Where the hell is that?" asked Pajetic. Marco said nothing. He seemed incapable of a response. He had withdrawn completely into himself, and was useful for nothing more. He just sat on the floor, slowly rocking back and forth.

Pajetic was about to question further when Lance grabbed his arm and pulled him upwards. Quickly the two rose through the roof of the room, easily passing through the barrier, and emerged on top of the building.

Night blanketed the landscape, and clouds obscured the moon. The hum on the spiritual plane, ever constant but distant in the building, seemed to intensify in the outdoors. Pajetic angrily wrenched himself from Lance's grasp and took a few steps away.

"What did you do that for? We weren't finished!" he snapped. Lance replied rapidly, trying to prevent Pajetic from returning.

"You said you would leave after you asked that last question. Besides, he's done. We'd only be wasting our time with more questions."

"We can't just arbitrarily decide that Lance!" Pajetic spat back angrily. "As pathetic as that creature is, he is our only path to Prufias! We need to find this Chapel!"

"We don't need his help with that, Pajetic," responded Lance. "I know where Mercy Chapel is."

"What?" said Pajetic, astonished. "How do you know?"

"This city," said Lance, gesturing around himself as he spoke, "Was the city I was raised in." Pajetic regarded Lance curiously, apparently taken aback by this information.

"Abyss did say you were an expert in this area. I just never figured it meant-" Lance interrupted, in an effort to divert the topic away from himself.

"Yeah, Mercy Chapel was all over the news several years ago. There was a fire. The interior was destroyed and the rest of the building was made unstable and unsafe. No one was willing to pay to fix it, so it's remained in disrepair."

Pajetic nodded, although he continued to stare at Lance thoughtfully. Then to Lance's surprise, he saw a slight smile stretch across Pajetic's face. "So, you can be useful after all, Lance. Where is Mercy Chapel?"

Lance pointed north. "It's just outside the main city. Follow me." And with that, he took to the air, cruising through the black sky, directly towards the remains of Mercy Chapel.

He did not wait or check to see if Pajetic was following, for he sensed the power of his partner right behind him. As they flew, Lance felt his disgust and anger over the revelations at the guardian society fade away, like water running through the drain. If the past day had taught him anything, it was the importance of letting go.

Instead, Lance began to feel a new emotion, one which had been unfamiliar to him in his time as a reaper, back when he believed he was a masterful hunter. Fear.

This was it. They were heading towards a demon. It would be the first time he would square off against something as strong, if not stronger, than he was.

Lance realized that there was actual danger here. Prufias wouldn't run and cower like a human soul. He wasn't stunted and slow like a revenant. Prufias could fight back. It's a strange feeling, being at the apex for so long, and then encountering a foe that is on even footing.

Despite the warm lights of the city glowing underneath them, Lance felt a chilling sense of foreboding. The shadows of the night, something he had once embraced as a hunter, suddenly felt constricting, suffocating. He had to remind himself that he was not alone, and that Pajetic and he had the advantage by making the first move. The hunt was over. The battle was about to begin.

Chapter 11

They arrived at the Chapel in no time. It sat at the top of a large overgrown hill, surrounded by a small forest. Lance alighted on the road at the foot of the hill, near a long path which lead up to the building.

They were almost at the city boundary, and the vibration of the plane had greatly diminished. The entire area was quiet and desolate. Lance had not seen a car since they had passed the North End Mall, several miles away. That was a big reason why Mercy Chapel had never been restored; it was too remote. No one seemed to use it in the first place.

Pajetic alighted beside Lance and hastily surveyed their surroundings. He shook his head in disgust.

"Could this guy have picked a more cliché hideout?" Lance smiled, caught off guard by Pajetic's humour.

"It is amazingly stereotypical isn't it?" he responded. Pajetic nodded vigorously and made a motion with his hand towards the remains of the Chapel, which consisted of a charred wooden frame, burnt walls, mangled furniture, and exposed rooms.

"It's literally a haunted house. I think I see tombstones!" Lance nodded, and, upon observing the hill a little more closely, noticed several headstones dotting the property to the far right.

"I suppose it makes sense. There would be no interruptions here, no humans coming to distract or annoy him," Pajetic mused. "Plus the travesty of a demon living in a desecrated church. Prufias probably finds that amusing." Pajetic spread his arms wide, initiating a stretch,

"I think Prufias has a flair for the dramatic." Yawning slightly, he beckoned to Lance. "Come on, let's finish our job." Lance nodded, and they both began to walk up the winding path. A serious mood settled in, subduing their slightly merry arrival.

"Where are the barriers?" asked Lance, wondering why they couldn't see the telltale blue glow of Marco's defensive constructs. Pajetic shrugged.

"Marco's not strong enough to put one around the entire place, He'll have erected one, or a few, even, on the inside of the building somewhere. My bet is the dungeon."

Lance grinned again. Even when serious, Pajetic could be funny. His grin evaporated as he refocused on the task ahead. The church dominated the landscape like an ancient ruin, and looked like it had the structural integrity of a sheet tent. In the gloomy night, with the clouds hanging over the sky, it oozed trepidation.

They scaled the path to the door of the chapel hastily, and without sparing a second thought, passed through. The inside was exactly as one would expect.

There was debris everywhere, with random scorched pieces of furniture, somehow avoiding complete destruction, still standing erect in the ashes of the rest. Some areas of the building had collapsed, blocking hallways and leaving only one pathway available: forward and to the right.

A staircase, with most of its steps broken and shattered, lay ahead of them, allowing precarious passage both up and down. A thick layer of dust covered the entire area, and cobwebs stretched over every surface.

Lance shuddered inwardly. The church was straight out of a horror movie. "Where do we go?" he whispered. Pajetic pointed to the staircase.

"Down. I doubt this church has a dungeon, but those stairs lead to a cellar or basement. That's where Prufias will be." He sank through the floor, ignoring the staircase, wishing to check his hypothesis.

Lance swiftly pursued him, not really wanting to be left alone in such a place. It was ironic, how someone who so often used fear as a weapon was now its target. Lance's entire body was on edge as they moved, straining his senses to try and detect Prufias. They were in the demon's very lair. And demons hated guests.

The reapers sank into a cavernous underground room, covered on the floor, sides, and ceiling by dark stone. The place was damp and lit by a familiar faint blue light.

Suddenly, a shiver went up the back of Lance's spine. He felt a power, a presence somewhere. It was very near. He flinched and nudged Pajetic.

"Did you feel that?" Pajetic nodded, his whole body rigid and focused. Abruptly, Lance realized that during this entire time, they had failed to check and see if they were being followed.

He spun around in alarm, but calmed down instantly when he finally spied the blue haze of one of Marco's barriers. No actual demon... yet. Lance spoke, turning his head over his shoulder.

"Here it is."

Pajetic, who was about to probe further into the opposite direction, turned and joined Lance.

"That was easy," he said nonchalantly. Lance shrugged, not letting his guard down one inch. This was confirmation of Marco's story.

Their entire flight, Lance had wondered if Marco had spun them a grand yarn. He could have sent them on a wild goose-chase, only to give this fellow spirits time to run and hide. Of course, Lance didn't think that any more. Prufias was here.

Wary, Lance entered battle-ready mode. His anxiety was pressing against him. Beyond that barrier, they would presumably find Prufias. And the fight would be on.

"Before we go in," warned Pajetic, "there are a few things you should know." Lance looked at Pajetic expectantly.

"We need to work as a team. There is only one demon, but there are two of us." Lance nodded. "Next, we can't be distracted by anything it shows us or tells us. Demons are manipulative."

Lance nodded again, he knew all about the tricks and deceptions of demons. They were told and retold in the stories he had heard. "Ok," said Pajetic, for the first time his voice revealing a hint of uneasiness. "Be ready. As soon as we break this barrier, he will know we are here! Let's go!"

Pajetic and Lance exchanged glances and prepared to step through the barrier. They never made it through.

Instead, they froze in their tracks as they heard a sinister laugh echo through the sombre chamber, originating from directly behind them.

The sound was raspy, inhuman, and undeniably evil. Panic immediately set in. Lance whirled around, his eyes blazing with spiritual power, and from the burst of green beside him, he knew Pajetic had done the same. There, standing in front of them, was Prufias.

The demon was the very definition of a monster. He was a towering presence, looming far above the reapers in the cavernous cellar. He had a muscular, male form, with scaly red skin. His face was that of a dragon, with an elongated snout and teeth protruding from the lower jaw. Spikes jutted from his shoulders, and along his spine.

He possessed a long tail, which ended in a serrated, deadly looking pitchfork. Two long black horns sprouted from Prufias' forehead, and his eyes, his completely human eyes, glowed crimson, a much deeper red than Lance's. The colour of blood.

Prufias did not react to the threat from the reapers, but merely stood there, passively observing their actions. Lance knew that it was Prufias, himself, that they had previously sensed, and wondered how long he had lurked nearby, watching them.

Lance realized that this monster could have attacked them at any time, but had instead chosen to revealed himself. This was very bad news. Prufias was confident enough to play with his food before eating.

The demon spoke, his voice sending shivers through Lance. "Why the show of hostility? I haven't done anything to you." He cocked his head to the side as he spoke, as if perplexed. "I was just coming back from my errands. And I find two little insects heading up to my house! I decided I would have to follow you."

"How long?" asked Pajetic, electing to keep his statements brief. Lance began to reach into himself, tapping into his deepest recesses of power. This demon was talking, not like it was a vicious bloodthirsty killing machine, but rather a deranged psychopath. Lance wasn't sure which was worse.

"Oh, who knows!" roared the demon, who then continued talking in a more subdued tone, apparently not caring about maintaining a consistent volume. "You are just here to kill time until your superiors arrive anyway, and I got bored with waiting! Besides, I need to warm up!"

After saying this, the demon twisted in a massive convulsion, emitting a sound like he had just cracked every single joint in his body.

Pajetic shook his head. "*We've* been sent here to kill you. No one else is coming." The demon glared at Pajetic, his burning eyes boring into the reaper.

"What?" the monster shrieked in disbelief. "Kill *me*?" The creature then unleashed another demented cackle and brought his gaze back to Pajetic. Lance instantly noticed something was different.

It was as if the *crazy* he had been sensing from the demon had been switched off. The rust coloured eyes now gleamed with calculation. Had it all been an act?

The demon continued talking, almost to himself. "This situation in the city must be more serious than I thought. No angels sent to handle me? That's insulting."

He then regarded Lance and Pajetic, sizing them up like he was looking at a particularly unappetizing meal. "You two aren't hiding any special powers, by any chance?" he inquired, and then, upon viewing Lance and Pajetic's unchanging faces, answered his own question.

"No, I guess not." He shook his head dejectedly. "Oh well. If we are to be adversaries, I would like to know who the hell you two are. I am Prufias, demon extraordinaire."

As he said this, the demon bowed. Lance was mystified. Why was this demon acting like this? He knew demons had no honour. Neither Lance nor Pajetic spoke, and the demon took a step forward. Lance and Pajetic's spiritual powers intensified, and they assumed ready stances.

The demon grinned. "Whoa now, don't be so eager, reapers. I'll be destroying you momentarily, don't worry. But before I do, I just want to talk. I haven't spoken to anyone capable of keeping a decent conversation in a long, long time." He then winked and asked, "So, how did you find me?"

Pajetic shrugged his shoulders. "We came here to kill you, monster. Not to talk."

"So it was Marco, then?" said the demon, smirking as he saw the slight shifts in both Pajetic and Lance at the mention of their informant's name. "I knew I should have devoured him, but he was so useful to me! What did he tell you? Did he tell you about the experiments

I've been conducting? The ones for which he so generously supplied the raw materials?"

Horrified by the malicious claim, Lance responded with undisguised loathing.

"We don't care what you've done Prufias, or what game you've been playing. All we care about is stopping you. You will pay for your crimes for eternity!"

As Lance spoke, he decided to try intimidation. He focused his power in the space in front of him and felt it pulse through his body. He shaped it, pressured it, until it became the luminous outline of a scythe. He was forming his manta.

Prufias laughed. once again. "A manta? How cute. I was hoping I could show you the results of my experiments; after all, seeing is believing! It's quite unbelievable what I've achieved. I've taken Marco's poor rivals, and merged them into a brilliant combination of spirit and revenant! It's astounding, and the possibilities are endless, you know. Although it is a rather painful, and slow, process..."

Lance finished summoning his manta and grasped it, remaining in his ready stance. His focus on the manta had blocked out the demon's boasts. Pajetic, however, had paid attention.

"Rivals?" he asked. Lance cursed inwardly. They needed to attack, not talk!

The demon nodded and bared his teeth, which seemed to be his equivalent to smiling. "Ah, Marco didn't tell you that, did he? Unsurprising. That spirit has been sending anyone who challenged his leadership to me, to be, shall we call it, rehabilitated. Anyone who argued with him, became mine. It is so much fun seeing his inherent dark side. Humans are wonderfully vicious."

Lance shuddered as he realized that the demon probably wasn't lying. He had expected the two of them to know of Marco's treachery already. But it didn't matter anymore, Marco wasn't here.

Lance had to clear his mind: Prufias was trying to distract them. Delay them. Now they needed to attack! Lance had heard enough. This creature had obviously inflicted irreparable and horrendous damage to a large number of spirits. His experiments were a threat to humanity, reapers, spirits, and all existence in both planes. He had to be stopped, and it was up to him and Pajetic to do so.

The demon studied Lance, and saw the fury in his eyes. "Wait, don't you-" he started, but was interrupted by Lance yelling, "ATTACK!"

With this battle cry, red power burst across Lance's body, forming a barrier around him and his manta. Pajetic followed his lead, summoning his own manta while green power suddenly whipped around him like a windstorm. Prufias, realizing he had a fight on his hands, began to laugh uncontrollably. His voice dropped several octaves and became noticeably more violent as he chuckled. When he next spoke, he sounded like the monster he truly was.

"I will be sure to give you a slow death, reapers! You think that you are the only ones with weapons!?" With that, ominous power glowed around him as a bracer formed on his wrist.

Out of the top of the armament sprouted a long blade, which protruded at least three feet outwards. It pulsed with power, and disconcertingly, dripped with blood. Its appearance left no doubt in Lance's mind: this was a demonic manta.

Lance roared with anger and charged at the demon, who stood firm.

"Come and die, reapers!" the monster taunted.

Lance and Pajetic reached the demon simultaneously. Prufias clasped his hands, placing the arm bearing his menacing blade on top. The reapers swung their weapons... and collided in mid-air.

The demon had completely disappeared! Lance whirled around to see Prufias on the other side of the room, hands still clasped. Pajetic swore loudly.

Lance glanced at him and noticed, with a start, that Pajetic was not wielding a scythe, but instead, two magnificent swords. Their green handles were adorned with skulls, and their blades were black, but pulsed with green energy. Lance didn't understand. Where was his scythe? He stared at Pajetic's weapons in confusion.

Suddenly, Pajetic cried. "Lance, look out!" Lance dived forward, narrowly dodging Prufias' blade. The demon had magically appeared behind him while he was distracted.

Lance recovered and aimed a wild blow at Prufias, but the demon had already begun clasping his hands, and he disappeared as Lance's manta swung through empty space. Lance saw the demon rematerialize behind Pajetic, who had become separated from him following Lance's desperate dive.

The monster stabbed with his blade, attempting to gut Pajetic. The reaper, sensing Prufias' reappearance, brought his weapons back to parry just in time. The swords warded off the strike of the demon, as the two mantas exploded in a shower of green and dark red brilliance.

Lance projected a blast of power at the demon, a beam of red energy, at the same time as Pajetic spun and sliced out with his swords. The attacks whizzed through empty space, inflicting no damage. Pajetic swore again. Lance yelled in frustration, "How do we hit him?"

The sound of the demon's guttural laughter floated in from above them. The two reapers looked up to see the demon hanging, feet attached to the ceiling. They both jumped back without delay, firing attacks upwards at Prufias. Lance sent another beam of red power, while Pajetic hurled crackling green lightning. The two attacks collided with each other in an explosion, and nothing could be seen for a moment afterward as the area was engulfed in spiritual debris.

The demon's malevolent voice drifted fearsomely from the stairwell, sounding completely unaffected by the reaper's most recent attack.

"This is my unique power, Ghal'zrag!" bellowed the demon triumphantly. "Teleportation. I cannot be defeated. Not by whelps like you!"

With this, he clasped his hands again, and appeared directly behind Lance, who brought his manta back to block, but met thin air as Prufias vanished once more. He emerged behind Pajetic this time, and slashed at his side.

Pajetic brought his blade up just in time to block the thrust but was knocked over by it's pure force. Lance raised his hand to send a barrage of power at Prufias, but the demon had already disappeared, attacking the still falling Pajetic, now from his other side.

Moving with alacrity, Pajetic tumbled across and successfully blocked the attack. The demon clasped his hands and disappeared again, and in a fraction of a second Lance felt the demon appear to his right.

Lance brought his manta to the side and, with his shaft, forced the demon's stabbing blade arm up, making him motion futilely over Lance's head. This was the first positive in the battle. Finally they had made contact with the demon.

At once, Prufias brought his free hand up to meet his raised weapon hand, and disappeared, only to reappear instead on Lance's left! Lance had time to create a shield of power at his side, but it was obliterated by the demon's blow.

Lance threw another explosion of power, hoping to deal great damage at such close range, but the gesture was useless. Prufias was already gone, quickly rematerializing directly before him. Green lightning shot behind his back, and Lance realized Pajetic had vainly attempted to anticipate Prufias' next position.

The world slowed down as Lance became aware that he had absolutely nothing protecting him—he was completely vulnerable. He lacked the strength to erect another shield, and there was no time to move his manta to deflect the blow.

Lance watched as Prufias' blade sped towards him, and he knew he had no way to stop it. He tried to collect a mass of energy in front of himself, in a panicked attempt to avert the blow. He failed.

The blade pierced through the centre of Lance's body, and pain like he had never experienced before exploded through his mind, completely incapacitating him. He fell to the ground in shock, barely conscious.

"NOOOOO!" howled Pajetic, seeing Lance fall. Prufias chuckled, pulling his blade casually out of Lance's limp body. "How odd. It looked as though that reaper had fairly significant stores of power. What a weak showing."

Prufias turned his gaze to Pajetic, who glared at him with pure hatred in his eyes. "I promise your death, reaper, will be much slower." With this he clasped his hands together, preparing to teleport.

What Prufias had not realized, however, was that Lance was not dead. He lay there on the floor forgotten, his power slowly seeping out of him. Dying, certainly. But not dead.

Lance's first death had been sudden, his life had been snuffed out like a flame. This one was drawn out. He was still conscious. The world had become unhurried for him, as if time were slowing down so he could squeeze every drop of life from it.

Lance wasn't cognisant of much, but for some reason, he focused on Prufias' hands, clasped together to teleport once more. His thoughts floated to all the people he cared about, all of them, who would be menaced by those scaly hands. The people of the city, those innocent souls, even Pajetic, would be crushed by them. He had failed. Failed again in his duties.

Despair was creeping up on him when he witnessed movement in the hand that the demon had clasped underneath his bladed arm. The knuckles, facing directly towards Pajetic twisted slightly. To the left and up. Lance had a feeling this was significant, but he couldn't deduce why. His mind was foggy, and nothing made sense.

Prufias disappeared, and as Lance watched he reappeared, behind and to the left of Pajetic. Directly where the knuckles had pointed.

Prufias stabbed his blade and Pajetic brought a sword back, parrying once more. He sliced his other blade around, striking at Prufias in a flash of green.

Pajetic's attack was so fast that Lance could barely see it, though he wasn't really paying attention. Instead he studied Prufias intently, as the demon clasped his hands and rotated his bottom knuckles again, this time up ever so slightly. Pajetic's attack hit air as Prufias appeared at Pajetic's front, repeating the tactic he had used to dispatch Lance.

Pajetic brought his swords down in an x and blocked the oncoming blade. Lance struggled to attach meaning to what he observed. Part of him knew that what he was seeing was important, but he couldn't figure it out.

It made Lance angry, and he frowned as he watched his partner fight. It was amazing how fast Pajetic was. Lance watched as Prufias clasped and rotated his knuckles to the left, and up ever so slightly. He appeared to Pajetic's right and attempted another strike, which Pajetic just barely fended off.

Pajetic couldn't keep this up for much longer. Lance knew this, as he watched Prufias clasp and attack again and again. Pajetic parried with blistering speed and skill, but each attack got closer and closer to home. Pajetic was getting tired.

Prufias teleported behind Pajetic and aimed an overhead swipe at him, which Pajetic blocked with one sword. A shield of dark red power surrounded Prufias as he, instead of clasping his hands, grappled the weary reaper's blade and wrenched it from his grasp. Pajetic grunted loudly and, twisting his other sword, stabbed behind himself.

Prufias, having abandoned teleporting to disarm Pajetic, would have taken the full brunt of the shot, but it was completely neutralized by his dark shield.

Even though Pajetic's strike thinned the demon's defenses considerably, Prufias simply smirked and brought his blade down on Pajetic's other hand. The wounded reaper's remaining sword dropped to the floor. Pajetic grimaced, let loose a cry, and jumped back, his body erupting into a green outline. He was on his last legs.

Prufias tossed the weapon he held to the ground beneath him, freeing up his hands once more. He chortled callously.

"Disarmed, reaper. You stand no chance now!" The demon took a step forward, and euphoria descended on Lance.

In that instant, he connected the dots. The clasping, shifting hands, it all made sense. The twist of the knuckles provided the direction for Prufias teleporting! Their movement up dictated how far forward he would go! That was it! As strong as Prufias was, he couldn't teleport using his mind alone. He had to focus his power through hand gestures!

Lance felt his own power flood back through him in a rush of excitement. Prufias had been correct when he had said Lance had substantial reserves of spiritual power. It was returning.

Lance thought of all the people who were counting on him. He thought of Pajetic, and of Jessica. He thought of Gazardiel and Michael. He thought of Enigma. Would this be how he was remembered? Helplessly lying on the floor as a demon tortured his partner? Their faces played before Lance, faster and faster, until they became a blur. Lance's power flared back to life, surging like a stoked coal. He wasn't done yet.

A titanic wave of positive spiritual power erupted through the room, pushing Pajetic backwards several feet, out of harm's way. Prufias' most recent teleport attack, an attempt to impale Pajetic, failed spectacularly as his blade stabbed into the floor. Lance was filled with rekindled power, but it was also seeping from him, flowing rapidly from his wound. He didn't have much time. A shield of red power engulfed his frame once more, but this time much larger. Its intensity surprised even him.

Prufias turned to face Lance, eyes wide in disbelief. "Ah... so you're not dead. Let me fix that." He raised his bladed hand and shot a beam of blood red energy from his palm. It bounced off Lance's protective shell, accomplishing nothing. Lance roared with anger.

"Judgement has come, Prufias!"

The demon stared at Lance with a bewildered look. He had not expected Lance to survive his second assault. He clasped his hands together, and disappeared.

Lance swore inwardly. He hadn't seen where the knuckles had pointed. The spiritual power in Lance's hands surged outward, and he felt his manta appear once more.

Prufias' blade stabbed into the spiritual power field to Lance's left, and he wasn't fast enough to react. The blade thrust into his barrier, but didn't get to Lance.

His brilliant red outline faded slightly, but held firm. In an instant, Prufias was gone, only to reappear seconds later on Lance's right. He aimed at Lance, who was again to slow. Just like before, the stab was repelled by the barrier again, but this time only just. It exhausted almost all of Lance's remaining power, and as his shield broke, the red outline vanished from his body. Only his manta, wrapped in red energy, remained.

But luck was with Lance. He had his eyes on Prufias, lingering to Lance's right, and watched his hands intently. As the demon brought them together, he rotated his knuckles ever so slightly upwards, directing his hand to the left. Lance knew what this meant. The demon would appear directly behind him.

With this knowledge, Lance focused all his remaining energy into his manta. Channelling every drop of power he had left, he violently jabbed it over his right shoulder. Prufias disappeared from his sight as Lance's blade pierced the area behind him. Lance closed his eyes, preparing for his end.

It did not come.

A vicious cry tore through the stone cellar. No blade had penetrated Lance's body. His remaining energy, all used in his attack against Prufias, dissipated. His manta shimmered, and then disappeared, leaving him alone and defenceless.

Lance fell to his side, turning to look behind him. There, rigid as a statute, stood Prufias.

His arm was brought back, ready to deal a final blow. But he did not move. He couldn't. Dead in the centre of the demon's forehead, was a massive, gaping hole. His mouth was open, and he was roaring in agony, eyes wild. Slowly, cracks appeared from the wound in his head, spanning to his entire body.

The fissures glowed with light, morphing as they took the form of gold chains. Suddenly a white beam of light engulfed Prufias. This bore no resemblance to the illumination Lance used to reach Paradise, but was instead a blinding ray of pain. The demon's screaming intensified, then ceased entirely. The light faded and the room sank into silent darkness once more.

Prufias had been defeated.

Chapter 12

The fall of the demon was a sight to behold, and Lance rightly felt pride in his great accomplishment. Lance and Pajetic, two reapers, had managed to destroy one of the most malevolent spirits to ever exist.

Lance grinned, as the warmth of victory rushed over him. He was vaguely aware of a trickling sensation from his midsection, almost like bleeding, but did not bother to drop his head. He focused only on the pleasure of his conquest. Colours began to merge, blending into a swirling mass, as the world spun lackadaisically around him.

Lance could sense his spirit growing weaker by the second, but even that realization could not strip the smile from his face. It was a pleasant numbness, a sort of calm that seduced and suffocated him all at once. Lance held a vague notion of what was occurring, but remained in bliss. Nothing could spoil his triumph. Not even death.

His shifting vision changed slightly, as a green shape appeared in the middle of his field of view. Something, or someone, latched on to him. And suddenly he was moving, floating through the sky, immersed in a dark blur, tinged with light blue. The hue of an early morning, just before the sun rises.

The green glow slowly faded as he journeyed on, but Lance never felt separate from its presence. It was a constant for him, a pillar for the foundation of his soul. He felt protected.

The trickling sensation in his chest had slowed, but Lance's grasp on reality was rapidly washing away. He could neither hear nor see anything, anymore.

All his earthly senses abandoned him as he slipped further into nirvana. Now, all that remained was his spiritual sense of power, and that, too, was almost completely gone.

In spite of this, the pervasive feeling of comfort endured. Lance did not mind what was happening, not one bit. They had won. Together.

And with that thought, Lance's hold upon his life as a reaper completely failed. A cloud descended onto his mind as it drifted into a totally different plane of consciousness. It was alien to Lance, mysterious and intriguing.

There were lights, bright and sparkling, surrounding him in a galaxy of darkness. They resembled stars.

Arrayed before the lights, flashing before him, were visions of his life. Shreds of his reality, a library of all that Lance was.

He saw Jessica, twirling at a dance with an unknown boy, a teenager. He seemed familiar, but Lance just couldn't quite place him.

The picture shifted, and there was the same male teen, standing beside Lance's family, along with Enigma and Pajetic. Lance wondered who the fellow was, and why they were all together. The boy smiled encouragingly at Lance, his tangled brown hair arrayed messily across his brow.

The gaze was so friendly, so kind, that Lance never wanted to look away. To him, it was like looking into the face of a long lost friend. Time may have changed the face, sculpted and worn the features as life takes its toll, but there was always something that remained unchanged. And it was this something, this testament to the human inside, that Lance saw before him in this young, confident boy.

The more he looked, the stronger the feeling became until Lance was overwhelmed with recognition, and felt his heart soar. He knew who this stranger was. It was *him*. Not Lance, but instead Miles.

But this Miles was different; he was older, bigger, stronger. It was the Miles that never was. Lance's mortal self beamed happily at him, and Lance grinned back. Before him was the reason he had taken the path of the reaper. The boy he could never become. This Miles was so proud of what Lance had done. And all around them were Lance's family, silently supporting him in the weightless dark.

It was bliss for Lance, who tried to not speak, for fear of breaking the spell. He locked eyes with each person separately. They smiled encouragingly back. Then something changed. Slowly at first, then at a frenzied pace, the tableau began to move, not forward, or backward, but side to side erratically. Lance realized the world was shaking. What was happening?

Panic gripped him as he felt pressure on his chest, like a fishhook had implanted itself and was pulling him away. Pain erupted in the centre of his body, as he, for the first time, recalled the grievous wound Prufias had inflicted upon him. The tremor became violent, the tug on his spirit overcoming Lance's defences, and suddenly the image of his family and friends shattered before him.

Lance cried out, trying in vain to rush to their fractured images, but was held in place as the scene unfurled. Something else had risen from the blackness, taking their place.

It was the figure of a man, a spectre, with no discernible features except for dark purple eyes. Its entire body was a malevolent pitch of black, more dark than even the space between the myriad of lights. It reached a hand out for Lance, stretching onward, trying to grab him.

Lance recoiled, instinctively maneuvering to avoid this ominous creature. The shaking and pain increased in intensity as the figure lunged forward, until Lance felt he could bear it no more. Abruptly, a brilliant light flashed before him, and the figure vanished before its radiance.

***

Lance awoke, startled. He was lying on the floor of a room made entirely of concrete. The spiritual plane shook intensely, which led Lance to assume that he was in the city centre, or at least somewhere very near to it.

He was disoriented, but saw an open door just in front of him. The sun was rising, bathing a revealing view of the downtown in a red glow. It took Lance a few moments to gather his bearings. Once he grew more lucid, Lance stole another glance at the landscape and realized he had made a mistake. The sun was not rising—it was setting.

He tried to stand, but the pain in his chest flared angrily. Lance grunted and stopped trying to move. He gazed down towards his stomach apprehensively, but his fear was replaced with confusion as he surveyed the damage.

Instead of a gaping wound, there was a covering, and as far as Lance could tell, underneath it was a concentration of spiritual power. It was like his injury was an empty bowl, and that bowl had been filled with healing power. But Lance knew at once that this was not his power; it was coloured a dazzling gold and felt completely foreign. Lance had never seen anything like this before. Was it some kind of spiritual bandage? It was a mystery.

At the very least, Lance felt it had kept him alive. The room he was in had a decidedly mortal feel to it; there was nothing celestial or heavenly about dingy, concrete walls.

The shaking of the world around him supported his theory. And if this were the city centre as he suspected, and not some kind of after-life, then he was in a lot of trouble. The highest concentration of revenants would be here, in this neighbourhood. If a single one found him right now, Lance would perish. He was in no condition to defend himself.

He had never been hurt this badly before, but as he felt he had stabilized, Lance wasn't altogether worried. His strength would return to him in short order. It didn't take spirits long to regain discharged spiritual energy; in fact, Pajetic had probably entirely recovered from the fight, if this sunset marked the passing of almost a full day.

The thought of his partner reminded Lance of the green energy he had felt near him, and the sensation of flight through the darkness.

Pajetic most certainly wasn't present with him now, but Lance had a feeling the reaper had something to do with his safe arrival: there was no way Lance could have just randomly appeared in this room.

And Pajetic was probably coming back; he knew how vulnerable Lance was in this situation. At least, Lance *assumed* Pajetic was coming back, and that the reaper, whom Lance now looked upon as a friend, hadn't abandoned him as soon as their mission was complete.

Either way, he really only had one option. Wait. Wait until Pajetic returned, or his power was restored, or a revenant found him and devoured him.

Meanwhile, he marveled at the sight of several skyscrapers etched in shadow in front of the setting sun, outlining the breathtaking skyline of the city, and sighed out loud. Lance really hoped that his strength would return soon. He had never been patient.

Lance did not have to wait long.

As the last rays of the sun disappeared, he felt a familiar presence drawing near. It was Pajetic's power, and soon the reaper strode into the room, none the worse for wear.

He noticed Lance sitting upright, fully conscious on the floor, and a barely perceptible smile flickered across his face.

"So you're finally awake, sleepyhead?" Lance nodded, sporting a full-fledged grin.

"What the hell, Pajetic? You left me alone? I could have died!" he accused, half joking, but still acutely aware of just how vulnerable he had been by himself in the room.

"You almost did," responded Pajetic. "That was quite the blow you took Lance. And I was never far away. I kept a constant vigil on this building. No one was getting near you. Besides, I had to leave to get you more of this."

Pajetic finished by showing him a ball of gold energy, the same composition as the material currently filling the hole in his abdomen. Lance was intrigued.

"What is that stuff?" he asked.

Pajetic replied, "Seriously? How can you not know what this is?" He then raised both his hands and gestured around the room. "It's everywhere!"

Now Lance understood what the energy was, and why it had felt so familiar. It was the power that permeated the spiritual plane, the source of the ever-present shaking, just in an extremely condensed form. Lance was impressed.

"How long did it take you to gather it? Is that why you took me to the city centre?"

"Yeah," said Pajetic, "you were in really bad shape, and I wasn't exactly at one-hundred percent, either. So I used my last bit of strength to get us both here, figuring this essence was powerful enough to speed our recovery. I don't quite understand why your spirit didn't consume the power, though."

Lance nodded in agreement. That was bizarre. Typically, non-volatile energy exposed to a damaged spirit would be automatically absorbed. This material had just moulded to him like a cast. It refused to be controlled. Lance shrugged, then continued his questioning.

"I get it, I can't seem to absorb it, but it stopped my power from escaping, and allowed it to regenerate, so it worked. But why didn't you just take me to Paradise? You know, go to the top and get help from an experienced spirit when my life was on the line."

Pajetic shrugged nonchalantly.

"I didn't have the energy," he responded in a calm tone. "Besides, the angels have their hands full, Lance. And you're doing fine."

"Now," he continued, placing the ball of energy down beside Lance, "I need to know what the hell happened in that fight. Where did all that power come from?"

Lance copied Pajetic's easy manner and shrugged his shoulders.

"I'm not sure," he said. "I've got a lot of power. Enigma told me it was the highest quantity of latent energy he had ever seen in a mortal. And sometimes-" Lance's voice trailed off as he became lost in his musings. Lance thought about what he had seen before his power had flooded out. His family, and Jessica, and how he was needed. What a corny way to summon it.

"Go on," encouraged Pajetic, impatiently

"And sometimes," resumed Lance, tentatively, "I can find more power, like it's hidden within me. And all I have to do is think of the right things to bring it out."

"That's it?" snorted Pajetic. "That's what the whole super-power mode thing was? Just hidden power?"

Lance nodded weakly.

"Huh," said Pajetic. "So how did you end up finishing him off? Lucky guess?" Lance shook his head again.

"No, I figured out where he would be after he teleported."

He could see Pajetic's interest was piqued, so he continued. "It was his knuckles. They were his *tell*. Whenever Prufias brought his hands together, he rotated the knuckles of his bottom hand and then tilted them up. The knuckles pointed in the direction he wanted to go, and the degree of tilt controlled how far he went."

Lance looked at Pajetic, who clapped his hand to his forehead, as if he couldn't believe his own stupidity.

"Of course!" exclaimed Pajetic. "I can't believe I didn't see that." He then regarded Lance more seriously. "Why did you wait until after he had stabbed you to take advantage of this?"

"I didn't realize it, at first, for the same reason you didn't," responded Lance. "It took everything I had just to parry his attacks. There was no time to analyze his hand movements."

"No kidding," agreed Pajetic, obviously remembering, like Lance, the fury of Prufias' initial assault.

"But when he struck me down, he left me on the ground, and I saw what he was doing." Lance glanced out at the skyline illuminated with artificial light as evening set in. "He must have thought I was done."

"He wasn't the only one," murmured Pajetic, quietly. "Your power was gone Lance, there was just a sliver left. I swear, you were done."

Pajetic left this statement hanging in the air as he dropped his gaze to the ground, engrossed in thought. He then glanced up at Lance, with curiosity. Lance wasn't entirely sure what he was thinking, but the keen attention made him nervous.

"I guess you've felt it, right?" Pajetic finally asked, in an awkward fashion, as if he didn't know exactly how to phrase his question. Lance shrugged his shoulders, perplexed. "You know," Pajetic continued, before evidently deciding to be more direct and blurting out, "Feelings."

Lance felt an interesting combination of hope and fear. How did Pajetic know he had feelings? Had it been that obvious? What would he do? Lance was worried that he would be reported to Enigma, or even Abyss.

"How-" began Lance, in a troubled tone, before Pajetic cut him off.

"I have them too. I think the seal has been broken for every reaper who has been near this power." Lance's eyes widened, realizing the implications. "So Enigma, Abyss, everyone... has feelings too?"

"Yeah, I think so," responded Pajetic. "I guess it's something about this energy, it cancels out our pact in some way. I doubt Abyss would reveal it to anyone; she'd be afraid of losing her position. And Enigma isn't exactly a big talker. Other than the four of us, I don't know of any other reapers who have been exposed."

Lance agreed whole heartedly with what Pajetic said. He nodded thoughtfully.

"Has noticing this changed how you think? Knowing you're human again?"

Pajetic recoiled out of habit, expelling an audible breath of air.

"I was never much of a human to begin with."

Lance stared at Pajetic but was able to decipher nothing. He was impenetrable. But you didn't have to be a psychologist to notice his negative reaction. Lance wanted to know more, but Pajetic had stiffened, and Lance did not want to fall back into their previous routine of insults. He prepared to change the subject, when to his shock, Pajetic spoke.

"It's not like anyone really wants to know," he muttered, turning away from Lance.

"I want to," Lance replied confidently. "I want to know more about my partner, my *friend*."

The word sounded so odd coming out of Lance's mouth. Just twenty four hours ago, the two of them were at each other's throats. But now they were a team—they were demonslayers.

Lance had saved them both in combat, and Pajetic had carried his wounded comrade to safety. They had formed an indestructible bond, one forged in battle. Lance's words seemed to have a powerful effect on Pajetic, who asked, almost innocently, "Friends? Is that what we are?"

Lance nodded with conviction. "Yeah." He paused for a moment, considering Pajetic's response. "You talk like you've never had one."

Pajetic shrugged. "I've never needed one."

"You've never had a friend?" exclaimed Lance incredulously. "Not even a member of your own family?"

"No," said Pajetic simply. He remained calm and in control, ever the foil to Lance. But, for the first time, Lance sensed some vulnerability behind the reaper's tough exterior. There was something in those eyes, just out of reach. Could it be… regret?

"Why?"

Lance's question hung in the air, while Pajetic considered it for a few seconds. He steepled his deft hands and furrowed his black eyebrows, pondering the implication of Lance's words.

"Do you really want to know?"

"Yes," confirmed Lance emphatically.

"It's not that interesting," dismissed Pajetic, but Lance was tired of waiting.

"Pajetic. Tell me."

The reaper rolled his eyes and walked over to Lance.

"Why tell you, when you can see it for yourself."

Pajetic reached out with one hand and a fine mist of acid green energy wafted from his fingertips, surrounding Lance. "I'll show you from the start," he explained, as Lance's vision faded.

***

The first thing Lance saw was a ship. A weathered watercraft constructed of rusted metal and the improvisation of its crew. Its motors groaned as it cut through a choppy sea on a clear, bright afternoon.

The smell of salt-water was in the air, as the strong wind blew the tops off waves onto the deck, which was packed with a crowd of people. They were all Asian, like Pajetic, and wearing the clothing of tired travellers.

Suddenly, Lance's view zoomed, as if he were watching some kind of movie. It focused on three people, huddled near the centre of the boat.

A middle-aged man, with graying hair, and a gentle, thin woman. And between them, a small, frightened boy. Lance knew immediately who it was. Pajetic.

The man reached down to the boy, who was clutching his mother's leg, and pointed to the horizon ahead. Lance spun around, to see a massive coastline, lined with buildings. He recognized the harbour. This was his country.

Time jumped forward, and in a jolt Lance was in a small, undecorated room. It was sparse, with only a cot and desk for furniture, and a single window overlooking a busy suburban street. The young Pajetic sat on his bed, downcast.

A woman's voice rang out from below. She spoke in a different language, but Lance was able to understand the meaning of her words perfectly.

"Jacob, come down for dinner!"

"My name is not Jacob!" cried Pajetic angrily, in the same language.

There was a pause, where Lance could just make out the murmur of voices from down below.

"Jacob, come down and eat your hamburger right now," demanded a male voice, sternly.

"NO!" screamed Pajetic. "My name is Yao, and I don't eat stupid hamburgers!"

The scene melted away, and Lance prepared for the next. But instead, he was treated to an array of sights and sensations. Conflict between Yao and his parents. Yao at school, laughter directed at the awkward boy who couldn't speak English. Yao slowly learning the language, against his own will. Frustration. Anger. Yao, sitting alone, as days melted into years. Loneliness. Desolation.

Then, like a ray of light, hope. Yao, joining a volunteer program going to his homeland. A chance to be where he belonged. Joy. Happiness. Sitting in the airport terminal, ticket in hand. Apprehension. Excitement.

Lance felt a grin creep across his face at Pajetic's enthusiasm. But it was not to last.

Laughter. Derision. Locals complaining about Yao's accent. Confusion. Humiliation. Young kids, his own age, teasing him about being "whitewashed". Yao running away, selling his things, and getting a ticket back home. Despair. Devastation.

Anger. Resentment. Yao, now a teenager, snickering at a student who answered a question wrong in class. Spending afternoons all by himself, playing videogames on an old computer. Cynicism. Apathy. Yao easily passing tests and jeering at those who failed. Contempt... Hatred.

The slideshow stopped as suddenly as it had begun. It took Lance a moment to regain his bearings. Yao was walking along a secluded city street, with a backpack around his shoulders and a scowl on his face.

Approaching him on the sidewalk was a gang of teenagers, about Yao's age, dressed in cheap shirts and torn jeans. Lance saw the confrontation coming a mile away.

True to Lance's prediction, Yao refused to step out of their way, and collided with a member of the group. Immediate chaos. The youths rounded on Yao, encircling him and shouting insults.

"You want to start something, kid?" taunted the ringleader.

"I don't waste time with peasants," spat Yao, refusing to back down. There was a second of silence, where Yao appeared to realize the implications of his wisecrack. A shadow of fear flickered across his face as the gang fell upon him.

Yao was outnumbered, unable to fight off four adversaries at once, but held his ground admirably. The group showered fists upon him, until Yao was incapable of standing, then rained down a storm of kicks. The beating lasted less than a minute, but it seemed to stretch on for a lifetime, as Yao's blood splattered across the pavement.

Lance seethed as he witnessed the cowardly assault, his vexation multiplied by his inability to take action to stop the injustice. He was only able to watch as the assailants pummelled the helpless Yao, before fleeing down the side of the street.

Lance tensed, wishing he could reach out past time and space to enact retribution, but his vengefulness was shortlived. Instead, his heart filled with sorrow as he heard Yao start to move.

Yao could barely see, his eyes swollen shut and his vision clouded with his own blood, but that did not prevent him from trying to stand. He struggled briefly on the ground for a second, marshalling his strength, before staggering to his feet. He swayed uneasily, his spirit desperately trying to hold on to life. But the battle was already lost.

Lance felt his heart ache when with a horrible gurgle, Yao collapsed back to the ground. Lance's view was quickly focused to Yao's head, where he saw an inflamed blood vessel burst. There, all alone, Lance's friend took his last breath.

The scenes began to scroll by faster and faster, each one shorter than the last. Lance saw Pajetic's spirit awakening from his body, extremely confused and uncertain. Predictably, Pajetic was unaffected by the pull of Paradise. He was too strong.

Subsequent days were spent exploring and experimenting with his new world. Pajetic quickly discovered that he was on a separate plane of existence, and before long, was able to fly. Lance could barely believe what he saw. Pajetic had mastered it without a teacher.

When Lance had first awoken, he had been weak. Unable to move, dependent on Enigma to show him the way. Pajetic was nothing like that.

Pajetic was strong, from the very beginning. Far stronger than any human soul Lance had ever seen, stronger even than some of his colleagues. This meant the tables were turned, and that Pajetic would have a chance... when the inevitable reaper came.

The first time it attacked, it surged menacingly from the shadows of night, swinging at Pajetic with a great scythe, a foreboding weapon decorated at its head with a skull. Pajetic reacted instantaneously, catching the reaper by surprise, and flew into the air just in time. Pajetic took off, racing away into the dark sky, leaving the reaper behind, standing resolute in the darkness below.

From that point on, Pajetic was constantly alert. His pursuer was unrelenting. Time after time it tracked Pajetic down, but time after time, through a combination of luck, skill, and power, Pajetic evaded capture. The cat and mouse chase went on for several days, until finally, the reaper cornered his prey.

The two engaged in pitched battle, Pajetic fighting brutally with all his might. Despite his great ability, Pajetic was still not match for a reaper, who finally smote him to the ground.

Pajetic lay there defenceless, prone on the floor of an abandoned parking garage, pinned beneath the reaper's knee.

"Finish it," Pajetic panted, scowling at his foe. "Kill me."

The reaper paused there, atop its prize, and slowly the shadows which obscured its appearance began to clear. Lance gasped as a familiar face emerged from the darkness.

"Kill you? I want to recruit you," said Enigma, pleasantly.

***

And with that, the vision was gone. Lance was again seated in the golden sunset in the city centre. He blinked, mouth agape in shock. Pajetic really had shown him everything.

His partner stood across from Lance, his back turned, watching the city slip into night. The two remained there in silence for a few seconds, as Lance marshalled his thoughts.

"I was trained by Enigma." He offered, still surprised by the common link between his and Pajetic's paths.

"That makes one of us." Replied Pajetic simply. "Enigma never got to teach me."

Lance frowned. He wanted to know more about Pajetic's training, but he felt like it would be inappropriate to pry further after such an intimate explanation.

"Pajetic..." He began, hoping to lend some support to his friend, but was cut off by a curt laugh.

"Oh come on," Pajetic grinned exasperatedly. "Don't you want to ask who taught me?"

"I... I do." Replied Lance, choosing his words carefully, trying not to sound corny or stupid. "But... I don't want to force you to talk. I want to show you that I'm sorry for what you've gone though, and that I'm grateful you would tell me about it."

"You already have." Explained Pajetic, his grin fading slightly. "You're the only person to ever ask." He paused for a moment, before continuing.

"It was Abyss. I was taught by Abyss."

Lance almost didn't believe what Pajetic said. If he hadn't just seen Pajetic's history first hand, he would have dismissed this most recent claim as a complete lie.

But Pajetic's story was so incredible, so intense, that it did not seem too far-fetched to believe this last statement. And Pajetic had no reason to mislead him.

Abyss... as a teacher. Lance shuddered at the thought, and new questions burned within him, he opened his mouth, about to inquire further, but was stopped by Pajetic.

"I've talked enough Lance." He stated firmly, and Lance reluctantly nodded his head in agreement. Pajetic had never talked to anyone in his life, and now Lance was practically interrogating him.

"Just one last question then," Protested Lance, observing his new partner in a new, gentler light. Pajetic rolled his eyes.

"Was it Abyss who gave you your weird manta?"

The question had been in Lance's mind ever since he had seen Pajetic wield the two swords against Prufias. Perhaps Abyss wanted her pupil to be treated differently. "Is that why you weren't given a scythe?"

Pajetic chuckled dryly. "Mantas, Lance." He emphasized the plural aspect of manta. "And Abyss did, in a manner of speaking. I suppose Enigma was never allowed to teach it to you."

He then appraised Lance. "You look a little better. Do you think you can travel if I assist you?" Lance nodded and slowly stood up.

"I can manage on my own, I think." And to prove his point, he took a painful step forward.

"Not where we're going, tough guy," said Pajetic, smiling. With that, he sent two tendrils of green energy to wrap themselves around Lance, pulling him towards Pajetic. Lance grimaced. He did not want to be carried around like some weakling.

"Where are we going?" he asked, curtly.

"Outside of the city," said Pajetic, as they soared away from the room, revealed to be a compartment in a skyscraper under construction, and into the twilight. "We need to get away from this spiritual power, so I can make a portal."

"To Paradise?" asked Lance, confused.

"No," answered Pajetic. "To the Grim Reaper's Tomb." Lance did a double take. The Grim Reaper's Tomb? That made no sense.

"The Grim Reaper was a spirit," said Lance, challenging Pajetic. "He wouldn't have a tomb."

"Spirit's don't," agreed Pajetic as they continued to fly through the air, "but remember, he was human before he ever became a reaper." Lance nodded. Pajetic had a point.

"But what is significant about his tomb? Why would it affect the creation of a portal?" Pajetic ensured they were secure, and free from any prying ears, before answering.

"I think we are safe from revenants. I guess I should really start from the beginning. The first thing you should know is, there is a lot of important stuff in that tomb."

"So?" Lance stated, somewhat rudely. "Tell me we aren't tomb raiding, Pajetic."

"Of course we aren't," he responded. "You don't understand the whole story. You want to know about my mantas, right?" Lance nodded eagerly.

"Alright," explained Pajetic, "then you need to know that mantas are used by all powerful spirits, not just reapers." Lance nodded,

"Angels use them, and demons, too." Lance thought of the long blade of Prufias as he spoke, and felt the mostly-healed wound in his chest twinge painfully.

"Correct," agreed Pajetic. "mantas for angels and demons can take on many forms; you saw Prufias' weapon." Lance nodded once again in agreement; things were starting to fall into place.

"So why do you think reapers are any different?" prodded Pajetic. "Turns out, we aren't. Summoning a true manta is incredibly difficult and requires three things: a deep knowledge of oneself, a highly tuned level of control, and an immense store of spiritual power. This is beyond most novice reapers, so instead they give us a pre-formed spiritual weapon, and call it a manta. Your scythe is an example."

Pajetic paused, surveying the scenery again. "But your scythe really isn't a manta at all. It's some other spirit's power, probably an angel's, which you're free to use. The angels have no other options. Spiritual weapons are the only way we can send rogue spirits to Paradise."

Pajetic's discourse made sense to Lance. He knew how essential his manta— or, as Pajetic called it, his spiritual weapon—was to his job.

"So all mantas are different?" Lance inquired.

"Yeah," answered Pajetic. "They are extensions of the spirit, they fit their summoner perfectly. I'm just naturally inclined to use two blades."

Pajetic then grinned at Lance, "I'm sure if you learned to summon one, your weapon would be a big shield. You love that power barrier stuff."

Lance's face lit up at the potential of Pajetic's revelation. Ignoring Pajetic's little jibe, he visualized himself holding a massive golden sword, light to the touch, carving enemies before him. He had never really liked using a scythe.

"How do I learn to do this?" asked Lance eagerly, turning his face to Pajetic, who had stopped moving.

"I'm going to show you." As he spoke, Lance felt Pajetic's energy unravel, and noticed they were at the far outskirts of the city. There were a few buildings here and there, but for the most part this area was devoted to smooth farmland, dotted by the occasional tree.

It was natural, a nice departure from the artificiality of the city.

"Hopefully the spiritual plane is settled enough for me to do this," continued Pajetic.

His eyes began to glow bright green as he focused on his task. Pajetic raised a hand and stood utterly still, straining to call forth the portal. Lance quickly appreciated why they needed to leave the city. It was hard enough to conjure up one in this calm environment, let alone in the midst of a spiritual earthquake.

However, Pajetic was more than up to the task, and before long a green circle opened up before them. Lance could see nothing through it, but trusted Pajetic and the mechanics of portals. After all, he had used the same concept to get to Paradise. But before he stepped through, he wanted to know more about their destination.

"What does the tomb have to do with summoning a manta?" he asked Pajetic.

"The Grim Reaper was the sole mortal spirit capable of independently summoning his own manta. The only way reapers can do it themselves is by being exposed to his energy, which lies in several items in his tomb. Now let's go." As he uttered this last statement, Pajetic stepped through the portal, disappearing from Lance's sight.

Lance sighed inwardly. He had assumed that any spiritual items, like a manta, would dissipate when their creators died. After all, it was a spirit's energy that sustained it. But then again, he had also thought that the weapon he had been wielding this entire time was a manta.

Why did he have so little knowledge? Lance pondered the question irritably. He had never before felt as if Enigma's teaching had been mediocre; the reaper had prepared him for every challenge he had met. That is, until he encountered Pajetic.

Now it seemed like Pajetic was constantly explaining new facts to him. Was all this taught to him by Abyss? Did Pajetic know more than Engima? But he seemed so young, not at all as wise as Lance's tutor. Deciding against asking, Lance grit his teeth and stepped through the portal.

It took Lance a short while to collect himself when he surfaced. There was little light, and he had still not recovered from his wound. He let out a deep breath. Today was not his day for clarity or sharp thought.

Pajetic silently acknowledged him through the dark. They stood out on a platform, in a massive underground cave. Across from them was a mountain of rock, not large enough to fill the empty cavern, but more than large enough to be classified as a hill.

At its bottom was the black entrance to a tunnel, with an oppressive and almost otherworldly quality to it. On either side of the tunnel's entrance were great etched statues, each clasping hulking stone weapons. Their grim presence guarded the passage into what Lance assumed was the actual tomb of the Grim Reaper.

"Where are we?" asked Lance, who was unnerved by the disturbing atmosphere. It was very reaper-like.

"The tomb," responded Pajetic respectfully, as one would whisper in a church. "Or more specifically, the tomb's entrance. It's somewhere in Egypt, deep below the sands. This is where the angels put the Grim Reaper's artifacts. Now, come on."

Pajetic stopped just before the entrance way, so Lance was able to observe its features in greater detail. The statues flanking it appeared to be angels. They both had sculpted wings sprouting from their backs with halos of stone circling above their heads. Lance believed that, at one time, their facial features would have been elaborately carved. But over the course of history, erosion had worked its own uncontainable magic, and the faces were now blank ovals, with just the bare suggestions of a nose, or eye sockets. Perturbed, Lance wondered why they appeared weathered, since they were sheltered underground.

The overall effect was disconcerting, with the guardians a symbol of decay and darkness, as opposed to the typical angelic concepts of light and justice.

"Let's go in," said Pajetic brashly, as he was swallowed by the void of the tunnel's mouth. Lance was about to follow him, when something above the doorway caught his eye. There, high on the stone wall, was a sinister carving of a skull.

Lance had not seen it from across the subterranean hole, but now that he was closer, it was hard to miss. The surface was embellished with ornate details, and strange runes danced across the forehead, with uncanny onyx eye sockets and a wicked grin stretching across its teeth. There were no signs of erosion on this adornment; each line seemed fresh, as if it had been etched earlier that day.

The sight of it thoroughly creeped Lance out, and he became acutely aware of just how alone he was, standing outside of the tomb in the eerie outer-cave. Lance stepped into the shadows quickly, hoping that Pajetic had not gone too far. The leering skull remained prominent in his mind.

The corridor was dim, and Lance, ignoring all walls and pathways, simply floated to where he could sense Pajetic's energy. He eventually reached him, standing in an illuminated room, observing the source of the light. As Lance arrived, Pajetic held out an arm, barring him from progressing further. Lance saw immediately what had stopped Pajetic in his tracks.

There, blocking their passage further into the tomb, was a spiritual barrier. This one was pure white in colour and pulsed with strong energy.

"This wasn't here last time," mused Pajetic, a note of worry audible in his voice. "That's the work of an angel, for sure. The burial chamber is just beyond it." Pajetic pointed towards the barrier as he spoke. Lance agreed. The white hue and the power definitely attested to the influence of an angel.

"Are we supposed to be here?" queried Lance, anxiously.

"Not really," answered Pajetic. "I think only senior spirits are allowed." Lance shrugged.

"So, time to leave?" he asked. The eeriness of the skull and the oppression of the tomb were getting to him. As much as reapers like the whole doom and gloom motif, Lance found this mausoleum to be a bit much.

"We already came all the way out here," rationalized Pajetic. "Besides, this barrier doesn't seem to be too strong. We can get through."

"Are you sure?" said Lance hesitantly, while Pajetic boldly strode into the barrier and began to force his way through it.

"Come on," he grunted. "Help me out." Lance sighed, and surveyed the room one last time. He fervently hoped their actions would not release any ancient curses or immortal guardians.

He stood beside Pajetic and pushed. Fighting through the barrier was like trying to push through tar: it stuck and impeded the reapers' movements. But eventually, despite Lance's weakness, they broke through and emerged onto the other side.

Immediately, Lance could tell something was not right. This part of the room possessed walls and a floor, not of natural rock, but of great sandstone blocks. The blocks even extended up over the ceiling, making it clear that this section of the cave was not a natural phenomenon. Torches lined the walls and spewed not red fire, but flames of dark purple. Lance was instantly reminded of the figure with purple eyes that had appeared in his near death visions. He felt a chill ripple through his body.

At the end of the room, which was several meters long, lay a casket. Behind it was a wall, again constructed of sandstone, with several shelves. Carved in the wall were a number of depressions that from where Lance stood, looked like outlines of weapons. One of the spaces took a form that was impossible to mistake. It was chiseled in the shape of a scythe.

"Uh oh," breathed Pajetic, in a decidedly nervous tone. He surged forward, heading towards the back wall. Lance followed, somewhat pleased at how easy his movements were now, compared to earlier in the night.

Pajetic reached the far wall and swore loudly. Lance recognized at once what the problem was. The depressions were clearly where the Grim Reaper's artifacts had been placed, creations Lance had heard of repeatedly. They were the armaments of legend, weapons of fantastic and terrible power. But Lance did not get to see them now. The depressions were empty—the items were all gone.

"Uh oh" repeated Pajetic, numbly.

"Where are they?" asked Lance, worried.

"I have no clue," stated Pajetic, equally as worried. A few moments later, he stared at Lance, wide-eyed, "Tomb raiders, it has to be tomb raiders."

Suddenly, a source of spiritual power emerged into their senses, moving along the rock tunnel they had taken. Lance jerked his head towards the barrier, which still shone brightly. He could tell that Pajetic had done the same.

"Someone is coming," whispered Lance, frantically.

"I know," answered Pajetic. "Whatever happens, don't fight Lance. You won't survive another battle in your condition. Just surrender. I'll handle this." Pajetic's eyes flared into acid green, as he and Lance awaited the appearance of the approaching spiritual power, which was drawing closer and closer.

A dazzling light appeared on the other side of the barrier. It fizzled and disappeared, revealing the spirit on the other side.

Gazardiel the angel stepped forward, weapon ready, with an exceedingly stern expression on his face.

"Entering this tomb was a very poor decision, thieves!" he cried loudly, but before he could say anything else, he saw Pajetic and Lance.

His expression froze for a second, before shifting to recognition, then shock, and finally, steely determination.

"Pajetic. Lance. I did *not* expect to find the two of you here," he said quietly, with a tinge of regret in his voice.

Lance opened his mouth to speak, but Gazardiel raised a finger, silencing him.

"I was under the impression that you were striving to redeem yourselves by destroying a demon. I never expected you to be responsible for this." Gazardiel covered his face with his hand, as if he were terribly disappointed. "Where did you take the relics, Lance? Speak!" His last command was brisk, and full of authority. Lance felt as it he had to mount a defense.

"We did kill the demon sir!" stated Lance, somewhat defiantly. "Prufias has been destroyed."

"Really?" asked Gazardiel, in disbelief. He took several steps towards Lance, "You stole the Grim Reaper's weapons, stole from the angels themselves, to defeat a demon?" Lance shook his head vigorously; the angel had misunderstood him. Pajetic, however, understood clearly, and spoke before Lance had the opportunity to respond.

"No Gazardiel. We defeated the demon by ourselves. Together." Lance felt a surge of pride at being recognized by Pajetic, in front of Gazardiel. "I used my own, real, mantas in the battle," continued Pajetic quickly, "and Lance was curious. He wanted to learn to summon his own too. I brought him here so he could. Everything was gone when we arrived. Trust me."

Gazardiel was silent as he slowly processed Pajetic's information. Then he sighed, audibly.

"Michael has dictated that anyone who enters the tomb is to be apprehended, Pajetic. The contents of this resting place were pilfered a few short days ago, and it was believed that the thieves would return to try and take the Grim's casket. Do you have any idea how guilty you look? I have no option but to detain you."

Pajetic stiffened. "I don't want to be detained. Are you going to fight us Gazardiel?" he challenged, the green hue of his eyes intensifying. Lance could not believe what Pajetic was saying. There was no way they could defeat an angel. Gazardiel laughed; it was a boisterous and powerful sound.

"Fight you? Pajetic, do not deceive yourself. You may be strong, you may even have defeated a demon, but a contest with me is not one you could ever win."

"Please Gazardiel," pleaded Lance, trying to prevent a fight. "You have to understand. We have done nothing wrong."

Gazardiel studied Lance, who could once again sense his compassion. But now there was another emotion clearly evident, one which had been absent in their meeting in the alley. Pity.

"I am sorry Lance. But this is the end. Even if you did not steal the items, you have trespassed upon sacred ground. And you cannot prove what your true intentions were. If it were up to me-"

Gazardiel paused, and for an instant, Lance thought that perhaps Pajetic and he would be allowed to leave. "Well, we've had this conversation several times now. It is a pointless observation. It is not up to me."

He then turned his back on Lance and Pajetic, so the reapers could no longer see his face. A pit formed in Lance's stomach as he realized what was about to occur. "I cannot protect you from Abyss this time," said Gazardiel with finality.

Two tendrils of blinding white power extended from the angel's shoulders and faster than they could react, coiled themselves around Lance and Pajetic.

Pajetic cried out loudly, as green power sprang ineffectually from his hands. Lance merely sank to the floor, unable and unwilling to resist.

"Lance and Pajetic, reapers of the spiritual realm, I, Gazardiel, under the authority of the Archangel, hereby find you guilty of trespassing and accuse you of theft. You are therefore relieved of your duties and placed under arrest."

Overcome by the tendrils of power, the two of them had no way out. Gazardiel's strength dwarfed their own. Lance looked up, trying to plead their innocence once more with the Archangel, but Gazardiel refused to acknowledge them. The coils began to constrict, squeezing tighter and tighter and tighter.

Then, the world was no more.

Chapter 13

Lance awoke not long afterwards in yet another unfamiliar setting, but this time with a thankfully clear mind. The restful sleep, induced by Gazardiel, had not allowed his consciousness to drift. Lance had seen no visions of past family members, or dark threatening figures. Now it was just him. All alone.

Or so it seemed.

To Lance, there was literally nothing around him. He could sense nothing, not even his own powers. Just complete, all-encompassing nothingness. He felt strangely disembodied, and the idea bothered him.

Worried, Lance tried sending out tendrils of his spirit to probe his surroundings. Maybe he could feel that which he could not sense. To his surprise and alarm, he could extend nothing. It was like not being able to breath. In a panic, Lance pushed out again, straining with all his might. Nothing came forth. He was powerless.

He tried to move forward, to flee this constricting place, but he was immobilized. He couldn't even feel his own body, let alone move it.

"Let me go!" he roared, throwing his voice as far as he could. He waited for a second, as his plea echoed in his mind. Despair insidiously crept in, the complete loss of autonomy bothering him far more than any battle ever could.

Then, like a ray of sunshine piercing through a cloud, he heard the sound of Pajetic's voice. It was weak, as if it came from a long distance away, but audible and clear nonetheless.

"Lance? Is that you?" Lance smiled. Or at least he would have if he could have moved his face. Misery loves company, and knowing that he was not trapped alone comforted him greatly.

"It is," he responded, then continued. "What is this Pajetic? What's happened to us?"

"It's the void," replied Pajetic, dejectedly. "We are in the outer ring-" his voice trailed off, as if distracted.

"The Outer ring… of *Abaddon*?" finished Lance in horror.

"Indeed," confirmed Pajetic, gravely.

Abaddon. The mere name of the realm of the damned was cloaked in a sense of dread. The halls of judgement. Lance was well schooled in this subject, as like every being, he was naturally curious about the ultimate punishment. So, when Enigma instructed him, he had paid very close attention.

When spirits are sundered on the mortal realm by a manta, or some similar spiritual technique, their fragments are carried up towards Paradise where they reassemble and then pass into their reward.

Unless the souls are marked by evil. Those souls, weighed down by destructive flaws such as anger, greed or cruelty, arrive at a markedly different destination.

They are not given a happily ever after, but instead an eternity of damnation, solitude, and punishment. They are left in Abaddon, for the remainder of time. It is not a pleasant thought, but Lance understood that exceedingly few souls were deemed monstrous enough to be warded in the spirit prison.

The fact that the two of them were trapped in there was devastating news. Lance knew that no one had ever escaped from Abaddon before; the mere thought was madness. It couldn't be done.

Abaddon is built in concentric rings, with the least dangerous offenders, by Abaddon standards, incarcerated in the outer circle. As the rings of the realm progress inward, the atrocities committed by the wards become increasingly vile. Its corridors are patrolled by several angel-wardens, but their services are a mere formality, because of the dungeon's first line of defence: the void.

A lack of anything. That was the base description Enigma provided to Lance when explaining Abaddon's most valuable weapon. As Lance trained and studied, he gained a greater understanding of the pure nothingness that was the void.

Humans believed that they had already found the lack of anything and had named such a thing a *vacuum*. But despite their efforts, Lance knew that a *vacuum* actually existed.

That was the fundamental difference between it and the void. Void is what everything used to be, before the Creator instilled its divinity upon it and shaped it. It is the total opposite of spiritual power and existence. In fact, it fully absorbs any power near it. Because all spiritual movement and action is controlled by exerting power, it effectively paralyzes and restricts any spirit nearby.

Despite its threatening qualities, Lance also knew that void could be manipulated, and even created. Michael could bring it into being, Lance was sure of that, as could the wardens.

He understood the basic process; to produce void, one needed to undo the work of the Creator. He liked to think of existence as some kind of elaborate machine. To create void, you simply removed the bolts, gears and springs of life. How void was shaped into life, however, he could not say.

Enigma had implied that not even the angels could perform such a feat. The void's use in Abaddon was simple. Offenders were deposited in a designated place and then the entire area around the spirit was turned to void. There was no escape; the victim was powerless, trapped. And nothing could undo the void.

His thoughts about the void made Lance curious about his conversation with Pajetic.

"Pajetic," he inquired, "if we are both stuck in void, how can we communicate?" Silence followed for an instant, and in his mind's eye, Lance visualized Pajetic shrugging.

"I don't know," responded the reaper. "It might be that spiritual communication is telekinetic, and not contingent on an exercise of power. All I know for sure is that we can speak to one another, thankfully."

"Then we need to take advantage of this! We need to talk!" stated Lance.

"About?" asked Pajetic dryly, foreseeing the direction Lance was headed.

"Escape!" exclaimed Lance, proudly. He heard Pajetic chuckle lightly.

"It's over Lance," replied Pajetic, with a calm and even tone. "There is no escape. You know that. We're done. End of story. You know the power and intelligence of some of the things in here... deeper in the rings. There is no way we can succeed where they have failed."

"You just want to give up?" cried Lance incredulously. "You just got your human emotions back, your hopes and your dreams, and you want to give it all up?"

"I told you," said Pajetic coldly. "I was never much of a human." He paused for a moment, and then added, "and I never said anything about giving up."

"Never said anything?" scoffed Lance indignantly, "Then what was the whole 'it's over' thing about? That's not giving up?"

"Resistance is not the sole method to solve a problem Lance," advised Pajetic. "Use your head, think for a few seconds. Things aren't as negatively aligned as you may think."

"What do you mean?" asked Lance, not really wanting to think, seeing as Pajetic clearly understood something he didn't.

"Well," stated Pajetic, "for starters we know we are in the outer ring." He paused then, and apparently predicting a potential question from Lance regarding his conclusion, continued.

"We know this because we are talking, Lance. I bet our individual voids must be close to each other, perhaps in the same room. That leads me to believe that we probably aren't in the actual Abaddon, just a holding area on the outside."

"But in their eyes, we are criminals who stole some of the most powerful and threatening weapons in existence," countered Lance. When he thought about it, he completely understood just how suspicious Pajetic and he had looked in that cave.

"Your fault, coincidentally," said Pajetic, in a slightly peevish manner, which managed to aggravate his already irritable partner.

"My fault?" said Lance, practically yelling. "Pardon me for not knowing that my guide was leading me into a crime scene."

Pajetic laughed, and Lance, slightly surprised by his partner's reaction, chuckled as well.

"I guess it's immaterial. The point I was making is precisely what you said. The angels think we are thieves. And they have absolutely no idea where those items are, and who is in possession of them. Plus they probably think their theft is linked to the spiritual disturbance in the city. They are going to come to question us Lance. We still have a shot at proving our innocence. After all, we did kill a demon."

Lance tried to shake his head, realized he couldn't, and that Pajetic wouldn't see him even if he did, and then stated, "We can't negotiate or prove anything Pajetic. They've given us plenty of chances."

"Well, we can try," said Pajetic, bluntly.

"Sure we can," agreed Lance, "but we should also try to take advantage of our time to talk now, before our jailers show up."

"Talk?" asked Pajetic mockingly. "You want to have a heart to heart? Gossip, perhaps? Maybe we'll talk about the weather?"

"No." Lance laughed, then added, "We need to figure out what to do, in the event of escape."

"I already told you," said Pajetic in a dispirited tone, "We can't escape."

"I know. You said that. But they said we wouldn't be able to kill a demon, and that didn't stop us."

"Killing a demon was unlikely, but possible," countered Pajetic. "Escaping the void is not."

"Still," mused Lance, "it does us no harm to make a plan. We need to figure out how best to clear our names."

"The best way," answered Pajetic knowingly, "is to peacefully stay put. We didn't steal anything. We trespassed, but that's no reason to overreact and imprison a spirit in Abaddon. We just have to wait until they catch the real culprit."

"That could take decades," lamented Lance. "We have to prove it ourselves."

"But we-," Pajetic tried to once again remind Lance that they were not in a position of power, when Lance interrupted him.

"I think the theft and the appearance of that power aren't attached, but I bet if we solve one of those issues, the angels will believe our side of events. It will give us some credibility. For me, specifically."

Lance recalled what Enigma had said about killing the demon as being a chance to prove himself. He had actually managed to make his reputation *worse*.

"That's true," agreed Pajetic slowly. "But we know nothing about the theft, except that the items of power are no longer there. That's not much of a lead."

"But," interjected Lance, "we were the ones who triggered the defences, not the real thief. That means the spirit had to be exceptionally powerful in order to evade whatever safeguards the angels originally had in place."

"Wow," said Pajetic, sarcastically. "A strong spirit was the one who stole the *most powerful spiritual artifacts in the mortal realm.* How did you figure *that* one out, Lance?"

"It's better than nothing," responded Lance, somewhat subdued. Now that Pajetic had pointed it out, he realized his conclusion was pretty obvious.

"I think we know a bit more about this disruption in the city," said Pajetic.

"Yeah," agreed Lance, brightening up. "We know it disrupts power."

"And masks all other energy in the area. Not only that, but it doesn't seem to affect the mortal realm," added Pajetic. "It also was the most potent essence you had ever encountered, correct?"

"Uh, yeah," affirmed Lance, adding sheepishly, "It took me completely out of commission, and it didn't even come close to hitting me. It flew right over me."

"It's nothing to be embarrassed about. It's strong enough to keep the angels totally clueless," finished Pajetic. "They've been working on it for days and haven't figured it out. I've never seen them at such a loss."

"So, what do *you* think?" asked Lance, earnestly. His partner had proven to be very good at guessing things correctly.

"It's definitely a spirit," answered Pajetic. "An inanimate source of power would be located easily." He paused here, thinking for a second, before shouting excitedly, "I know! It's a demon."

It's definitely NOT a demon," said a third voice. It was arrogant, and lacked the clarity and majesty of an angel. It spoke again.

"What? Do I sound weird? I just wanted to join in on the conversation!"

"Who the hell are you?" growled Pajetic. "You're not an angel, that much I can tell."

"Well, aren't you brilliant! And here I was beginning to fret that I had been unceremoniously dumped beside two idiots!"

After neither Lance nor Pajetic answered, the voice continued unphased. "You two didn't think you were the only spirits in Abaddon did you? I'm your block-mate! My friends call me Bee!" it stated, jovially.

"Right," said Lance. "So you've been eavesdropping this entire time?"

Naturally," replied Bee happily. "But I'm afraid I couldn't continue doing it for any longer. I've wanted to talk to somebody, anybody, for ages you see. And besides, I think I can help you."

"Help us?" stated Pajetic angrily. "We don't want your help, heathen."

"Heathen?" queried Bee, feigning hurt feelings. "What are you, from the middle ages? Why would you call me that?"

"You are imprisoned in Abaddon," Snapped Pajetic. "We know what kinds of creatures are kept here."

Bee giggled, then replied, "So, then, you are monsters too?" Lance started, he hadn't really thought of that. He had been thinking exactly along the lines of Pajetic, that those in Abaddon are the purest of evil. But Bee had a point. Pajetic and he were in there too.

"We've been wrongly imprisoned," protested Pajetic.

"Ah!" cried Bee, "As have I! It's terrible!"

"Really?" inquired Lance, derisively, although he was still contemplating the possibility in the back of his mind.

"Really!" exclaimed Bee.

"Well then, what kind of spirit are you?" said Lance, continuing the enquiry.

"That is neither here nor there, *reaper*," announced Bee, shocking Lance by his knowledge about who he was.

"How do-" began Lance, before Pajetic quickly cut him off.

"What a genius you are, figuring out that two prisoners, conversing normally with each other about how innocent they are, are reapers. You know angels don't get thrown into Abaddon, and demons wouldn't worry about how to solve the world's problems. I'd give you a gold star if I had one."

Pajetic then continued, "Since we've established that you just state the obvious, *demon,* I see no point in continuing this conversation."

"Fine," said Bee resignedly, "You figured it out master reaper, I am a demon, at your service."

"We need no service from your kind," stated Lance, firmly and angrily. "I'll let you know we killed one of your brothers less than a day ago."

"Really?" asked Bee, now sounding surprised himself. "Who?"

"Prufias," stated Pajetic coldly. Bee chuckled softly, not showing a hint of remorse or sadness.

"That old dog was still out in the mortal realm? I'm impressed by his resilience." His tone was softer, as if he were speaking only to himself. "And by you two? If you managed to handle him by yourselves, I'm impressed. Prufias is no pushover."

"Thanks," said Pajetic. "We're done talking."

"But why?" complained Bee forlornly. "I can help you two!"

Lance snickered and Pajetic snorted.

"Help us?" said Pajetic, incredulously. "Every word you say is a lie. And even if not, you're still of no use to us."

"I disagree on all counts," replied Bee. "First, you seem to inherently distrust me. And yet you said it yourselves that you are as far out of Abaddon as you can get. That is true. I've timed the wardens' rounds, and we must be on the outside. Or Abaddon is much bigger than I think it is. But by your own logic, this means that I can't be a serious offender, because my cell is near yours.

"Secondly, I've been around for a really, really long time. There aren't many things in this existence that have escaped the notice of old Bee. That's why I can tell you with assurance; whatever it is you were talking about is definitely not a demon."

"Regardless," said Pajetic. "Why would you help us?"

"Because," explained Bee, "I've missed having someone to talk to. And being a demon, it tickles me to think of two reapers being able to solve this big conundrum that has the angels so upset. I don't really like angels."

"Fine," said Pajetic. "What do you think Lance?"

"We should at least listen to him," said Lance. "We know he is probably lying, so it's not like we will follow him blindly."

"Exactly!" said Bee, gaily. "Now listen, it's not a demon. Our energies don't work that way. I've been near some really nasty ones before, some big names like Oni, and Cerberus. Sure they had massive power, but it was so destructive that it ripped everything apart! Mortal, spiritual, it made no difference. This thing sounds too passive to be a demon. Where did this power come from?"

"We don't know," responded Lance. "It came out of nowhere one night."

"Ah," mused Bee. "Then it *could* be a spirit emerging from some kind of energy shield, but I doubt it. All the ones strong enough to do that are accounted for in here. Or are lounging away up in Paradise."

"Indeed," stated Pajetic evenly.

"That rules out spirits," surmised Bee, "but it could still be some powerful item. You two said you stole some really important stuff, right?"

"We stole nothing," said Lance flatly, before adding, "but someone else stole the Grim Reaper's scythe and some of his other treasures.

"Ok," answered Bee, "so those could-"

"Argh," interrupted Lance suddenly.

A sharp twinge had just coursed through his body, and he felt... he felt!

"What is it?" asked Pajetic, concernedly. "Are you hurt?"

"No, I don't think so," Lance mumbled, sounding confused, "But I feel something!"

"Feel?" queried Pajetic. "You're speaking nonsense."

Lance focused for a moment; his soul was pumping and moving about. Was it regenerating? It was as if his body had fallen asleep, and it was only now just awakening. He was aware of a sensation at the centre of his chest. His energy could expand and move, although he could still sense nothing elsewhere.

"I can feel Pajetic!" he exclaimed jubilantly, "I can control my power! It's stemming from my chest!" In the excitement, they had totally forgotten about Bee.

"Your chest?" asked Pajetic, a sense of realization dawning on him. "But that's-"

"Yes! Where you put some of the energy from the disturbance!" said Lance excitedly, beginning to grasp the implications.

"You can feel it." said Bee in a quiet tone, breaking his silence. "You must know that means."

"The void is gone!" said Lance, breathlessly.

"Your essence must have healed and pushed that power bandage off," stated Pajetic.

Lance now concentrated again, trying to summon his power once more, but focusing it towards the area of his body he could feel. He tried to force a tendril out, and to his surprise, it slinked out of his midriff, although it did not get far before it met the cold void again.

Elated, Lance expanded it as far as he could in every direction and noticed a small tunnel existed in the void, straight down. Lance's power flowed down the tunnel until it connected with a pulsating, familiar energy.

"It drilled a tunnel through the void!" Lance cried out, in amazement.

"Quick!" exclaimed Pajetic, "Bee, how much time do we have before a warden comes? You said you timed their rounds."

"You've got about thirty minutes. Go!" said Bee, sounding equally energized.

"Lance, move the essence about, try to mop up the void!" commanded Pajetic. Lance did as he was told, using the voidless space as a base to move the power. It sucked up the void like a sponge, providing even more space for Lance's form as he moved it around.

"It's working!" he said with delight. This was their big chance. "It's obliterating the void!"

"You realize there is only one source of power capable of undoing void, don't you, reapers?" asked Bee, whose voice trembled with anticipation.

"The power of a Fragment!"

The statement hung in the air for a few seconds, as Lance digested Bee's startling proclamation.

"Ridiculous." Pajetic dismissed the notion outright.

Lance, who had now cleared much of the void from around his face, nodded his head in agreement.

"Impossible. It can't be a Fragment of the Creator."

"What other explanation is there!?" demanded Bee. "What other source of power exists that can undo void, fundamentally alter reapers, and even elude discovery by angels? I know of no other answer."

Lance shook his head, the void almost completely gone. "The Fragments are relics, hidden away in Paradise. They could never reach the physical plane."

"There are three of them, you know," said Bee, "kept under lock and key by the angels themselves. The Creator could never die, but it feared that its massive power would destroy everything that had been built! So the Creator broke itself apart, splintering itself into three Fragments, each a third of the Creator's glory."

"I'm well aware of what a Fragment is," responded Lance, who had successfully removed all the void from around himself, and could now see his surroundings.

He was in a cold stone room, with a door at each end. The design of the place left no doubt in his mind as to which exit would take him deeper into Abaddon. The door to his left, constructed of iron, had haunting etchings of screaming faces, visages of the damned. The door to his right was made of simple wood.

Lance breathed a sigh of relief, thankful they had not been taken further into the prison. On the other side of the room were two sizable vortices. Simply put, they resembled dark-purple clouds, with crackles of black energy zapping around them, sporadically.

Or perhaps the correct term was crackles of black *lack-of-energy*, so to speak. "So that's what void looks like," he said aloud. Then he added, "Pajetic, say something."

"Huh? Why?" asked Pajetic, confused. But it was exactly what Lance needed. He walked towards the void to his right, in the direction of Pajetic's voice.

"What I don't understand about your hypothesis, Bee," stated Lance, "is what a Fragment, one of the three most sacred objects in all of creation, guarded by all the angels of Paradise, is doing in the centre of a city!"

"Isn't it obvious!" replied Bee. "The angels tried to absorb it for themselves!" Bee's words tumbled out gleefully. "They finally broke! They are going to do something horrific to the mortal realm. I knew it was coming, knew it all along. Something is rotten with the angels, there always has been. But Fragments are clever. They can detect negative intent, evil residue. This one would have repelled itself from the usurpers! It is probably still evading them as we speak!"

By the end of his rant, Lance had freed Pajetic from the void. His entire being was shaking with excitement. They had just escaped Abaddon! The jail of the damned! Pajetic smiled at Lance, then cocked his head towards their block-mate's cell.

"That sounds like the exact thing a demon would say." observed Pajetic, coldly.

"I can't believe you are still on that!" whined Bee, sounding hurt. "Everything I've told you has been in good faith! I told you about the Fragment, and I gave you the correct time for the guard's rounds. I've been nothing but a loyal friend and advocate!"

"We can't totally discount what he's saying," stated Lance, "but we have to go. I think avoiding the angels, for now, is the best plan. A warden will get here soon, and next time we're caught, we won't escape."

"Yes!" cried Bee, "I beg you to release me, so I may help you further! I can be a distraction; I can prevent the angels from catching you! Hurry, we don't have much time left."

Neither Pajetic nor Lance said anything. The awkward silence lasted for a few seconds, until Bee said, "Oh..." in a heartrending tone. "But I helped you."

"And we're grateful, but there's still a problem," said Pajetic. "You warned us about the guards, but we have not escaped yet. Since we're accused of being thieves, we don't want to doubly damn ourselves by setting a demon loose. Especially since we know exactly what your kind is capable of. Lance, we have to go."

"You manipulative little wretches!" howled Bee, instantly exploding in violent fury. "You won't be safe for long! I will tear you apart! You liars! You jailbreakers! I'll get you!"

After this rant, he stopped for a second, then began screaming as loudly as he could, "WARDENS!! THERE'S AN ESCAPE!!! WARDENS!!"

"Run!" yelled Pajetic, and the two of them bolted for the door. Lance dropped the ball of Fragment power on the ground as he went, knowing that it would massively complicate their escape. The darn thing was incandescent!

They sprinted towards the wooden door, away from Abaddon's depths, and charged toward freedom. The ball of power slowly rolled into the corner, where its radiance gradually dimmed, silently sinking out of sight and mind.

Chapter 14

The door opened to a winding stone staircase, which Lance and Pajetic easily flew up, now free from the void. Spiralling upwards at a frantic pace, Lance felt a little dizzy.

He could never handle spinning rides as a human, the inertia was just too much for him. As the stone flashed by, Lance called out to Pajetic. "What's the plan?"

"Improvise," shouted his partner.

Lance couldn't help but smile. Pajetic and Lance, the only spirits ever known to escape the void, were hopefully about to burst out of Paradise in a storm of glory.

Or at least, in something that somewhat resembled glory.

They reached the top of the staircase and encountered another door, once again constructed of just simple wood. Pajetic stopped and held out his arm, barring Lance from bursting through. Lance regarded Pajetic nervously from behind.

"We can't stop!" he breathed. Pajetic nodded.

"I know," he responded, "but we need to be prepared for whatever is out there. We keep going until we get to the main terrace of Paradise; I'm pretty sure that's where this path will eventually end. When we get there-" he paused. "We will need to overcome any and all attempts to restrain us. No exceptions."

"Fight the angels?" asked Lance in disbelief. In the excitement of their escape, he had forgotten about their circumstances. They were now fugitives. And he couldn't shake Bee's explanation of the spiritual disturbance, and his opinion on the guardians of Paradise. Instinctively, Lance thought Bee was a liar. The angels would never betray the Creator. But he couldn't know for sure.

"I don't want to, but there may be some truth in what Bee was sayin, so I'm not about to give one a hug." Explained Pajetic tacitly.

Lance understood, what Bee had said made sense. The Fragment theory was perfect, it explained everything. Fragments had something approaching a consciousness, and would definitely flee from a would-be usurper. It could easily use its power to hide itself. It also explained why the energy had allowed him to heal so rapidly. It all fit. Except the bit about the angels. Something just wasn't right.

"I know," said Lance, weakly, "but I don't know if I could fight an angel." He shook his head, knowing attacking an angel would be hard for him. They were supposed to be the protectors of truth and justice!

"Let's just hope we don't run into any," said Pajetic, as he pulled his hood up over his head and turned to stare at Lance. "For their sakes."

His eyes came to life with their acidic green glow. Despite the seriousness of the situation, Lance couldn't help but smile. Pajetic and he were joined at the hip. They had been to hell and back, literally, and done it together.

Here, once more, they would stand or fall, as brothers. Lance was ready to fight, be it angels or demons. He was armed with courage and conviction, and his eyes blazed with crimson fire. Pajetic smiled approvingly.

"On the count of three," he said. "One."

"Two," counted Lance.

"Three!" yelled Pajetic, who threw the door open, and rushed forward into a blinding white light. Lance charged alongside, but found himself overwhelmed by its hue. The glow quickly dimmed, as a sudden rush of white energy engulfed both he and Pajetic, immobilizing them in mid-air.

"You two!" boomed a voice, loudly, harshly, and recognizably.

Lance knew it the second he heard it. He struggled against the power, but his efforts only seemed to tighten the hold it had upon him. It constricted, slowly crushing him in its vice, but giving him at least some room to speak.

"Gazardiel!" he gasped in shock.

Sure enough, as the brilliant white light dimmed, the Archangel strode forward, wearing the same white tabard and golden armour as always.

His features were arranged in a stern, solemn expression, with his bushy eyebrows knotted together fiercely. It was an angry expression, and yet not as menacing as the circumstances seemed to merit. Lance saw something odd in Gazardiel's face, and had a sense that the angel was experiencing some internal conflict.

"You two!" The Archangel exclaimed again. "Why is it always you two!"

Pajetic snarled angrily, and there was a flash of acid green energy. Pajetic dropped to the ground, the white power that had bound him severed, and crouched into a ready stance.

"You won't imprison us again, Gazardiel!" he declared defiantly.

Lance quickly examined his surroundings, and noticed that they were in a long, beautifully decorated room with light streaming in from gorgeous stain-glass windows. At the far end was what looked to be a final, great door.

Lance instinctively knew what lay behind it. They were almost out. But Gazardiel would never let them pass. The angel shook his head, his long hair swaying. His handsome features, so fierce a second ago, now seemed quite sombre.

"Always you two," he repeated, almost to himself as he glanced at Pajetic, who was wasting no time.

Seeing that Lance was still ensnared in power, Pajetic shot two razor sharp lines of green towards his ally, rescuing him from Gazardiel's grip. Lance landed heavily on the ground, then, obeying Pajetic's commanding look, reluctantly allowed his red power blaze into life.

All of Lance's motivation had disappeared the instant he saw his opponent. He did not want to fight Gazardiel. Of all the angels, Gazardiel was the one who had helped him the most. When no one else believed in him, Gazardiel did. When Abyss wanted him dead, Gazardiel had protected him. Gazardiel was the last person Lance imagined would forsake his duties.

"So you mean to fight me?" asked Gazardiel, his blue eyes staring into Pajetic's. They then flicked to Lance, who looked away. "Lance?" insisted Gazardiel, quietly.

"We won't let you stop us," said Pajetic. "So unless you let us pass, there is no other option. We've dealt with a demon. You know our power." Gazardiel sighed heavily.

"But you have no grasp of mine. This is what it's come to? The two brightest stars of the reapers, the two challengers to Abyss, now about to attack an angel? For what, some backhanded, pathetic attempt to escape?"

His voice escalated with rage "I have spent the last day lobbying for your release! And now you flee like cowards? I expected so much better." The fierceness had dissipated by the last sentence, and was replaced by pure disappointment. Lance squirmed inside. The last thing he wanted to do was displease his former advocate.

"Lobbying for us?" spat Pajetic, clearly less bothered by Gazardiel's admonishment than Lance. "Don't lie."

"Lie?" said Gazardiel, caught off guard. "We do not *lie*, Pajetic! You know this!"

"Ha," laughed Pajetic. "Evidence proves otherwise." He turned to Lance and nodded his head slightly. Lance knew what Pajetic meant by this signal. Pajetic was about to make this move, leaving Lance with no choice. He had to attack. Leaving Pajetic to assault alone would not only be weak, but would probably result in his friend's capture. Or worse.

So when Pajetic sprang forward, acidic green enveloping his fists, Lance had no options. He leapt forward as well, allowing his crimson energy to course through him. Gazardiel did not react, and Pajetic and Lance reached the angel in the blink of an eye.

Pajetic struck towards the angel's shins, letting his energy slice out of his hand in a great band. Lance forced his power into his fist and aimed a herculean blow at Gazardiel's chest, to temporarily disable him.

The explosion of their intense attacks engulfed Gazardiel in a cascade of power, a radiant light-show which again rendered Lance's senses useless. Everything was hidden behind red and green energy. Lance fell to one knee. He had no idea what had just happened. As the glow faded, the scene slowly revealed itself.

There, standing in the same position as before, was Gazardiel. He was encased in a bright bubble of power, which had fully absorbed Lance and Pajetic's attacks. The angel sighed once again.

"Please, stop." He turned his gaze first to Pajetic, then Lance, exasperated. Lance looked to Pajetic, hoping to see some sign from his ally. Pajetic was crouched on the floor, on the opposite side of Gazardiel.

He seemed weakened, although green energy still flowed around his hands. His hood remained up, obscuring his features. He spoke, his voice still carrying significant strength.

"We won't let you stop us." Pajetic stood, his eyes dripping with green light once more. Lance rose with him, eyes crackling crimson.

"We are not *cowards*, Gazardiel!" Lance declared, emboldened by Pajetic's words. He had thought of something; a way out. "We would rather fall here, fighting to stop your shameful plan, than be locked into the void for eternity."

"That-" responded Gazardiel slowly, "is an eminently mortal way of thinking, Lance."

"It is the only way. We will stop the scheming angels," declared Pajetic, following Lance's lead.

"Stop whom?" demanded Gazardiel, incredulously, "From what? You've referenced a plan, what are you talking about? And remember, lying will not serve your cause, Pajetic!"

"Cut it out, Gazardiel," said Pajetic curtly, to which Lance added "We know about the Fragment." Lance took a step forward, and added, "That's what's in the city, and you've known it all along." Immediately, Gazardiel started to laugh.

"A Fragment? In the city? Inconceivable!" Gazardiel chuckled again. "A Fragment, do you have any idea what that is? The three Fragments are our most precious treasures! They are the Creator's very essence!" Gazardiel threw up his hands, to emphasize his point.

"Besides," he mused, "they are under Michael's exclusive protection. And-" Gazardiel's voice trailed off suddenly.

His gaze shifted, as though he was now looking past the two reapers, his mind racing as the implications of what he had just said sunk in. "Wait," he said apprehensively, the colour draining from his face, "How *did* you escape from the void?"

"How do you think?" responded Pajetic grimly. Lance was at once worried and hopeful. He could feel the tide of the argument shifting in their favour. Gazardiel had always listened before. But, the notion of the principal Archangel, Michael himself, as their enemy made him feel queasy.

The best he could do now was convince Gazardiel. They didn't have much time; the Wardens could arrive at any second, but he decided to risk it anyway.

"When we battled the demon, Gazardiel, I was badly injured. Prufias inflicted a mortal wound in my abdomen, and my power leaked from me in an unstoppable tide. I was going to die," Lance looked at Pajetic. "But Pajetic saved me. He gathered energy from the city centre, concentrated it, and used it as a type of bandage to stem the flow. It was still there when you captured us, and when we awoke in the void." Lance turned back to Gazardiel, and saw naked fear across his face. "It completely dissolved the void, Gazardiel."

Gazardiel stared intently into Lance's eyes, and at once, Lance felt completely exposed, as if the spirit were reading his mind like a book. Lance refused to look away. He wanted to know the truth, to hear it from an angel.

"There is no other power on earth, other than that of the Creator, which can remove void. Of that I am certain," declared Gazardiel, solemnly. He face was in turmoil, and as the Archangel shook his head, Lance saw, for the first time in his service as a reaper, a distraught angel.

"It can't be Lance." he continued. "You must be mistaken. Michael couldn't! Where is the power—the so-called Fragment? Proof is needed for such outlandish accusations!" Lance took his turn to shake his head. "I left it in my cell. I couldn't take it with me Gazardiel, it was a dead giveaway." Pajetic spoke up, having been mute thus far during the revelation.

"Gazardiel, you know how powerful the spirits that have been locked in Abaddon are. We are ants compared to some of them. Our escape is proof enough. Fragment power is the only answer."

"We go back," said Gazardiel sternly, "If there is proof, I will show it to the other angels, and we will adjudicate this matter swiftly."

"No!" yelled Pajetic. "The wardens will be here at any moment Gazardiel. And we have no idea who is involved. If Michael is bold enough to attempt to control the Fragments, he may have recruited other angels to his cause. He could be working alone, but it's not worth the risk!"

"Your logic is flawed," argued Gazardiel, convincingly. "If that were the case, how are you to know *I* am not involved in the plan?"

"We have no choice!" growled Pajetic. "You've reminded us time and time again that we are no match for you. If you are in cahoots with the conspirators, our run is already over. You're our only hope!"

Lance came to a sudden realization, while Pajetic was talking.

"Where is Michael, now?" he asked. Gazardiel's eyes opened wide.

"He is several floors above this room, which exits into the main section of Paradise."

Pajetic stepped forward purposefully.

"He could come down at any moment Gazardiel! We have to go! We can help you!"

"Without evidence we are nothing, Pajetic! I cannot simply act impulsively!" said Gazardiel, although Lance could hear doubt and confusion in his voice. They were convincing him.

"You can gather evidence later Gazardiel! You can conjure void by yourself! When we escape, you yourself can test our theory. If the power in the city dilutes it, it will confirm our claims and our innocence. If it doesn't, you can easily return us to Abaddon" explained Pajetic. "Just take us away from here, before Michael ends us all."

Gazardiel looked past Pajetic and Lance, to the doorway behind them. Strain lined his face. He clenched his fists, and said aloud, "Lord, forgive me!"

Suddenly there was an explosive flash. In a wave of force, Pajetic and Lance were both pinned against a wall, surrounded in a white nexus of light. It pushed in on Lance's power, shaping his form.

Trust me. Don't be afraid. Don't do a thing! Gazardiel's voice echoed mightily in Lance's mind. Lance relaxed, and no longer fought the now familiar strength of the angel. He and Pajetic were not the only ones capable of improvising. They had won Gazardiel over, and now the Archangel had a plan.

A crash sounded as three armoured angels burst from the stairwell. Their faces were unfamiliar and were marked with sky blue paint. Their golden locks fell down to their shoulders, and they clutched elegant yet deadly weapons: one, a rapier; another, a long and sharp pike; the third, a bow.

They halted their charge as they saw Gazardiel, stopping almost comically, tumbling into one another as they tried to slow.

"Gazardiel!" the one with the rapier exclaimed breathlessly.

"I already know!" cried Gazardiel. "Their trail grows dead here! I just came from the high quarters, they had to have run into the main temple! Go! I'll follow with my hounds!" The assembled wardens regarded Pajetic and Lance for a brief moment, before returning their attention to Gazardiel. But, to them, they did not see two reapers. They saw two animals.

For that is exactly what Pajetic and Lance had become, their energy completely cocooned in one of Gazardiel's signature abilities, his spirit-hounds. They had been transformed into dogs of pure white, with short hair and golden runes etched along their sides. Their teeth were lined and sharp, with massive canines sprouting from their lips.

The wardens wasted no time and immediately rushed out of Abaddon, exiting to the main terrace of Paradise, although the one with the bow lingered behind.

He looked back to Gazardiel and asked, rather brashly in Lance's opinion, "Has Michael been informed?"

Gazardiel shook his head. The angel motioned toward Pajetic, concealed in the hound's form. "Send a hound to alert him, Michael will catch them." Gazardiel again shook his head.

"You, inform him right now. I must try to stop them. By the time Michael is informed it could very well be too late!" With that, Gazardiel took off, out the door, and into the main pavilion of Paradise.

His voice boomed into Lance's head. *We leave now. We will talk more when we are in the city, safe from others.* If Lance could have, he would have thanked him.

Gazardiel walked forward briskly, Lance and Pajetic trotting alongside. Lance wondered to himself if senior angels ever ran. Paradise looked the same as when he had last, although Lance noticed that they had just exited from the tall tower that he had observed on his last visit. So that's how one gets to Abaddon, he mused.

The temple itself was still utterly empty, save for the two wardens who were now at the gate, talking animatedly to Peter. The guardian made a sign, and the wall of power that surrounded Paradise, normally a light and almost invisible gold, turned an angry shade of orange, pulsating with power. It did not take long for Gazardiel to reach the group.

"Anything?" he asked. Peter shook his head.

"I saw nothing, Gazardiel, but there is no way of knowing if they escaped the boundaries," he replied in a defeated tone. "The barriers are to keep spirits from coming in, not leaving. Now the way is barred both ways, but I fear it is too late."

Gazardiel slammed his fist into his hand, and Lance found himself impressed by the acting. Hadn't Gazardiel said that angels did not lie?

Lance spent a moment thinking about recent events, and realized Gazardiel had not actually said or done anything that was untrue. But he certainly had withheld truths, extremely important ones. Did all angels work that way? Lance's contemplation was interrupted by Gazardiel.

"I'll head into the city," he stated authoritatively. "I sent Dumah to Michael, he will be here shortly." He then looked at Peter, who seemed visibly upset.

Gazardiel put his hand on the gatekeeper's shoulder. "You did nothing wrong, Peter. These reapers caught us all off guard. Nothing was ever supposed to escape from the void. And you are but one spirit." Peter nodded.

"I depart. I will return when I am able!" With that, Gazardiel charged out through the gate, and in one fluid movement, summoned a beam of white energy directly ahead. In less than a second his silhouette, along with that of his hounds, disappeared into the ether.

The remaining angels stood by Peter, at the gates, and watched silently. The two wardens slowly turned away and walked back towards the main tower of Paradise. Abruptly, the door to the tower flew open, as Michael emerged with the third warden, Dumah, trailing behind his left shoulder. The Archangel was still garbed in his golden armour, with his flowing platinum blonde hair. But his eyes were no longer baby blue. They were, instead, blazing pure white.

There was a quick flash of white energy, and Michael was immediately standing beside Peter, flanked by Dumah, who looked slightly disoriented.

Michael stood as straight as ever, his face completely devoid of emotion. The two wardens, having halted their approach to the tower at the sight of Michael, backtracked for further orders. Peter opened his mouth to speak, but Michael interrupted. "I know everything up to the warden's meeting with Gazardiel." Michael paused, waiting for the two wardens to arrive, before he spoke further. "Peter, anything new?"

Peter shook his head, heavily. "No, Archangel." Michael nodded knowingly.

"I expected as much, you can't be tasked to both protect and seal Paradise. Not with the amount of power present here." Michael turned, regarding each of the assembled angels sequentially.

"Where is Gazardiel?" he asked, calmly.

"In the city, in pursuit," replied one of the wardens, "but we won't be able to track him because of the disturbance. He predicted they would flee into the city."

"Flee exactly where they know we would look for them," added the other, dubiously.

"Which is correct of Gazardiel to assume," snapped Peter. "Those two have always associated with that city. Almost all of their assignments have been in that area, it's where they are comfortable. And they know how difficult it will be to find a fugitive, cloaked in the mess down there."

"A fact made even more certain by our opinion that those two are linked with the disturbance," concluded Michael. "Gazardiel is our best hunter. He will find them."

"And he's angry," added Dumah. "He had his hounds out, I have never seen him use that signature ability before."

"His hounds?" asked Michael, in surprise.

"Yes," replied Dumah.

"Well then, he *is* taking this very seriously." The Archangel mused. Michael stood silent for several moments, apparently lost in thought.

"What should we do?" asked Peter. Michael crossed his arms.

"Call all our forces to Paradise. From here we will descend upon the city. This situation is getting out of hand; and we will need everyone to help Gazardiel, and finally solve the mystery of this power."

Dumah nodded, and he and the other wardens again headed back to the tower, presumably to summon the other angels. Peter lingered at Michael's side for a moment, then slowly walked to his post at the gate.

When he arrived, he studied Michael, who had not moved. He stood stoically, arms crossed, and face impenetrable. Peter thought the Archangel looked like a statue, frozen in time, contemplating the world.

Or, at least, the spirits of the world.

Or, at least, two very specific spirits.

Chapter 15

Lance felt Gazardiel's controlling magic release him as soon as they had passed through the angel's portal. His form expanded, reassuming its lean, human, shape. His robe once again covered his body, with the hood high and over his face. But there were some slight changes to his attire.

Now, glittering on his shoulders, were two silver pauldrons, and clasped around his waist was a red and silver sash, which accented his robe quite nicely, he thought. Lance was ready for war.

Both Pajetic and Gazardiel were standing beside each other, or rather, floating. For as Lance quickly noticed, they were high in the air. Below the midday sun, but above the glittering skyscrapers that marked the center of the city.

Lance could see the large brownstone, with the gargoyles, where this entire adventure had begun. Out of the corner of his eye, Lance watched the pure nothingness of the void spring into the world, presumably from Gazardiel's own hand.

Lance had been facing slightly away from his companions, so he did not witness the look of shock on Gazardiel's face as the void melted away before the overwhelming aura of the spiritual disturbance. He was convinced. It had to be a Fragment.

Lance barely paid attention to Pajetic's proud proclamations about how he and Lance had been truthful, because his mind was racing. He was still unsettled about their escape from Paradise, and felt exposed in this open space high above the city. He met Pajetic's eyes, and then as the reaper opened his mouth to speak, took off without a word.

Lance tore through the sky, flying as fast as he could. He heard Pajetic swear and knew his partner was in pursuit. He banked sharply to the left and rapidly dropped his altitude, heading towards the cover of buildings.

"Stop Lance!" yelled Pajetic, angrily, "We were fine up there!" But he was ignored. Lance continued to fly, lower and lower, until they were at street level. He contemplated going underground, but decided against it since it was so far out of a spirit's element. The pull of earth made him feel sick.

He banked around a street corner and flew east. He maintained this direction, making only a few slight changes in order to follow streets and avoid melting through buildings. He didn't want to confusing Pajetic and Gazardiel. After a few blocks he heard the angel call out.

"Where is he going?" Gazardiel's voice sounded apprehensive, almost worried. Lance knew the angels were not always comfortable in the mortal plane, which made sense. After all, they did not truly belong.

He contemplated stopping, but felt driven to continue on his path. In truth, he did not really know where he was going. It felt like he was on autopilot, the feeling you get when you commute to work for the thousandth time. His mind knew where it was going.

"I'm not sure," answered Pajetic, adding "just follow him, he knows this city, he must have something in mind."

Gazardiel didn't respond, and the two continued to follow Lance, who was still moving at warp speed. Buildings flew by, and as the time passed, greatly diminished in size. They became smaller and smaller, until the largest building was only a few stories high. The harsh colours of neon signs, ever present in the city centre, were slowly replaced with the pleasant green of trees as the city relented to suburbia.

Lance eventually alighted, standing on a gray concrete sidewalk, slightly surprised at his destination. Last time he had been out this far, there was no vibration of the spiritual plane. But now, it appeared nowhere was safe from the tremors.

Lance simply stood there, with his hands on his hips, and waited. Pajetic and Gazardiel arrived just seconds after him, alighting deftly onto the concrete.

"You took us to a building in the outskirts of the city?" asked Pajetic, curiously.

"A school, to be exact," explained Gazardiel. "I would presume it was his."

Lance nodded his head in confirmation. He stood at the foot of several stone steps, the same steps he had sat on a lifetime ago, which led up to a brick, two story school.

"Jackson Secondary School: Senior Spelling Bee today at 12!" proclaimed a simple lettered sign at the base of the steps. The name Jackson Secondary School was echoed in gold lettering on one of the front walls of the building. It was large and rectangular, with one floor wings stretching out from the main two story structure to either side.

"So why are we here, Lance?" asked Gazardiel, in a gentle tone. Lance turned away from the school, back to face Pajetic and Gazardiel. Pajetic's arms were crossed, his hood covering his eyes. Lance noticed he also sported pauldrons, along with a green and silver sash. His face was hidden in shadows. Gazardiel stood with his arms at his side, and he looked somewhat concerned.

"I'm... not really sure," responded Lance. "It felt like I should come here." He shrugged his shoulders, unable to come up with a better explanation.

"Seriously?" asked Pajetic, annoyed. "We chased you across the city on a whim?" He shook his head. "Let's get back to the city, now that you're done with your sentimental baloney. You remember that place right? The one where the Fragment *actually* is?"

He prepared to leave, but stopped when Gazardiel reached out and squeezed his shoulder.

"There's nothing wrong with this," said Gazardiel calmly, letting his hand drop.

He turned his head away from Pajetic, looking back to Lance, who had been watching the two of them with a guarded expression.

"This school can actually work out to our advantage, Lance. It's far enough away from the city that revenants won't be a threat, and the pulsing of the realm is insignificant here. It would have been difficult to talk and plan in the city centre in any case, with all of the activity going on there. Did you feel all of the entities, Pajetic?"

The reaper nodded slowly, "My tracking is not nearly as developed as yours, Gazardiel, but I did feel a lot of spirits. Certainly more than I've ever felt anywhere else."

"Besides," said Gazardiel, continuing, "We will need a spot to meet in any case, since we will have to split up to perform my plan."

"Split up?" asked Lance, incredulously.

"What exactly is the plan?" inquired Pajetic, curiously. "I was of the opinion that we had no plan."

"We didn't," responded Gazardiel. "But I came up with one as we followed Lance on his little trip," he shook his head. "I can't believe what I saw with the void. Something terrible is happening."

He gazed, distracted, towards the school for a moment, engrossed in thought. "At this point," he continued, "contacting the other angels is a risk I'm unwilling to take. We do not fully understand the situation, so naturally our first step is to gather information. I have an idea of what we need to do."

"So do I," countered Lance, "but my plan doesn't involve us splitting up."

"Very well," answered Gazardiel, gesturing to Lance politely. "Please share, Lance."

"Well-" started Lance, who had not actually invented a full plan beyond not splitting up, "we, uh, we should stick together."

"We know that Lance," said Pajetic, exasperated.

"Yeah," continued Lance, mind racing. "Stick together and move through the city in a unit. We won't be troubled by any revenants we meet, and as a group, we could disable an angel or two, whereas if we separate, we wouldn't have a chance." He stopped as he looked at Gazardiel, realizing that he often forgot just how much power the angel possessed.

"By us, I mean Pajetic and me, Gazardiel," he quickly explained, before going on. "We will use Pajetic's tracking, and yours Gazardiel, to find this Fragment. It will know that we have good intentions, so it won't evade us. Then we can protect it!"

Gazardiel smiled, "A good plan Lance, but unfortunately, we would be more efficient if we were to split up."

Pajetic nodded, "Gazardiel is right. We will cover three times more ground apart than we would together."

"But I can't track, unless there is a trail somewhere I can follow. I won't be able to find anything!" remonstrated Lance, who added self-consciously, "Am I just a liability?"

"No," answered Gazardiel, forcefully. "We all have a part to play Lance, regardless of specialty. Besides, we actually can't track this Fragment either."

Pajetic nodded vigorously in agreement. "Lance, you already have basic tracking abilities, we can just sense spirits further away because we have more experience. But Gazardiel is right, this Fragment is untrackable."

"Untrackable?" asked Lance, taken aback.

"Correct," replied Gazardiel, "or else Michael and I would have found it from the start. Well, technically we have found it."

Lance stared at Gazardiel, not understanding at all.

"The power is located directly on top of the city, but even you could track that Lance," explained Pajetic.

"Ok, so we go to the center of the city!" exclaimed Lance loudly, forgetting his initial meeting with Michael, Abyss and Gazardiel when much of this had been explained. "The Fragment will be in the direct centre." Pajetic shook his head.

"Don't you think the angels would have thought of that Lance? The Fragment is protecting itself. Its power is like a fog, the fragment could be anywhere in the area, and we wouldn't know where."

"Exactly," agreed Gazardiel. "Which brings me back to our plan. If we mean to find it, we must maximize our resources. And get very, very lucky."

"Well," asked Lance, "how hard can it be to find a stone?"

Gazardiel regarded Lance strangely, before saying, "The power of the Creator is the ultimate embodiment of energy. The Fragment won't just be lying free on a street somewhere; it will combine with his creation."

"The city?" asked Pajetic.

"No," said Gazardiel, "the people."

Comprehension dawned on Lance.

"Oooh, so we are looking for a person!"

Gazardiel nodded in affirmation. He took a few steps towards the school, before hesitating. "The Fragment would have been drawn to a human, someone free of evil and powerfully good. It would have bonded with that person."

"But why hasn't anyone found this guy yet?" said Lance, "If he's running around with that much energy, he must have an incredible aura."

"No, Lance," said Gazardiel, "this vibration," as he talked he gestured around the area, which trembled with spiritual energy, "*is* the aura."

"So how on earth do we locate this person," asked Pajetic, determination settling into his voice.

"It's a needle in a haystack kind of thing," responded Gazardiel. "The person will feel incredibly hot to the touch, and their eyes will emit pure gold light."

"That's it?" asked Pajetic, disconcerted. "No wonder no one has found it yet," he grumbled.

Gazardiel nodded. "It's what we must do. And why we must split up. If we all look, use all our resourcefulness, I have faith we can do this."

Lance smiled, enjoying Gazardiel's approval. He noticed Pajetic still seemed uninspired.

"How many people live in this city Lance?"

"Around a million." replied Lance, wincing at his considered the mind-bafflingly low probability of finding the Fragment.

"This is impossible," stated Pajetic flatly. "No one is ever going to find the Fragment."

"But we must," replied Gazardiel simply. "The consequences of the Fragment falling into the wrong hands are far too great. The task ahead is difficult. But we must succeed."

"They told us we would never kill a demon, Pajetic." Lance offered, encouragingly. Pajetic responded by rolling his eyes, but Lance could see his posture straighten, slightly.

"We will meet back here at dawn," Announced Gazardiel. "Each one of us has the ability to find this Fragment." He stretched his arm out, with his palm facing the ground. Lance smiled as he recognized the angel's gesture. He placed his palm on top of Gazardiel's. The two of them both stared at Pajetic, who shrugged and added his hand to the stack.

Lance glanced from Gazardiel's face, handsome, rugged and wise, to Pajetic's, with its keen eyes and dark shadows. What a team, he thought: the best of the young reapers, an angel and himself.

"Together?" asked Lance.

"Together," confirmed Gazardiel, a twinkle in his eye.

Pajetic, who was not so big on the whole team spirit thing, reluctantly nodded his head, before adding his "together".

With that, Lance pushed his hand down, and then abruptly spun about, taking off back towards the city center. He would meet up with them at dawn. Having found the Fragment, of course.

***

The sun had almost set, as Lance stood, perched on his favourite spot on the brownstone in the centre of the city. He felt attuned with this place, and though he justified his presence here with its high volume of traffic, Lance knew he just wanted to return somewhere familiar to gather his thoughts. It had been a futile exercise.

The day had gone by without any sort of success on the reaper's part. He had begun, filled with enthusiasm and vigor after Gazardiel's speech, by scouring the city for places he associated with great good and purity. He had looked at the nurseries, had searched schools and hospitals. He investigated churches, even tracked down an orphanage and a soup kitchen. Nothing.

He had searched the eyes of thousands of people without luck and had become fairly frustrated. So now he sat, on top of his brownstone beside one of the large stone gargoyles, mindlessly staring into the stream of people, hoping to see a flash of golden light.

It was hard to stay motivated, as each time he saw a flash, his hopes rose like helium, only to crash down again upon further investigation. It was always a false alarm. Always the glow springing from a car light, or a golden watch, or one of a thousand cellphones.

His frustration was compounded by the ever constant presence of revenants. Lance could see a few of the spirits from where he sat right now. They were flying in the air, a fair distance away from him.

He suddenly was very happy to be in the midst of such a mass of power. While he was near the city center, he was nearly impossible to track. Revenants could only find him by seeing him directly, and Lance had been able to hide whenever they drew too near.

There had been some close calls already today, and although he was not afraid of one revenant, he knew more would come like sharks to blood. And, gauging by the hundreds of different revenants he had seen already, he had little doubt he would be overcome. Weren't the angels supposed to be reducing their number?

He turned back to the steady stream of people, noticing the tall man in the red jacket once again. That guy had walked through the city centre about five times already, and his stupid bright jacket kept distracting him. Lance shook his head.

He wondered if Pajetic or Gazardiel were having more success than he was. He hadn't seen either of them since their talk, which slightly surprised him. He figured he would see one of his friends, diligently searching. After all, he was in the centre of the city.

Lance shrugged. He had never really grasped how huge this city was, until he had to look for someone without his ability to sense spiritual power. It must be even more frustrating for a guy like Pajetic, being so talented in tracking and yet unable to find his quarry.

Lance looked back to the crowds of people, trying to detect any hint of gold in their eyes. To find the Fragment here would be like winning the lottery.

Lance shook his head, and turned around to face the roof of the building, fed up with watching. There had to be a better way, something he wasn't thinking of. He grit his teeth and spun around in frustration.

A creeping fear that he had felt since he had escaped Paradise took ahold of him, and he sat down on a gargoyle angrily. He really *was* useless. He couldn't track like Pajetic. He wasn't powerful like Gazardiel. And if the moment came, where there was a confrontation with Michael, he would just be a liability.

Lance felt his blood boil as he thought of Michael, the smug overlord of the angels, dispatching him easily with his utterly careless face. There was nothing Lance would be able to do about it.

Furious, Lance glared over the roof of the building, littered with various air vents and chimneys. He silently berated himself for heading to such a fruitless location, but his downward spiral of deprecation was abruptly put to an end, as he saw something emerging over the building's far side. Lance could not make its form out clearly, but he knew what it was. A revenant.

Lance grinned wickedly. He wanted to fight.

Chapter 16

The emergence of a revenant did not bother Lance as much as it should have. His grin faded as he let his spiritual power flare into life. Red energy bled through his eyes and flickered along his hands.

He scowled at the revenant, but on the inside, he was thrilled. He needed a fight; the monotony of this stakeout was going to be the death of him.

He didn't care how packed the area was, nor how difficult it might be to control power in the city centre, or even how easy it would be for him to be seen. The past long hours had acclimated him to the vibrations of the plane, and he needed an outlet for his frustration. He wanted to destroy something.

"I guess I'm human, after all," he said to himself, smugly. He allowed his power to build, concentrating it into a ball of energy in his right hand. "Bye-bye." He whispered as it shot from his hand.

The revenant had just emerged fully, beyond the lip of the rooftop, when the blast of energy flew at him. The creature appeared humanoid to Lance, although it had some unique features. It possessed the body of a human, but its entire left side was disfigured.

It was larger than the right, and seemed to be covered in some sort of black exoskeleton, like the carapace of a scorpion. This image was further reinforced by the revenant's left arm, which hung down to the ground, and ended not in a hand, but two gigantic pincers.

The creature saw the blast coming, an instant before it hit and dropped like a stone, sinking through the building's roof. The ball of energy flew harmlessly over the cityscape towards the setting sun. Lance was upset with his miss, but excused himself given the instability of the spiritual plane. It was hard to aim!

Predicting what would come next, Lance flew into the air, staring intently at his previous position on the rooftop. He focused his power again, and slowly, a bar-like shape of pulsing energy began to form in his hands.

Just as he had suspected, a huge claw, glowing a dark brown, ripped up from underneath the roof, directly where Lance had been standing just a moment before. The entire revenant followed, surging out of the building, which remained completely intact on the physical plane.

Lance was impressed by the revenant's speed, but knew he was far more skilled than his opponent. Swinging his now fully-formed manta back, he flew down towards the revenant like a diving falcon. The revenant looked up, too slow to react, and a flash of recognition hit Lance.

Distracted, and flying too fast to adjust, Lance mistimed his descent. He slammed into the revenant, throwing it towards the ground awkwardly. Trying to recover, he lashed out with his weapon, trying to land at least a partial strike, but the impact had moved his target out of reach.

"You!" growled Lance, furiously. "What are *you* doing here!"

The revenant, which had stopped his downward motion and appeared to be standing on the roof, looked up to face Lance again. Lance could clearly make out his slicked back hair and thin mustache.

Marco scowled and bared his teeth at Lance, who took absolutely no notice of his attempt at intimidation.

"Marco! I was hoping for some kind of punching bag, but this is too perfect!" said Lance violently, remembering what this spirit had done to his compatriots. "When I obliterate you, I'll be doing the world a great service." Lance stopped for a moment, sizing up Marco's mutated body. "What the hell is wrong with you? Or did you just decide to make your exterior as ugly as your soul?"

Marco responded by swinging his clawed hand and shooting an arc of brown energy at Lance, who didn't even bother moving. The band collided with Lance, who had erected his familiar energy field. The attack was absorbed, but to Lance's astonishment, demolished his entire shield. Lance couldn't believe it. How was Marco capable of such a powerful attack?

"Reaper!" cried Marco, in an anguished tone Lance was not prepared for. "I'll kill you reaper! I swear it!" He swung another arc of energy towards Lance, who this time dodged underneath the band, landing on the rooftop.

Lance looked around hastily, this big display of power would be visible to other revenants. The combat, now recognized by Lance as serious, had drained him of his fury. He was beginning to realize the consequences of his actions. Their fight was sure to draw more attention, and Lance was in no mood to fight thirty or forty enemies at once. Or catch the eye of Michael. He had to finish Marco off quickly, but his curiosity stayed his attacks.

"I spared you Marco, back in your little clubhouse. Looking back on it, I think that was an error." Lance prodded coolly. "Thankfully you've come to help rectify my mistake. Suicide by reaper."

"This isn't self-destruction. This is vengeance you monster!" howled Marco, who maintained his fierce demeanor while unleashing another strike. Lance sidestepped, uneager to absorb another attack.

"Vengeance?" said Lance, incredulously. "You wish to avenge your master, little spirit?"

"You killed the demon!" yelled Marco, as he threw another wave of energy at Lance, who easily leapt over it.

"And the world is better off because of it!" snarled Lance.

"He was the only thing keeping Maria alive, you murderer!" said Marco, nearly crying. "She's dead, it's your fault!" With that accusation, Marco launched himself at Lance who, distracted again, dodged a second too late.

He hadn't thought of that, the consequences of killing Prufias. But when the demon had died, any work he had done on Maria would have been undone. Marco said she had cancer. When the magic was gone, it would have raged like a fire in her body.

Not that this fact excused what Marco did. Maria could still go to Paradise, while those souls that Marco had betrayed never could. Marco was a monster, and yet, Lance couldn't help but feel a tinge of guilt. He truly was responsible.

His reflections did not last long, as Marco tried to slice his head off with his claw.

Lance grabbed the arm at the wrist, and then using his other, grasped the spirit's throat. Lance marveled at Marco's strength. He was clearly no longer human.

Lance could sense his rage, and for a moment pondered what such intense negative emotion could do to a regular human soul while exposed to so much spiritual energy. Based on Marco, it could cause an empowering mutation. It could make a monster. Some kind of human-revenant hybrid.

Lance cared little for Marco's origins, because although he was surprised at Marco's strength, he knew the spirit had poor control. Tightening his grip around Marco's neck, Lance hurled the creature away, into the sky above the roof, and followed his throw with a blast of his own energy.

Marco couldn't dodge in time and was engulfed in an explosion of red. Lance bowed his head and heard a thump as the body hit the rooftop. His aim had been true. Marco was badly damaged, so hurt that he no longer had enough energy to float.

Lance regretted lowering his guard when he heard the buzz of another attack crackle through the air. Lance barely had time to react, and had to drop to the ground instantly to avoid another band of brown power. Lance returned to normal height and stared at Marco. It was an unnatural sight.

Marco lay prone on the roof, face uplifted towards Lance. There was pure, undiluted hatred in his countenance. His body was ruined, missing several limbs and a good portion of his face. Dirty brown residue oozed from his open wounds. But his imminent demise did not deter Marco, who struggled to move towards his adversary. Lance was unnerved.

"How did you get this power?" he asked, frightened by Marco's grim resolve. Lance did not like things that did not die.

"I was willing to do anything," spat Marco, through gritted teeth, "so I could destroy you!" Weakly, he shot a beam of energy at Lance, who easily sidestepped the attack.

"If I go to your society Marco, what am I going to find?" Lance, who was still holding his manta, walked towards Marco and held his scythe up menacingly. "What have you done!?"

Marco spat, then said, "Death." Lance nodded knowingly. So the society was gone. That's how he had done it. Marco had attacked and consumed his friends, in a bid to grow stronger.

"I even got revenants!" said Marco, defiantly. "I can kill you!" His last two words were accompanied with an explosion of dark spiritual energy that rippled from Marco in a massive balloon of power. Brown light enveloped the rooftop, obscuring all from sight.

Slowly the glow faded, revealing Marco, still lying there, but very clearly dying. And, standing over him, with red energy flickering across his frame and his manta held high, was Lance. Red light continued to shine in his eyes as he looked sternly down at his foe.

"But I am a reaper."

A growl sounded in the distance, halting Lance's death blow. He looked up from Marco, and surveyed the surroundings. He saw nothing, only tall buildings reflecting the golden light of a setting sun, until suddenly, movement.

Emerging into Lance's line of sight from behind a tower was a monstrous horde of spirits. Another deafening growl came directly from it, and Lance stared in awe at what was quickly headed his way.

A swarm of revenants was charging towards the brownstone. It had to be several hundred strong; it was as dense as a cloud of locusts. Lance could barely believe his eyes; he had never seen anything like this before.

A host that size could overwhelm him in seconds. He cursed inwardly, knowing he had taken too long. Of course their battle, with the powerful explosions and attacks, would attract revenants. He just did not realize how many.

He watched the throng for another moment, following their movements. Although he knew revenants sometimes moved in packs, the sheer size of the congregation was overwhelming.

They filled the air, all different shapes and sizes. Hundreds of sharp fangs, scaly wings, and horned heads all jostling about as they rushed towards the roof. For not the first time since this ordeal began, Lance felt acutely weak.

Thrusting his arm forward, Lance launched a thin but powerful beam of spiritual energy towards the group. It collided with a flying-snake-like revenant, which squealed and fell down to the street. As Lance looked on, the revenants halted their advance and dove towards the wounded revenant, ripping at its essence in a cannibalistic frenzy as it fell.

Lance looked down at Marco, who still glared malevolently at him, having lost the strength to talk. An idea dawned on the reaper. Lance detested himself for even considering it but, as he looked down upon Marco, Lance felt his resolve harden. It was what Marco deserved.

Lance knelt down, bending his head right to Marco's ear, mocking the reaper with his proximity. He met the spirit's hateful gaze before speaking, with venom in his voice.

"As bad as this will be, I can guarantee-" he paused for a moment, still refusing to look from Marco's eyes, which bulged with hatred. He saw in those eyes innocent spirits. Spirits of the guardian society, unaffiliated souls, even humans. All had been betrayed. Lance felt not a single tinge of guilt. "You deserve worse," he finished, summoning a small but bright ball of energy upon Marco's chest as he turned away from the broken spirit.

The revenants would not miss him.

Lance launched himself into the air, flying away at top speed. He did not look back, but knew that Marco would keep the swarm occupied. He was safe.

Marco earned himself this fate. Lance expected a scream, perhaps some further attacks, but heard nothing of the sort. Just a few more howls from revenants and a chewing sound, which quickly faded as Lance put distance between himself and the swarm. He shook his head slowly as he continued on, surging through the city on an irregular route, to ensure that no revenants could be following him.

The sun was dropping low into the sky, and its fat golden rays reflected off the glass and steel of the many skyscrapers, making the city glow as Lance flew.

It surprised Lance just how much of the day had gone by, with such little progress. He knew he could not have planned for the attack by Marco, but right now he needed to attend to a more pressing issue. The city was getting too crowded. It was becoming nearly impossible to avoid conflict.

And Lance was fighting out of his league.

Chapter 17

Inspiration, imagination, innovation. The words danced in Lance's head, a mantra learned in an English class in another lifetime. The cornerstones to any solution.

If he focused, hopefully they would help him find the answers he was desperately seeking. Lance continued to fly through the city, paying no attention to where he was going, but instead, concentrating intently. *How could he find the Fragment?*

"Think, Lance!" he muttered, alighting on a ledge of what appeared to be a hotel.

Rows of flags extended just a story below him, declaring the place receptive to foreign patrons from across the globe. Lance paid no heed to their actual insignias or colours, but found himself following the flow of the fabric. Countless brightly decorated strips of cloth moved in unison, coiling and elongating with the wind, which had picked up throughout the day. A storm was coming.

"In more ways than one," said Lance. He glanced towards the hotel's lobby. It was clean and orderly, with an attractive tiled floor and marble accents. Just outside the building was a secluded pavilion for new arrivals, who could park their car on a cobble-stone driveway.

It was a calm place, especially compared to the tumultuous city streets and sidewalks. Several cars were parked there, and one family of four— a mother, a father, and two girls—were struggling to load their luggage onto a cart.

Lance smiled as he watched the father reach down and take a suitcase from the smallest girl, who couldn't have been more than ten.

He observed the happy foursome for a few seconds, as his smile slowly melted away. A pang of grief shot through him as he was reminded of his past life. It had been great fun going to hotels, or just about anywhere, with his family.

There was so much excitement, so much wonder at being in a new place, so much potential for new things. Lance knew it would never happen again. Maybe it was best for the reapers to let go of their old lives. Remembering the past was so painful…

Lance shook his head dejectedly. It would probably have been better if he had just let himself sink to the bottom of the river after the accident. What was the point of going through all this? Even with his powers, he couldn't solve anything. He had no idea where to even start looking for the Fragment. As Gazardiel had warned, those elusive golden eyes were the proverbial needle in a haystack. And he was running out of time.

On the street below, he impassively watched a rotund gentleman who had emerged from the hotel. The man was talking furiously on his cell phone, an arrogant frown pasted on his face. Lance didn't bother checking to see if he was the Fragment. Lance knew the angry gentleman did not fit the bill. He shrugged and sat down on the ledge, allowing his legs to dangle.

Even Marco, a weak human soul, had outdone Lance today. Sure, Lance had defeated him in the end, but at least Marco had a chance to fight. Marco had found what he was looking for.

Meanwhile Lance had absolutely nothing. He looked out over the street again and, upon observing all the people, felt hopeless. How was he supposed to find someone out there, in a city of *millions*? This was impossible: he wasn't a detective! Lance's mind froze for a second, as the implications of what he had just thought dawned on him.

Humans tracked humans all the time. Private investigators and police officers had tons of tools and techniques to find people, based on partial or even misinformed descriptions. The local police department even sent speakers to his high school to explain how easy it was to find someone with present-day technology.

Lance's mind raced; if they had the ability to locate someone, so could he. The framework was all right there for him, ready and waiting. And no angel would ever think of using it.

Slightly giddy now, Lance stood up and took one last look at the scene down below. He saw that the gentleman was now intently staring at his phone, cupping it with his fingers and clicking icons on the screen with his thumbs. Everything fell into place. The phone was his answer.

Once he realized the man was searching for something on the *internet*, he knew exactly what he had to do. Like a bolt of lightning, Lance took off.

He had half a mind to just swoop down and steal the device from the guy, hang the consequences, but knew that would be wrong. There was a better way to handle this. He knew of a place where he could go for a public computer and free internet access.

He dove through the streets, twisting around corners and keeping a sharp eye out for any lurking revenants. He had gone there several times before, but only because his mom insisted that he borrow books for research projects.

Lance rounded a large glass skyscraper and faced another busy avenue which ended in a massive limestone building. It was imposing, with a centre section topped by a dome, and two rectangular wings, extending to the north and south of the main structure. A tree-lined walkway led to its front doors, although the trees were practically invisible in the evening light.

It was the Memorial Library, still standing in the dense city centre because the municipal landmark committee had refused to let commerce raze one of their most historic locales. Lance paused for a moment, quietly appreciating their stubbornness.

Surveying the avenue itself, he found what he was looking for. Along with the array of cars, shops and pedestrians, there was a set of stairs leading below ground to a subway.

Lance immediately headed for the stairway and disappeared into the underground. It didn't take him long to find a public restroom, and in there, a vacant stall. The bathroom was empty of patrons, but was also beyond disgusting.

Gum covered the grungy tile floors, and the sinks were all clogged with drenched brown paper towels. Lance carefully peeked out of his stall one last time, checking first for people, and then for any kind of surveillance equipment. Even though he was in a restroom, he couldn't be too careful. Once he was satisfied that he was truly alone, Lance focused and brought his power forth.

In seconds, his robes were gone, as was his hood and all traces of his spiritual persona. Instead, they were replaced by the getup of a teenager. In fact, it was the same outfit Lance had worn at the Guardian Society a short while ago.

His black sneakers stuck on the bathroom floor, making a rubbery, squishy sound as he took his first steps out of the stall, holding his breath. The odour was rancid. Lance had always disliked public toilets, but this one was the worst. Ever. It didn't help that he hadn't used his sense of smell since he had died.

Gagging, Lance sprinted out of the men's room, throwing the door open wide, and bending his head over his knees. He felt like he needed to vomit. He stood there in the doorway, heaving, before coming to a sheepish realization.

His body wasn't real. He didn't actually have a nose, a stomach, or any bile. It was just a reflex, like breathing. Comforted, Lance stood up straight and saw that a heavy-set man was watching him intently. The man had a goatee and wore a pair of rimmed glasses with a blue vest. Embossed on the fabric in reflective print was a single, unfriendly word: *Security*.

Lance smiled meekly and said in a pained tone, "That place is disgusting." The security officer nodded and continued his trek through the mostly empty station. Lance realized that the workday was over, and most people had already completed their commute home. He began to worry that the library might be closed.

Lance quickly climbed the steps leading to the sidewalk and headed straight for the building, weaving swiftly through the crowd.

He was happy with how well he could still move in the physical plane, but that did little to ease his distress about the time. The library's exterior was well lit, and judging by the glow spilling from the windows, a fair number of rooms remained illuminated inside. Lance hoped this meant it was open late.

He reached the main steps in a minute, and in five more seconds was standing in front of the entrance's modern glass doors. Lance's heart sank as he saw a bright, but completely vacant foyer. Just beyond it, a second room and part of one bookcase. Also unoccupied. He reached out and grabbed the door handle, trying to pull it open. It didn't budge.

Lance sighed, then melted into the shadows behind a tree planted in front of the library, slipping into the spiritual plane once he was hidden from sight. He immediately flew into the main building, through a wall, to begin his search for a computer lab. The library was spacious, with one cavernous room dedicated to book storage and then a series of hallways leading through the wings, connecting to smaller meeting areas and classrooms.

He didn't bother entering the main book room, but instead, searched the peripheral areas. It didn't take long before he was able to locate a computer lab, in a sterile, windowless room in the north wing.

Lance hastily re-entered the physical plane, took a seat at a computer and pounded on the space bar. Slowly the computer screen came to life, showing a bright blue background and a popup window that made his heart sink.

"Please input Username and Password," it demanded coldly. Lance stared at it for a second, wondering why a public computer would require a username and password. He pressed *Enter*, but was stopped by a further popup message, "Error: Incorrect Password." He swore angrily and moved to a second computer, bringing it out of sleep mode, but was again faced with the same obstinate security message.

Lance stormed out of the computer lab and headed for the exit. His idea had been such a good one—and now it was falling apart. He was wasting time. He'd just have to steal a cellphone or something equally dramatic; he had tried to do it the right way with no luck at all.

Lance reached the main foyer and could just see the avenue outside when he heard a sound that made him pause. It was a loud *thump*, as if someone had just dropped a pile of books on the table. Cautiously, Lance walked towards the centre room. There, at one of the tables in between the many bookshelves, stood a lady.

She was wearing jeans and a red top, and was intently flipping through the top book on the stack she had just placed on a simple wodden table. Lance was already thinking librarian, and his suspicion was confirmed when the lady came upon a big coffee stain on one of the pages. She shook her head in dismay, sighed, then muttered aloud, "Another one ruined."

Lance knocked loudly on one of the bookshelves. The librarian turned to face him, revealing a middle-aged face wearing a pair of glasses with thick lenses and rims.

"Ahhhh!" she yelled, knocking her stack of books down as she reached back to grab the table. Lance put his hands in the air as he advanced, sputtering apologies and becoming acutely aware that his current clothing made him look like a thug on the physical plane.

"I'm so sorry," he apologized, profusely, "I didn't mean to frighten you. I was wondering if you could help me."

The librarian took her hand off the table and pressed it against her chest. "My goodness you scared me! Don't worry, dear, but unfortunately, we are closed for the night. Come back tomorrow. We open at 8." Her eyes narrowed suddenly. "How did you get in?"

Lance thought quickly and said regretfully, "I didn't realize you were closed. The door was unlocked, and I saw lights." He gestured back at the door while he spoke.

The librarian responded, "I must have forgotten to lock it! Silly me, here let me show you out." She took a few steps towards Lance before he stopped her and pleaded his case.

"It's just... I have a project that's due, and I need to use a computer to do some research for it. And-" Lance paused for effect, trying to appear as pathetic and humble as possible, before adding quietly, "I don't have access to a computer at home."

As he confessed this, Lance made slight modifications to his outfit. His white muscle shirt was now dingy; his hat was frayed at the edges; his shorts were torn; and his shoes were full of holes.

The exact moment Lance's revised appearance was achieved, the librarian looked him over. Judging by the pity in her eyes, she had taken notice of Lance's poor attire. Lance hoped this would help.

"Can you not just use books, dear?" asked the librarian, who admonished him gently. "It is always a poor decision to leave your studies so late."

Lance was on a roll and had no problem coming up with an answer to her questions. "My teacher wants us to use at least three electronic sources, and I already got my books from the school library," he replied, before continuing, "I just got off work."

The librarian nodded pensively, "Fine, let me take you to a lab." Lance smiled before responding.

"I already wandered through the library and found a lab. I just need a username and password." She glared at him sternly, clearly not pleased with the idea of someone wandering through the library after hours. "I thought the library was open," rationalized Lance.

The librarian nodded, then leisurely walked over to another desk in the centre of the room, this one devoid of books, but covered in pens and paper. Lance followed her, noticing how slowly she moved. The physical plane would always seem sluggish compared to the high-paced action of the other dimension.

However, he did appreciate the shelter from the constant shaking and trembling of the spiritual plane. The normal world was entirely cocooned from its impact.

As Lance waited, the librarian scribbled two phrases on the corner of a piece of paper, before ripping it off and handing it to him. "Thank you," he said, truly appreciating what she had done.

"You have thirty minutes before I turn the power off, so make it quick!" responded the librarian, who turned back to her stack of books.

Lance didn't need to be told twice. He sprinted off and made it to the computer lab in no time at all. He had hoped for longer, but he would do his best. At least he had a chance, one last shot before daybreak came, when he had to return to the school.

He sat down at the first computer and entered the username *Public1* followed by the password, *quest4knowledge*. Lance pressed enter and was greeted by the beautiful sight of the computer loading.

Encouraged, Lance muttered aloud, "Good luck!"

Although he had been dead for some time, Lance had no difficulty launching the internet browser or finding a search website. This fact served to motivate him further, as he had worried there might have been drastic changes during his time away from technology.

Clicking onto the search bar, Lance paused for a second. What should he search for? Gazardiel had told him to look for golden eyes and skin hot to the touch, neither signs that would be visible to humans. So what could he use to help his search?

A few seconds was all it took for Lance to come up with the answer. Confidently he reached out, quickly inputting the words *Good Deeds*. The Fragment would go to someone powerfully good. The internet could help him find that someone.

A string of titles popped up, none of them useful. One was about a newly released movie, another, a database asking people to submit their good deeds, and a third was a list of someone's good deeds, although when Lance clicked on it, he realized it was just a self-promotional blog.

Undeterred, Lance tried a few other terms but *good person*, *altruistic acts* and *save the world* also produced nothing. Lanced paused here, to regroup. He was looking too broadly, at the entire internet. He needed something local. Wracking his brain, Lance typed into the search bar, "*The Gazette*", which was the name of the city's local paper. It was the third link and he eagerly clicked on it.

The front page was a glossy photo of a high-rise construction site downtown with the title "New Ground Broken," which Lance entirely ignored. What he wanted was a small bar, which he found in the top right corner of the webpage, just above a bright yellow button that screamed, "Advertise your company with us!" The website had its own search feature.

Lance glanced at the clock at the bottom of the computer screen. It was 8:43 pm. Twenty minutes had already passed! He frantically typed *good deed* into the search feature, pressed enter, and was treated to a list of articles. The first one read, "No Good Deed Goes Unpunished," the next one boldly proclaimed, "The Death of the Good Deed,", the third one simply stated , "The Good Deeds," and the final one read, the same as the first, "No Good Deed Goes Unpunished." Lance sighed. *The Gazette* clearly employed *very* creative writers.

Each article had a summary, so he didn't have to go through them fully, but as he read on he began to notice a theme. Not one article was about a good deed. Instead they focused on murders, injuries acquired while attempting to perform a good deed, and on legal battles regarding land deeds and property ownership.

Lance rapidly pressed the *next* button in frustration, accessing results page after results page of articles. That's all the media seemed to publish nowadays—sensational and depressing news. How could he find anything about *good* when all humans wanted to talk about was *evil*?

He paused his clicking frenzy and stared at the current results page. There, the fourth article displayed had a title that caught his eye, "Local Heroine Hospitalized." Intrigued, Lance clicked on it, accessing the article in its entirety.

He scanned the pages feverishly, trying to speed read, as his computer clock gave him about three more minutes before his time was up. Lance guessed the librarian would check on him when the time elapsed.

The more Lance read, the more excited he became. The article was fascinating and packed with information. According to the reporter, a young woman named Emma Whitfield had been hospitalized for an unidentified illness.

Apart from the symptoms—graphic, horrifying hallucinations and a high temperature—she appeared healthy. This definitely piqued his interest, but the article went further, detailing Emma's contributions to the community, including the founding of five different charities.

She had been born to a life of privilege and said it was her calling to share her good fortune with others. Ms. Whitfield had created a women's shelter in her own home where her team provided hot meals, beds and counselling for needy families. On the world stage, she had been involved in humanitarian work in Haiti and educational initiatives in Zimbabwe.

Renowned for her tireless philanthropic efforts and selflessness throughout her short lifetime, she had received international accolades, the admiration of the entire community and even the key to the city. On top of all that, the article, somewhat irresponsibly, actually listed the hospital where she had been admitted.

As soon as Lance read the line about the hospital, he leapt into the air while simultaneously transitioning to the spiritual plane. It was reckless, but Lance felt giddy.

This was the best lead he'd had all day. No one could possibly be closer to Gazardiel's description of a worthy Fragment bearer than young Emma, and Lance knew that if she were confined to bed, none of the other spirits would have been able to find her.

He cleared the outside wall of the library effortlessly, and took off into the night. He flew up until he was high in the black sky, dense with storm clouds, and away from the congestion and fluorescent lights of the streets below.

As he climbed, Lance kept a sharp eye out for any sign of revenant or angel. Excitement had the tendency to make him feel invincible, and now, more than ever, he needed to stay alert. He was so close.

Lance halted his ascent once he had passed above the tallest skyscrapers and was satisfied there was no threat of hostile spirits. The view from this height was incredible. The city was bathed in golden streetlight, with miniscule little accents of green, white, and red everywhere. The sight reminded Lance of a crown, the small lights sparkling like jewels. Not even the constant shaking of the spiritual plane could ruin the majesty of the scene below.

It took Lance a moment to orientate himself, as it was harder to navigate in the dark. From this height, all the buildings looked the same.

Lance was thankful the rain had held off so far. As soon as he had his bearings, he flew downwards, heading into a steep dive that took him closer to the exposed streets and his goal.

He had never been to Bishop's Hospital, as there was a local health centre where he had been cared for when he had his appendix removed, or when he had broken his ankle playing football. However, he still had a basic idea of where to go, and after weaving wildly through the various streets, he alighted at his destination.

He had landed in front of a towering square building, painted bright white, with rows upon rows of windows. Some were lit up, but most were dark, their occupants asleep for the night.

Lance stood outside in a gigantic parking lot. It surrounded the hospital, boasting manned parking booths and even a four-tiered parking garage.

The garage itself was connected to the hospital by several extended walkways that spanned the gap between the two buildings, hanging in the air like a massive concrete spider web.

Beneath these overhanging passages, near the sliding glass entrance to the main hospital, stood a bright red sign that read *Reception*.

Lance wondered where to start looking for Emma. Try as he might, he couldn't detect her presence. The Fragment's essence saturated the entire city, and Lance felt neither closer to it, nor farther away. There was nothing that would lead a spirit here. He supposed it was a good thing; if Emma really were the Fragment, and she left a trail...

Lance shuddered to think of the terrible power Michael would wield, if it had only been easy for him to find the Fragment. The second fallen angel, a desecrator of his original charge. The extent of Michael's strength alone was hard to fathom. Lance was just a reaper, and an inexperienced one at that.

Lance whacked his forehead with the heel of his hand, trying to put a stop to such a negative train of thought. He shouldn't be thinking like that. After all, he had killed a demon! And escaped Abaddon. He was a force to be reckoned with!

And now, he had a job to do. Lance glanced around furtively; he was standing near some trees, and just in front of the Bishops Hospital sign. He took a few quick steps into the grove and re-entered the physical plane. This time, he was wearing much nicer clothes.

His hair was combed and fell back behind his ears. Instead of a muscle shirt, he sported a clean navy blue polo, and over it, he wore an elegant leather jacket. On his legs were tight black jeans, and his shoes were now shiny brown loafers.

He walked towards the hospital, content with his new wardrobe. Now at least the hospital staff wouldn't think he was trying to rob the place.

He passed the parking booth without any problem—the security guard, engrossed in a sports magazine, absent mindedly waved him on. Lance reached reception soon after and stepped in through the automated sliding doors.

They whooshed closed behind him. There was always something unnerving to Lance about harsh fluorescent light in rooms when it was late at night. It was ruthlessly economical, with no ambience or life to it. Lance didn't envy the tired patients, all waiting inside for assessment and treatment. He hated hospital waiting rooms.

The wall to his left had four small cubicles labelled *Receptionist.* He headed towards the first one, and was disappointed to find an empty chair. Undeterred, Lance walked over to check out the other three cubicles and saw that they too were vacant.

Annoyed, he scanned the room, to see if he were missing something. He quickly noticed that one of the men sitting in the waiting room was staring at him.

It was disconcerting for Lance, being watched by a human; he was so used to being invisible. The man was of average size, with a chubby face, wrinkled forehead and curly gray hair. When Lance made eye contact with him, the man blushed and pointed to the first receptionist desk.

"You can ring the bell for help," he said, quietly.

Lance looked over and saw the silver bell, plain as day, sitting on the desk. Before going over, he paused for a moment. "Thanks." he said simply. The man nodded respectfully, and Lance headed for the desk and enthusiastically rang the bell.

It took three rings before anyone emerged from the other side. It was a worn-out looking gentleman, wearing a blue hospital uniform. "How can I help you?" he asked, unenthusiastically.

"Well," responded Lance, "I'm here to visit a patient, Emma Whitfield."

The man nodded, "It's a little late for visitors, sonny, don't you think?"

"For sure," agreed Lance, "except she wanted to see me, so here I am."

"Ok," said the man, typing into the computer.

"So can you please tell me her room number?" asked Lance, politely.

"I'm afraid not," he answered, still typing. "I can't just give patient information out, I'm looking here on her declared visitors, and there's no one on the list for tonight. You aren't a member of her immediate family, are you?"

"What?" asked Lance, confused.

"Her... brother or husband, maybe," explained the receptionist, a hint of contempt clear in his voice.

"Oh... no," replied Lance, his mind racing. He needed to have a look at that screen; he was sure her room number would be displayed on her *Declared Visitors* page. He studied the receptionist in more detail, and after noticing how badly the man had shaved this morning, saw his name tag: *Frank*. That might work.

"Could you possibly call the desk on her floor?" asked Lance, adding, "She just asked for me, like an hour ago. Maybe your system isn't updated." Frank agreed, reaching for a telephone.

"I'll just give them a quick call, then," he said, smirking, obviously believing that he was calling Lance's bluff.

With the distraction in place, Lance sprung his trap, "Oops, I forgot. I was given a message for a staff member working at reception." Lance then made a big show of looking at Frank's nametag, as if he hadn't seen it before.

He smiled before continuing, "Apparently it's for you! Unless there is more than one *Frank* working reception tonight?" Frank shook his head. "The guy at the toll booth, I don't know his name, said Frank needed to come out to see him. Apparently someone hit his car." Lance held his breath after he said this, hoping that the toll booth guy didn't have a radio or a telephone.

"His telephone is down again!" exclaimed Frank, clearly upset. He paused, before looking suspiciously at Lance. After regarding him for a second, Frank turned his head and yelled into the back, "Sheila, I'm going out to the parking lot. Apparently someone hit my car. Watch the front."

Addressing Lance, he said, "I'll be right back." Lance nodded, unperturbed, and watched as Frank ran out the door to the parking lot. Without hesitating, Lance turned the screen for a moment to see "Whitfield, Emma: Room 644" in the top right corner. Mission accomplished.

Wasting no time, Lance reclaimed his spiritual presence in the nearby patient bathroom, which, to his relief, was immaculate. He immediately floated up, through the ceilings, heading to the sixth floor. He almost wanted to see Frank's reaction when he came back, but time was of the essence.

It didn't take him long before he rose to the correct level. He emerged in a small room, with two male patients, both probably in their thirties. They weren't hooked up to any medical equipment, but Lance wondered how the one in the bed farthest from him could sleep. The patient nearest him was snoring like a bear.

Lance exited into the hallway of the sixth level. It was narrow and well lit, with windows at either end of the long corridor. He noted the room number, 632, then checked the door to his right, 634. He headed in that direction, scanning each door as he approached his target. 636...638...

As Lance drew closer, it seemed like the shaking on the spiritual realm was getting stronger. No, it was his imagination. He took a deep breath, trying to calm himself down. Even if Emma were the Fragment, her power was widespread. It wouldn't intensify around her... or would it?

640...642... Lance came to a stop at the very end of the hallway. He had reached his destination. 644 at last.

Lance stared at the door for a second, afraid to cross this final threshold. What if it was just a wild goose chase? What if he had just wasted the rest of his valuable time, and had to return to the school empty handed? What if all three of them had to?

An electric mix of apprehension and excitement coursed through Lance, who fought to steady himself. It didn't matter what was on the other side, he thought. He had to trust his instincts. This was his best lead yet. Drawing in yet another deep breath, that was actually pointless on the spiritual plane, Lance stepped into the room.

Chapter 18

Lance found himself emerging on the other side, into a run-of-the-mill hospital room. It was dimly lit, with bland walls covered in an uninspiring polka-dot pattern. The furniture was sparse and functional, with only a narrow single bed, not much larger than a cot, and a few scattered bedside tables.

It's only redeeming feature was a vast picture window in the far wall, which offered a spectacular view of the distant downtown centre. It still pulsed with life, despite the late hour. But Lance's focus was not on the room. It was on the person inside it.

Sitting perched in the bed, was a young woman in a washed-out hospital gown. In her lap was an open book, pages of text Lance could not decipher. She had long and curly chestnut hair, which was slightly untidy and frizzy. She wasn't a typical magazine beauty, but she had a hardy, earthy appeal, with sturdy cheeks and bold eyebrows.

Her eyes were luminous. Not the typical combination of white and iris, but instead, delicate shades of exquisite gold. They sparkled, independent of light. And they were staring, directly, at him.

Lance did a double take, startled and elated at the same time. It was her, there was no doubt. She was the Fragment. He wanted to scream with joy, to dance and cheer and congratulate himself on his good fortune, but there would be time enough for that later.

Now they needed to go, he needed to take her away. Yet, at the same time, he was mystified. Lance looked down, checking and re-checking his form in bewilderment. No, he hadn't made a mistake. He was still on the spiritual plane. So how then...

"Hello?" asked the girl gently, still watching Lance with her hands politely clasped over her book. He furrowed his brow, still perplexed. Her eyes were throwing him off. He had expected them to overflow with power, like his own crimson surge. And how on earth could a human being see him?

"Hi?" said Lance, in a confused tone, still not entirely sure what was happening.

"May I help you?" questioned the girl, quietly. She smiled encouragingly, aware of Lance's hesitation.

"Uh... Emma?" The girl's smile deepened.

"That's me!" she announced, before continuing "May I ask *your* name?"

Lance thought for a second before responding, truthfully, "It's Lance."

"I like that name," said Emma, "it sounds noble." She seemed sweet, and completely at ease. "What can I do for you, Lance?"

"Well," he mused for a second, unsure about how to tell her. "I... I mean we... Uh, we need your help, Emma." Lance felt relieved that he was still wearing normal clothing, even after slipping into the spiritual realm. His awkward diction would have been drastically amplified in his traditional reaper cloak and hood.

"How can I help?" asked Emma graciously, concern in her voice.

"I need you to come with me, Emma. My friends and I, we need you with us. We need you with us to help."

Emma looked at him curiously before responding, "Help with what?"

"I... I can't really say, it's hard to explain," Lance replied pausing between each word, then adding, "It would be easier for me to show you."

Emma shook her head, sadly. "I'm sorry, I can't go. I'm not allowed to leave the hospital."

Lance paused, he hadn't really considered that. He had forgotten he was in a hospital, to be honest, having been carried away by the thrill of finding the elusive Fragment.

Was he really asking this young woman, in the dead of night, to abandon a hospital bed and travel who knows where, to assist some complete strangers?

The more Lance reflected on it, the more absurd it seemed. The fact that Emma would even consider helping him was surprising. And she seemed genuinely upset that she could not.

Lance's thoughts turned to Emma, and he strained to remember why she was in the hospital.

"I'm sorry," he said, feeling foolish. "What exactly is your ailment? What is the reason for your stay here, I mean?"

"Don't be sorry." She paused, and Lance noticed a tinge of sadness in her expression. "It's a little embarrassing," she confessed. She looked at Lance, who said nothing, before continuing. "I've been hallucinating. Seeing things, crazy things. The doctors haven't come up with a diagnosis yet, so they want me to stay here." She gestured around the room as she talked. "I've been here for a while."

Lance nodded slowly. Things were starting to make a lot more sense to him.

"You've been seeing things you don't understand, weird things that shouldn't be possible," he said, in a steady tone.

"Yes!" she nodded, emphatically. She regarded Lance quizzically. "Would you, like an example?" Lance bowed his head in affirmation, so Emma confessed. "When you came into the room, it didn't look like you used the door. You just sort of melted in," she recounted nervously.

Lance smiled, in what he hoped was a big friendly grin. So she *could* see him. He chuckled lightly, before saying, "Goodness, that is serious. Next thing you know I'll be punching my hand through a wall and growing a moustache!"

While he said this, Lance stepped towards the wall to his right, closer to Emma. He pushed his hand through it, and being on the spiritual plane, his arm vanished up to his elbow. Simultaneously he added a bushy moustache to his top lip.

Emma yelped in surprise, pushing herself up against the headboard, staring wide eyed at Lance, who had not realized how startling his actions would be. Sheepishly, he resumed his normal form and pulled his arm out of the wall. He stepped slowly towards Emma, raising his hand.

"I apologize; I didn't mean to startle you, Emma." Lance said, kindly.

"Are you real?" asked Emma timidly, "or am I just imagining you?"

Lance chuckled again, shaking his head.

"I am as real as you are, Emma. Just in a different stage."

Lance continued his calm approach, remaining silent as he reached Emma's bed. He faded into the physical plane and reached out, lightly touching Emma's arm. She recoiled from his contact, but Lance was not offended. "As you can tell, I'm certainly not imaginary," he finished.

Emma searched Lance's face, and he could see she was calming down. "But...but..." she stammered, softly, "I can't trust what I see."

Lance shook his head. "Well, I'm asking you to trust *me*. Emma. I am not make-believe. Your visions are not fantasies. Everything you have seen, I have seen as well. All of it."

Emma eyes widened again, and Lance could tell what she was thinking about. He spoke before she had a chance. "Monsters," he said quietly. "Scary things, wings and claws and fangs and scales."

"I just keep seeing more and more!" Emma said, breathlessly.

"It's because they are multiplying," said Lance firmly. "They are the reason I have been sent here Emma. Those creatures are not figments of your imagination, but they are also not of your world. And they are getting dangerous. My duty is to protect you, and all of mankind, but I can't do it alone. I need your help! There are others, like me, who will shelter you. But we need to meet with them. Then, you will be able to help us."

"How can I help against those... things?" asked Emma, quietly.

"You have a rare gift, Emma," responded Lance, who grabbed her hand. "But I can explain later. We have to go."

He rifled through Emma's closet and handed her some street-clothes. Lance looked to the window again, then back at Emma. He wasn't sure, but he thought he heard the sound of footsteps getting closer. He remembered his earlier interaction with Frank, the hospital receptionist. Surely he would send someone to Emma's room when he returned and found Lance had disappeared. They needed to move.

"But what if this is all a trick!?" asked Emma, while she hurriedly tied her shoes. "How do I know for sure if I *can* trust you?"

Lance stared intently into Emma's eyes, and saw the worry and doubt in them.

"Sometimes, in order to live your life, you have to risk it!" he proclaimed with conviction. Without hesitation, he concentrated his power and pulled Emma along with him into the spiritual plane.

It took a great deal more strength than Lance anticipated. He had underestimated just how overwhelming her power was. Gathering all his might, Lance hurtled through the window with Emma in his arms, while her screams echoed into the night sky.

The trek back to the school was daunting. Lance had originally planned to fly there, but after the first few minutes of travel, his power had become drastically depleted. The effort required to move Emma through the spiritual plane was beyond belief.

He landed on a city street, close to the downtown, exhausted, and transitioned both of them back into the physical plane. After regaining a little strength, Lance directed Emma to follow him on foot. She had calmed down after the fright of the initial flight and pursued him without question. Their path led them directly through the city, and although Lance went to great lengths to keep them out of view, it wasn't long before they saw the first revenant.

It resembled a ghostly snake skeleton, with a huge dinosaur skull head, and wide bone wings. It was silently drifting through the night sky. Searching.

When Lance saw it, he immediately pulled Emma into a lane between two shops. She had seen it as well.

They raced through the streets, flitting from alleyway to alleyway, fear adding to their speed. More and more revenants became visible, as if they were attracted to Emma like a magnet.

Lance knew the two of them were well hidden due to the massive power fog in the city centre, but he did not let that slow them down. The revenants might not be able to sense them. The revenants might not even be able to affect them on the physical plane. But they could see them. And detection by them could lead to detection by others.

The seemingly endless backstreets and artificial lights blurred into each other, as the hours of darkness stretched on and on. Lance had to take cover regularly to allow Emma time to recuperate. He couldn't believe the resolve of the young woman, who had not once complained. She truly was extraordinary.

The threat of revenants, silently floating above, or stealthily patrolling the streets, was not the only danger they faced. Three times, they had dashed across a road, only to be narrowly missed by a car, and immediately assailed by the blast of a horn. Each time, Lance thought they would be found. There were some close calls, but they were never discovered.

After these occurrences, Lance and Emma had been more careful. The stakes were too high. They could not afford to draw attention to themselves.

Once, while navigating a particularly ominous alley, a desperate hand burst from the shadows, snatching at Emma. She screamed in fright, stumbling and falling to the ground. With a single blow, Lance sent the would-be attacker flying into a pile of garbage bags. It was just a haggard and dirty human.

Lance sprinted to Emma's side, and helped her to her feet before they took off again together. Lance noticed she was limping and saw a large cut on her knee. He examined it with concern, but noted it wasn't threatening.

"Almost there, Emma," he said encouragingly. "We can't stop now!"

The pitch black of the night sky had mostly faded by the time they reached Jackson High. It had been replaced by the purple and deep blue hues of an approaching dawn. Clouds of grey mist floated above the ground, transforming nonthreatening objects, like cars and houses, into malevolent shadows. Lance was lucky that he knew the area so well.

It felt like a miracle when they finally reached the familiar bottom of the stone steps. Lance let out a sigh of relief, relaxing his guard as Emma watched him curiously.

"This is it, we're here. We-" Lance stopped and instinctively stepped in front of Emma, shielding her from harm. Instantly, he shifted into the spiritual realm, his energy tense with expectation. He was sure he had felt it. Power had just been released.

Suddenly, the doors of the school flew open with a crash, and a green blur shot towards them. Emma screamed while Lance's powers flared into his familiar crimson shell, surrounding both Emma and himself in a protective cocoon of energy.

Abruptly, the blur came to a halt, hanging in mid-air. It was Pajetic, covered in flashy green armor, his two swords bared and ready for combat. "Lance!" he exhaled, "Jesus!"

"Jesus!?" cried Lance incredulously, extinguishing his power and immediately checking on Emma. "Are you out of your mind Pajetic?"

Pajetic looked shocked. "You'd react the same way. I had no idea what was out here; I've been waiting in the basement." He flew closer to Lance, examining Emma and dropping his voice. "What's going on here—what's with the lady?" Emma, who had moved up beside Lance, stared at Pajetic. Pajetic's eyes widened.

"No!" he whispered, his voice trembling in awe and excitement. "I didn't think we stood a chance!" He turned to Lance, his face full of wonder "Where?"

"A hospital," answered Lance, before addressing Emma. "Emma, this is my partner, Pajetic."

As he said this, Pajetic nodded coolly, and stated, "Proper introductions can wait. We need to get you inside, Emma,"

"Sounds like a plan," she agreed, and the three of them swiftly ascended the steps. The doors were locked, so they had to pull Emma through, into the spiritual realm. Lance noticed Pajetic's surprise with the amount of effort it required.

They walked along the unlit halls of the school, eventually going through a set of doors to the basement. It was a dark windowless room, with an old boiler and a variety of exposed pipes.

Lance sat Emma down gently on the floor, feeling a tinge of regret that there was nothing softer. "You can rest now, Emma, we are safe here." He did not have to tell her twice, as she sank into a relaxed posture and almost immediately fell asleep.

Lance turned to Pajetic, who was standing at the foot of the stairs, quietly eyeing Emma. He looked up to meet Lance's gaze, "You two ran the entire way."

"Yup. I couldn't fly with her, it was too much."

"She just followed you? Through all that?" inquired Pajetic, in disbelief. "Why?"

"Because she wanted to help."

Pajetic raised his eyebrows in surprise. "She is not like anyone else I've ever met," continued Lance. "It's clear why the Fragment chose-" Lance stopped mid-sentence. There it was, again. The sensation of spiritual power drawing near.

"I felt it too," said Pajetic, as the two of them immediately flew out of the basement, into the main level of the school. They floated into a classroom lined with windows, and strained to see through the thick fog, which was sluggishly lifting.

"There," whispered Lance, pointing.

A group of boys emerged from the mist, staggering through the street. There were six or seven of them, none older than seventeen. One had a skateboard tucked under his arm. They were yelling obscenities and laughing raucously.

"Man, I'm still drunk!" yelled one of the teens, happily. "School will be impossible today!"

"Like we're going to school, Joel!" cried another, as they all laughed again, continuing on their way.

Lance turned away from the scene, in relief. "False alarm, I guess, just some kids up all night." Pajetic shook his head slowly, his face ashen, and motioned back to the window. Lance spun around, to see another figure emerge from the remaining fog in silence.

As it moved forward, Lance felt his spine crawl. It was a monstrous revenant. It was massive, at least fifteen feet tall, with a huge eyeless head and a gaping mouth lined with giant sharp teeth. It was roughly humanoid, with gigantic shoulders and arms and disproportionately small legs. It walked on all fours, resembling some grotesque gorilla-corpse. Along its curved back, the vertebrae broke through its disgusting pallid skin.

"Look what it's doing" stated Lance, mortified. The revenant was stalking the boys. Each time one slowed down and separated from the group, it would move towards him. It would inch closer and closer, opening its jaws in anticipation, fangs slick with drool, until its prey strolled nonchalantly back to the main pack.

"It's been following them all night." said Pajetic, grimly.

Lance looked at Pajetic, thoroughly creeped out. "It can't do anything to them though. Can it?"

Pajetic shrugged, "Not right now." Lance shivered, acutely aware of Emma's vulnerability, alone below in the dark. "Let's get back downstairs." he said.

"Yes," agreed Pajetic. "Let's."

Chapter 19

The morning sun rose peacefully over the high-school, its warm rays refracted in the drops of dew that collected on the grass on the football field. A few random cars moved along the streets, although the full morning rush had not yet begun. The air was fresh, with the scent of spring in the air.

Deep in the basement, Lance and Pajetic continued their vigil. Emma slept quietly in the corner of the room, curled upon the floor. Her power pulsed through the spiritual realm, saturating it with her slumbering strength. The shaking, once constant, had abated. It was a welcome change.

Pajetic stood silently beside the girl, carefully studying her face. Lance hadn't seen him move for ages. He wanted to speak, to talk to Pajetic, but his friend's expression discouraged all communication. It was difficult to describe. Stern and rigid certainly, Pajetic always looked that way, but there was also something else. Maybe worry, or perhaps, even sorrow.

Lance cast his eyes around the dimly lit room, picking up every detail despite the shadows. It was largely a tangle of pipes and circuitry, with low ceilings and piles of old desks and chairs heaped against the walls.

The only light came from a few spartan lightbulbs, which hung forsakenly from the ceiling. Lance had flicked them on earlier in the morning, thinking Emma might appreciate the light. Cobwebs and dust layered every surface, save for the trail Emma had made upon entering.

"It will never be the same." Pajetic announced.

"What will never be the same?"

"For her," said Pajetic, tilting his head towards Emma. "She can never go back."

Lance stared at Pajetic for a few moments. "Of course she can, Pajetic."

"No," responded Pajetic, shaking his head and looking directly at Lance. "She will never be the same. She's seen too much." Pajetic walked a few steps away from Emma. "This has never happened before."

"Obviously," answered Lance. "It's not everyday a Fragment-"

"No," interrupted Pajetic, dismissively. "She's seen everything. Spirits, revenants, you, me. All of it."

"Ah. It doesn't matter, Pajetic, no one will believe her, even if she talks about it."

"So she is doomed to be ridiculed, persecuted and called a liar."

Lance struggled for a moment before answering. "Well... uh... yes... in a manner of speaking. If she says nothing, there's no problem." He paused before continuing in a more subdued tone, "I've never seen you like this before."

Pajaetic shrugged. "I know what it's like to be truly alone. It destroys you." Lance couldn't argue. Pajetic had firsthand experience with solitude. Even in his darkest moments, Lance had someone to lean on. His family, his friends, and then later Enigma, Gazardiel and Pajetic. Pajetic had had nothing.

Lance was about to try and console his friend, but stopped as he felt an immense spiritual entity enter the area, strong enough to sense over the Fragment's power.

"Someone is here," said Pajetic, whose eyes began to glow softly.

"Shall we check it out?" whispered Lance.

"No, we stay here together and protect her." Lance nodded, scanning the room continuously. He could feel the power, but had no idea where it came from. Pajetic and Lance stood there for what seemed like a lifetime, before they heard a voice.

"Lance? Pajetic?" called out Gazardiel. Lance let out a sigh of relief.

"Here, Gazardiel."

The angel emerged from the ceiling and dropped to the floor. His face was grim as he dejectedly shook his head.

"Nothing, my friends."

He continued his disappointed gait until he observed his two partners. Then he noticed the grin on Lance's face. "Did you find it?" he exclaimed excitedly, a spark flaring to life in his eyes.

Lance nodded, while motioning to Emma, still fast asleep. "You're sure?" questioned Gazardiel.

"See for yourself," replied Pajetic. "Lance found her. We've been waiting for you for the entire morning."

"I apologize," responded Gazardiel, eagerly moving towards Emma, before briefly entering the physical plane and delicately touching her cheek. He raised his eyebrows, now fully comprehending the extent of Emma's strength. He murmured quietly, "I can't believe I've found you."

"Where were you?" demanded Pajetic, a little more harshly than Lance felt necessary. Gazardiel turned to Pajetic.

"Searching. I couldn't just give up."

"What's the next step?" inquired Lance excitedly. "This proves what we've said all along, right?"

"You are absolutely correct, Lance, But it's too early to celebrate. The most powerful spirit in existence has broken his most sacred promise." Gazardiel knitted his bushy eyebrows together and frowned. "We weren't the only ones in the city last night. They are hunting for us, and her, as we speak."

"But now you'll fight *with* us, right?" continued Lance, hopefully. Gazardiel hesitated, his mouth still firmly set.

"I cannot defeat Michael," he stated plainly. "Not even with the two of you at my side." Pajetic nodded.

"So we'll need more help."

"Exactly," confirmed Gazardiel. "It is very unlikely Michael will have many angels supporting him once we expose his treachery. If we can bring the Fragment to Paradise, and prove his breach of duty, we will have enough support to confront him."

He sighed before continuing in a resigned tone. "Maybe he has some explanation for this."

Pajetic shook his head violently. "There will be no redemption Gazardiel. There is only one motive for proceeding like he has."

"Regardless," said Gazardiel, returning his attention to Emma, "We need to move her to Paradise." He reached towards her, but Lance interrupted.

"You can't fly her anywhere, she's too unstable," he said quickly. Gazardiel nodded distractedly as white power flew from his outstretched hands, enveloping Emma in its soft glow. "What are you doing?" Lance asked apprehensively.

"It is impossible to move a power like this through conventional means, Lance," answered Gazardiel. "I need to create a perfectly stable portal, and to do that I'm going to need time."

"How much?" asked Pajetic.

"I'm not sure, but it will require my full attention. We are lucky she is asleep!" Gazardiel closed his eyes and began to chant quietly, the glow of his power intensifying as he worked.

"Well... what should *we* do?" questioned Lance. Before Gazardiel had a chance to answer, chaos engulfed the room.

Emma's body flew up from where she lay, becoming suspended in mid-air. Her hair and clothes whipped around her, and her power became a torrent of energy.

Lance floated into the air, struggling against the force. He had never seen anything like it before. Without warning, a pulse of power exploded from her body. The wave collided with Lance, and he fell hard to the ground.

It didn't take long for him to leap up, his eyes wild with shock. He felt the dirt on his back and the cobwebs sticking to his skin—he was undoubtedly in the physical plane. He and Pajetic exchanged distressed glances.

"Gazardiel!" cried Lance in alarm. He looked to the angel, and noticed Emma was once again lying peacefully on the ground, surrounded in a cocoon of Gazardiel's strength.

"It was too concentrated!" Gazardiel said. "I needed to release some of her power. It won't happen again." The angel seemed somewhat disoriented—his mind was clearly elsewhere.

"But Gazardiel!" interjected Pajetic, "That knocked us into the physical plane!"

"What?" exclaimed Gazardiel. The muffled rumble of an explosion outside reverberated menacingly through the basement. Lance looked to Pajetic, suddenly coming to a horrifying conclusion.

"Pajetic, if it knocked *us* into the physical plane, then-"

"Revenants!" shouted Pajetic, who immediately slipped back into the spiritual plane, and rose through the ceiling like a bullet. Lance tore after him, leaving Gazardiel alone with Emma.

They flew through the school in a second, flowing out the front doors, and into a scene of complete mayhem.

The front driveway was packed with cars, all in various states of collision. The carnage extended to the intersection nearby, where four crumpled vehicles lay strewn, one engulfed in flames.

The two great trees in the schoolyard had fallen over, taking all overhead hydro wires with them. Their frayed remains swayed in the wind, sparks leaping from their exposed ends. The sidewalk was cracked, and massive jets of water gushed from ruptured pipes.

The school day was about to begin, so the entire area was packed with people. Panicked teenagers bolted in all directions, along with teachers and parents while sirens wailed in the distance. Wild shrieks and harsh yells engulfed the air the entire crowd fled for their lives, retreating before a horrible, monstrous creature.

Near the intersection, slowly ambling towards the school, was the same cadaverous revenant they had spotted earlier in the morning. It had seemed menacing in the spiritual plane, but in the physical plane it was full-on terrifying.

It was as tall as a house, with fists easily stretching five feet across. They crushed the ground as it lumbered forward. The monster paused when it noticed a school bus lying on the sidewalk, blocking its path. It roared, a horrifyingly deep sound, revealing its enormous, sharp, teeth.

It raised one gigantic arm to the sky, and slammed it down upon the bus, cleaving it in two. Then, with a heave, it flung the back half directly at the school. The screams of the crowd intensified as the metal smashed through the hallways, flinging debris and glass everywhere.

Lance cried out in shock as the carnage unfurled around him. This was what he had always feared. The terrors of the spiritual realm reaching to the physical.

"Go!" ordered Pajetic, as acid green energy crackled around him. Lance followed suit, channeling his crimson power, coalescing into a red orb which glowed between his hands. Once enough was gathered, a red beam of energy exploded from his palms, travelling directly at the revenant.

"No!" cried Pajetic, as he watched Lance's attack streak towards the revenant. Fast as lightning, it crackled right to its target... and simply passed right through. Astonished, Lance gaped at the creature, stupefied. Pajetic pushed Lance forward, beginning his own charge. "Physical plane, Lance!"

Lance ran behind Pajetic, unsure of their next step. The revenant, having cleared his path, was beginning to advance towards the school again, completely oblivious to the charging reapers.

Pajetic reached the revenant first, and transitioning into the physical plane, leapt into the sky. The revenant raised its eyeless visage, tracing Pajetic's trajectory as if suddenly aware of the reapers presence, and began to swing it's first.

Right before connecting with a blow, Pajetic put both hands together and let loose a massive jet of green power, which had to travel about three feet before it made contact with the revenant.

A bellow of astonishment came from the crowd of running people, many of whom had ceased running to watch the supernatural spectacle before them.

The monster roared in surprise, flinching away from the assault but continuing its arm swing. Its massive hand flew towards Pajetic, who noticing his peril, immediately returned to the spiritual realm.

With a great woosh, the arm swiped through the air Pajetic had occupied just a second before. The reaper dropped to the ground in a catlike pose, panting heavily. The revenant stumbled backwards, trying to regain its footing.

Lance took his opportunity, now entering the physical plane himself. Pajetic's attack had done little damage to the revenant, and he knew why.

It's incredibly hard to maintain and direct power in the physical plane, and the more distance that needs to be covered, the more power you had to sacrifice. So Lance simply needed to close the distance.

Lance felt crimson energy crackle in his right fist, as he sprinted towards the revenant who had staggered back to the intersection. This time, it had no defence.

Lance's full-strength punch connected directly with the creature's scaly white belly. It flew backwards, crashing into a small house, demolishing it like it was made of cards. Lance prepared to deliver a final blow, when a second wave of screams made him pause.

A mob of people, about thirty strong, was running down the street with a monstrous fiend in pursuit.

This revenant was very different from the first, as it moved with great agility, leaping from rooftop to rooftop as it stalked the scrambling people below.

It was roughly the size of a car, with extremely dark black fur, a hunched profile, and beady, orange eyes. It had a long, ugly, hairless tail and massive fangs protruded from its lip. Suddenly, the thing pounced onto a larger man who had fallen behind the group. He let out a bloodcurdling cry as the revenant mauled him to the ground.

Pajetic immediately took off, and Lance was preparing to follow when he heard yet another round of shrieks pierce the air, this time from the school parking lot. He spun around, and watched in dismay as a second crowd scrambled in every direction, yelling and screaming, while a menacing shape landed with a thud on top of a car.

This revenant was avian-like, with a disproportionately large and bony triangular head. It had the body of a starving bird, with a large expanse of wings and dirty feathers. Its feet featured long black talons, which were currently embedded in the roof of the vehicle. All said, it was as if someone had taken an armoured angelfish and stuck it where the head normally goes on a vulture, then made it huge and deadly.

The sound of a girl's distressed cry rang out above the others, and the creature shrieked with fury. Lance charged, his soul spiking with adrenalin. He knew that voice. He'd recognize it anywhere. Jessica was in the car!

As Lance neared, he could see her, huddled in the passenger seat of the vehicle the revenant had latched on. She shrank into the car's interior; hands upraised covering her face, cowering in fear.

The revenant reared up and plunged its beak-like jaws into the roof of the car, parting the metal like it wasn't even there. Jessica screamed as the nose tore right beside her, barely missing its target. The revenant lifted its head into the air and screetched once more, preparing to strike again.

Lance reached the car before the revenant could, and roared as he body-checked the bird, hurling it off its perch. One of its wings smashed into a tree, which cracked violently. The creature then spun into the vacant sports-field behind the school, where it collapsed heavily.

Controlling his body as he rebounded from the impact, Lance alighted smoothly on the pavement directly in the front of the vehicle. He heard a cheer from somewhere nearby, but paid it no attention. He was entirely focused on Jessica, who was staring, wide-eyed, right back at him.

Lance began a shy grin, but his flourish was interrupted as a large branch fell from the tree that had been damaged during the fight. The branch whacked down upon Lance, who fell to the ground with an indignant thud.

He lay on the ground for a moment, woozy and weakened from the impact. The pain from the branch was bad, but the agony from his pride was far worse.

He could not believe his luck. A random tree branch had flattened him? Him? The slayer of demons? And it couldn't have happened at a worse time.

Lance staggered to his feet, facing away from the car in embarrassment, but more screams meant he had little time to reflect. In the distance Lance saw that the first revenant had recovered. It had resumed its steady march on the school, and was presently terrorizing everyone in its path.

It roared angrily, and to his horror Lance made out the figure of a young boy, clutched tightly within its foul grasp. The boy's cries were heartwrenching as the creature slowly brought him to its steadily opening jaws.

Lance had no time to react. Desperately searching for some way to save the child, Lance spied a large concrete telephone pole just a few feet away. It was planted in the ground and had a pointed tip. Lance reached it in the blink of an eye.

Gritting his teeth, he heaved, ripping the pole from the earth, ignoring the whipping cables and menacing sparks. Lance instantly hurled the makeshift missile like a javelin, directing it point first at the revenant.

The weapon impaled the creature through the chest, causing it to drop the boy, who unceremoniously plopped to the hard ground. Lance winced, but knew that broken bones were far better than being eaten. The revenant bellowed in pain, convulsing into a heap on the pavement.

Lance had barely watched the revenant fall before he was caught off guard by a massive impact which sent him flying forward, skidding along the street. He rolled and recovered in the middle of the two lanes, turning to face his assailant.

Streaking towards him was the enraged bird-creature, wildly flapping its wings and out for blood. It charged forward, leading with its pointed beak, but at the last second Lance dodged to the side, pushing the razor-sharp end away from his form.

The monster's momentum carried it forward, and it stumbled awkwardly ahead of Lance. Searching furiously for a weapon, the first thing Lance noticed was the mangled body of a car.

"You'll pay for that!" he shouted angrily, picking up the car and charging towards the creature. In two steps, he had caught up to the revenant, despite lugging his new weapon.

With a cry, Lance lifted the vehicle over his head and brought it down upon the revenant. Revenant and roadway crumpled before him as his force carved out a crater in the asphalt.

Recalling the recovery of the first revenant, Lance continued his assault relentlessly. Drawing the vehicle back, Lance swung it like a golf-club at the revenant's prone form. It hit the creature with a sickening crunch, as it was lifted up off the pavement and propelled towards the school. Lance watched the trajectory for a split second, before throwing the vehicle after the revenant. His aim was true.

The bird crashed into the wall of the school and was immediately pulverized by the vehicle-turned-projectile. Its body slumped down to the ground, shuddering woefully before becomming still. Gradually, its form began to glow. The dark plumage and skin brightened, as the body dissolved into bright gold flecks of power. They fluttered away into the wind as gradually, the revenant was no more.

Lance turned back to where the first revenant had been impaled, just in time to see Pajetic slash its throat with a long blade. The creature slowly crumbled away into nothingness as Pajetic stood steadfastly above, admiring how his weapon caught the sun. The battle was over.

Lance relaxed, allowing his power to fade and making his way back to the parking lot, ignoring the stares from the relieved and awestruck survivors who now watched his every move.

The area was quieter—the only sounds came from the crackling of flames and the hiss of water from the broken pipes, with the steady backdrop of sirens droning distantly in the air. It sure was taking emergency response a long time to arrive.

Leaving his partner, Lance walked to Jessica's hiding place, and noticed with concern that the passenger seat was now empty. He glanced about, searching. It didn't take him long to find her.

Jessica was sitting huddled on the broken sidewalk, close to a collapsed wall of the school. Lance hadn't the chance to get a good look at her during the chaos, but now he could plainly see that she was as beautiful as ever, despite her face being swollen from crying and covered in muck. Lance suddenly felt very nervous.

As he got closer, his nervousness morphed into confusion as Lance realized he had missed an important detail. There, with his arm around Jessica, *was some boy*. Lance had assumed her companion was just another terrified pedestrian, but this notion was dispelled when the boy began to speak.

"Thank God you're safe!" he murmured tenderly. He was fairly big, with broad shoulders and long brown hair that fell to his neck. He wore a simple t-shirt and jeans and started gently rocking Jessica, and to Lance's surprise, kissing her upon her forehead.

Lance suddenly felt very awkward, aware he was in his residual self-image and wearing the robes of a reaper. The two seemed oblivious to everything around them, but in a few more seconds of walking Lance would be practically on top of them.

"I'm just glad I was brave enough to run in and get you out of the car. You mean everything to me. I love you, Jessica." Lance rolled his eyes.

It took *so* much bravery to run in and undo a seatbelt after the monster bird had been dealt with. Lance's jealousy mounted and he prepared to say something, some devastating and witty remark that would clearly show Jessica what an amazing guy he was, when incredibly, Jessica reached up and kissed the boy on the lips.

"I love you too, Henry," she cooed softly. Lance felt like vomiting.

The lovebirds then appeared to wake up to the rest of the world, for they looked away from each other for a moment and noticed Lance standing directly in front of them, with his arms crossed before his chest.

"Oh my God!" said Jessica, in a slightly ditzy voice Lance did not remember her having. "You're the guy who tackled the bird!" Lance stared at her for a second before nodding slowly.

"Thank you for saving my girlfriend, man," said the boy breathlessly. "While you distracted that thing, I was able to get her to safety!" Jessica gazed at him with complete adoration as he spoke, and then pecked him on the cheek as he finished and beamed.

Lance almost laughed. The two had moved maybe twenty feet from where Jessica had originally been hiding, and were now in the middle of an exposed parking lot, alongside a structurally damaged building and surrounded by flaming wreckage. That was quite a generous interpretation of safety.

"I'm her knight, you know. I came in and saved her!" the boy bragged.

"Right," Lance replied slowly, holding his tongue

The boy smiled, and then offered his hand for Lance to shake. "Maybe we could team up, you know?" He offered before continuing, "You're not great at the saving people thing, but you tackle pretty well!"

Lance did not move toward the outstretched hand. He merely looked confusedly to Jessica, who had been nodding as the boy spoke, then to Henry, and then back to Jessica.

He felt disillusioned, a little bit wounded, and was shocked at how out of touch the boy seemed. He stood in silence, trying to figure out what to say next, when to his relief he felt someone else approach and heard Pajetic's voice.

"Well, it's been grand seeing everyone, but we have to go. This was all a big misunderstanding. A gas leak." Pajetic placed his hand on Lance's shoulder and yanked him into the spiritual plane. Jessica and the boy gasped as they disappeared from sight.

"What was going on?" asked Pajetic, in a slightly playful mood.

"Just talking," said Lance, still watching Jessica and Henry. Then he shook his head.

"About what?" laughed Pajetic, apparently amused.

Lance shook his head again, "Something stupid. It doesn't matter anymore." Changing the topic, he added, "Is that your manta?" as he motioned towards the sword Pajetic held in his right hand.

"Yeah," responded Pajetic calmly, letting the sword melt away into nothing. "One of them."

They stood there for a moment, listening to the mumble of people and the growing sound of sirens. Pajetic broke the silence first.

"I figured I needed an advantage; my ranged attacks did nothing. The manta was actually way easier to use than I thought. How'd you handle that bird creature?"

"I beat it with a car."

"Ah," responded Pajetic, as emergency vehicles finally arrived on the scene. Lance watched them invade the area, until the entire place was engulfed in flashing lights and brightly coloured vehicles. Their attention was quickly diverted back to the spiritual plane as the sound of humming energy abruptly filled the air, emerging from the school.

The reapers turned back to the ruined structure, only to see a bright beam of white light spring forth in the spiritual plane, directly into the sky. It seemed both serene and powerful. Neither Lance nor Pajetic moved, as they silently watched the beam emanate from the ground. It was just like the energy used to transport any other spirit to Paradise.

The beam grew in girth, until it eventually covered the entire area of the school, filling the air with a strong but harmless vibration. Lance stared into the light and felt a strange, foreboding feeling seep into his gut. Something did not feel right. Abruptly, the energy shifted.

What was once a peaceful strength turned into a horrific pressure as the beam slowly darkened, transforming from pure white into a dark shade of purple. A knot formed in Lance's stomach. He had seen that colour before.

Then with a flash, the beam was gone, leaving the reapers, and the school, behind. Lance spoke up immediately.

"What was that?" he said, angrily. Pajetic looked at him, surprised with his tone.

"What do you mean? That was Gazardiel moving Emma to Paradise. Can't you feel the difference?" Pajetic was right, there had been a marked change. The spiritual realm felt completely normal now, free of the Fragment's overwhelming power.

The shaking was gone. All that remained of Emma's presence was a slight bit of residue, drifting lazily in the air. It was very peaceful, but Lance was not placated.

"But why was it that colour?"

"The beam? You're kidding Lance. Maybe purple is the Fragment's natural colour," he dismissed while shaking his head.

"The Fragment's colour is gold," said Lance, defensively.

"Then maybe purple is the colour needed to transport a Fragment!" countered Pajetic.

"I doubt it," said Lance, dully. Pajetic sighed.

"Who cares?" responded Pajetic, putting a reassuring hand on his partner's shoulder. "We've dealt with enough problems, there's no need to imagine any more. Don't you get it? We won, Lance! We did it!"

Lance noticed his friend was grinning. He felt a weak smile spread across his face. Pajetic was right. It was over. They *had* done it.

"That's better!" said Pajetic, beaming.

"Well, what do we do now?" asked Lance, his smile becoming a full-on grin. "Retire?"

Pajetic laughed. "It's in Gazardiel's hands now. We should probably hide until he calls for us."

Lance nodded, finally letting the pleasure of victory wash over him. He stepped forward, raising his arms. "I've always wanted to go to Mexico, you know!"

Continuing his gaiety, Lance dropped his arms, expecting a chortle from Pajetic. Or at least a sympathetic laugh. When nothing came, he turned back to his partner in confusion. The reaper's face was stony.

Quietly, Pajetic whispered, "We might not want to get tickets just yet, Lance."

Lance turned, following Pajetic's gaze, and felt his heart sink. There, hovering about a hundred feet off the ground, was Michael.

Covered in golden armor, the Archangel glared directly at them, not moving a muscle. He was surrounded by a host of angels, at least fifty strong. Directly to his left, floated Abyss, Enigma and several other reapers. They all floated in the air, observing the two fugitives in deathly silence.

"There are more pieces on this board than we anticipated," muttered Pajetic, darkly.

Chapter 20

Lance stared at the crowd of spirits in disbelief. It couldn't be! So many. Each one, a party to Michael's nefarious scheme. So many! He whipped his head around to dart a glance at Pajetic, who gazed furiously onward. His eyes narrowed and blazed into acid green light.

Following Pajetic's gaze, Lance noticed that Michael was rapidly approaching, his own eyes bathed in a pure white glow. Power leaping through him, Lance prepared for their last stand.

"We did it, Pajetic," he said, bravely, squaring his body towards the throng. "With Gazardiel's escape, there is at least hope."

Pajetic only nodded curtly, before issuing a warning to Michael.

"Not one foot further."

Lance was shocked by the menace in Pajetic's tone. Surely he knew intimidation would not work. But Pajetic maintained his threatening posture, allowing an ominous globe of green to coalesce in his right hand.

Michael halted his advance, hovering in midair, silently observing the two. His voice rang out, clear and powerful as thunder.

"Valiant Pajetic. Reckless, but valiant."

Pajetic snarled in response. Michael nodded sadly. A second voice then rang out from the assembled spirits, a distraught voice which Lance knew only too well.

"Why, Lance? Pajetic? You have deceived and disappointed everyone," lamented Enigma, as he moved forward to flank Michael. To Lance, it felt like a punch in the gut, seeing the ancient reaper at Michael's side. Was there anyone left for Gazardiel to marshal?

"Silence, fool!" cried Abyss angrily, her voice still sending chills up and down Lance's spine. "They are criminals. They are still dangerous."

"Dangerous?" yelled Lance, incredulously. "You cowards would never know, bringing fifty to fight two!" He glared into the billowing smoke cloud that obscured Abyss' face, but she made no further move.

"Cowards!" he yelled again, his fury washing over him. "Betrayers, oath-breakers and back stabbers!" Lance pounded his fist into his hands. "We may be out numbered, but we will never stop fighting those who have destroyed a sacred trust."

"Trust?" scoffed Enigma, ignoring Abyss' recent command. "Is the irony of betrayal lost on you, Lance? Look at what you've done! We will not allow you to create any more havoc-" Enigma stopped his rant as Michael raised his hand in the air, commanding silence.

"Let Lance speak," he said calmly, staring directly at Lance. It seemed as though the power that flickered in his eyes intensified. "But do not, for a second, doubt my honour, reaper."

"Honour?" growled Pajetic. "There is no honour in thievery, in subterfuge and deceit, Michael!"

"So come," challenged Lance, preparing for battle. "Michael, the fallen angel."

Lance's last comment sparked some unrest in the crowd of spirits; many of the angels became visibly agitated. They whispered together, looking concernedly between Lance, Pajetic and Michael. The Archangel himself barely reacted, mustering only an almost imperceptible shake of the head.

"Some time from now, I should very much like to know how you twisted your minds to arrive at this conclusion," he responded, and Lance was surprised to hear a distinct note of sadness in Michael's voice. It was a far cry from the total logic of their earlier meeting.

"But we cannot idle here. Now tell me, Lance." he continued, his tone hardening as tendrils of pure white energy leapt from his body and raced towards the reapers. "WHERE IS GAZARDIEL?"

Lance reacted, and brought his energy-engulfed fist down upon the tentacle that had snaked its way through the air towards him at lightning speed. He made contact, but it had no effect. His defence broke in an instant, and Michael easily wrapped his energy around Lance.

Lance struggled, but was unable to free himself from Michael's grasp, which was steadily tightening, slowly crushing him. He screamed in anger and fear, and heard similar sounds emerge from beside him. He saw from the corner of his eye that Pajetic had been trapped as well.

"WHERE IS HE?" commanded Michael, his voice no longer calm, but booming with menace and authority. The pressure upon his essence was almost unbearable, and Lance felt his soul breaking. He roared, summoning his power to push Michael's strength back. A crimson surge flooded over his form, and he felt the pressure lessen, although not evaporate. Lance smiled ruefully at Michael, through gritted teeth.

"He's... gone!" he managed, fighting to get the words out. "You've failed Michael! We found it FIRST!"

"What!?" cried Michael, who took a step back. Lance felt the pressure suddenly weaken, almost as if Michael's focus was broken. Lance decided to seize the opportunity. Crying out again, he let his full power spill forth, as he shredded the encircling tendrils and dropped to the ground. To his right, he saw that Pajetic had done the same.

"That's right, Michael. You're too late," Pajetic said with confidence. He then turned and addressed the gathered spirits, raising his voice. "You are here supporting Michael, and yet, I implore you to listen. The source of this disturbance, this incredible energy that has engulfed the town... is a Fragment!"

Uproar immediately sprang from the crowd, as the spirits turned to each other, to Michael, and openly argued amongst themselves. The cacophony faded quickly as Peter, who was stationed at Michael's right side, spoke out above the others.

"This was no hunt for fugitives, was it Michael?" Each voice stopped as the assembled spirits turned to their leader, awaiting an explanation. However, Michael did not respond; he simply stared at Pajetic and Lance in shock.

"Ah," said Pajetic. "So they didn't know, *Archangel*." He spat out Michael's title with disgust. "That's right," he continued, now speaking to everyone, "Michael has failed in his duty to you all! He tried to take the power of the Fragment as his own. He violated his vow! He has deceived us ALL!" Lance looked to Pajetic for an instant. Could it be that these spirits were *not* in the conspiracy with Michael? Was there still hope?

Lance decided to speak up. "But Michael has not yet won! The Fragment is safe, away from *him*!" He glowered defiantly at Michael and was disconcerted by the stark fear he saw plain on the angel's face—completely the opposite to the rage and disdain he had expected. A lull in the conversation followed, with nary a sound, not even a whisper, as all awaited Michael's response.

Michael spoke, each word trembling softly with... rage? Or something... else. "Where is the Fragment Lance? Where did you take it?"

Lance smiled. "Just a few moments ago it was here! But Gazardiel has taken it under his protection. Those of you still loyal to your purpose, you can join with him! And stop this heresy!"

As Lance concluded, he stretched out his hand and pointed at Michael. "You're finished."

Silence returned to the empty parking lot. Lance stood beside Pajetic apprehensively, anxiously awaiting the surrounding crowd's reaction. A reaction that would decide the fate of their worlds.

His patience waned as the seconds flew by, grains of sand in an hourglass that was all but spent. Surely they would respond! He needed something. Anything! Applause, cries of woe, or perhaps indignation.

He witnessed none of this; instead there was only a subdued kind of... sadness. Were they all involved in this scheme? Lance noticed confusion playing across Pajetic's face. Had they been mistaken? The absolute quiet stretched on, until Michael finally spoke.

"Brothers... Sisters... We have been betrayed." His voice was heavy, almost weary. Lance did not understand; they had known from the beginning, hadn't they? What was going on?

Peter floated forward and put his hand softly on Michael's shoulder. "Did you know?" he asked, sombrely. Michael sighed.

"Of course he knew," accused Lance, with righteous indignation. "It was his idea!"

Michael brought his hand to his head and ran it through his hair, "Despite his... enthusiasm, Lance is correct about one element. There absolutely was a Fragment in the city." He studied Lance, who noticed the white glow had faded from his eyes. Instead, he saw two clear spheres of cerulean blue, buried in distress. "But why do you think it was I who released it?"

Lance furrowed his brow, exchanging a troubled look with Pajetic. He had not spent much time thinking about Michael's involvement since Gazardiel broke them out of Paradise. He turned back to Michael, feeling unsettled.

"Well... Gazardiel confirmed our suspicions," he answered, slowly. He thought about his response for an instant, dread gathering in his heart. He immediately remembered the purple flash as Gazardiel escaped the school, and the dreadful presence in his vision. A horrible realization slowly dawned on him.

"No!" he said, in disbelief. "No!" he repeated, more forcefully this time. Michael nodded sadly.

"Lance," he said, "it was not I who was charged with guarding the Fragments."

"NO!" asserted Lance again, shaking his head and breaking eye contact. He felt his heart being torn apart as he braced himself for the worst. How could Gazardiel, his hero, be the traitor? He was always there for him, had always believed in him. It couldn't be true! The pain was overwhelming and the world was spinning. Disoriented and somewhat faint, Lance dropped to one knee. Pajetic simply stood there, speechless.

"Gazardiel has betrayed us." Michael proclaimed. Lance scrambled, desperately searching the other spirits' faces, hoping for someone, anyone, to refute Michael's condemnation. He looked to Enigma, his trusted his mentor, the reaper who had taught him everything.

Returning his gaze, Enigma nodded sorrowfully in confirmation. Lance was beginning to understand. It explained why Michael had such unanimous support, why Enigma and Abyss were here.

Lance and Pajetic had been played, possibly since the first time they had met Gazardiel. They had been fools, idiots, naïve children, who had been in Gazardiel's pockets from the beginning. And they had never even questioned him, or his motives!

To a part of Lance's mind, it seemed so clear now. It was too convenient, for Gazardiel to be right there when they had escaped, and practically waiting for them in the Grim Reaper's tomb. But another part refused to believe it. Gazardiel had been part of their team. He, alone, had listened. He, alone, had helped.

On the spiritual plane, tears serve no purpose. There are no physical eyes to moisten, no tear ducts, and no face to run down. And yet,

Lance felt drops of his essence spill forth from his eyes, as the depth of the betrayal cut into him. In his time as a reaper, since his emotions had been restored, he had never truly despaired. But he did now. He felt pathetic, weak, malleable.

Gazardiel had seen Lance's desire for approval. He knew the reaper had spoken the truth that morning on the alley. After all, he was the one who started the event in the first place. And so he kept Lance involved, on the off-chance that a disgraced, inexperienced reaper might just find a Fragment.

And Lance had happily delivered it right to him. His greatest triumph had been a dupe. Lance's form roiled as he imagined the horrors Emma would endure at Gazardiel's hands, and the dark purpose behind Gazardiel's acts. It was all Lance's fault!

The pressure of a hand on his shoulder broke Lance's reverie. He turned and looked up, to see Pajetic staring back down at him. No tears fell, but he was obviously distraught. Lance felt Pajetic's very being wavering. They stood there for a brief moment, united in support of the other, until they were interrupted. Another spirit joined them, placing a soft palm upon each. It was Michael. Lance was relieved to see a tender expression upon the Archangel's face.

"We have *all* been deceived," he said, gently. "I am sorry Lance. I should have listened to you from the very beginning. I arrogantly discounted what you said based on your inexperience. And now look where it's got me. Do not blame yourselves young reapers. Blame me."

"Michael!" exclaimed Peter, anxiously. "What do we do now? Why would Gazardiel betray us?"

"I had thought... no... I had hoped, that there was some explanation for his actions Peter. But faced with what I now fear is the truth, I can only think of one possibility."

"What could that be?" asked Peter. Michael sighed again, and turned to the other spirits, who had drawn in closer.

"Conquest. I shall endeavour to explain everything, to the best of my knowledge." Michael paused, taking a deep breath to steady himself before continuing.

"Gazardiel's greatest duty was to safeguard the Fragments of the Creator. In that, he has unquestionably failed. The Fragment escaped, and landed here, in this very city. Those facts alone are sacrilege. But I believe the ploy runs deeper. The Fragment is sentient, it thinks, it feels, it can even exercise control. It knows Paradise is its home... and would only leave if it absolutely had to. Only if there was no other choice"

A gasp rose up amongst the spirits who hung on every single syllable. "Gazardiel must have attacked it, attempted to steal its power, to force a Fragment to react so drastically. Luckily, Gazardiel appears to have failed in his plan. To absorb the Fragment is a task beyond a single spirit. It escaped his clutches and fled here."

Michael paused before continuing.

"When Pajetic and Lance made their escape and Gazardiel left in pursuit, I visited the cache of the Fragments on a hunch. That was when I confirmed that the first Fragment was indeed missing. Gazardiel's secrecy damns him... and clouds my perception. There is but one purpose for taking such power. He intends to wield it against us." There was silence for a few seconds, which was finally broken by Abyss.

"Gazardiel is mad then. Surely the steward of the Fragments knew he could never absorb its strength. Even now, in hiding, it's useless to him. Only a lunatic would attempt something so impractical!" There was a murmur of agreement amongst the angels. Lance noticed, however, that Enigma was unconvinced.

"Perhaps he is not as mad as we assume," the old reaper said, calmly, deferring to Michael.

"Abyss, what action brought these two reapers before us to Abaddon in the first place?"

"The plundering of the Grim Reaper's ancient tomb" replied Abyss, curtly.

"We did no such thing!" cried Lance angrily, remembering the accusations of the angels. He could feel Abyss preparing to argue, but she was silenced by Michael's raised hand.

"At this point, Lance, there is evidence to prove your innocence. Does anyone recall what was taken from the tomb?"

"Several items, including the reaper's belt," stated Enigma. A second gasp ran through the assorted spirits, as Michael inclined his head in agreement.

"So that's his plan then?" said Peter, in a bewildered tone.

Lance felt completely out of the loop. Enigma, noticing, gestured towards him. "Lance, the reaper's belt was an item the Grim used millennia ago, to assist in the gathering of souls. It was an incredibly powerful spiritual gatherer, so strong that the angels actually used it to develop the pull of Paradise itself."

"Precisely," responded Michael. "It was a wonder to behold. A force I doubt this planet has seen since. A force so powerful... that I believe it could break down and absorb the power of a Fragment." Just as Michael finished, a strange sensation came over Lance. It started out lightly at first, then quickly grew.

The feeling was impossible to ignore. It was a tug, a steady suction towards the centre of the city, which pulled on his soul. Michael's eyes opened wide, flaring back to life as white power engulfed them. The other angels followed suit, and Lance felt a surge of energy as he prepared. The belt was calling them.

"And so it begins!" cried Michael, soaring into the air. The angels cheered loudly and headed after their leader, towards the city centre. Without warning, as quickly as it had begun, the tug ceased. Lance lurched backwards, mystified. Had Gazardiel given up?

He saw that Michael had also stopped his advance. The angel was paused before them, head tilted upwards, observing the sky. One by one, the angels followed his gaze, They looked up and stood transfixed, frozen in disbelief. Curious, Lance followed suit. His jaw dropped.

Rushing towards them, at an incredible speed, was a massive golden wave of spiritual power. Even higher than the sun in the sky, its peak crested thousands of miles above the tallest towers of the city centre. As it approached the group of spirits, the roar of energy began to grow, beginning as a distant rumble but growing more like thunder by the second.

"What is that?" asked Lance, mesmerized, before quickly realizing no one could hear him. He looked at Michael, who had his hands clasped in front of his face, eyes closed, chanting frantically. The wave was almost upon them, its apex directly overhead and golden energy frothing all around. The spirits cried out in fear, as the frothing tsunami bore down upon them.

"Brace yourselves!" ordered Abyss above the din. Lance stood his ground and amassed his power into a shield, hoping he could blunt the devastation, but knowing there was nothing he could do.

Gritting his teeth and preparing for the worst, the entire world dyed an insane yellow from the approaching cataclysm, Lance's attention was diverted by second energy. Rushing into view faster than even the oncoming Armageddon, a titanic sphere of strength bloomed around the spirits, enclosing them in its pure white radiance.

Lance had no time to ponder its emergence, for as soon as he saw it, the end arrived. With an explosion that reached the atmosphere, the two forces collided. White and gold and sound and force twirled together in a calamitous singularity which assaulted each and every sense.

And then... there was total silence.

Chapter 21

Have you ever been knocked off your feet by something you didn't see coming? Or accidentally smashed your head into a wall? Lance felt as though he had just been tackled by a hot air balloon made of bricks.

He could see, slightly, but everything was a blur and nothing made sense. He was awash in a sea of sensations, with odd colours and sounds waxing and waning around him. He was reminded of basketballs and the repetitive thudding sound they made.

"Get up, Lance!" The words rang persistently in his ears but meant nothing to him. He turned his head to the side and felt sick. The world spun about him, wildly and irregularly. To say he was disoriented would be an understatement.

A tingle cut through whatever befuddled and perverted consciousness he currently possessed, and Lance felt heat being applied to his shoulder. The temperature quickly intensified until it seared his spirit. Lance lurched to the side, his senses sharpening as he desperately tried to escape the scalding torment.

He landed on his shoulder, and felt more pain shoot up his arm. Lance shook his head, trying to clear his mind from the cobwebs of confusion. His movements were successful, as finally, his perception ground into gear.

Lance was sprawled on the hard asphalt of the school parking lot, surrounded by angels and reapers he did not recognize. With a heave of panic, Lance remembered the earth shattering wave and bolted upright. Had he survived? He must have; the scene was too familiar, and he felt too grounded. It was nothing like that time, long ago in the rain.

As he surveyed his surroundings, Lance spied Enigma standing nearby, watching him bemusedly. The old reaper's hand was outstretched, and his index finger was smoking. Lance rubbed his shoulder, wincing.

"So that was you?" he asked. He thought he saw a sliver of a smile cross his old master's face.

"Energy was hemorrhaging from you Lance— it was serious. I needed to rouse you, somehow."

"And you figured pain was the best bet?" Enigma shrugged and chuckled.

"It was the first thing that came to mind."

Lance looked beyond him, observing the rest of their party, searching for Pajetic. It took him a few seconds before he located his friend, who was perched on top of the school, staring intently to the west—the origin of the wave. Lance suppressed the urge to call out. If Pajetic was watching for further attack, he needed to focus.

The only other active spirit in the area was Michael, who Lance knew was the source of the white sphere that had saved them. Seemingly unaffected by the immense use of his power, Michael flitted amongst the group, kneeling and whispering to the strewn bodies of the other angels and reapers. His words appeared to carry great power, as after he spoke, each spirit began to rise. Lance shook his head in wonder.

"I've never witnessed such an overwhelming assault," he said, while turning to Enigma. The reaper nodded his head in agreement.

"Nor such a defence. To stop such energy requires... impossible strength."

Lance shook his head again. He had always had the impression that he was a powerful being. But compared to what he had just seen, he was about as significant as an ant. He heart sank as he contemplated the implications.

"Will Gazardiel attack again?" asked Lance, fearfully, knowing he was at the mercy of the strength of the two god-like beings. A cold laugh rose behind him, and Lance twisted to see Abyss, sitting on top of a ruined car.

"Unlikely," she snorted. Lance knotted his eyebrows. He did not appreciate her intrusion, but his curiosity quickly got the better of him.

"How do you know?" he asked, preparing for a rude rebuke. He was surprised when Abyss responded frankly.

"That attack wasn't Gazardiel's doing. Only the Fragment could cause such an anomaly." Lance felt even more confused.

"But why would the Fragment attack us? We're trying to help Emma!" Abyss tilted her head, which remained shrouded in roiling clouds of black smoke.

"I assume Emma's the name of its host? I doubt what the Fragment did was an attack. It was so broad, so far reaching. The wave crashed across the horizon, and who knows how far it's travelled since passing us. It seems more like a defensive tactic."

"A defense that indiscriminately pulverizes all nearby spirits?" asked Lance, sceptically.

Abyss did not have a chance to reply before a voice called out from across the parking lot, and Lance noticed a small group of disheveled humans approaching. They were young, perhaps students at the school. Their faces were dirty, with torn clothing covered in soot, rushing towards the spirits.

Their haste was justified, for in their arms they were supporting a wounded youth, barely old enough to be in high school. Blood dripped from a horrific gash in his abdomen, and Lance thought he could see intestines protruding from it.

"You! You saved me from that monster!" called out an older boy who stood slightly ahead of the carriers, arm outstretched and finger extended. He was pointing at Lance. "You've got to help Terry! We can't reach anyone!" Lance started, uncertain as to how the youth could see him.

"You fool!" hissed Abyss. "Get into the spirit realm, now!" Lance complied immediately, transcending his soul into the spiritual realm, but was nonplussed by the kid's reaction. He still seemed to be staring right at him. Something was amiss.

The teen kept approaching despite Lance's hesitation, switching targets to look directly at Abyss. "Are you with him?" he asked , a note of panic in his voice. "Please, one of you needs to help, Terry could die!" Lance had no idea how to react, and gazed at Abyss, who stood as rigid as a statue—the only movement was a thick billow of smoke rising in front of her face.

"They can see us," observed Enigma, calmly. He took a slow step forward before continuing, talking almost to himself. "And yet we are certain we are in the spiritual realm." He brought a hand up to his chin and stroked it, thoughtfully.

"Notice how not a single spirit is off the ground right now?" Lance nodded. He hadn't, but after Enigma's comment he realized that none of the spirits were levitating.

"Strange," murmured Abyss, whose dark fushia eyes started to glow from within her shrouded face. Lightning crackled around her as she rose several feet into the air. "I can still control energy and move as I would in the spirit realm."

The human, at first intimidated by Abyss' actions, moved forward again. "Please!" he begged. "Use your magic to heal him!" Abyss twisted to face him, and the boy yelled, ducking as a stream of purple energy flew over his head, just missing him.

"Silence!" she commanded, her voice sounding shrill and other-worldly. Lance sprung forward angrily. He knew Abyss had intentionally missed, but her actions infuriated him nonetheless.

"What are you doing Abyss?" he growled, angrily. Abyss faced him, her eyes glowing with energy. Her voice was low and trembling menacingly, as if one wrong move could ignite her.

"I could not hear myself think with his badgering," she said.

"That kid needs help!" argued Lance, ignoring the warning in Abyss' voice.

"And he should get it from his own kind," answered Abyss, curtly. Lance shuddered. Where was her empathy? Had she not also been human once? Ignoring the thought lest he become further distracted, Lance questioned the group.

"Where are the emergency vehicles, anyway?" He looked about the parking lot, but only saw destruction. It was littered with the twisted bodies of cars, broken trees, rent sidewalks and downed power lines.

But no people. Lance could not even see signs of life in the houses that lined the street adjacent to the lot. The area was altogether much too quiet.

"They took as many wounded as they could and left," said Enigma. "They were gone before we were confronted by the wave. It must be hard for them to react."

"Then we need to fly him to a hospital." Lance announced, heading for the group of kids.

"Stay where you are, Lance," ordered Abyss cruelly. "We must solve this puzzle before any more action is taken." Lance glanced at her out of the corner of his eye, and saw Abyss raise her arm threateningly. Incredulity filled him. Could she actually be preparing to attack *him*? Before he could take another step, he heard Michael's voice.

"How lucky, then, that I have solved it, Abyss." Lance watched as Michael, followed by Pajetic and Peter, strode towards the group of humans.

Lance made eye contact with Pajetic, who nodded in response. He appeared unhurt, but Lance knew Pajetic would not show it even if he was. Michael reached the youths, who seemed frail compared to his might. They stared at the Archangel with wide eyes. Lance knew they could see his halo.

"Have no fear," he said softly, as he approached the injured one. The child flinched, but lacked the strength to move away. White energy flowed from the Archangel's hands, drifting lazily in the direction of the gaping wound. As it landed, it spread into small sparkles of light, rapidly circling the injury, and entering into the abdominal cavity, filling the spaces where Lance assumed muscle once was.

The lights moved faster and faster, eventually melding into a solid white line. Lance gasped as the edges of light faded and revealed pink, unblemished skin. In seconds, the wound had been completely healed.

The boy opened his eyes, gazing in astonishment at Michael. He prodded his stomach timidly before smiling, tears of relief in his eyes. "Thank you," he whispered, his words echoed by his friends.

Michael smiled before speaking, "Retreat young ones, find shelter and contact everyone you can. Tell them to flee the city." As the humans scattered, he walked back and stood beside Lance and Abyss.

"As you can see," he stated, in a calm but resonant voice, "everything has changed."

Lance watched as the other reapers and angels closed in, all having now recovered. "The division between earth and the spirit world is no more. There is no spiritual plane. There is no physical plane. There is just this. The violence of the impact was too great for a realm already saturated to its breaking point by the Fragment."

Michael paused and beckoned to the surrounding spirits, inviting them to come closer. "Paradise itself was shaken by the explosion," he continued, "and the consequences will be felt forevermore. But now we have a more pressing concern. The Fragment's power may have stalled Gazardiel, but I very much doubt that it dealt him a fatal blow. He will recover soon."

For the second time, as if on cue, Lance felt a lurch in the pit of his stomach. The inexorable force of the reaper's belt was, once again, exerting a gravitational pull.

"Protect the humans. Defeat Gazardiel." Michael commanded. "Worry about nothing else, for it will only serve to weaken you." He then addressed Pajetic, who was standing behind his left shoulder, staring towards the source of the disturbance.

"Have you had any success? Is he there?" he asked, evenly. Lance realized Pajetic had not been on the lookout for an attack. He had been using his considerable skills to locate Gazardiel. Pajetic nodded in response. "He's there alright. But he's not alone. There's a lot of activity there, Archangel. Multiple, massive spirits."

Michael nodded grimly. "Very well, there is no time to waste. To the skies!" Without a second look he took off like a bolt of lightning, streaking through the air, in the direction of the city centre. The spirits shouted a battle cry in unison as they embarked, following their leader's course.

Lance flew as fast as he could, comforted by how easy control remained, and yet still worried about the situation. Michael flew so quickly that it was a strain on his reserves just to keep up. Lance had no resources to spare for thought. Perhaps the Archangel wished it to be so.

But as he grew more comfortable with his trajectory and pace, Lance found himself unable to ignore the million questions burning in his mind. Try as he might to subdue them, they assailed his consciousness.

Why was Gazardiel giving his position away? Why was he pulling them in now, so quickly after acquiring the Fragment? Had Gazardiel taken control of Emma already? Lance gritted his teeth angrily. What had he gotten her into?

A muffled boom sounded in the distance, a gigantic explosion of some sort, forcing Lance to become aware of his surroundings. They had traversed miles in mere seconds, and were now flying directly above the outskirts of town. A dark plume of smoke rose on the far side of the city, obscured by the skyscrapers within its centre.

Archangel Michael turned sharply, dropping towards the ground, shadowed by his cohorts, moving like a great flock of birds. Lance heard the roar of engines sound above, as a formation of seven fighter jets rocketed past, heading right for the explosion.

The display of militarism worried Lance almost as much as the blast itself. He understood why Michael had dropped; the fog of war had enveloped the city, and Michael was fearfully of becoming mistakenly engaged in battle by humans.

They dipped towards a multi-lane highway, which wound like a snake around the far south side of the downtown. Michael levelled as he reached it, and pursued its contours, maintaining an altitude just above the vehicles. Screams filled the air, and Lance noticed that there were hundreds of people standing in the streets, clustered together in groups, now gaping at the sky and pointing feverishly. Traffic was at a standstill.

A dreadful, terrifying, deafening roar echoed through the city. It was low, but rough, like the world's largest anchor was scraping against the world's largest rock. It slowly rumbled away as a second explosion thudded in the distance. Lance anxiously strained his eyes, searching between the buildings for the cause of the commotion, but able to see only black smoke. Michael doubled his speed, from extremely fast to positively ludicrous.

Lance half expected flames to erupt from behind him, and he felt the friction of the air actually breaking away parts of his energy. They rounded a bend in the road, curving around the city and finally revealing its farthest side. Their break-neck pace came to a bowel-clenching stop.

Directly in front of them was a layered convergence of highways, all weaving in various directions. Overpasses and underpasses and a myriad of access roads created a messy web of asphalt and concrete that spanned several stories into the air.

Behind this haphazard meeting of roads was a broad building, perhaps the most impressive in the downtown, though certainly not the tallest. Lance recognized it as the domed sports stadium, capable of housing almost one-hundred-thousand people.

It was rectangular, with a retractable silver dome that extended a few hundred feet above the main building. The corner closest to them had been completely demolished, and was consumed by flames. They had found the source of the choking smoke.

If Lance had looked closely, he might have seen a flash of gold inside its black and obscured corridors, along with a haze of dark purple. But Lance was distracted by a more immediate threat.

There, directly before them, stood a living mountain, poised in the midst of the network of highways.

Lance had never seen a creature of such scale. Its form stretched into the air, dwarfing the skyscrapers of the city centre. Far above, practically scraping Paradise itself, the beast's face leered down at the city. Six eyes, each glowing a murderous shade of orange, seethed in the heavens.

"God help us," breathed Lance in disbelief.

Chapter 22

The line of angels wavered, unnerved in front of such a nightmarish creature. Its gigantic head was larger than a house, and shaped like an inverted diamond. The lower part was much wider than the top to accommodate two sets of menacing jaws, one above the other. Each was lined with a row of massive razor-sharp fangs, dyed a dreadful orange, jutting from its scaly black skin.

Spines the size of billboards erupted from its sides and top, and ran down its neck, shoulders and arms, which terminated not with fingers, but instead in a pair of colossal pincers. It looked somewhat like a demented, alien, dragon, with all its scales and spines. And pincers. And two mouths.

Lance peered again into the smouldering orange eyes, and was filled with dread. He was aware that for revenants, creatures of poor discipline and control, size was directly correlated with power. And this monster stood head and shoulders above the skyscrapers. It was by far the most imposing revenant Lance had ever encountered, larger even than any creature of legend. The implications did not bode well.

The leviathan had apparently not noticed their group, as Lance was certain it would have attacked on sight. Lance focused on his surroundings, just in time to see the seven jets, which had passed by earlier, break formation and launch a barrage of missiles straight at the beast. A swarm of angry red explosions engulfed it, and it recoiled as flames enveloped its form, letting out a bellow loud enough to shake the concrete beneath their feet.

Dense smoke permeated the area, as the jets hooked away from the creature, withdrawing to a safe distance to assess the damage. A momentary calm descended upon the scene, as the sound of the blasts faded and all sight of the monster was completely obscured by smoke. Lance stood still, stunned. Surely, the humans could never inflict enough damage to defeat it. And yet, they were determined.

Suddenly, out of the inky veil, an ominous orange glow shone forth like a search light, blazing in the darkness. It grew brighter by the second, growing like the headlamp of a train emerging from a tunnel. Lance reacted instantly, hurtling himself in front of the group of spirits who watched as if in a trance, desperately erecting a wall of crimson energy around his allies.

His red was immediately surrounded by white, and Lance realized Michael was augmenting his defence. In less than a second, the attack was unleashed.

With a massive crackle of electrical energy, an enormous ray of power erupted from the bright point in the smoke, blasting the murky vapor away as it streaked forward, gushing from the now revealed revenant's jaws. It was aimed high, and streaked above Lance, just as the human jets flew overhead. They tried to veer away in a panic-stricken attempt to evade the assault, but were far too late.

The blast set the skies above ablaze, as the distinctive drone of untamed energy buzzed all around. The force of the attack shattered all of the glass in the vicinity, igniting anything flammable nearby, and reduced the fleeing jets to ash.

Lance watched his crimson shield shudder, and then before he could direct power to repair it, collapse entirely. Lance flinched instinctively, but Michael's shining wall stood firm, protecting them from harm. Lance stared in horror at the monster and saw the murderous orange eyes methodically turn to them.

Admittedly, Lance had not thrown all his strength into his shield, but that had seemed reasonable at the time. The monster's attack had not even been aimed at them. And yet its mere proximity had been enough to undo his defenses. Lance's thoughts were racing, how could the creature be so powerful?

He had no time to think, as Pajetic yelled, "Where did *those* come from?" Pajetic sounded as worried as Lance felt. Alerted by his partner, Lance now noticed a swarm of revenants now circling the arena. There had to be over a thousand of them, flying in every direction around the huge beast. They were all fairly substantial, at least the size of a large human. Lance gulped.

"The big one was hiding them," stated Enigma in wonder. "The explosions must have broken its concentration, or that blast was so powerful it stunned itself. Either way, it's going to recover soon."

Lance diverted his gaze, looking back to where the jets had been obliterated. "Thank you for your sacrifice," he said, quietly and gratefully. At least the horde of revenants no longer had the element of surprise.

As he stared into the space where the humans had been destroyed, he thought he saw a flicker of blue, clouds of energy, swiftly floating towards the arena.

"What?" said Lance aloud, confused. He pointed to the strange apparitions in the sky. There's no way they could be...

"Souls," confirmed Enigma, in a matter of fact tone that belied the seriousness of his statement. "They're being pulled in."

So preoccupied by the challenges in front of him, Lance had forgotten the barely noticeable tug, leading them towards the arena. *That* was strong enough to pull the spirits in? Then again, he did not even feel the pull of Paradise.

"It's Gazardiel. His use of the reaper's belt is gathering them," concluded Michael. Things were quickly spiralling out of control. Lance knew that absolutely nothing good could come from the gathering of souls. He could sense dissent in the ranks, as the wills of the angels splintered. The longer they lingered, the more time the monster had to regain its wits.

"I will enter the building," said Michael, in a commanding tone. "Enigma, Abyss, Peter, you focus on the revenants. Lead the remaining spirits against the swarm." Enigma and Peter nodded somberly, but Abyss spoke up.

"Don't be foolish, Michael. We should ignore the revenants and overwhelm Gazardiel. He is the true threat here," she said, casually.

"Did you *see* that thing?" Lance was speaking impulsively, angry at the thought of the massacre Abyss was implying. "Nothing in the city would survive!" He heard a murmur of agreement from the assembled spirits and was emboldened.

"Humans reproduce quickly; the city is a sacrifice that must be made," countered Abyss, indifferently. "They have not the strength to defend themselves, and thus, will die."

"That is precisely the reason we are here, Abyss," Michael's voice was adamant, and more commanding than anything Lance had ever heard. "Above all, we defend the defenceless."

The monstrous revenant roared, a horrible, artificial sound, which assaulted the mind and interrupted the conversation. "The city must be guarded," he concluded sternly.

Peter spoke now, putting his hand on the Archangel's shoulder. "You need not go alone."

"I must, my friend," he responded, sadly. "We are not mighty enough to take others away from the battlefield."

"Gazardiel is not who we thought he was brother. Who can say what dark secrets he has turned to, what newfound strength he has," cautioned Peter, refusing to relent. "We cannot lose you!"

"Then I shall not fail." Michael looked deeply into Peter's eyes, placing his hand on his shoulder in kind. There was a sadness, shared between the two of them, that was beyond Lance's understanding. Their faces were stoic and brave as they said nothing, but Lance felt much more was being communicated nonetheless, as quiet fell over the group.

"I'll go," volunteered Lance, breaking the silence, as Michael and Peter turned to him in surprise.

Lance wasn't entirely sure why he said it. It could have been guilt about Emma, or his desire to safeguard Michael, with whatever small strength he had. It could have been his bravery, or his rashness, or his unquenchable desire to make Gazardiel suffer. It could have been anything, but as soon as he said it, Lance knew he was going. He could sense the approval of the gathering of angels.

"He knows the Fragment bearer, Michael," argued Pajetic. "You'll need to be free from distraction to fight; he can manage Emma."

"And he has the power to survive the conditions in there, whatever they may be; his strength of body, mind and soul will protect him," added Enigma. Not even Abyss spoke against it.

Michael's gaze stiffened, as he searched Lance's face. Lance met it boldly, refusing to look away, even though he ached to do so. It felt like Michael was staring inside his mind, stripping from it secrets that Lance didn't even know he had.

Never before had he experienced such an intimate link, and Lance doubted very much he ever would again. After a brief moment, the connection broke, and Michael nodded his head contently.

"Very well," he said softly, before raising his voice to address everyone.

"Harden yourselves, friends," commanded Michael, as he boldly strode ahead of the group of spirits. "For only those who stand firm can hope to survive such might." Michael remained still for a second as the giant revenant roared once more, a hideous metallic sound that would make lesser beings flee. Lance fidgeted nervously.

"Today marks the end of an age, the end of our way." Michael was facing the group now, and he began to pace back and forth across the highway.

"For millennia, we've faithfully stood sentinel as Life blossomed before us. Now this one greatest creation is threatened!" Michael brought his right hand to his chest, closed in a fist.

"We love humanity. We have guarded it faithfully since Creation. Many have forsaken their well-deserved afterlife in this service." Lance noticed a few reapers nodding their heads.

"Why?" Michael spoke as if posing the question, but continued before any could respond. "Because we've seen the love in humanity, we *know* of the good in their race, and we will never allow their opportunity to flourish and evolve to be undone!"

Michael spoke with great conviction; each word was laden with passion. Lance had never heard the Archangel speak in this way, but he felt a stirring of emotion, a powerful motivation that fed his energy, erasing his doubts.

"Choice is the greatest gift given. And we will never allow it to be taken away! Evil, opposition, the shadow in the light. It has risen once again, after ages of hiding."

Michael brought his first away from his chest and flung it into the air, where it began to crackle with sparks of luminous energy. "We shall remind it why it fled so many years ago!"

There was a buzzing of power, as the assembled spirits summoning their many mantas. Scythes filled the hands of the revenants, as the angels displayed a wide variety of instruments.

At the edge of his vision, Lance saw Pajetic's green swords pulsing eagerly. He reached into himself, brought forth his great scythe, instantly feeling stronger. He clutched it in his hands, reassured by its form.

"Today, we fulfill the oaths we have made and protect those who have not the strength to protect themselves. TODAY WE FIGHT." Lance smiled a ferocious smile as Michael spoke, and began to pulse up and down in anticipation. He was ready for the next step.

"FOR CHOICE!" bellowed Michael.

"FOR CHOICE!!" cried Lance, his call merging with the shouts of the other spirits.

"FOR LIFE!" Michael continued, his hand high in the air, clutching a gorgeous sword with a blade of pure, heavenly, white.

"FOR LIFE!!" echoed Lance.

"AND FOR JUSTICE!" cried Michael, who turned, his garments fluttering about his armoured torso, and charged towards the revenants.

"FOR JUSTICE!!"

Lance instantly joined in the pursuit. The spirits surged forward in a stampede of colour and bravery. Over his shoulder, a barrage of spiritual energy flew towards the revenants, who had assembled behind their giant leader.

A flurry of dark orange and brown energy answered the angel's assault as the revenants scattered from their ranks, arcing through the air and descending savagely upon the charging spirits. The two forces collided, and in an eruption of noise, chaos overtook the battlefield.

Chapter 23

Lance charged forward, desperately trying to keep up with Michael, who moved with speed greater than he had imagined possible.

The swarm of revenants attacked relentlessly from above, but Michael persevered undeterred. All antagonising energy directed at him simply bent away at the last second, careening harmlessly into the sky, as if refracted by a mirror. They had almost reached the behemoth, which now seemed more like a mountain than a living thing, towering ominously over the battlefield.

With a great strike of his sword, Michael cut a blinding white slash of power through the air, creating a crescent of energy which sliced towards the enemy host. Rays of white light crackled from the blade, arcing into their ranks and connecting lethally with at least five. They screeched in pain as they fell to the ground, incinerated in chastising white flames.

Lance took to the air, rising above Michael, heading towards the airborne monsters. Knowing he was exposed, Lance encased himself in protective energy.

His plan instantly paid dividends as he absorbed a number of attacks that were immediately thrown his way. The two groups clashed in a violent hurricane of force, and Lance could only tell friend from foe based on the different colours of energy and the monstrous guises his enemies had adopted. It was mayhem.

Lance quickly collided with one revenant. It lashed out at him with its claws and large beak, but Lance managed to dodge, stabbing it in the chest with his manta.

The creature tumbled to the ground, energy dissipating from it as it streaked downward. Lance fell with it, trying to use its dissolving body as a shield. He sprang from his temporary shelter just as a new revenant dove at him. Lance swung his scythe at the creature, this one resembling a demonic monkey with bat wings, but it dodged under the blade.

However, Lance had anticipated the move, and had swung the manta with his right hand only. Now using his free left, which held a pulsing ball of red energy, Lance twisted and delivered a haymaking punch to the monkey's face. It connected, and the force of the blow carried the two spirits to the ground where they landed in a crater.

Grunting, Lance pulled his fist out of the defeated foe's head while scanning the combat zone for Michael. He saw the Archangel, a ways ahead, carving a path through the revenants and having almost reached the damaged corner of the arena.

Dark purple hazed there ominously, preventing the combatants from discerning its interior. Michael was too far ahead. Lance needed to catch up!

"RUN LANCE!" It was Pajetic's voice, warning him from nowhere. Lance instinctively bolted forward as two black silhouettes extinguished the sky ahead. The monstrous revenant's two pincers were dropping from the sky, poised to crush him under their sheer mass.

Lance swore forcefully and doubled his speed. The first appendage pulverized the roadway where he had just been standing, collapsing the pavement and unleashing a tirade of water from broken underground plumbing.

Straining with every bit of power he had, Lance willed himself onward racing to beat the other pincer—a second descending shadow, the size of a street.

The surroundings meshed into a blur as Lance ran for his life, fighting to maintain control. Right as the actual pincer came down, he leapt forth, diving through the air with his scythe held above his head. His form spun one-hundred and eighty degrees as he moved, keeping the threatening extremity in his sights.

Flying feet-first, Lance concentrated his energy into the tip of his manta. He completed his flip just as he cleared the claw, and brought his weapon slashing into its scaly edge. It easily rent the scales, creating a long gash along the pincer's side. Lance heard the monster scream in agony. He landed in a crouch, his scythe held in his right hand, with its shaft against his back.

Lance's pride in his cool landing was short lived, as he realized Michael was now inside of the arena, hidden from his view. Lance headed towards the building, barely noticing the blast of energy that landed exactly where he had just been crouching. Flitting across the combat zone as swiftly as he could, Lance completely ignored the revenants, now hoping only to dodge them. They dove past him as he spun and weaved, dancing between their strikes, focused only on reaching Michael. The real battle was about to begin.

***

The beast roared savagely as Pajetic yelled. He saw a flash of power as Lance tried to avoid the falling pincer. It pounded into the pavement, shattering pipes and throwing dust and water into the air, jarring sounds that quickly mingled with the din of battle.

Pajetic strained, trying to sense as he veered through the sky, but he could track nothing on the saturated battlefield. He wanted to go forward, to check the wreckage for Lance, but knew better. He couldn't afford to stop. He had to keep moving, keep fighting. Lance looked like he was going fast. He should have made it. No, he *did* make it.

Pajetic stared angrily ahead at an approaching revenant. His twin swords flashing, he dropped slightly, twisting to face the sky, and slashed his swords through its underbelly.

The creature moaned and fell to the ground, while Pajetic brought his right sword down upon the head of yet another revenant, this one flanking him from below. Getting into a rhythm, Pajetic brought his left sword to his face, deflecting a beam of rust-coloured energy which had been flung at him from across the skirmish.

Pajetic continued to move, eyeing a revenant that was flying perpendicular to his path. It was buglike, with large compound eyes and mandibles. He reached it just as it turned to face him, unleashing a spray of sickly green energy. Pajetic dispersed the attack with his own acid green, and then beheaded the monster with his blades. He watched the lifeless body plummet to the earth before surveying the area.

Reapers and angels were scattered around the arena's grounds, fighting for their lives against swarms of their enemies and dodging the random, pulverizing strikes of the leviathan. Pajetic thought it looked confused, as if the huge revenant was overwhelmed with all the activity. Its attacks, though devastating, had thus far done more damage to its own kind than its opponents. Pajetic hoped that it would stay that way. If the beast's technique improved, they had little hope.

Pajetic was suddenly hammered on his right hand side and driven to the ground in a crash. Stunned by the impact, he felt pressure on his chest. A vague shape stabbed at him, and Pajetic flinched his head to the left, for his body was pinned, feeling the rush of something streaking past. His mind clearing, Pajetic concentrated on his attacker.

A revenant, this one resembling a spider with wing-like folds of skin stretching between its legs, was scrambling on his chest. It had ugly brown eyes, a hairy carapace covering its head and a formidable set of jagged fangs. It lunged at his face again and again, each time coming closer to him as Pajetic struggled to dislodge it from his torso.

The attack was relentless, but fortunately, Pajetic was able to liberate one arm for protection, wrestling the teeth away from his face. Summoning all of his strength, he finally freed both legs, bringing them up to his chest.

He delivered a mighty kick to the belly of the spider, propelling it into midair. He was on his feet immediately, reminded now of the perils of standing still.

Keeping them linked to his wrists by thin cords of acid green, Pajetic hurled his mantas into the belly of the repelled revenant. Using these tethers of energy, Pajetic yanked himself upwards into the air, just as a rush of energy shot behind him.

Pajetic closed the distance between he and his target in an instant, clutching the handles of his swords with a typical overhand grip. Spinning, he flung his foe beneath him, sending its corpse streaking toward a new enemy that had pursued him from the ground. They collided, the momentum of the second overwhelming the first, and shot past Pajetic into the sky.

Mantas in hand, Pajetic fell, controlling the pace of his descent. He spied a revenant with the body of a man, and the head and wings of a hawk. It was banking towards him, dirty talon-like nails outstretched. At the very last moment, Pajetic dramatically increased the rate of his fall, dropping just below the revenant. He raised his swords, which struck into its chest as it streaked overhead.

To his surprise, the blades did not easily slice through this revenant's energy, instead abruptly lodging inside its torso. Pajetic was violently lurched to his side and dragged along by the bird creature, which screeched horribly, scratching at its chest and labouring to stay airborne.

From this vantage point, Pajetic had a panoramic view of the battlefield. The swarm of enemies had dispersed, with many packs surrounding and assaulting individual combatants. He saw an angel fall to the ground, every inch of his body covered by scaly spiked revenants, biting and clawing at him mercilessly. The sight of an angel's demise deeply unsettled him.

Pajetic grunted, enraged and energized, ripping his swords out of his prey's body, and then using them to cut it in half. It fell away from him in two pieces as Pajetic was left alone, far above the battle.

A new development on the front immediately grabbed his attention. There, near where the assembled spirits had charged the revenants, calmly stood Abyss, Enigma and Peter. They clustered together, shouting orders to the ranks of tiring reapers and angels.

Purposefully, the three turned to face each other. They grasped one another's hands, forming a circle that slowly rotated as they rose into the sky. Arctic blue, deep fuchsia and forest green energy merged together, as the circle revolved faster and faster until it was a blur. With a groan of power, the circle expanded into a gigantic tornado of energy, which, although not as wide as the monster, reached almost as high.

Streaks of crackling energy, a mix of pink, blue and green, fired from the tornado, lashing out at the revenants. They were like guided missiles, as each one found its mark, instantly maiming its target.

The bolts fired at an incredible rate, annihilating entire sections of the horde as the storm turned mercilessly. Pajetic saw a reaper, whose arm was in the mouth of an alligator creature, become freed just in time to fend off the stab of the tail of a winged scorpion.

Many revenants wheeled away from the tornado, abandoning their fight as they tried to flee its devastating assault. A cheer sprung up from down below, and Pajetic added his voice in jubilation. He had never seen such technique, such a display of power. The three were singlehandedly destroying the entire enemy army!

Watching the revenants flee, Pajetic came to observe the large revenant, whose face traced the tornado's path. Its six eyes appeared to narrow, and its mouths began to open. It held not a single scrap of fear. Comprehension dawning, Pajetic realized that the revenants were fleeing, but not from the tornado.

"Shit!" cried Pajetic as the mouth continued to open, small particles of orange energy collecting within it. The tornado continued to spin, still spitting lightning. A group of spirits had congregated around the base, shooting their own beams of power at the retreating revenants.

"MOVE!" shrieked Pajetic, with a sense of déjà-vu. How could they have forgotten? This monster didn't only attack with claws. He charged, shooting green energy from his mantas at the huge revenant, trying to distract it, aiming for its eyes. If only he could blind it for a moment, alter its aim!

He managed only a few bursts before the assault was unleashed. A gargantuan blast of orange energy, with the same sound as before, erupted from the leviathan's mouth and streaked towards the tornado.

The revenants were not retreating before the Tornado – they were running from this attack. The explosion was colossal, engulfing the entire area with its force. Pajetic lost consciousness for a second, and felt himself plunging to the ground. He was able to shield himself from the impact just before he hit the concrete, but there was nothing he could do to alleviate the emotional shock.

Carnage. Almost the entire host of angels and reapers had been in the direct line of fire. Desperately, he reached out with his senses to try and find any of his comrades. He couldn't be all that was left.

Dread filled his heart as he could only sense five, lonely spirits still present. No Abyss, no Enigma, no Peter. *No Lance*. And still so many revenants.

The few survivors would be overwhelmed in seconds. Pajetic heard the titanic revenant roaring triumphantly, and he felt a sense of profound sadness wash over him. Their defeat was absolute. They had lost.

Chapter 24

Lance rushed through the crowded battlefield, deftly avoiding attacks as he raced to reach the ruined corner of the arena. He sprinted inside, hoping the confines of the building would give him some shelter from the swarm of revenants.

This part of the stadium was eerie, a maze of cracked concrete and sparking electrical wires. Flames licked the corner's edges, but lingered in the light of the exposed edge, as if afraid of the building's onyx depths.

Multiple floors of corridors lay open, but very little could be seen within them. Lance chose the one on the lowest level, to the right, and bolted down it before spinning, facing back towards the entrance, manta held ready.

There was nothing there. No revenants pursuing him from the battle, no Michael, and no shadowy Gazardiel. Lance resumed his walk into the stadium, his entire being tense with apprehension.

The corridors were wide, with walls of concrete and ceilings that reached about twenty feet into the air. Due to the damage to the electrical system, the lighting was malfunctioning.

A few bulbs flickered on and off randomly, but the majority were dead. The darkness and sporadic flashes of light had a disorienting effect on Lance, as shadows crept and shifted around him, tricking his vision and blurring the line between enemy and imagination.

Lance tried to expand his senses; he had to find Michael. He scowled as he stepped gingerly along the corridor. There was something unsettling about this area, but Lance had difficulty putting his finger on it.

He continued onwards, entire being on edge as he crept forward delicately, straining for something, anything, that might indicate he was not alone in this dilapidated arena.

Lance seized in place, taking in a sharp breath as he felt something emerge from afar. He paused, straining to see into the dim corridors. He felt strong energy up ahead. And it seemed like it was... moving. Lance scowled as he felt it approach, tensing and preparing the worst. Was it friend or foe? He was about to find out.

Suddenly, a broad wall of dark purple energy erupted from the darkness, charging rapidly towards him like a river. It covered the entire corridor, leaving Lance no possible avenue for escape, only a chance to retreat.

Lance had seen enough of this purple colour to know that bad things were about to happen. He fled from the rushing barrier, retracing his steps at top speed. But the energy was too fast. Lance could feel it behind him, unmercifully closing in. He pushed with everything he had, but even at his fastest Lance could not escape. He was going to be overtaken.

"No, Lance!" A great power grabbed him around his shoulders, and yanked him through an open door in the corridor. Miraculously, the room was extremely well lit. Lance heard the energy rush past him in the corridor and stared, wide-eyed, into Michael's face.

They were in what appeared to be an industrial kitchen, with clean ceramic tile and an array of cooking utensils and appliances. Lance had landed flat on his back, on what appeared to be a simple counter.

As Lance attempted to get his bearings, he realized that the hallway was completely engulfed, top to bottom, in purple energy. It was hovering before, but not entering, the room. It just remained there statically, ominously flowing like a thick liquid.

"It's his barrier," commented Michael calmly. "From this point on, nothing will be able to move in or out. Fortunately, we're on the right side." The angel stepped back and said, with warmth in his gaze. "I'm glad you were able to make it in time."

Lance leapt from the table and resummoned his manta, which he had dropped when Michael wrenched him away. "Do you know where they are?" he asked the Archangel breathlessly. Michael nodded.

"The middle of the field, in the centre of the stadium. Both of them."

"Let's split up, go from different angles. With a well-timed surprise, we will-" Michael placed his hand on Lance's shoulder and shook his head.

"No, Lance," he said, quietly. "There will be no surprises. He knows exactly where we are." He lightly steered Lance away from the barrier, facing him towards the centre of the arena. "Come with me. We'll stay together. When I make my move, secure the human."

Michael squeezed Lance's shoulder, reassuringly, before continuing. "Protect the bearer Lance, but please allow me to converse with Gazardiel, no matter what he says. I know he was once your friend, but do not let him beguile you."

"He may have been my friend, once," admitted Lance. "But Michael, Gazardiel was your brother!"

He studied Michael's face after speaking, but as usual was able to discern nothing from the smooth visage with blazing white eyes. He wondered if the handsome look was really a front, a mask, a show of strength that concealed the pain that Lance thought the angel was feeling. Or perhaps Michael felt nothing at all. Lance would never know.

Without another word, Michael strode forward, and Lance followed suit, lingering slightly behind. It wasn't long before they emerged onto the main terrace, which was lit at midfield by a faint golden glow, leaving everywhere else shrouded in blackness. Even the tiers of seats were hidden from view.

In the epicentre of the glow, Lance could see Emma. She floated gracefully, her hair lightly bobbing. It was obvious that she had suffered great trauma. Her clothing was torn and marked, her hair dishevelled, and her face was contorted in a wretched expression. Emma was in pain.

And there, towering above her, was Gazardiel. Or at least, a being that once might have been Gazardiel.

His right side was completely normal, with the handsome and hardy face that Lance knew so well. The left side, however, was no longer recognizable. It had a roughly humanoid silhouette, but was pitch black. It was so dark that it actually stood out against the contrasting gloom of the arena. It reminded Lance, forcefully, of the void.

The form flowed in and out of focus, twisting through the air like Abyss' smoke. There were no discernible features, except for the left eye, which burned with the purple fluorescence that Lance knew he was about to face.

Abstract plates of energy floated along the side, like pieces of armour. They were triangular and the same colour as the eye. An unusual pattern of lines and dot-like circles adorned them, reminiscent of an artist's depiction of computer circuitry.

Two triangles floated on his face, one directly above his eyeline pointing up to the sky, and one below, its tip directed at the ground. They left a narrow slit of shifting dark at exactly eye-level, where the lavender eye shined brilliantly. It gave Gazardiel's side the appearance of being helmed. Lance wondered if it were the Fragment's energy that had changed him, or merely Gazardiel's own will.

"Ah, damn," Gazardiel spoke. His voice sounded the same, but it was followed by a second intonation. The echo was deeper and distorted, almost robotic. "I had hoped the barrier had been erected in time."

The right side of his face grinned, as he glared at the Archangel. "Michael, I always knew I'd end up fighting you today." His eyes then focused on Lance, his mouth stretching into a taunting leer.

"But I had honestly hoped I had sensed *his* presence incorrectly," he said, shaking his head derisively as he turned back to Michael. "I am dismayed that you brought that failure to help. I am insulted, Michael. I figured you would at least have Peter with you. Or even Abyss, or that geriatric reaper Enigma. Anything but *Lance*. He is a hindrance, a handicap, Michael—more likely to kill you, and himself, than be of any use. Him being here means I don't get the pleasure of defeating you at your total strength."

Angrily, Lance met Gazardiel's gaze for a moment, before instantly regretting it. The betrayer's humanoid eye was filled with hostility and madness. Into its depths had been poured an eternity of malice, and now it was quivering and shaking on the breaking point, ready to finally explode in a tempest of violence.

At that point, any memory Lance had of Gazardiel was forever changed. Any doubt he had, any reservation about fighting him, was gone completely. It was clear; it had been an act. All of it. Lance immediately looked to Emma, resisting the urge to cry out. Gazardiel laughed as he followed Lance's look.

"It's a shame you weren't here earlier. Her screams were deafening." He reached out a hand and played with her hair, before slowly stroking her cheek. "It seems she has fallen unconscious, I'll have to wake her."

Pulsing purple energy crystallized around one of his fingers, which he suddenly sliced across Emma's face, drawing blood. "Having the energy removed from her body in such a way... it's excruciating. Like being ripped *limb from limb*."

Lance shook with rage. It took every ounce of his self-control, control he had lacked just a few days ago, to keep himself from attacking right now. But he remembered the Archangel's words. Not yet.

"Gazardiel, what you have done is beyond forgiveness." Michael moved to his left as he spoke. Comprehension dawning, Lance slowly inched to his right, further away from his ally. Gazardiel was entirely focused on Michael. To him, Lance was less than an afterthought, a fly to a bull. But Lance's path to Emma was beginning to clear.

"That revenant could destroy the entire city!" the Archangel continued.

"Oh, did you like him?" taunted Gazardiel, a smirk stretching across his half-face. "It was all too easy to form, you know. There is enough hatred in this infested slum of a city to raise a hundred of its kind!"

"You will not harm them."

Gazardiel's eye narrowed, his smirk melting from his face.

"We will see, *brother*; after I destroy you, I plan on slaughtering *every, last, one*."

Michael shook his head, an act that appeared to annoy Gazardiel greatly.

"Despite any dark energy you have turned to, you lack the strength to defeat me."

Gazardiel chuckled darkly.

"That's where you are wrong. I have absorbed the power of the Fragment. I AM A GOD!" Purple lightning flashed from his hands as Gazardiel emphasized the last few words.

"The Fragment would reject you," said Michael, matter-of-factly.

"Wrong again, Michael!" cried Gazardiel, gleefully pointing towards his waist. "The belt of the Grim Reaper! The loser over there almost foiled my plan in the tomb, but no matter, for I persevered. Don't you see Michael? The belt is the catalyst. You're right, I couldn't absorb the power myself. But the Grim could, back before the world was rotten, and his legacy can still! I have feasted on the energy of the Creator while you fools searched and seeked. And now, I am too strong to lose."

Lance continued to move slowly to his right. Gazardiel had said little that they did not already know, but now Lance wondered about the timing of his visit to the tomb. Had they arrived mere seconds after Gazardiel?

"Why?" It was a simple enough question, but from the moment Michael asked it, Lance knew it was one Gazardiel had been dying to answer.

"Because creation must be protected! I will not permit you, or the other angels, to allow the destruction to continue!"

"Your plan to protect creation is to destroy a city?" Lance could not tell if the Michael was taunting Gazardiel or was genuinely confused.

"Not just a city. Humanity!" answered Gazardiel brashly.

"Gazardiel, you fool!" chastised Michael, his voice increasing in volume as he spoke. "Humanity *is* creation."

"No, Michael! Humanity is the scourge of it! You've seen what they've done, to their world, to each other. They desecrate everything the Creator gave them. They are a plague, an infestation." Gazardiel stole a quick, malevolent glance at Lance before looking back to Michael, not noticing or caring about their change in position. "One I intend to eliminate"

"Humans are the greatest of all creation," proclaimed Michael.

"You *would* say that. Your compassion for them has always sickened me. They are a mistake, the Creator's biggest failure. They will destroy the planet; they will consume its beauty. They could even overwhelm Paradise as they multiply endlessly. Even amongst themselves, they cause pain. They have no redeeming qualities."

"If creation is to destroy creation, then so be it," stated Michael, the passion in his voice evident. "It would be as intended, but you know there is no such future. Humanity continues to inspire, to improve and to protect." He chuckled to himself, startling Lance, before continuing, "And they have no shortage of redeeming qualities. Just look at Lance."

"Hah!" snarled Gazardiel, annoyed with Michael's rebuttal. "He is the posterchild for the human condition. A perpetual disappointment, a worthless weakling who has no control. He fails at every turn, latching onto luck, or the success of others. Gifted with power that he lazily squanders through lack of discipline. He is incapable and incompetent. Beyond that, he is the reason for my success. Lance handed me the Fragment!"

Lance felt sick. He tried to ignore Gazardiel, to disregard his words. But they had reached him, and they stung. It was true. He had handed Emma over to Gazardiel. He would never forgive himself for that. And he hadn't done a thing on his own, not since the Fragment first landed. Pajetic was always there to help him, or Enigma, or...

His thoughts were interrupted by Michael who yelled at the top of his lungs, his outraged voice booming throughout the stadium.

"Lance is all that is bright in humanity. He has latent power which he works tirelessly to control. He is imperfect, yes. But he listens when needed and never gives up. He has unquenchable hope. More importantly, Lance loves fiercely. He cares, and that caring nature brings him the strength he needs. It brings strength to all those around him."

Lance's face was still, as he strained to show absolutely no emotion.

"I noticed it from the minute I met him, and it is something you will never understand, Gazardiel, twisted and broken as you are." Michael planted his feet, and Lance could see the glow of his sword-manta being called forth.

"You must fail if you are to learn. You must fall before you can rise. And you must be harshest on those you see with the most potential. Humans like Lance are the reason why they have such a promising future, and why I would die for them." There was a flash of purple lightning, and Lance knew Gazardiel was summoning his own weapon as well. Another mighty sword.

"Pathetic," he said disdainfully, apparently regaining his cool. "Lance wasn't loving and caring when you met him. The seal removed his emotions. You grasp at straws Archangel."

"That is my greatest regret," acknowledged Michael. "Denying reapers access to their greatest tool, and allowing myself to be swayed by *you*, Gazardiel. Treating just one case, the selfish acts of the first reaper, as an indictment of the entire group. But they've been freed now. And their emotions make them more powerful than you could possibly comprehend."

"You're referring to the emotions that lead them to genocide? The emotions that cause greed and revenants and pain? Those emotions?" Gazardiel shook his head, violently. "They are better off without them."

"No, Gazardiel. Emotion brings hope, emotion gives for no reason, emotion allows humans to achieve more than anyone thought possible. In fact, it is their emotions which will help us to defeat you, fallen one." White energy was crackling from Michael's fully summoned weapon and Lance could tell the battle was imminent.

Gazardiel laughed, a crazed, maniacal sound that sent shivers down Lance's spine. "There is no stopping me! I have the power of the Creator! I grow in strength every second that passes! Why do you think I've even bothered speaking with you? Each moment you waste in mindless chatter brings me more strength from the Fragment! I am the curtain that falls over the age of man! I AM GAZARDIEL! I AM THE NEW DAWN!"

Massive bolts of purple lightning flashed from Gazardiel's fingertips as he reached upwards to the skies. Lance was puzzled. Had Gazardiel not noticed? He looked at Michael, and was relieved to see that the Archangel was smiling.

"Interesting theory, Gazardiel, except I have sensed no change in your power since we started," said Michael confidently. Gazardiel's eyes widened, as if coming to a realization. "And why has the pull of your belt disappeared?"

"What? You stopped it?" cried Gazardiel, looking down in disbelief at the Grim Reaper's belt.

With a roar, Michael launched himself at Gazardiel, sword held high. Simultaneously, Lance streaked forward, his eyes set on Emma.

Chapter 25

Turning slowly, Pajetic moved to confront the leviathan He had always wanted to see his own death coming. He had done it once before, and he would do so again. The reapers were gone, Lance was gone, and confronting his end was the only triumph he could muster.

It was fitting, in a way. The futility of it all. There was a thunderous crack of pavement and concrete, as the creature clumsily shuffled towards him. It towered overhead, focused exclusively on Pajetic. He held out his swords once more, and a steady stream of acid green energy emanated from his body. "If I am to die, it will be fighting," he said, aloud.

Looking around, he noticed there were very few revenants left, flocking about and shoulders of the great beast. The triple-attack of the angelic force had decimated their ranks. And yet, there were still far too many.

He studied the giant revenant, looking up to its smug face. To his surprise, he realized that one of its six eyes had suffered significant damage. The orange glow had faded, and raw energy gushed from the deep black fissures that now permeated its ruined surface.

Pajetic grinned. He might not have been able to kill it, but at least, he had hurt it. The monster bellowed mightily, and Pajetic raised his swords.

"I AM NOT AFRAID!" he cried, preparing for his final battle. The creature stared down at him malevolently. Its lower jaw slowly opened, as it prepared to bring Pajetic to his end through a final, devastating attack.

Suddenly, out of the corner of his eye, Pajetic saw a rocket streak towards the beast. Then another, and another. In seconds, a barrage of missiles filled the air, hammering the beast's torso in a crescendo of explosions. Smoke engulfed the creature as with a roar of noise, the humans arrived.

A formation of jets engaged the revenants, launching their projectiles in complicated patterns while banking from the flailing leader. Next, a mighty fleet of helicopters swooped low, machine guns mercilessly peppering into the flock.

Pajetic watched in surprise as revenant after revenant fell towards earth, bodies dissipating in the wind, squawking and squealing as the explosives ripped them apart.

A deep boom sounded, and Pajetic nodded in approval as a tank, accompanied by several jeeps and a contingent of soldiers, advanced from the main city. Smoke trailed from the tank's main gun. Filled with new purpose, Pajetic raced towards the ground troops.

His intuition was correct, for with a bloodcurdling cry, a pack of revenants attacked the land-borne soldiers, tearing at those exposed and crushing steel vehicles between their claw. Pajetic watched help-lessly as the tank exploded, raining debris on the humans. The men fired chaotically, some at Pajetic. He ignored them all, heading for the largest jeep, which had two vulture-like revenants perched on its roof.

Arriving just in time, Pajetic cleaved the first one in two with his mantas. It fell to the ground in a twitching heap. The other was faced away as he arrived, and reacted slowly. Pajetic rewarded its sluggish-ness with a quick blast of energy. It toppled backwards, its face charred and its power spent.

Desperately ripping the roof from the jeep, and still ignoring the flying bullets which simply bounced off his form, Pajetic searched inside. Within the frame were several soldiers, pressed as far against the floor of the vehicle as they could be.

Pajetic instantly recognized his target. A white-haired man cow-ered at the front of the jeep, wearing a fancy uniform adorned with countless medals and stars. A leader.

"Tell them to attack the monsters!" yelled Pajetic at the com-mander, who stared at him uncomprehendingly. Pajetic realized, with annoyance, how brightly his eyes were glowing. "Those of us who look human, we are here to help! We are angels!"

He rose above what was left of the vehicle to survey the scene. Many of the soldiers were gaping at him, open-mouthed, while others were fighting the revenants. He realized that they had stopped shoot-ing him.

"ATTACK ALL NON HUMANS" he shouted, repeating his message. He looked back at the one in charge, who was now clutch-ing a radio, relaying his words. "The big one," Pajetic added, hurriedly pointing to it. "It charges an attack that could level a city.

Everyone and everything needs to avoid those blasts or it *will* be the end." The man nodded, and spoke even faster, rattling off orders and coordinates into the radio.

The revenants had been taken aback by the sudden arrival of support. The few that remained were on the run, flying about in a panic as they frantically tried to flee from the weapons and aircraft.

Unfortunately, the principal one appeared unfazed and unharmed, impervious to the missiles and bullets. It swiped its massive pincers angrily at the passing aircraft, who were for the most part more than agile enough to avoid his cumbersome gambits.

Continuing his surveillance, Pajetic's heart leapt as he saw flashes of spiritual power amongst the flailing bodies and gunfire. There were at least some spirits still fighting. "Attack him!" He yelled, gesturing at the main revenant and trying to fill the leadership void now that the senior spirits were gone.

Rushing up to the giant, Pajetic shot a flurry of emerald power at the creature's scaly abdomen. He might as well have thrown a rock at it, for all the damage his moves did. Pajetic cursed and flew up to its head. He knew the eyes were vulnerable. As he approached the face, he noticed a cluster of orange energy gathering in its lower jaw. *SHIT.*

"RUN!" he cried, immediately retreating from the line of fire. He dropped backwards as the assault unfurled before him. The mouth was pointed towards a particularly substantial formation of helicopters, which soared to the right without delay. Pajetic smiled. The beast was too slow. The humans should be able to dodge its deadly payload, there was no doubt.

However, Pajetic high hopes were quickly dashed. Just as the assault was unleashed, the revenant twitched to the left, zeroing in on the flight path of the helicopters at a startling speed. It was a small shift, but it made a huge difference. Although the beam still missed its targets, it streaked close nearby. Pajetic winced as the shockwave battered the machines, sending most of them careening out of control.

Shuddering, they struggled against gravity as they rode out the force. Pajetic expected the worst, but watched in amazement as the pilots successfully stabilized their vehicles, regaining altitude and resuming their flight pattern.

"Yes!" cheered Pajetic jubilantly, as the revenant roared in frustration. He then looked back up to its mouth, any confidence quickly melting away. There was already another gathering of orange power.

"That soon? What?" said Pajetic, in shock. He remembered Enigma's words about the monster's need to recharge after an attack. The reaper had been wrong. And that was not all that wasn't the only bad news.

The behemoth's mouth was pointed, not towards enemy troops, but instead towards the atmosphere above, where not a single jet or helicopter lingered. "What is it doing?" Pajetic gaped in dismay as the ball of energy grew larger... and larger... and larger. It consumed the monster's entire face, looking like a second sun in the hazy city sky. For all his skill, Pajetic was no prepared for this.

The humans scrambled as the attack charged, flying in confused, haphazard circles. They continued to bombard the revenant, but it completely ignored them as the orb reached blinding levels of luminescence. Shivers running through his form, Pajetic hastily erected a shield of green energy and braced himself. Something big was on its way.

With a blast ten times the magnitude of any other, the attack erupted into life. But there was no massive beam aimed at the sky, as Pajetic had anticipated. Instead, a rain of orange rays of energy erupted from the orb, hurtling erratically in every single direction.

Or maybe not as erratically as Pajetic had thought. With horror, he quickly diagnosed their movements. *They're tracking*.

The assembled forces broke ranks, attempting to dodge and flee from the deadly projectiles. None were successful. Helicopter after helicopter, jet after jet, each was pierced with the overpowering shafts of force, and each disappeared, consumed in a fiery explosion.

Pajetic whirled about, searching for the one with his name on it. He was almost too late; it had curved around from behind and was blazing violently towards him.

Pajetic stared at the attack, not moving a muscle. Projecting where it was headed, he hurriedly formed a small, intensely concentrated shield and placed it right between himself and the imminent danger. Pajetic readied for what would come next.

An enormous impact flung him backwards, but miraculously, his shield held. The missile of orange energy had evaporated, converted to pure force. Pajetic laughed out loud in relief. Just above the battle-field, a few lonely helicopters hovered in the air, having somehow persevered through the armageddon.

Everything else, entire city blocks, the pavement and roads, the stadium, was all destroyed. It was engulfed in an inferno, searing in great pillars of fire which towered above the rubble. Pajetic had never witnessed such devastation. He breathed heavily; projecting the shield had taken almost all of his strength. He would not survive another as-sault.

He had to act decisively, or the battle would truly be lost. Pajetic remained calm. He had despaired once already, and the human army was spent. Now he had to think. His adversary stood tenaciously be-fore him, jaws bared. It was just the two of them, a sliver of green and a bastion of orange, painted onto a canvas of brick and flame.

It glared right at him once more, loathing apparent in its cruel or-ange eyes. Pajetic was certain it remembered him. He hurt it. Now he needed to kill it. Quick as a whip, Pajetic bolted for the nearest gigan-tic pincer. He had a plan.

"Aim for the big one, wait for my signal!" he yelled, projecting his voice as far as he could, hoping there were enough survivors to carry out his plan. He slashed at the creature's nearby pincer with his mantas, immediately banking up, narrowly out of reach.

The revenant roared angrily, and Pajetic felt it slashing upwards in an uppercut motion, a wall of scaled flesh chasing him as he as-cended. "Come on! COME ON!" taunted Pajetic, through clenched teeth.

Upon reaching the monster's face, Pajetic darted to the side, al-lowing the claw to extend up to the monster's eye level beside him. He regarded the claw for a second, his plan revolved around it not moving an inch. He bravely faced the creature, whose six eyes stared hatefully back at him. Its two mouths were beginning to open, slowly.

"ME VERSUS YOU!" cried Pajetic, raising his mantas to a point above his head. A sphere of green formed at the tip of his swords, pulsing and growing in size. "Come on!" he said, ready to move at the slightest act. A globe of expanding orange energy again appeared in the creature's mouth. "Is that all you've got? Is that the best you can do?" challenged Pajetic, carefully watching the orb.

It seemed to Pajetic like time itself slowed down. Every detail was sharpened before him. Pajetic could see each scale on the leviathan's face and count every jagged fang in its vicious jaws. Its ball of power grew at an agonizingly slow pace, as fleck after fleck was added to its mass. Pajetic didn't move a muscle.

Everything snapped back to full speed as Pajetic suddenly surged to his right, towards the upraised claw of the revenant. He had to move at the perfect speed—just slow enough that it thought it could kill him.

As he had hoped, the mammoth beast twitched, ever so slightly, to follow his trajectory. But the dumb brute had forgotten where its other limbs were, particularly the one that was upraised, right near the height of its firing mouth. Now, in its haste to murder Pajetic, it pointed its assault directly at its own upraised pincer. Pajetic wished he could have seen its eyes, to know if, at this very point, confusion and fear clouded the burning hatred.

Too late to alter its course, the massive beam of orange shot from the monster's jaws, missing Pajetic, and destroying the behemoth's own claw. A nauseating burnt odour permeated the air as the extremity burnt away. All that remained was a fractured, broken stump. The revenant howled in pain, for the very first time.

"FIRE!" shouted Pajetic, who had shielded himself from the shockwave of the attack. He rushed back up to the creature's head and sent blast after blast of acid energy at its face. Defenceless and bewildered, it staggered backwards. A flash of blue energy shot towards the beast's chest, as did a streak of yellow lightning, followed by a burst of indigo flames. The effect was multiplied as the remaining humans deployed their arsenal. Their missiles found their target, burrowing deep into the gigantic revenant's suddenly permeable hide, as it stumbled back another step.

Pajetic brought his mantas together, crossing them over his head, and used the last of his power. He began to spin, faster and faster, until he became a green cyclone of energy. Following up the other's assault, Pajetic whirled with alacrity into the revenant's already weakened eye.

He stabbed into it with the point of his swords, drilling into the revenant, plunging himself into total blackness. The blinded leviathan screamed, and Pajetic felt its defences crumble, allowing him to burrow deep inside, into its very center.

He corkscrewed for another second, then stopped, releasing every ounce of his power in a colossal storm of energy. He even threw his swords, letting them tear through the soft inside core.

In an instant, the screaming stopped. Slowly, pockets of light pierced the dark as his victim's head dissolved. Fine strands of energy lightly wove away from the monster as Pajetic lingered in the air, even as the great being's body crashed down towards the ground far below. It landed in a heap and slowly disintegrated, in front of what used to be the stadium. It had been completely demolished, revealing now a globular shield of purple energy.

Pajetic hovered alone in the sky, far above the carnage wreaked by the battle. It seemed peaceful up there, but he knew he had to move. He heard a faint cheering, as if a million voices were all joined together, drifting from the direction of the city. Lazily, he let himself float down to the ground, where he knelt, exhausted, facing the shifting purple barrier.

Barely conscious, Pajetic lacked the strength to even contemplate trying to break in, and had a strong sense that he would fail, even if he did. He watched it passively as the energy shifted slightly, gurgling and buzzing as it moved.

"That's where Michael is," he said aloud, to no one in particular. "And Lance," he added. "And Lance," he repeated with greater certainty. He knew Lance was in there. There was no spiritual sense telling him this, nothing altogether reasonable, or calculated. Just a feeling. But he knew it. His friend was in there.

The sound of a helicopter interrupted Pajetic's reflection. He turned to watch as one dropped low, rushing right to his side. A rope was flung from a doorway, and a soldier rappelled hastily down. Pajetic did nothing, merely observing. Humans were not spiritually strong. They could not summon mantas nor project power. But they could fly regardless.

The soldier reached the ground and struggled for a moment to detach himself from his harness, before approaching Pajetic. Once he had removed his helmet, Pajetic recognized him as the white-haired commander he had saved earlier.

"We did it! We got the bastard!" cried the captain, joyously. Pajetic merely nodded calmly. He wondered, mutely, how the human had managed to survive the destructive tracking attack. The captain turned to follow Pajetic's gaze and stared in astonishment at the shield which, to him, looked like a big purple mass of jelly.

"We can't get in there?" the captain asked anxiously, adjusting his helmet, absent-mindedly.

"No," replied Pajetic, calmly, still observing the oval of purple energy. "It's a sphere that extends underground."

"What's in there?" the captain asked, curiously.

"Everything" answered Pajetic simply.

Come on, Lance.

Chapter 26

Michael heaved a mighty swing at Gazardiel, slashing at the monster's dark side, near his head. Distracted and bewildered by the ineffectiveness of the Grim Reaper's belt, a clever trick of Michael's, Gazardiel was not properly prepared.

However he reacted quickly, barely bringing his own manta up in time to parry the assault. He gave ground, moving backwards as Michael launched strike after strike relentlessly.

Ducking behind the battling titans, Lance swooped over to Emma. He snatched her from her hovering position in the air and pulled her tightly into his arms.

Immediately he set off, tearing across the field as he fled from the warring angels. He breathed a sigh of relief when he saw her chest expand and contract slightly, proving that Gazardiel had not managed to destroy her—yet.

Although curious about the melee behind him, Lance dared not pause to glance behind. Without hesitation, he directed his movement towards the outer wall of the building. He had to get Emma out of here, somewhere safe from Gazardiel's madness.

The fallen angel retreated a few steps further before Michael's onslaught, but the Archangel's advantage of surprise has been lost. Gazardiel seemed to be clearing his mind, deflecting each slash with progressively greater ease. Before long, it was Michael who was on the back foot. And Gazardiel had time to think of more than his immediate opponent.

He stared past the Archangel, noticing Lance's flight. Planting his feet, he lashed out with his manta, imbuing it with purple energy. Michael leapt to safety, avoiding impact, and landing roughly fifteen feet away. He never took his eyes from Gazardiel, who had shifted his onto Lance.

"Where do you think you're going, whelp?" the dark angel yelled angrily, as two sinister shadows started to emerge from his shoulders. Michael immediately charged Gazardiel, who was at once forced to the defensive, but not before two huge, feral, wolves had dropped to the ground at his sides.

They paced menacingly, growling as they slowly turned towards Lance. Their forms were as dark as Gazardiel's left half, with jolts of purple highlighting their fur and glowing eyes and fangs to match.

"Run Lance!" called Michael, redoubling his efforts as the wraith-like canines tore after the young reaper. Lance instantly bolted from the arena as the conflict between the angels resumed.

Michael's assault was tremendous. He attacked at the speed of light, interweaving strikes with crackling blasts of spiritual energy. Tendrils of white energy stretched from his body, wrestling with Gazardiel as Michael tried to gain some toehold against his foe's defences.

But Gazardiel was indomitable. The betrayer matched Michael's pace, meeting every single advance with his sword and repelling Michael's spiritual attacks through his own dark purple energy. Streaks of white and purple lightning flashed through the stadium, illuminating the entire field.

And yet, bit by bit, Gazardiel's defence grew less frenetic, as he once again adjusted to Michael's fighting style. After easily blocking a wild slash by Michael, the rhythm of the battle shifted markedly as Gazardiel went on the offensive.

He stabbed out with his own sword, a strike Michael managed to deflect off course. Gazardiel swiftly followed up with another great strike, and all of a sudden, it was Michael losing ground. The Archangel twisted and turned, his platinum hair flying through the air as he moved in a blur of speed, fending off the vicious barrage.

The two blades suddenly froze, as they met energy crackling in midair, directly between Michael and Gazardiel. The angels trembled with effort, each determined to push the other back, but neither able to gain the upper hand.

"You cannot defeat me," said Michael, in a strained voice.

"That remains to be seen, *brother*," breathed Gazardiel, breaking the guard and resuming the battle.

***

Lance fled, melting through countless walls and rooms, until he and his precious charge reached the very edge of the building. He was thankful that melding through physical objects was still possible in this new merged realm, but continuing to do so came at a cost: it consumed more energy than flitting between the physical and spiritual plane ever would.

Resolving to avoid this tactic unless it was absolutely necessary, Lance came to an abrupt halt. Gazardiel's purple barrier shimmered before him. He stole a quick glance behind and saw nothing. That did little to ease his nerves, as he could sense the wolves closing in on them. He hadn't much time.

"Damn," he cursed to no one in particular, as he imbued his manta with his crimson energy. Mindful of Emma, whom he held protectively with his left arm, Lance struck at the barrier with all his might, hoping to somehow break through.

He achieved nothing, as the barrier held firm, rippling around the point of impact. It glowed resolutely, taunting Lance with its ominous purple hue. A low growl caused Lance to spin around.

There, gradually emerging from the wall, were his two pursuers. Lance stared at them, meeting their deadly purple gaze. He let the crimson in his eyes intensify, perhaps subconsciously attempting to intimidate them. Crouching and carefully placing Emma on the ground behind him, Lance prepared for the pounce.

At once, the two lunged forward, purple teeth snapping. Red energy bloomed around Lance, engulfing him in a familiar barrier of strength. He charged to meet them, hurrying to keep their inevitable collision as far from Emma as possible. It was a very one-sided affair. With a single swipe of their massive paws, Lance's best defence evaporated like water.

Shocked, Lance was forced to dart away or be mauled by their fierce claws. He rushed downwards, flinging his body on top of Emma, just in time to have the two beasts fly over them, crashing with a thud into the powerful purple wall.

Crying out, Lance slashed at the closest one with his manta, trying to bury it in its black flank. Its tip simply bounced off, as if he had struck at rock with a butter knife.

At that point, Lance grabbed Emma, turned, and fled. They were too powerful. He could not fight these avatars. But maybe he could run.

Manta in one hand, Emma in the other, Lance hurtled through a wall, attempting to put distance between him and them. He dashed through room after room, Emma's glow softly illuminating each one as they went. He saw a merchandise stand, then a restaurant, and then another industrial kitchen. He could feel the wolves closing in.

Panicking, Lance leapt upwards, through the ceiling of the room he was in, and onto a large concrete concourse. Sprinting along the curved path, Lance was afforded the occasional view of the field, where the angels continued their epic confrontation.

He stole another glance behind him, and to his surprise, did not see any trace of the two beasts. Unfortunately, this did not mean they weren't hot on his trail. Lance realized this quickly as to his dismay a fearsome dark head slid up through the concrete floor before them. It blocked Lance's path, its jagged teeth bared angrily.

Wheeling around, Lance backtracked, fleeing from the threat. Out of the corner of his eye, he saw something burst through the wall to his right. He dropped to the ground with a crash as a black and purple blur shot above them, fierce purple claws raking the air where they had just been.

An enormous tremor of spiritual power suddenly shook through the stadium, causing the entire structure to tremble and jarring Lance as he rose to his feet. He kept moving, not devoting any time to thought. The two spirits, however, paused.

***

"You have already failed!" cried Michael, a triumphant smile crossing his face. "They did it. They felled the giant." Gazardiel scowled, his face obscured.

"It makes no difference. I will kill your comrades, personally, once I absorb the rest of the Fragment's strength. They merely delayed the inevitable."

Energized by the success of the angels, Michael seized the opportunity to attack, lashing out with his manta again and again. Each strike grew in intensity, and his momentum lost, Gazardiel was forced once again to give ground.

Leaping into the sky, Michael let his coils of white energy coalesce into beautiful wings of divine light. He hung in the air for a second, a brilliant star amidst the night of the looming grandstands.

Then he dove, streaking towards Gazardiel, who erected a barrier of energy similar to the shield that surrounded the stadium. Slashing with his sword, Michael hammered at the obstacle, shattering it like glass into a million Fragments of power. Charging through the rain of energy, Michael prepared to stab Gazardiel, but was unexpectedly interrupted as he was rebuked by an unmovable mass.

Gazardiel stood below him, suddenly much taller, easily grasping the Archangel's cloth tabard with an outstretched arm. A latticework of purple energy threaded out from his hand, ensnaring and immobilizing Michael.

Gazardiel stared into his rival's eyes, and grinned wickedly, revealing horrible cracked and pointed teeth. "I'm more powerful than you could possibly imagine," he taunted, raising his manta and preparing to administer the death blow. He watched Michael impassively for a moment, before dropping his blade in a vicious slice.

With a sound like fabric ripping, the purple web of energy imprisoning Michael disintegrated as he unleashed a staggering torrent of strength.

The lines of energy shredded apart, as the Archangel fell to the ground, aiming his manta at Gazardiel's thigh. His sword connected, tearing into his adversary while Gazardiel's weapon swept only through air. Howling in pain, he recoiled from Michael, who challenged him fearlessly.

***

Lance moved with renewed vigor. Pajetic and the angels had done it! Now he had to fulfill his end of the bargain. He rounded a corner, refusing to rest and give the wolves a chance to catch up. He heard Gazardiel cry out in pain. Lance cheered inwardly.

He knew that sustaining his two minions taxed Gazardiel greatly. It sounded like the stress was taking its toll, and Michael was finally gaining the upper hand in combat.

A burst of black melted through the concrete beneath him, and Lance launched himself upward, to the third level of the stadium, as a set of jaws snapped at his ankles. Lance spun, preparing for another attack from below.

Without warning, Lance was tackled from behind by the second wolf. Crying out, Lance twisted round, desperate to protect Emma. Purple claws tore into his essence, but finally Lance was able to shed the wolf's grasp.

Just as he made his escape, the first wolf emerged from floor below and stampeded towards Lance. He had no time to dodge. The beast collided into his chest snout first, knocking Lance and Emma through the roof of the third floor, onto the highest level of the stadium. The wolf fell away from the two, but Lance's momentum carried them through the fourth level concourse, back to the inside of the arena. They crashed out onto the stadium seats, far above the dueling angels below.

***

Michael's attacks continued, each one drawing closer to home. Gazardiel laboured to defend himself, fighting both Michael and his own injury. Exhausted, he parried each advance a little later as wisps of Michael's white energy bore down upon him, his mouth agape, and his face showing not disdain or rage… but unconcealed fear.

***

Lance rolled to the side, ignoring his injuries and taking hold of Emma, whom he had dropped during the impact. He had used his energy to protect her as best he could. Thankfully, she was still breathing, but her body was now scraped and bruised.

Up above them, Lance could see the two wolves, descending inexorably towards him. Lance and Emma had landed in a low row of seats, so the pair was a fair distance from them. He looked quickly to Michael, who appeared to have Gazardiel on the ropes. "Hurry!" he pleaded desperately, settling into a crouch position.

***

With a roar, Michael struck at his enemy with such force that he knocked the dark angel to the ground. Gazardiel frantically fended off blow after blow, tendrils of white energy almost completely surrounding him.

***

The first wolf darted at Lance, who cut to his right. The creature skidded through the stands, swiping futilely at him as it passed. It crushed the seats before it, spraying metal and cheap plastic through the air. Lance reasoned it no longer had the energy to stay incorporeal. Gazardiel was nearly through.

The other one pounced, and Lance spun, trying to keep Emma out of harm's way. At the same moment, the first minion jumped up from below, teeth barred. Lance immediately abandoned his twirl, now pushing Emma to his left and using the inertia to dive to the right. The first wolf careened between them, missing both, and demolishing more seats. Lance immediately rose, hastily trying to locate Emma. Instead, all he could see was a mass of black as a great paw swept towards his face.

Lance didn't have time to move.

Wham.

The impact sent him flying through the air from the highest level of the stadium. He dropped like a stone, propelled away from Emma before crashing down onto the main field. He had hardly laid on his back for a second before he saw two dark shapes leap into the air, hurtling in his direction. Lance felt a sense of relief; they had left Emma.

The two wolves bore down upon him, moving closer and closer together until they merged into a single cloud of black and purple energy, which fluidly formed into the rough shape of a lethal spear.

Lance was transfixed, and powerless to move. He remembered the sensation of being trapped on the bridge, with death approaching unstoppably. He traced the weapon's trajectory through the sky as it descended upon him. This time, he would not close his eyes.

"Lance! No!" In a flash, Michael appeared directly beside him. Brandishing his manta, Michael met the spear head on and sliced into it, dividing the former spear into two useless streams of black energy.

The power dissipated into the air, fleeing Michael's blade in every direction. With relief, Lance struggled to his feet to meet the Archangel. His reserves were seriously depleted.

"Thank you, my friend," he said, with a feeble smile. Michael stood before him, completely motionless. Not a single limb moved, and the filaments of energy that had blown about around him earlier were now apathetically slumped to the floor. Lance's smile immediately faded. "Michael?" he asked, his voice betraying his fear.

To his horror, a cruel purple blade slowly poked through the centre of Michael's chest, and the Archangel fell to his knees, revealing Gazardiel's spectral frame. He was looming over the pair of them, his manta fully implanted within Michael's back.

"NOOOOOOOOOOO!" Lance quickly jumped to his feet and sprang back, still screaming, as Gazardiel pushed Michael to the ground with his foot, extracting his blade disinterestedly. Raising his free hand, Gazardiel again shot out a web of purple energy towards his victim, who was soon imprisoned by an immobilizing mesh of power.

Shaking his head slowly, he turned to Lance, who had knelt to the ground, tears falling from his eyes. *Why did Michael save him? He could have defeated Gazardiel! They would have won.*

"It always was a weakness of his," observed Gazardiel coldly. "He tried to hide it with bare logic and regal power, but I knew." The monster strode towards Lance, who still sobbed quietly. "He cared so much about humans, about others. We almost lost to the Grim Reaper because of his moronic attempt to save Gabriel."

Lance screamed and charged at Gazardiel, swinging his manta with all his might. Gazardiel effortlessly blocked the attack with his free hand, before bringing his manta down upon Lance's scythe, shattering it.

"How dare you lift OUR gift against me, impudent rat," he growled, gripping Lance's head and using it as a handle to whip him through the air violently. "We are the ones who gave you the mantas!"

Lance hit the ground and collapsed, having used the last of his strength in his strike. He knew what was coming, and struggled to get up as Gazardiel approached, but failed; only managing to get to one knee.

The traitor paused, towering above the hunched reaper. "And, one again, he has sacrificed himself for someone else. Look where it's got him." He nudged Lance with his foot, a force strong enough to knock the reaper sprawling over. "He could have let you die, destroyed me, and claimed victory." Gazardiel raised his hand into the air, pointing his manta down, in stabbing position, glaring at Lance.

With enormous effort, Lance raised his head, meeting the terrible angel's wrath with dignity. "The Archangel himself gave his life for you, worthless boy. But now... now there is no one left to be your shield. Finally, you are alone. Finally, your luck has run OUT!" With that last word, Lance watched helplessly as the blade began to descend.

He *did* love. Michael had been right. Lance had loved his family. He had loved his friends, those he had known back when he had been alive. He loved Enigma, his teacher and mentor. He loved Pajetic, his partner and friend. He loved life; he loved humanity—despite his own death, despite his own pain.

He had agreed to a great sacrifice, what seemed like ages ago, when he had first heard of the reapers. He had made it, not for power, fame or fortune, but because he wanted to protect those whom he loved. And despite all the trials he had gone through, all of the difficulties, he had not once doubted his decision.

It had always felt right to him, protecting the ones he loved. He saw them now; each of their faces appearing in perfect detail within his imagination. His dad's brave gaze, his mother's tender smile, his brother's confident smirk. But it was not only humans. He saw Enigma, with his bemused, wise expression. He saw Pajetic's with a slight grin—just towing the line between amusement and annoyance.

He thought of them as the blade plunged through his abdomen, puncturing his essence. The pain was excruciating, but he was comforted by the realization that his life had been one of purpose. Nothing could take that away.

Gazardiel chuckled and yanked his blade out while Lance convulsed pitiably on the ground. He victoriously turned his back from the defeated reaper, walking casually back to Michael, savouring his triumph.

Lance lay there, waiting for the pictures and memories to fade. For death to finally claim him as his spiritual being broke apart and scattered on the wind. But it did not happen. On the contrary, the images dancing through his consciousness grew stronger, more powerful.

All of a sudden, Lance realized that the pain from his wound was gone. Fresh power flooded through him, as he visualized one final face. The calm Archangel, Michael, who had sacrificed everything to save him.

"Get up Lance." Commanded the Archangel. "Fight him Lance."

He would not fail him.

"Stand again Lance."

He would not fail them.

"Save us Lance."

HE WOULD NOT FAIL.

Struggling, his form wavering like a poorly tuned television, Lance lifted himself off the ground, crimson energy flowing about his body. Essence seeping from his wound, Lance took his feet to battle once more.

The situation was bad. Even with a second wind, Lance knew was still outclassed by Gazardiel. And he didn't even have a weapon. Lance watched his enemy pace away from him, ignorant of his recovery, as his mind raced.

His manta was gone, but maybe... He scanned Gazardiel, looking for the artifact he knew the dark angel wore. There it was, around his waist.

The Grim Reaper's belt.

Pajetic had told him that *any* item of the Grim would be enough. He might not have a weapon, but perhaps he could summon one.

"You missed me," he said, with a voice much stronger than he felt, a plan developing in his mind.

Gazardiel whirled around, a look of incredulity flashing over his face. "You just don't want to die, do you?"

Reapers

"Like Michael said, you can't defeat us."

Gazardiel let out a sinister chuckle, "Well, at this point, it's clear he was wrong. How many times must I kill you to make you understand? You, and those you fight for, are scum."

"Take that back," roared Lance, assuming a ready stance.

"You. Fail." said Gazardiel, ignoring Lance's command. With a howl, Lance charged Gazardiel, trying to tackle his foe around the waist. This was it. All he had to do was touch it. Just touch it Lance! He reached out his arm, fingertips tantalizingly close to the belt's buckle. Come on!

But Gazardiel was too fast, and saw through Lance's gambit in an instant. Expertly wielding his manta, Gazardiel swung his sword through Lance's waist, cleaving him in two. Lance once again fell to the ground, again gripped in agony.

"Fool," taunted Gazardiel, smugly, looking from his belt towards Lance's rent form. "You hoped to free your own manta? Pitiful. You wouldn't even have the strength to summon it." He took a few steps away from Lance, towards Michael, before pausing to yell violently, "NOW STAY DEAD."

Lance lay there on the ground, decidedly not dead. He felt his two halves knitting together, bringing him back once more. His energy felt strained—he was spent—like when you run for hours then force yourself to sprint. But he had not achieved his goal, and he would not falter. Not yet.

There, in his mind, was one final option. One last desperate bid to stop this fiend. In the history of the world, only one reaper had managed to summon a manta without any assistance. If Gazardiel was to be stopped, Lance would have to be number two.

He had no idea how to do it. Hell, he could barely summon the fake manta the angels had given to him. He never studied the weapons, or knew the theory behind their conjuring. He didn't know any of that. But it had to be done.

Reaching deep into his soul, Lance thought of the people he cared about. He thought about his desire to protect them, his love for them. He saw his friends once more, along with hundreds of other faces. Humans, reapers and angels. They swarmed his consciousness; their survival depended upon him. With a mighty battle cry, Lance reached into his power, trying to shape it one last time.

"Impossible!" cried Gazardiel, furiously.

Time slowed to a crawl as the monstrous angel rounded on Lance, unleashing violent volleys of black and purple energy, trying to disrupt his plan. Lance saw the power streaking towards him, but paid it no heed.

He remained focused entirely within himself, straining to summon his own manta. Seconds dragged on as Lance drew closer to his goal. He could do it, Lance knew he could. But could he do it now? The manta lay just beyond his reach, each time he felt like he was close his hold upon it melted away, like he was trying to grasp a hilt of water.

Gazardiel's projectiles were almost upon him, and the manta still was not there. Lance felt his body buckle beneath him. He had nothing left. No power, no strength left to resist. But it didn't matter. He didn't need anything. He would *never* stop fighting.

Lance suddenly expanded his power outwards, in a final, self-destructive attack. If he was to die here, he would die fighting. His body exploded, torn piece by piece in a cascade of pain as he sacrificed his very self to sustain his last offence.

Lance felt a twinge of regret as he accepted that he couldn't do it. He couldn't summon a manta. His power was too heavy, it was too much to shape. He could not pull his manta from it. But that did not break his resolve. No, he might not be able to pull a sword from a stone. But he sure as hell could throw the stone!

His attack ballooned outward, finally making use of his immense strength in an unstoppable tirade. Pain and pride twisted through his mind as the last vestiges of his being burnt away. He wasn't strong enough to fight Gazardiel alone, he never had been. He had needed help.

He had needed Michael.

But he would try his best to make do without. He was stronger than even he knew.

As his consciousness faded at each passing metre, Lance felt something solid materialize in his hands. What was left of him smiled.

He could no longer see, but as destruction rained around him, he knew what he held. His own manta.

Finally, Lance understood. That was what it meant to be Lance, that was why he had said that name so long ago in the rain. He truly was a knight, always willing to give. And now he would give it all.

His assault bombarded Gazardiel, extinguishing the dark angel's ranged attacks in a tirade of strength. Gazardiel was engulfed in a crescendo of spiritual force, as he struggled to hold on, obscured within the whirlwind. The explosion reached its outer limits as Lance exhausted his, engulfing the entire stadium in its crimson glory.

And there, at the critical threshold of Lance's final act, a new power intervened.

Maybe it was his unquenchable hope. Maybe it was his great act of martyrdom. And maybe it was because he needed help. But, for the first time since it took refuge within Emma, the Fragment stirred.

With a deafening hum, a beam of golden energy suddenly sprang from a dark, forgotten point in the stands. It flowed into Lance, producing a glorious light, blinding in its intensity.

"What?" growled Gazardiel, emerging unscarred from the explosion, appearing shaken for the first time since Michael nearly ended their fight.

The light surged forth until it had completely engulfed Lance in a vortex of golden power. Energy streaked through the stadium, replacing the violent red glow of Lance's attack with a divine gold.

It burned with holy radiance, blinding any who could see with its incomprehensible incandescence. When it had faded, Lance one more stood in front of Gazardiel, this time with a confident smile on his face. In his hands, he held a staff.

It was fairly long, with a constant breadth throughout its golden shaft. Each tip was adorned with three ruby rings, giving it the appearance of a double-ended mace. The shaft was encrusted in jewels of every description and inscribed with a variety of runes. Some were in English, clearly spelling out the words, *Brave*, *Just* and *Pure*.

But the weapon was far from the only change. Lance himself had been transformed. No longer was he wearing a reaper's robe; instead, he was covered in shining golden plates of armor, much like those worn by the angels. On his forehead was an exquisite gold band, runed to match his staff and his hair had shifted colour, from silver to gold streaked with ruby. Grand wings of crimson flame burst from his shoulders, illuminating the field in a blaze of red.

"Only once..." murmured Gazardiel, "The Grim." Lance's smiled broadened, and clutching his magnificent staff in his right hand, he pointed it at Michael. A beam of red light, rimmed with gold, shot towards him.

The purple web of Gazardiel shredded before its strength, liberating the Archangel. The glow encircled Michael's form, dancing about his limbs and sealing the grievous wound in his chest. He sprang up to face Gazardiel, strength renewed, white tendrils whipping about his body.

"I told you," Michael boasted, his passionate voice full of pride. "Lance is everything that is good in humanity! You said he was undisciplined, and yet he summoned his own manta—only the second reaper in history to do so unassisted! You said he was weak, and yet *he is the one* who absorbed the power of the Fragment! A task beyond even you, for all your beloved *strength!*"

The Archangel and Lance both approached Gazardiel who stumbled as he retreated before their fury.

"This cannot be," he whispered in terror. His fearsome stature, his insidious duplicity, all were now gone. Gazardiel was nothing more than an empty shell, broken before Lance's triumph. There was no fury, and certainly no remorse. All that clutched to the former Archangel was madness.

"You've fallen short of our glory Gazardiel. May someone stronger than I take mercy on your soul!" cried Michael, advancing upon him. Lance charged ahead, reaching the betrayer first.

He swiped his manta through the air, leaving a magnificent trail of red and gold sparkling behind. Gazardiel meekly raised his weapon in defense, and as the mantas made contact, his purple sword shattered, just as Lance's scythe had moments before.

The shaft of Lance's manta slammed into Gazardiel's humanoid shoulder, forcing the angel to drop to his knees. Lance then stepped back, deferring to Michael for the finishing blow.

"I'll pray for you. Brother."

The Archangel brought the hilt of his sword back past his shoulder, then stabbed Gazardiel in the centre of his breast. Releasing the handle, Michael stepped back.

For a moment, the dark angel remained still, on his knees, with the sword planted through his body. His mouth gaped open in surprise, his expression one of complete shock.

Then gradually, his form stirred. The void-like parts of his body spread, slowly invading the last vestiges of the old Gazardiel. It corrupted like a disease across arms, legs, body and mind. When it had finished, all traces of Gazardiel were gone. All that remained was Michael's sword and dark, fleeting shadow.

With a crash, the floating sections of Gazardiel's armor fell to the ground, dissolving into a thousand miniscule pieces. The point where the sword had pierced his torso began to glow pure white, pulsing and growing in size. The shadows roiled, as if trying to flee from the scorching light. There was a bright flash; and then the sound of a sword clattering to the floor. And Gazardiel slipped into memory. Forever.

A cheer rang out, and Lance was startled to see a jubilant group of at least twenty spirits, as well as a larger group of humans, all standing within a few hundred yards, near an end of the stadium that had been obscured by Gazardiel's now extinguished purple barrier.

Lance saw that the arena outside the barrier had been completely pulverized, but paid it no heed. Ignoring everyone else, Lance softly drifted into the air, propelling himself to the upper level of the stadium.

There, amongst a multitude of obliterated seats, lay Emma. Her curly brown hair dirty, her clothes torn and her pale skin bruised. Lance reached out tenderly and lifted her up in his arms. He looked down upon her face, and saw not worry, nor confusion, nor torment, but peace. Her chest moved, but did so laboriously. The Fragment was gone. Her strength was gone. And she had been through enough.

Lance reached into himself, tapping into the gift she had given him, and slowly transferred some of his strength back into her. Her body shook as the rejuvenation occurred, bones and bruises mending in seconds.

Then, with a flutter, Emma opened her eyes. They we no longer an overwhelming shade of gold. Only a simple hazel. Although, if Lance looked hard enough, he might just be able to make out a glimmer of what she once was.

"Lance?" She managed to ask, tiredly. Lance nodded encouragingly. "You look... different."

Lance laughed happily. "So do you."

Emma managed a weak smile before taking in her surroundings. "What happened?" She asked, too tired to be anything but mystified. "Did you save me?"

Lance firmly shook his head.

"No Emma. You saved us all." And with that, Lance carefully took to the air, gently bringing Emma down to the ground as he descended back to Michael. There were a few others he wanted to see.

Down below, four of spirits had detached from the main group, and were swiftly rushing towards them. It was Pajetic, Abyss, Enigma and Peter. Lance landed quickly at the Archangel's side and looked to Pajetic.

His friend's face split into a goofy grin as he recognized Lance from the new outfit. Pajetic pointed, in amazement, at the new staff; Lance laughed and mouthed, "Later!"

Michael was the first to speak, directing his query Peter. "So you defeated it?" Peter shook his head, chuckling. "It was close. We were nearly destroyed by a direct hit." He continued, noticing Michael's inquisitive gaze. "Enigma shielded us from most of the damage, but we were still blasted miles away. It's a wonder in itself that Enigma didn't die."

"I nearly did." Said the old revenant craftily. "It actually came down to a lucky guess. At the last instant, I estimated the composition of the revenants attack, and managed to convert it into pure force. Incredibly, by the time we returned, Pajetic had annihilated the monstrosity."

"You?" questioned Lance, happily shoving Pajetic with his elbow. Pajetic nodded, weakly.

"I had some help. There were other spirits, and humans. It was a joint effort—together we took that monster down."

Lance looked past Pajetic, to the throng of euphoric humans, who were still rejoicing wildly along the edge of what used to be the arena. They stretched back as far as the eye could see, clambering all over the rubble. There were soldiers, but also thousands of everyday people. Men and women, parents and children, all celebrating their tri-triumph.

"We'll never be able to cover *this* up," said Lance dryly, addressing Michael who bobbed his head in agreement.

"No, we certainly won't," he said calmly.

"So then, what does this mean?" asked Abyss, who for once, almost sounded happy.

Michael shrugged unconcernedly, before letting his form swell, growing in stature so he would be visible to all. The cheering of the humans intensified as he addressed them, voice booming. "This means it is the beginning of a new era!" He spread his arms wide, and the jubilation intensified.

Michael looked down upon the spirits, quietly repeating to them. "A new era." They all nodded in agreement, confident in the future and believing in one another. Michael then turned back to the crowd and smiled, revealing his perfect white teeth. "An era... of hope!"

Epilogue

All alone, in a corner of a holding cell in the outermost ring of Abbadon, lay a single golden sphere of the Fragment's power. It had been left behind by two inexperienced reapers, who had brought it with them to their prison, and had been missed by all the angels who had rushed by since. It remained there in solitude, dormant within the silence.

Down below, on Earth, an unstoppable wave of spiritual energy collided with the immovable shield summoned by Michael, sending shock-waves of stupendous force shuddering through the spiritual plane.

The fall-out was beyond contemplation, and with a horrendous crash, the spiritual and physical collapsed into one another. There, in that moment, the impenetrable barriers between human and the divine were shattered, altering the course of the world.

The impact hit Paradise like an earthquake, with tremors running through its outer gates, vacant courtyard and empty tower. Even Abbadon itself trembled before its magnitude, the outer holding cells shaking and swaying drastically.

The vibrations caused the sphere to roll, slowly at first, then faster, along the floor of the room. It swerved to one side, before being redirected again with another violent shake of the realm. As the rumbling ceased, its momentum carried it forward—towards a shifting and swirling black cloud of void.

It passed through the void, sucking it up like a sponge, until it was brought to a halt by a scaly, clawed foot. The energy suddenly recoiled, as if it were trying to flee from danger. In the blink of an eye, the foot was replaced by a red-skinned hand. It snatched up the sphere, and wordlessly withdrew into the nothingness.

It did not take Bee long to liberate himself from the void. He strode confidently out of his cell, crushing the Fragment's energy in a vice-like grip. He grinned victoriously.

Bee had assumed a humanoid form, and stood about six feet tall. He wore fine leather shoes, black dress pants, and a short-sleeved white dress shirt, with a garish and poorly knotted red tie. His long black hair was tied back in a ponytail, and on his nose rested a pair of semi-rimmed glasses, which flashed in the orb's light. A digital watch displayed the time: 12:21 pm.

That was the end of Bee's resemblance to a human, as his skin was bright scarlet. Almost every inch of it was tattooed with strange black runes. Sprouting from his head were two sharp horns, which curved a few inches out of his forehead. All in all, he looked like a bizarre cultist accountant, although it was obvious that Bee didn't really care.

He smiled and stretched, free after thousands of years of imprisonment.

"Unbelievable," he chuckled softly, staring hungrily at his prize. "Chance," he said wondrously, before setting off for the inner catacombs of Abaddon. As he moved, Bee took care to conceal his essence, making sure no spirit could sense his presence. Being detected now would ruin *everything*.

He crept forward, slowly, through the iron door and into the shadows. The first thing he noticed upon passing the exterior threshold of the prison was the heat, which seemed to double with each step he took. The second was the insufferable noise.

Moans of agony rang through the hallways, a symphony of suffering. It was an ode to madness; such sounds of torment that would break a lesser spirit. To Bee, it was merely a distraction. He was uninterested in the babbling of broken minds. He shook his head in annoyance. "Weak spirits, incapable of resolve," he muttered heartlessly.

Advancing still deeper into Abaddon, he arrived at a second steel door, far more imposing than the first. It loomed over Bee, stretching more than twenty feet into the air, a simple cross clearly etched into its surface. Bee observed it for a moment, speaking quietly to himself.

"The guards may be gone, but I can't risk forcing it open. Maybe if I-" Slowly, cautiously, Bee turned the handle. The door swung inward, allowing him to progress further.

Bee grinned broadly and passed through, tut-tutting to himself amusedly. "Careless of them."

He carefully advanced through the corridor, and noticed a marked shift in the scenery. What had been a prison of wood and stone had morphed into a fortress of void and iron. The walkways were a reddish, rusted metal, but everything else; walls, ceilings, and floor, was shifting, malevolent void. Bee shuddered. He was glad to be free again.

Bee paused, directly before an intersection of four walkways. He could sense something coming. He focused his attention, detecting an angel steadily approaching from the pathway on his right. Bee's view of him was blocked by the void, but they were just steps from one another, on a collision course. They had left a guard in here, after all.

The angel strode confidently along the walkway, each step echoing on the iron. In his right hand, he appeared to be holding a torch, although it threw no light onto the void. He turned the corner, heading directly into Bee's path. There was a cry, a feral roar, a loud clang of metal, and then, silence.

Bee emerged from the corner, licking his lips and now carrying an elegant key.

As he descended further into the depths of Abbaddon, the wails of spirits vanished, replaced by the sinister whispers of evil beings. They intruded into Bee's thoughts, trying to bewilder, seduce and terrify.

He was grateful for the change. Bee preferred the whispers of his kin to the maddening drone of the eternally broken and condemned. He ventured further along, until he came to another iron door, again inscribed with a cross.

It took him a short while to locate the keyhole, but after he did, the door swung open smoothly. "Too easy," he said, walking into the chamber he had been seeking.

The room was immense, with walls of fire engulfing each side. A narrow, rickety iron walkway led to its centre, where there was a massive, solitary tower of void. It was flanked by four pillars of ancient stone, one at each corner. The blistering heat was scalding, searing away Bee's body as he moved. The demon was forced to expend his considerable energy stores just to survive in this hostile environment. He wouldn't last in here for very long.

As Bee stepped briskly towards the void, a final voice spoke out to him. It dominated his thoughts, brushing all other sounds and sensations away as easily as one may sweep crumbs off a blanket.

It was a horrific sound; an abomination to all that is natural. It was neither male nor female, sometimes shifting between the two. It conveyed every emotion, seemingly sad and overjoyed and furious and tender, all at once. Beelzebub paused; it had been lifetimes since he had heard this voice.

"Who dares approach me?" The question echoed in the air before fading, leaving Bee alone to approach the great prison in momentary silence, before returning once again.

"Beelzebub?" said the voice, terrible and beautiful at the same time.

"Indeed, my lord," Beelzebub answered, and he took the final steps to reach the tower. It had been a long time since he had been called by his true name.

"They have brought you here to share in my torment?" demanded the voice. Bowing his head low, Beelzebub pushed the ball of golden energy into the pillar, parting the choking cloud of void.

"Better. I've come to free you... Lucifer."

www.ingramcontent.com/pod-product-compliance
Lightning Source LLC
Chambersburg PA
CBHW020235260626
47156CB00002B/690